Advance Praise for Matt Cardin and *What the Daemon Said*

"This is the perfect companion piece to Matt Cardin's fiction omnibus *To Rouse Leviathan*. We're lucky that Matt exists in our world at this particular time and place, in which the weirdness of our day-to-day reality is in dire need of his deeply humanistic criticisms, ideas, suggestions, and presence."

—Jon Padgett, author of *The Secret of Ventriloquism*

"*What the Daemon Said* is more than a must-read collection of essays; it's the ultimate handbook for anyone with an interest in horror. More specifically, it's about how horror, philosophy, and religion have combined to create an ever-evolving tapestry of our existence on planet earth, a layer of human consciousness that Cardin peels apart like a celestial onion with an army of dark gods hidden at its core. This book is a mind-blowing mandala that will take you by the hand and show you wonders and secrets you never could have imagined. Matt Cardin is one of the genre's greatest minds, and this collection is essential reading for every writer and reader in the field."

—Philip Fracassi, author of *Beneath a Pale Sky*

"For my money, Matt Cardin is the most interesting voice in horror criticism of our time. His investigations into the intersection of religion and horror get to the root of what makes this literary mode so potent and so profound. The arrival of this book is an event to be celebrated. It belongs on the shelf of every reader who cares about the human mind, creativity, and how they relate to this bleak and beautiful literature."

—Nathan Ballingrud, author of *North American Lake Monsters* and *Wounds*

"A fine, wide-ranging exploration of the deepest wellsprings of nightmare and chthonic revelation; of the roots of the monstrous and mythopoetic. A look at the bases and the underpinnings of our deepest fears and some of our finest dark literature. Mystagogic initiation from Matt Cardin."

—John Shirley, author of *The Feverish Stars*

"Matt Cardin is a rare genius whose essays are as rich as his fiction. *What the Daemon Said* is a feast for the psyche. Cardin empowers his readers with startling new means of perceiving horror, theology, and the art of writing. This is a profound and magnificent book."

—Richard Gavin, author of grotesquerie and
The Benighted Path: Primeval Gnosis & the Monstrous Soul

What the Daemon Said

What the Daemon Said

Essays on Horror Fiction, Film, and Philosophy

Matt Cardin

Hippocampus Press

New York

Published by Hippocampus Press
P.O. Box 641, New York, NY 10156.
www.hippocampuspress.com

Cover artwork and design by Dan Sauer, dansauerdesign.com.
Hippocampus Press logo designed by Anastasia Damianakos.

First Edition
1 3 5 7 9 8 6 4 2

ISBN 978-1-61498-362-0 trade paperback
ISBN 978-1-61498-370-5 ebook

Contents

Epigraphs in Lieu of a Preface

When I have fears that I may cease to be
    Before my pen has gleaned my teeming brain,
Before high-pilèd books, in charactery,
    Hold like rich garners the full ripened grain.

—John Keats

Of making many books there is no end, and much study is a weariness of the flesh.

—Ecclesiastes 12:12

There lives a creative being inside all of us and we must get out of its way for it will give us no peace unless we do.

—M. C. Richards

A writer is not so much someone who has something to say as he is someone who has found a process that will bring about new things he would not have thought of if he had not started to say them. . . . I know that back of my activity there will be the coherence of my self, and that indulgence of my impulses will bring recurrent patterns and meanings again.

—William Stafford

And now there poured from that limitless MIND a flood of knowledge and explanation which opened new vistas to the seeker, and prepared him for such a grasp of the cosmos as he had never hoped to possess . . . the multiform entity of which his present fragment was an infinitesimal part . . . that final cosmic reality which belies all local perspectives and narrow partial views . . . the ultimate background of that riddle of lost individuality which had at first so horrified him. His intuition pieced together the fragments of revelation, and brought him closer and closer to a grasp of the secret. . . . Curious concepts flowed conflictingly through a brain dazed with unaccustomed vistas and unforeseen disclosures. . . . He knew that in this ultimate abyss he was equidistant from every facet of his archetype—human or nonhuman, earthly or extra-earthly, galactic or trans-galactic.

—H. P. Lovecraft and E. Hoffmann Price,
"Through the Gates of the Silver Key"

The end of my labors has come. All that I have written appears to be as so much straw after the things that have been revealed to me.

—Thomas Aquinas

> Those who know do not speak.
> Those who speak do not know.
>
> —*Tao Te Ching*

The wisdom of this world is foolishness with God.

—1 Corinthians 3:19

The Ligotti Papers

Thomas Ligotti's Career of Nightmares

Thomas Ligotti is arguably the preeminent living writer of horror fiction. This reputation has grown up around him over a period of twenty years, during which time he has remained paradoxically obscure in the mainstream literary consciousness and even, astonishingly, among some segments of horror fandom. Probably more people are acquainted with Ligotti unawares through his editorial work for The Gale Group—the academic publishing company where he worked for more than twenty years—than are acquainted with his stories. Nevertheless, he has produced a substantial body of fiction that has generated a passionately devoted fan base, and his work has been soundly praised by critics and readers alike. Reviewers have written glowingly of his books, and his publisher has mined these reviews for blurbs. (From the *New York Review of Science Fiction*: "Ligotti is probably the genre's most committed purist. He perfectly expresses the 'disorienting strangeness' that is the hallmark of the weird." From the *New York Times Book Review*: "If there were a literary genre called 'philosophical horror,' Thomas Ligotti's [*Grimscribe*] would easily fit within it . . . provocative images and a style that is both entertaining and lyrical." From the *Philadelphia Inquirer*: "Thomas Ligotti has had one of the most quietly extraordinary careers in the history of horror fiction." From the *Washington Post*: "Thomas Ligotti is the best kept secret in contemporary horror fiction . . . the best new American writer of weird fiction to appear in years." From *Interzone*: "Ligotti is wonderful and original; he has a dark vision of a new and special kind, a vision that no one had before him.") His admirers are inclined to call him the best author the horror genre has ever produced, and while such sweeping statements are always questionable at best, it has become increasingly difficult to deny at least the possible validity of the claim. At a bare minimum, it seems undeniable that Ligotti has secured for himself a unique and lasting position of importance in the world of horror fiction, and probably in the wider world of literature in general.

His career as a professional horror author dates back to the early 1980s, when his work first began appearing in such small-press mainstays as *Nyctal-ops*, *Grimoire*, *Eldritch Tales*, *Fantasy Macabre*, and *Dark Horizons*. These stories spoke with a shockingly distinct voice, and their subject matter was unique. For example, "The Chymist," first published in 1981 in *Nyctalops*, speculates about the cosmic forces underlying the world of matter itself—"The Great Chemists," as the narrator calls them—and offers a glimpse of what happens when these forces decide to "dream" an individual into new and nightmarish shapes. "Dream of a Mannikin," first published in 1982 in *Eldritch Tales*, offers a horrific take on the eastern philosophical idea of multileveled selfhood. "Dr. Voke and Mr. Veech," first published in 1983 in *Grimoire*, poses disturbing questions about the nature and possible consciousness of puppets, dolls, mannikins, and other effigies of the human form, and also about the relationship of these effigies to their makers and manipulators. "Notes on the Writing of Horror: A Story," first published in 1985 in *Dark Horizons*, offers exactly what the first part of the title would seem to indicate: a series of notes on how to write horror stories. But then the narrative pulls an ingenious roundabout on the reader by revealing that the narrator is not as safely removed from the subject matter of his notes as he has led himself and his reader to believe.

The profoundly dark philosophical slant of these early stories had the seemingly inevitable effect of creating a cult following for Ligotti. His outlook was despairing, even nihilistic, and this proved to be a point of contact with many readers who, while they may not have explicitly shared his outlook, still found themselves resonating deeply with the dark and dismal truths about which he so powerfully wrote. Quite a few such readers had the unsettling (and somehow exhilarating) impression that Ligotti was expressing in his stories their own most secret and horrifying insights.

He also brought to his stories a distinctive literary voice. By his own account, he was for a time a "fanatical student of literary styles, the more bizarre and artificial the better" (Bee). An example of this stylistic obsession can be seen in the fact that when he conceived the maniacal narrative voice of most of his early stories, he was consciously emulating Nabokov (Paul and Schurholz 17). In spite of this imitation—or perhaps, somehow, because of it—his stories were in the end wholly original. When his first fiction collection, *Songs of a Dead Dreamer*, was published in a mass-market edition in 1989, having been published three years earlier in a limited small-press edition, readers encountered no less a genre heavyweight than Ramsey Campbell saying in the introduction that "despite faint echoes of writers he admires . . . Ligotti's vision is wholly personal. Few other writers could conceive a horror story in the form of notes on the writing of the genre, and I can't think of any other writer who could have brought it off."

In the same introduction, Campbell wrote that *Songs of a Dead Dreamer* "has to be one of the most important horror books of the decade," and with these words the proverbial cat was let out of the metaphorical bag. Ligotti's readership still remained relatively small compared to the Kings and Koontz-es of the world—as should have been expected, considering that his work was highly literary and idiosyncratic, and was most certainly not written for a mass audience—but his early reputation as the reigning dark magus of the horror world began to precede him, and more and more horror fans began to realize that this was a writer they simply had to read. In one of the more bizarre and amusing incidents of his literary career, Ligotti's innate reclusiveness, combined with the mysterious reputation he had gained from his fiction, gave rise to the rumor that he did not really exist but was instead a pseudonym for some more famous author. When Poppy Z Brite asked in her foreword to Ligotti's 1996 omnibus collection *The Nightmare Factory*, "Are you out there, Thomas Ligotti?" (ix), she echoed thousands of readers who were asking the same question, readers who wondered what the man was really like or whether he was even real.[1]

At the time of this writing (April 2000), Ligotti has five more collections of stories to his credit after *Songs of a Dead Dreamer*. In chronological order, these are *Grimscribe: His Lives and Works* (1991), *Noctuary* (1994), *The Agonizing Resurrection of Victor Frankenstein and Other Gothic Tales* (1994), *The Nightmare Factory* (1996), and *In a Foreign Town, In a Foreign Land* (1997). The last was written in conjunction with the experimental music group Current93 and was released with an accompanying CD of music to supplement the book. (Since the exact relationship of the book and CD has never been specified, it is also theoretically possible to view the former as supplementing the latter.) Ligotti's story "The Nightmare Network" was published in editor John Pelan's 1996 anthology *Darkside: Horror for the Next Millennium*, and in late 1999 Ligotti gained his widest exposure yet when his story "The Shadow, the Darkness" was published in editor Al Sarrantonio's high-profile anthology *999: New Tales of Horror and Suspense* alongside works by such genre icons as Stephen King, Peter Straub, and William Peter Blatty. In February 2000, Current93 released a CD titled *I Have a Special Plan for This World* in which the narrated text was written entirely by Ligotti.

For the uninitiated who are thinking of delving into Ligotti's work, or for

---

1. I say more about this phenomenon, including its real origin as a hoax perpetrated by one of Ligotti's close friends and colleagues, in "Of Masks and Mystagogues," q.v.

those who have not yet made up their mind, or even for those who have read some of his work and are wondering where to go next, there are a number of pertinent factors to consider. First, it should be mentioned that Ligotti has repeatedly cited Lovecraft and Poe as the two most important influences on his life and work, respectively, and many devotees of these authors have discovered in Ligotti a kindred spirit. In particular, the Lovecraft connection has continued to bring Ligotti a steady stream of new readers. He is very open about the fact that it was Lovecraft who originally inspired him to try his hand at fiction, and although he has said that Lovecraft's influence on him is more personal than literary, most readers find a strong Lovecraftian element in many of his stories. An example of direct Lovecraftian influence can be found in "The Last Feast of Harlequin," the earliest-written of Ligotti's stories, which is dedicated "To the memory of H. P. Lovecraft." Another direct influence can be found in "The Sect of the Idiot," where Ligotti mentions Lovecraft's infamous tome of occult magic, the Necronomicon, and makes reference to Lovecraft's "blind idiot god" Azathoth. Perhaps the most important and pervasive Lovecraftian influence in Ligotti's fiction is found in his repeatedly reworked idea of a mystical, ontologically absolute evil—in "Dream of a Mannikin," "Masquerade of a Dead Sword," "Nethescurial," "The Tsalal," "The Shadow, the Darkness," and others—which bears at times a similarity to Lovecraft's mythology of certain monstrous extracosmic entities or forces that continually impinge upon the little world of human interests and emotions. While there are significant divergences between the two men's literary styles and personal visions, many Lovecraft fans have felt that, in a way, Ligotti "takes up" where Lovecraft left off—that is, that Ligotti is saying what Lovecraft might have said if he were alive today—and it may not be too far off the mark to consider the bulk of Ligotti's fiction as a kind of distillation and expression in contemporary terms of what was best in Lovecraft. In short, those who appreciate Lovecraft will almost certainly find something to appreciate in Ligotti.

Second, when approaching any writer for the first time, there is always the question of what to read first. Fortunately, in Ligotti's case the answer is obvious. *The Nightmare Factory,* as mentioned above, is an omnibus of his work, reprinting most of the stories from the previous collections and adding to them six new stories in a section titled "Teatro Grottesco and Other Tales." As such, it forms an ideal introduction. The only drawback is that some of his best and most cherished stories from past collections have been omitted. Gone are his two metafictional explorations from *Songs of a Dead Dreamer,* "Notes on the Writing of Horror" and "Professor Nobody's Little Lectures on Supernatural Horror." Gone also is the entire final section of *Noctuary,* titled "Notebook of the Night" and consisting of a series of nineteen prose poems or vignettes that, in the opinion of this author, represent some of Ligotti's most powerful work. Not even mentioned is the wonderful *The Agonizing Resurrection of Victor Frankenstein and Other Gothic Tales,* which consists of a series of vignette-length reworkings of classic literary and cinematic horror tales, and which may in fact be Ligotti's best book when measured against his other books purely in terms of their overall success as collections. Having said this, *The Nightmare Factory* is still the single best book for the Ligotti neophyte to purchase, as it presents a sweeping overview of his perennial thematic and stylistic obsessions, and the new stories in "Teatro Grottesco and Other Tales" represent him at the height of his powers. The book also contains a valuable introductory essay by Ligotti titled "The Consolations of Horror," in which he considers the question of why readers read and writers write such things, and why it is that horror, "at least in its artistic representations, can be a comfort" (xi), He considers and rejects several alternative answers to this question, arriving finally at the conclusion that artistic horror offers only a single valid consolation: "simply that someone shares some of your own feelings and has made of these a work of art which you have the insight, sensitivity, and—like it or not—peculiar set of experiences to appreciate" (xxi).

A final consideration the prospective reader ought to bear in mind is that Ligotti's stories tend to have a profound emotional impact. His vision is exceedingly dark, and it is possible for his stories to infect the reader with a mild-to-severe case of depression. It is even possible for them to effect a change in the reader's self-perception and view of the universe. This warning is not meant to be sensationalistic, nor is it meant to turn new readers away. It is simply a statement of fact based on the experiences of actual readers. Ligotti writes about the darkest of themes with an amazing power, and he means what he says. Often his stories seem to communicate a message below the surface, a sort of subliminal statement that should not rightly be able to traverse the barrier of verbal language. This has not gone unnoticed by his fans and peers in the horror community. For example, Brian McNaughton, winner of the 1998 World Fantasy Award for his fiction collection *The Throne of Bones,* dedicated his story "ystery orm" to Ligotti, and in the story, which appears in Pelan's *Darkside* anthology, he described Ligotti's literary power as follows:

> To translate dreams into plain prose, into the bald speech of post-literate America, seemed impossible until he read the tales of Edward F. Tourmalign [a fictionalized Ligotti]. In Tourmalign's stories, wind-blown leaflets, clinking light-stanchions in empty streets, neon signs with missing letters—

such banal images assumed, in waking life and in cold print, the horrific significance they so often radiated in nightmares. It had been said of many pathetic hacks that they should never be read at night, but it made no difference when one read Tourmalign, for his work was a poison that infiltrated the bloodstream and changed the structure of the brain.

To illustrate the point from one of Ligotti's own works, let the reader consider the following long passage from "The Shadow at the Bottom of the World," in which the communal narrator of an unnamed rural town experiences strange dreams during an unnatural prolongation of the autumn season:

> In sleep we were consumed by the feverish life of the earth, cast among a ripe, fairly rotting world of strange growth and transformation. We took a place within a darkly flourishing landscape where even the air was ripened into ruddy hues and everything wore the wrinkled grimace of decay, the mottled complexion of old flesh. The face of the land itself was knotted with so many other faces, ones that were corrupted by vile impulses. Grotesque expressions were molding themselves into the darkish grooves of ancient bark and the whorls of withered leaf; pulpy, misshapen features peered out of damp furrows; and the crisp skin of stalks and dead seeds split into a multitude of crooked smiles. All was a freakish mask painted with russet, rashy colors—colors that bled with a virulent intensity, so rich and vibrant that things trembled with their own ripeness. But despite this gross palpability, there remained something spectral at the heart of these dreams. It moved in shadow, a presence that was in the world of solid forms but not of it. Nor did it belong to any other world that could be named, unless it was to that realm which is suggested to us by an autumn night when fields lay ragged in moonlight and some wild spirit has entered into things, a great aberration sprouting forth from a chasm of moist and fertile shadows, a hollow-eyed howling malignity rising to present itself to the cold emptiness of space and the pale gaze of the moon. (*Nightmare Factory* 352–53)

In this passage one can clearly feel Ligotti's magic at work. His careful choices of rhythm, sound, and vocabulary work synergistically to produce an oneiric effect, so that the "fairly rotting world of faint growth and transformation," hinting at a spectral presence that is a "great aberration sprouting forth from a chasm of moist and fertile shadows," becomes identified in the reader's mind with the world of dreams and nightmares. Here and elsewhere, Ligotti is remarkably successful in his attempt at using language to convey this most elusive of moods.

On a more philosophical note, we can discern three primary themes (although they are certainly not the only three) emerging from a survey of Ligotti's oeuvre: first, the meaninglessness—or possibly malevolence—of the reality principle behind the material universe; second, the perennial instability of this universe of solid forms, shapes, and concepts as it threatens to collapse or mutate into something unforeseeable and monstrous; and third, the nightmarishness of conscious personal existence in such a world. The stories in the "Teatro Grottesco" section of *The Nightmare Factory* provide a good example of these themes at work. In many ways they are the most personal of Ligotti's works, and as such they provide the literary equivalent of an intravenous dose of his mood. "The Bungalow House" is especially notable in this regard, for in it the narrator offers what might be taken for a Ligottian philosophical and artistic credo, if such a thing were possible. Upon discovering a series of performance art audio tapes in the form of "dream monologues," the narrator is surprised and gratified, and also somewhat disturbed, to discover that another person shares his own love for "the icy bleakness of things." He reflects:

> I wanted to believe that this artist had escaped the dreams and demons of all sentiment in order to explore the foul and crummy delights of a universe where everything had been reduced to three stark principles: first, that there was nowhere for you to go; second, that there was nothing for you to do; and third, that there was no one for you to know. Of course, I knew that this view was an illusion like any other, but it was also one that had sustained me so long and so well—as long and as well as any other illusion and perhaps longer, perhaps better. (*Nightmare Factory* 523)

This passage recalls Nietzsche's assertion in *The Birth of Tragedy* that "it is only as an aesthetic phenomenon that existence and the world are eternally justified" (52). In a universe reduced to those "three stark principles," the only pleasures one can safely enjoy—that is, the only pleasures one can enjoy without the threat of disappointment and painful disillusionment—are purely aesthetic. At the same time, the narrator is aware that this attitude is itself an illusion and that he holds to it merely because of its proven utility. But ultimately even this painfully worked-out maze of psychic defenses is not enough to shield him from utter despair. After a series of disturbing events, he finds himself unable to take any more pleasure from the works of this new artist and is left only with a desperate need to find release from "this heartbreaking sadness I suffer every minute of the day (and night), this killing sadness that feels as if it will never leave me no matter where I go or what I do or whom I may ever know" (*Nightmare Factory* 532).

This idea is foundational to Ligotti's fictional universe: there is simply no solace to be found anywhere in this or any other world. Nor is this merely a literary affectation; Ligotti is using the vehicle of horror fiction to express his actual experience of life. When questioned by one interviewer about the relationship between his writing and his personal outlook, he replied, "My outlook is that it's a damn shame that organic life ever developed on this or any other planet, and that the pain that living creatures necessarily suffer makes for an existence that is a perennial nightmare. This attitude underlies almost everything I've written" (Bee). The close connection between his personal perspective and his stories holds true for even his most extravagant fictional creations. In "Nethescurial," for example, he writes of an ancient pantheistic religious cult whose members discovered at some point in prehistory that their deity was evil and that their religion was in truth a sort of "pandemonism." As commentary to this idea, Ligotti has said,

> It seems to me that living beings on this planet suffer at the hands of an insatiable and wildly creative force—which has variously been referred to as Anima Mundi, Elan Vital, the Will (Schopenhauer)—that does not have our interests at heart, or the interests of any particular species for that matter, since it has extinguished more forms of life than it has created. From the point of view of individuals existing in this luxuriant world, this force must necessarily be viewed as inimical to our comfort and sanity, although almost no one holds to this attitude. (Cardin)

In the end, it is this direct connection between Ligotti's personal outlook and his fictional world that lends his writing such power. His technical literary skills are truly marvelous, but without the strength of his vision to empower them, they would amount to nothing more than a literary sound and light show. He has devoted himself to a career of nightmares, a career of expressing in literary form the demons that have afflicted him for most of his adult life. In interviews he has spoken candidly of his own "erstwhile craving for 'enlightenment in darkness'" (Bee), and the fruit of this craving can be seen in the fact that through his fiction he provides an aesthetic approximation of this very enlightenment for his readers. Christine Morris, writing in *Dagon* Nos. 22/23 (a special issue devoted to Ligotti), said, "Receptive reader, be forewarned—if you read for more than escapist entertainment, if you read to be challenged or enlightened, if you read to explore not only daydreams but nightmares, Thomas Ligotti's stories may transform you, too" (12). For those readers who already possess "the insight, sensitivity, and—like it or not—peculiar set of experiences" to appreciate Ligotti's vision, this transformation may already be well underway even before they encounter the master's books. In true Ligottian fashion, perhaps his stories will always speak most vividly to those rare persons in whom the seed of darkness has already been sown. In their own half-conscious pilgrimage toward a dark enlightenment, these sensitive seekers will follow Ligotti willingly into the depths of the nightmare, and there in the echoing stillness of the silent, staring void they will find that they are looking into the radiant black reflection of their own shadowed souls.

2000

Works Cited

Bee, Robert. "Interview with Thomas Ligotti." *Thomas Ligotti Online.* 11 April 2005 (originally published in 1999). www.ligotti.net/showthread.php?t=231.

Cardin, Matt. "'Nethescurial': Commentary." *Thomas Ligotti Online.* 5 April 2000 (interview conducted in 1998). www.longshadows.com/ligotti/ss-ne.html.

Ligotti, Thomas. *The Nightmare Factory.* New York: Carroll & Graf, 1996.

Morris, Christine. "Beyond Dualism: An Appreciation of the Writings of Thomas Ligotti." *Dagon* Nos. 22/23 (September–December 1988): 10–12.

Nietzsche, Friedrich. *Basic Writings of Nietzsche.* Ed. Walter Kaufmann. New York: Modern Library, 2000.

Paul, R. F., and Keith Schurholz. "Triangulating the Daemon: An Interview with Thomas Ligotti." *Esoterra* No. 8 (Winter/Spring 1999): 14–21.

The Masters' Eyes, Shining with Secrets: The Influence of H. P. Lovecraft on Thomas Ligotti

I. Introduction: The Shade of Lovecraft

Jonathan Padgett, the founder of *Thomas Ligotti Online,* relates the following anecdote in his Ligotti FAQ: "In a phone conversation I had with Mr. Ligotti in the Spring of 1998, he explained that Lovecraft's fiction had had the most profound influence on his *life* rather than his fiction, as reading HPL's work was the impetus for Ligotti's writing career. Aside from this fact, Lovecraft really has had very little to do with the subject or style of Ligotti's writing." From this, one might infer that Lovecraft's influence is not readily apparent in Ligotti's work. But if this is so, then what are we to make of the phenomenon noted by Ramsey Campbell, who in his introduction to Ligotti's first book, the short story collection *Songs of a Dead Dreamer,* stated, "At times [Ligotti] suggests terrors as vast as Lovecraft's, though the terrors are quite other than Lovecraft's" (ix)? In other words, if it is true that "Lovecraft really has had very little to do with the subject or style of Ligotti's writing," then how can we account for the fact that, as Ed Bryant has put it, "Hardly anyone seems to discuss or even mention the Ligotti name without evoking the shade of H. P. Lovecraft"?

It is tempting to try to answer this question simply by turning to the available Ligotti interviews and assembling a montage of quotations, since he has spoken repeatedly and extensively about his relationship to Lovecraft. But a more thorough and satisfying answer can only come from examining the evidence and extrapolating independent conclusions from it. This will also give us the opportunity to examine in depth some of Lovecraft's own writings and representative attitudes, and to compare and contrast them with Ligotti's in order to arrive at a general understanding of where both men stand in relation to each other.

We may begin, however, with the aforementioned interviews, and in perusing them construct a chronology of Ligotti's acquaintance with Lovecraft, and also with the field of horror fiction in general, that may prove instructive.

II. Dark Guru, Personal Presence: Lovecraft in Ligotti's Life

Thomas Ligotti was born on 9 July 1953. By his own account, he had no significant exposure to horror fiction, nor any serious desire to read it, until he was eighteen years old. That was when he accidentally discovered Shirley Jackson's *The Haunting of Hill House* at a garage sale in 1970 or 1971. In fact, prior to this he had never felt much interest in books and literature at all. In his own words, "Until reading Jackson's horror novel, I had read only a few works of literature in my entire life and almost all of those were reluctantly scanned under the duties of assignments in school. Having been something of a burnout in the late 1960s, I never really learned my way around a library and the concept of bookstores was wholly alien to me." When he began reading Jackson's novel, it came as a sort of revelation to him to realize that the book had served as the basis for a film he had liked, director Robert Wise's *The Haunting* (1963). Upon finishing the book, he "felt a definite hunger for more horror stories, but not necessarily those of the Jacksonian type." What he wanted to read were not stories about modern characters set in modern times, but ones more like the movies he had enjoyed as a child, "the more clichéd Gothic horror movies set in the Victorian era. . . . [T]his was the kind of horror fiction I was seeking, the progeny of Poe's tales" (Ford 31).

Before going on to describe Ligotti's successful search for this type of story, it is necessary to step back briefly and look to an event that had occurred prior to all this, and that had laid precisely the right emotional and philosophical foundation to render Ligotti exquisitely responsive to Lovecraft's fictional vision of the universe. The event took place when Ligotti was seventeen years old and under the influence of drugs and alcohol. He himself has described what happened, and also what his mindset was leading up to it, thus: "As a teenager I had a tendency to depression. To me, the world was just something to escape from. I started escaping with alcohol and then, as the sixties wore on, with every kind of drug I could get. In August of 1970 I suffered the first attack of what would become a lifelong anxiety-panic disorder" (Angerhuber and Wagner 53). Elsewhere he has described the event as an "emotional breakdown" and said that although it occurred "following intense use of drugs and booze," we should not assign a purely causal role to these intoxicants, since they "served only as a catalyst for a fate that my high-strung and mood-swinging self would have encountered at some point" (Schweitzer 30).

More than a mere panic attack, the episode involved a terrifying vision of the universe, and of reality itself, that permanently altered Ligotti's worldview in a direction that was, although he could not have known it at the time, pro-to-Lovecraftian. He has made this connection clear in several interviews, such as the one conducted by Robert Bee, in which Ligotti described Lovecraft's famous "cosmic perspective" as "the idea, as well as the emotional sensation, that human notions of value and meaning, even sense itself, are utterly ficti-tious," and then added, "Not long before I began reading Lovecraft's stories I experienced—in a state of panic, I should add—such a perspective, which has remained as the psychological and emotional backdrop of my life ever since" (Bee). Similarly, he told Monika Angerhuber and Thomas Wagner that he discovered Lovecraft "not too long after" that first attack and "found that the meaningless and menacing universe described in Lovecraft's stories corre-sponded very closely to the place I was living at that time, and ever since for that matter" (53).

So in August 1970—the very month in which, eighty years earlier, H. P. Lovecraft had been born—a seventeen-year-old Thomas Ligotti experienced a horrifying vision of the universe as a "meaningless and menacing" place in which "human notions of value and meaning, even sense itself, are utterly fic-titious." Shortly afterward, near the end of 1970 or beginning of 1971, he dis-covered Jackson's *The Haunting of Hill House,* read it, and hungered for a different type of horror fiction. Since he was not familiar with libraries or bookstores, his search took him in an unlikely direction that produced an equally unlikely, though fortuitous, result: "The first place I looked in my quest for horror literature was the local drugstore, of all places. What strange luck that contained in its racks was a paperback entitled *Tales of Horror and the Supernatural* by Arthur Machen. And I soon discovered that this was *exactly* what I had been looking for" (Ford 31). Shortly after reading the Machen col-lection, at some point in 1971, he returned to the same drugstore and bought another book. It was the Ballantine edition of *Tales of the Cthulhu Mythos, Vol-ume 1* (Bryant). And even though he had enjoyed the Machen book, the expe-rience of reading Lovecraft did what Machen had not: it set off an explosive sense of identification and inspired in Ligotti a desire to write horror stories himself.

The reasons for this are various, but they all center around the overwhelming sense of empathy that he felt for Lovecraft's outlook. Lovecraft was "the first author with whom I strongly identified . . . a dark guru who confirmed to me all my most awful suspicions about the universe" (Paul and Schurholz 18). Still fresh from the initial attack of his anxiety-panic disorder and still living in the grip of the horrific worldview it had opened to him, Ligotti felt "grateful that someone else had perceived the world in a way similar to my own view" (Angerhuber and Wagner 53). And although the inspirational connection may not be obvious or necessary, for Ligotti it was an organic part of his remarkably intense emotional response to Lovecraft: "When I first read Lovecraft around 1971, and even more so when I began to read about his life, I immediately knew that I wanted to write horror stories" (Wilbanks).

As it turned out, Ligotti did not actually undertake the writing of fiction or anything else besides school assignments until late in his college career, when he "found the required writing that I was doing to be very stimulating: it made me high, or at least distracted me from my chronic anxiety, and I wanted to do more of it" (Schweitzer 24). But his path as a writer had already been determined by that initial experience of responding to Lovecraft from the depths of his being, in the wake of which "there was never a question that I would write anything else other than horror stories" (Angerhuber and Wagner 53).

Recently (as of February 2005), Ligotti has provided a little more explanation about the specific nature of Lovecraft's inspirational influence upon him:

> As soon as a receptive mind discovers the works of someone such as Lovecraft, it discovers that there are other ways of looking at the world besides the one in which it has been conditioned. You may discover what kind of nightmarish jailhouse you are doomed to inhabit or you may simply find an echo of things that already depressed and terrified you about being alive. The horror and nothingness of human existence—the cozy façade behind which was only a spinning abyss. The absolute hopelessness and misery of everything. After publishing his first book in French, which in English appeared as *A Short History of Decay* (1949), Cioran learned from that volume's enthusiastic reception that his manner of philosophical negation had a paradoxically vital and energizing quality. Lovecraft, along with other authors of his kind, may have the same effect and rather than encouraging people to give up he may instead give them a reason to carry on. Sometimes that rea-

son is to follow his way—to communicate, in the form of horror stories, the outrage and panic at being alive in the world.[1]

From what has already been said, it should be obvious that Ligotti is speaking autobiographically here. Elsewhere, he has stated directly that he took Lovecraft not only as a literary model but as a model for living:

> It was what I sensed in Lovecraft's works and what I learned about his myth as the "recluse of Providence" that made me think, "That's for me!" I already had a grim view of existence, so there was no problem there. I was and am agoraphobic, so being reclusive was a snap. The only challenge was whether or not I could actually write horror stories. So I studied fiction writing and wrote every day for years and years until I started to get my stories accepted by small press magazines. I'm not comparing myself to Lovecraft as a person or as a writer, but *the rough outline of his life gave me something to aspire to.* (Wilbanks; emphasis added)

Thus it seems impossible to overemphasize the importance of Lovecraft to Ligotti, not just as a writer whose works he loves but as a human being with whom he feels a deeply personal sense of kinship. Ligotti himself has stated the matter definitively: "H. P. Lovecraft has been, bar none other, the most intense and real personal presence in my life" (Paul and Schurholz 18). And again: "I don't know what would have become of me if I hadn't discovered Lovecraft" (Wilbanks).

III. Notes on the Horror of Writing: Lovecraft in Ligotti's Work, and Vice Versa

What remains is the question of whether and how Lovecraft's influence can be seen in Ligotti's actual writing. Darrell Schweitzer offered a typical observation, and one that echoes Ramsey Campbell's sentiment expressed above, when he told Ligotti that "your stories only resemble Lovecraft's in the most tenuous manner, in that you too seem to depict a bleak and uncertain uni-

---

1. Thomas Ligotti, *The Conspiracy against the Human Race*, prepublication draft manuscript, 2005. (Note that the quoted passage does not appear in the published version of the book, which represents a comprehensive revision—amounting to a complete transformation—of the original version that Ligotti distributed to several individuals and briefly made available at *Thomas Ligotti Online* in 2005. When I originally wrote this essay in 2005, the book had not been published, and by the time it was, the passage quoted here had disappeared from it, along with the majority of the original version's content.)

verse in which human assumptions don't apply very far. But the more overt Lovecraftisms, from the adjectives to the tentacular Things From Beyond, are conspicuously absent" (25). This amounts to saying that Ligotti's stories recall Lovecraft purely in terms of mood and worldview, and for the most part this is correct, although a number of Ligotti's stories do incorporate specific Lovecraftian names and themes. One example is "The Sect of the Idiot," in which Ligotti mentions Azathoth, the fictional deity or cosmic principle that Lovecraft created to symbolize the ultimate ontological horror. Another is "The Last Feast of Harlequin," the earliest written of Ligotti's published tales, whose plot motifs explicitly recall Lovecraft's "The Shadow over Innsmouth" and "The Festival," and which ends with a dedication "To the memory of H. P. Lovecraft." But even in these and the few other stories in which definite Lovecraftian elements can be discerned—e.g., "Nethescurial," "The Tsalal," "Dr. Locrian's Asylum"—Ligotti does not mimic Lovecraft's prose style or call out a litany of fictional gods and monsters in the manner that has come to typify Lovecraftian "Mythos" fiction. Instead, he returns to the same psychological/spiritual source of nightmarish horror that animated Lovecraft's stories, and he works it outward into original tales told in an original style. This style itself may be decidedly non-Lovecraftian—Ligotti's stylistic masters, let it be recalled, are Poe, Nabokov, Burroughs, Schulz, and the like—but the spirit is Lovecraftian to the core.

And this is all to say that Ligotti nowhere apes Lovecraft, but instead, in a certain (purely metaphorical) sense, *embodies* him, or at least a version of him (see below). In my essay "Thomas Ligotti's Career of Nightmares," I speculated that Ligotti's writing may be taken "as a kind of distillation and expression in contemporary terms of what was best in Lovecraft." Regarding what qualifies as Lovecraft's "best," Ligotti has expressed a definite preference for the earlier, more poetic, dreamlike tales over the later, longer ones such as "The Shadow out of Time" and *At the Mountains of Madness,* in which Lovecraft attempted to build a combined atmosphere of cosmic horror and scientific/documentary realism. "I find Lovecraft's fastidious attempts at creating a documentary style 'reality' an obstacle to appreciating his work," he has said. "To me, reading a horror story should be like dreaming and the more dreamlike a story is, the more it affects me" (Ford 33).

Given such a literary predilection, we can appreciate why Ligotti has designated Lovecraft's dreamlike "The Music of Erich Zann" as his favorite among Lovecraft's works. "To me," he has said, "it was in 'Erich Zann' that Lovecraft came up with the perfect model of the horror story" (Ayad 109). He has described this story as "Lovecraft's early, almost premature expression of his ideal as a writer: the use of maximum suggestion and minimal explanation to evoke a sense of supernatural terrors and wonders" ("Dark Beauty" 82). "Erich Zann" has long been recognized as one of Lovecraft's most successful stories, and for our purposes here it is important to remember that Lovecraft wrote it in 1921, only four and a half years into his mature fiction-writing career, which had begun in 1917 with "The Tomb." When we recall his famous assertion from 1936, just a little over a year before his death, that "I'm farther from doing what I want to do than I was 20 years ago" (*Selected Letters* 5.224) and put this together with Ligotti's claim that he himself has "tend[ed] to take more cues from Lovecraft's earlier work" (Bryant), we can at last understand what it really means to say that Ligotti's writing distills the essence of Lovecraft's best. Specifically, Lovecraft himself felt that he had produced his best writing early on, and Ligotti agrees. Considering the deep affective kinship between the two men, it seems reasonable to regard Ligotti's writing as a continuation of the type of writing that Lovecraft produced early his career, before he made the changes in his approach that hindsight later represented to him as a misstep.

Perhaps this is the appropriate point to highlight the obvious fact that not everyone agrees with Ligotti's preference for Lovecraft's earlier work, and thus not everyone agrees that Ligotti's own authorial choices have been for the best. In the world of horror literature and entertainment at large, most people associate Lovecraft with, and venerate him for, the branch of his writing typified by "The Call of Cthulhu," *At the Mountains of Madness*, "The Shadow out of Time," and his other, longer stories told in a realistic tone and mounted as documentary-type expositions of cosmic and/or supernatural themes, as opposed to the earlier stories that Ligotti values most. S. T. Joshi is one prominent figure who believes that Lovecraft produced his most significant work in this later "supernatural realist" mode and that, moreover, this mode has characterized the greatest works in the supernatural horror genre as a whole. "Ligotti's own tastes notwithstanding," he has said, "few will doubt that Lovecraft initiated the most representative phase of his career when he adopted the documentary realism of 'The Call of Cthulhu' in 1926; if he had stopped writing before that point, we would have little reason to remember him" ("Thomas Ligotti: The Escape from Life" 152). By contrast, Ligotti believes that Lovecraft "was at his worst when he tried to be 'convincing' in the manner derived from the late 19th century realist-naturalist writers" and that these attempts failed to achieve the effect Lovecraft had intended. "Lovecraft," he says, "always veered off into a highly unrealistic, as well as highly poetic style," and it is this very deviation from the ideal of realism that Ligotti finds most laudable and valuable (Schweitzer 26). The upshot of the matter, generally speaking, is that Ligotti thinks Lovecraft was at his worst in the very stories where Joshi thinks he was at his best.

What we have here is a case of methodological and even philosophical disagreement, the details of which come out most clearly in the two men's respective assessments of "The Music of Erich Zann." Joshi, like Ligotti, notices something distinctive about this story. On the one hand, he praises it, saying that it "justifiably remained one of Lovecraft's own favourite stories, for it reveals a restraint in its supernatural manifestations (bordering, for one of the few times in his entire work, on obscurity), a pathos in its depiction of its protagonist, and a general polish in its language that Lovecraft rare;u achieved in later years." And yet he also expresses a reservation, already hinted at in the parenthetical aside quoted above, about "the very nebulous nature of the horror involved" in the narrative. "There are those," he writes, "who find this sort of restraint effective because it leaves so much to the imagination; and there are those who find it ineffective because it leaves *too much* to the imagination, and there is a suspicion that the author himself did not have a fully conceived understanding of what the central weird phenomenon of the story is actually meant to be. I fear I am in the latter camp." Although Joshi, like Ligotti, thinks Lovecraft was sometimes a bit too overexplanatory in his later stories, "in 'The Music of Erich Zann' I cannot help feeling that he erred in the opposite direction" (*H. P. Lovecraft: A Life* 271–72). But this is of course the complete opposite of Ligotti's opinion, since Ligotti, as we have seen, regards the same story as a masterpiece precisely because of its use of "maximum suggestion and minimal explanation" to evoke a specific type of philosophical-aesthetic response. For him, the story's refusal to give any hint of explanation regarding the precise nature of its central horror, in tandem with the skill of its telling, "suggest[s] to us the essence, far bigger than life, of that dark universal terror beyond naming which is the matrix for all other terrors" ("Dark Beauty" 80), whereas for Joshi the same quality merely hints at the author's underdeveloped conception of his own theme.

In light of this, we should not be surprised that Joshi has criticized Ligotti's own stories for falling short of the ideal of supernatural realism. In 1993 Joshi expressed concern at the fact that Ligotti "seems, apparently by design, not to care about the complete reconciliation of the various supernatural features in a given tale," which, in conjunction with several other problems he perceived in Ligotti's style—including obscurity, excessive self-consciousness and self-referentiality, and a lack of "spontaneity and emotional vigour"—he regarded as preventing Ligotti's work from ranking among the best in the supernatural horror genre. Joshi opined that Ligotti needs to produce more completed tales, as opposed to vignettes and the like, and more work in the supernatural realist mode of the later Lovecraftian stories "if he is to join the ranks of Lovecraft, Blackwood, Dunsany, Jackson, Campbell, and Klein, as he is on the verge of doing." Among Ligotti's works that already fulfill this order, Joshi counted "The Last Feast of Harlequin," "Nethescurial," and "Vastarien" ("Thomas Ligotti: The Escape from Life" 151–52).[2]

Ligotti, for his part, is quite self-aware about the choices he has made in matters of style and authorial philosophy. He has even employed a metafictional approach to incorporate his thoughts about such matters into some of his stories. "Nethescurial" is one such story, and ironically (in light of Joshi's praise) we can find within it an answer to Joshi's criticism of Ligotti's supposed over-vagueness. "Nethescurial" is constructed as a series of frame stories, and the narrator of the topmost frame is portrayed as possessing a certain savvy about the field of supernatural horror. In commenting on the contents of a manuscript he has found, which forms one of the lower-level frames, and which purports to give an account of a supposedly true quasi-supernatural/metaphysical horror story, he says:

> The problem is that such supernatural inventions [i.e., the god Nethescurial, a "demonic demiurge"] are indeed quite difficult to imagine. So often they fail to materialize in the mind, to take on a mental texture, and thus remain unfelt as anything but an abstract monster of metaphysics—an elegant or awkward schematic that cannot rise from the paper to touch us. (*Grimscribe* 82)

Although in this passage the narrator/Ligotti is not talking about the problem

---

2. More recently, Joshi has spoken positively of the increased stylistic realism evident in Ligotti's *My Work Is Not Yet Done* (2002). In this short novel, Joshi says, "Ligotti has tempered what in the past might have been regarded as his excessively tortured prose, and has instead evolved a smoothly flowing narrative style that, if perhaps a bit more spartan in its exotic metaphors than before, is nonetheless capable of powerful emotive effects" ("Ligotti in Triplicate"). The change Joshi notes is indeed prominent in *My Work Is Not Yet Done,* and is somewhat surprising in light of Ligotti's longstanding, self-avowed shunning of realism in favor of surrealism and oneiricism—which is a fact that Joshi also notes. But we may observe that Ligotti has clearly not abandoned his commitment to warped and fantastical narrative and prose styles, as evidenced by such relatively recent stories as "Our Temporary Supervisor" (2001), "My Case for Retributive Action" (2001), and "The Town Manager" (2003). Another tale, "Purity" (2003), represents an interesting hybrid, with Ligotti's typically oneiric thematic content couched in a realistic narrative style reminiscent of the one he employed in *My Work Is Not Yet Done.*

of authorial vagueness but about the ontological and affective barrier that separates the world of written words from the world of existential reality, we may still read these thoughts as addressing the former issue as well. This is especially true since the "demonic demiurge" Nethescurial, which forms the story's central metaphysical horror, remains fully and fundamentally as unexplained in the end as does the nameless horror confronted by Lovecraft's Erich Zann. Ligotti's concluding words at the end of the passage quoted above may thus be taken as an apologia not only for the power of literary horror to move us but for the power of a minimally explained supernatural premise to have a similar impact:

> Even if we are incapable of sincere belief in [the various stock narrative elements found in supernatural horror stories like the tale of the island cult of Nethescurial], there may still be a power in these things that threatens us like a bad dream. And this power emanates not so much from within the tale as it does from somewhere *behind* it, someplace of infinite darkness and ubiquitous evil in which we may walk unaware. (*Grimscribe* 82; Ligotti's emphasis)

Not incidentally, these thoughts were prefigured, and Ligotti's low opinion of the value and effectiveness of supernatural realism was given clear expression, in his words to interviewer Carl Ford in 1988, three years before "Nethescurial"'s first publication:

> I discovered some time ago that I am not necessarily interested in fictional confrontations between the so-called everyday world and the world of the supernatural. If I am affected by a writer's vision, it is never because he has caused me to believe during the course of reading that there is truth to a given supernatural motif. . . . What seems important to me is . . . the power of the language and images of a story and the ultimate vision that they help to convey. . . . Lovecraft's Cthulhu aided his expression of certain sensations that were profoundly important to him. The pure *idea* of such a creation—not if it exists or doesn't—is the only thing of consequence. That idea may be rendered poorly or with great power, and beyond that—nothing matters. (Ford 33; Ligotti's emphasis)

Obviously, Joshi is correct in believing that Ligotti cares nothing for "the complete reconciliation of the various supernatural features in a given tale." Instead, what matters to Ligotti is the evocation of mood and the conveyance, preferably with consummate literary skill, of an overwhelming artistic-horrific vision. In fact, we could substitute "Nethescurial" for "Cthulhu" in the above quotation to arrive at a viable statement from Ligotti of his own guiding philosophy as a writer. (For more on the parallels between Ligotti's personal aesthetic as a writer of horror fiction and his statements about Lovecraft, see the final section of this essay.)

If it is ironic that Ligotti has answered, after a fashion, some of Joshi's criticisms in one of the very stories that Joshi has singled out for praise, then it is doubly ironic that Lovecraft's own words indicate that by the end of his life he probably would have agreed more with Ligotti than Joshi on this issue. Although Lovecraft did begin employing a documentary-realist approach to fiction writing beginning in 1926, his self-stated ultimate goal in the writing of even these realistic stories was the evocation of mood, not the "complete reconciliation of [their] various supernatural features," which formulation may be taken as one of the hallmarks of supernatural realism. "[Weird fiction] must," he wrote in 1935,

> if it is to be authentic art, form primarily *the crystallization or symbolization of a definite human mood*—*not* the attempted delineation of *events*, since the "events" involved are of course largely fictitious or impossible. . . . A *really serious* weird story does not depend on plot or incident at all, but puts all its emphasis on *mood* or *atmosphere*. What it sets out to be is simply *a picture of a mood*, and if it weaves the elements of suggestion with sufficient skill, it matters relatively little what fictitious events the mood is based on. (*Selected Letters* 5.158, 198; Lovecraft's emphases)

In the case of Lovecraft's own writing, the point is illustrated by his 1931 short novel *At the Mountains of Madness*. He wrote this one in an ultra-realistic tone, complete with a generous overlay of scientific jargon, but as he said in a 1936 letter to his friend E. Hoffmann Price, at root his goal was simply "to pin down the vague feelings regarding the lethal, desolate white south which have haunted me ever since I was ten years old." In other words, he simply wanted to write a story that would express for him, and that would convey to others, an undefined *feeling*. This emotional closeness that he felt to the setting and subject matter of the story may account in part for the fact that when it received a hostile reception and was subjected to severe editorial mishandling, he was so discouraged that, in his own words, the episode "probably did more than anything else to end my effective fictional career" (*Selected Letters* 5.223, 224).

The point is reinforced later in the same letter to Price, where Lovecraft used similar mood-based terms to explain his motivations for writing "The Haunter of the Dark" (1935): "The sole purpose of this attempt was to crystallise (a) the feeling of strangeness in a distant view, and (b) the feeling of latent horror in an old, deserted edifice" (*Selected Letters* 5.224). Again, this ideal of mood, and not the achievement of a successful supernatural-realist effect, was so important to Lovecraft that his self-perceived failure deeply discouraged him. These words about "The Haunter in the Dark" are followed directly by his already quoted claim that he was farther from "doing what I want to do" than he had been twenty years earlier.

In a more formal vein, in his 1933 essay "Notes on the Writing of Weird Fiction," Lovecraft made the same point when he wrote:

> My reason for writing stories is to give myself the satisfaction of visualising more clearly and detailedly and stably the vague, elusive, fragmentary impressions of wonder, beauty, and adventurous expectancy which are conveyed to me by certain sights (scenic, architectural, atmospheric, etc.), ideas, occurrences, and images encountered in art and literature. (*Miscellaneous Writings* 113)

And if we look to the introduction to his classic essay "Supernatural Horror in Literature," which he wrote from 1925 to 1927, we see him flatly asserting that the "one test of the really weird"—that is, the litmus test for whether a supernatural horror story succeeds or fails—is simply whether it generates the right mood. More specifically, and to quote Lovecraft's famous words in full, "The one test of the really weird is this—whether or not there be excited in the reader a profound sense of dread, and of contact with unknown spheres and powers; a subtle attitude of awed listening, as if for the beating of black wings or the scratching of outside shapes and entities on the known universe's utmost rim" (*Dagon* 368–69).

At this point, the attentive reader may have begun to think that I am confusing categories in my argument. Supernatural realism, the reader might say, is a stylistic approach, whereas Lovecraft's weird-fictional ideal of evoking mood is a fundamental authorial motivation, prior to and separate from the selection of a literary style. In other words, supernatural realism was merely one of several stylistic vehicles that Lovecraft employed in pursuit of his emotional goal, and therefore to oppose the two is to commit a category error. In my defense, I do not think I have committed this error, because what I have been attempting to show is precisely the primacy of Lovecraft's emotional motivation for writing stories at all. My point is not that his stories can be discretely divided into "mood-based" ones and supernatural realist ones, but simply that he was more emotionally invested in the idea of writing stories to convey ethereal moods than he was intellectually invested in the idea of writing stories to create a convincing air of realism or to offer a coherent explanation or reconciliation of supernatural motifs. When he reached middle age and began to take stock of his writing, he felt that the work he had produced prior to adopting the realist approach had more successfully achieved and fulfilled his emotional goals. And in this opinion, he is at one with Ligotti.

Nor does this identity of opinion stop there. Although an author's assessment of his or her own work should not always be taken as valid, it is a telling fact that Ligotti's opinion about Lovecraft's fiction echoes that of Lovecraft himself. Late in life, Lovecraft maintained that he regarded "The Music of Erich Zann" and "The Colour out of Space," each of which in its respective way defies the conventions of supernatural realism by leaving the narrative's central horror utterly unexplained, as his most successful stories. Of course, Joshi, too, admires "The Colour out of Space," and he does so specifically—and also oddly, in light of his criticism of "The Music of Erich Zann"—for the way it "captures the atmosphere of inexplicable horror" perhaps more effectively than any of Lovecraft's other stories (*H. P. Lovecraft: A Life* 420). Ligotti, for his part, has said of this story that he admires the way it "delineat[es] a condition of pervasive strangeness and unease," the achievement of which is necessary for his enjoyment of horror fiction (Schweitzer 27). So on this point, regarding this story, Ligotti and Joshi are in agreement. But we have already seen that Joshi holds reservations about what he perceives as the possible overuse of underexplanation in Lovecraft's "The Music of Erich Zann," whereas for Ligotti the same story serves almost as an ur-text.

The overarching point that I have been laboring to make through all this is that Ligotti's sense of identification with Lovecraft is so profound, and their sensibilities so closely aligned, that the two of them even share Lovecraft's self-opinion as a writer, no matter whether this clashes with the expressed opinions of the world's foremost Lovecraft scholar or anyone else. If this seems an overstatement, I will at least argue for the heuristic value of the idea by pointing out that Ligotti's position enables him to offer an explanation for Lovecraft's late-in-life lament about his self-perceived failure to realize his authorial goals. The answer is really quite simple: Lovecraft's experimentation with supernatural realism may have produced the stories that he has become most known for, but they failed to satisfy him as much as his earlier work. For both Lovecraft and Ligotti, these later stories failed to approach the same summit of suggestive horror, and failed to capture and express the same delicate emotions, that his earlier ones had achieved, and thus both men prefer the earlier work to the later. It was therefore natural for Lovecraft to claim at the age of forty-five that he was farther from producing the work he wanted to produce than he had been at twenty-five. But Joshi can only be baffled by the claim and call it an "astonishing assertion" ("H. P. Lovecraft"). Or perhaps (and this is more likely) Joshi fully understands Lovecraft's subjective reasons for saying such a thing but still finds it astonishing because he considers the stories from Lovecraft's supernatural realist period to be patently superior, meaning more significant, meaningful, and mature, than the earlier ones. In any event, the question here is not that of the objective literary value of Lovecraft's pre- or post-1926 work, but of the way that he, along with Ligotti, felt about such things. And the answer is clear.

Perhaps most telling of all, in the same letter where he averred that a serious weird tale sets out to be "a picture of a mood," Lovecraft reflected on his then-current approach to writing fiction, and he expressed confusion over the most effective way to achieve his goals: "I'm pretty well burned out in the lines I've been following . . . that's why I'm experimenting around for new ways to capture the moods I wish to depict." He specifically classified "The Thing on the Doorstep" and "The Shadow out of Time," both of which he had written in his realist mode, as counting among these "experiments," and asserted, "*Nothing* is really 'typical' of my efforts at this stage. I'm simply casting about for better ways to crystallise and capture certain strong impressions . . . which persist in clamouring for expression." Then he makes a most interesting statement: "Perhaps the case is hopeless—that is, I may be experimenting in the wrong medium altogether. It may be that poetry instead of fiction is the only effective vehicle to put such expression across" (*Selected Letters* 5.199; Lovecraft's emphasis).

In this same vein, only a month after writing the letter to Price from which I have quoted extensively above, he wrote Price another one in which he disparaged his own earlier work, lamented the influence of pulp fiction on his thought process and therefore writing style, and then hinted indirectly, and tantalizingly, that he was groping toward yet another shift in his writing. And in this second expression of dissatisfaction, he made it clear that his lament from a month earlier referred not only to the quality of his work, but to its very form. "[F]iction," he stated, "is *not* the medium for what I *really want to do*." But regarding the type of writing he did want to do, he expressed confusion: "Just what the right medium would be, I don't know—perhaps the cheapened and hackneyed term 'prose-poem' would hint in the general direction" (*Selected Letters* 5.230; Lovecraft's emphases). Lovecraft, we will recall, had already written four prose poems earlier in his career: "Memory," "Ex Oblivione," "Nyarlathotep," and "What the Moon Brings." In keeping with the conventions of the form, each of these pieces is characterized by a poetic, dreamlike tone and an atmosphere of unabashed surrealism. In fact, we might anachronistically describe his prose poems as some of the most *Ligottian* things he ever wrote.

This is a clue worth following. Certainly, Ligotti himself has made extensive use of the prose poem form, or something resembling it, in what Joshi has described as "the vignettes, prose poems, sketches and fragments that so far [as of 1993] constitute the bulk of his output." It was Ligotti's repeated use of this semi-fragmentary form that led Joshi, with his preference for supernatural realism, to say that Ligotti "will, I believe, have to start writing more stories—as opposed to [prose poems etc.]—if he is to gain preëminence in the field" ("Thomas Ligotti: The Escape from Life" 152). Regardless of Joshi's judgment here, are we perhaps justified in speculating, based on the considerations already offered, that the different medium and/or style for which Lovecraft was blindly groping, the one that would have expressed to his satisfaction the poignant and powerful subjective impressions and imaginings that had dominated his life, the one that would have given him the same sense of creative fulfillment that his early works gave him in retrospect—are we perhaps justified in speculating that this new type of writing that he unsuccessfully sought to conceive may be found today in the works of Thomas Ligotti?

In pursuit of this idea, let us consider Ligotti's metafiction "Notes on the Writing of Horror," which stands as his quintessential statement on matters of literary style as they relate to the horror story. In this tour de force, he expresses, through the voice of the narrator, his thoughts about the various styles or "techniques" available to horror writers. These are, he says, essentially three in number. First is the *realistic* technique, which is simply another name for conventional supernatural realism. The description that he gives would serve well as a textbook definition: "The supernatural and all it represents, is profoundly abnormal, and therefore unreal. . . . Now the highest aim of the realistic horror writer is to prove, in realistic terms, that the unreal is real." The second technique is the *traditional Gothic* technique, which places characters and plotlines in a recognizably Gothic-fantastic setting and can therefore dispense with the strictures of realism by, for example, employing an "inflated rhetoric" that would seem hysterical in a more realistic context. Third is the *experimental* technique, which a writer adopts when the first two would fail to tell the story rightly, and which is defined by the writer's "simply following the story's commands to the best of his human ability. . . . [L]iterary experimentalism is simply the writer's imagination, or lack of it, and feeling, or absence of same, thrashing their chains around in the escape-proof dungeon of the words of the story" (*Songs of a Dead Dreamer* 104, 108–9, 110–11). By way of example, Lovecraft's "The Call of Cthulhu" and Ligotti's "The Frolic" may be cited as instances of the realistic technique. Lovecraft's "The Outsider" and Ligotti's "The Tsalal" may be cited as instances of the traditional Gothic technique. For the experimental technique, it is more difficult to pin down a Lovecraft story. Probably his prose poems are the best ones to single out, and perhaps "The Music of Erich Zann," which also qualifies as

Gothic. For Ligotti, so many stories fall into the experimental category that it is impractical to list them here. Examples include "Dr. Voke and Mr. Veech," "The Night School," "Mad Night of Atonement," "The Red Tower," the entire contents of "The Notebook of the Night" (the final section of his collection *Noctuary*), and the chapbook *Sideshow and Other Stories*.

Given Ligotti's assertion that a writer adopts experimentalism when the more traditional styles prove inadequate, we might speculate that it was this style that Lovecraft had in mind when he was searching for a new means of expression. Statements he made around the same general period that might seem to contradict this idea by cementing him firmly and exclusively in the role of scientific realist—such as his late-1936 claim to Fritz Leiber that one of his "cardinal principles regarding weird fiction" had always been the idea that "an air of absolute realism should be preserved (as if one were preparing an actual hoax instead of a story) *except* in the one limited field where the writer has chosen to depart . . . from the order of objective reality" (*Selected Letters* 5.342; Lovecraft's emphases)—may be taken simply as one more sign of the confusion he was then experiencing over stylistic matters, since it was this very approach that he had been expressing frequent and severe doubts over during the preceding months, almost to the point of repudiating it. Moreover, his words to Leiber are perhaps doubly suspect, since they echo sentiments he had expressed three years earlier in "Notes on the Writing of Weird Fiction," where he had counseled prospective weird fiction writers to "be sure that all references throughout the story are thoroughly reconciled with the final design," since "inconceivable events and conditions have a special handicap to overcome, and this can be accomplished only through the maintenance of a careful realism in *every* phase of the story except that touching on the one given marvel" (*Miscellaneous Writings* 114, 115; Lovecraft's emphasis). Throughout literary history, the descriptions that writers have given of their own compositional and creative processes, and also, especially, the prescriptions they have offered to other writers based upon these, have proved notoriously unreliable, in that these writers have not really practiced what they preach, or have not done so as casually and consistently as they make it appear. It almost seems as if the principles and points where writers present the greatest appearance of self-assurance are those where they should be most carefully interrogated, since these are the areas where they privately experience the greatest doubt and confusion. What we have already seen from Lovecraft should indicate that his words in "Notes on the Writing of Weird Fiction" and in the letter to Leiber are no exception to this rule, since they resound with a dogmatic certitude that conceals a very real, deep, and sincere uncertainty.

Having said all this, it may not be experimentalism alone that Lovecraft, or even Ligotti, was/is reaching for. In "Notes on the Writing of Horror," Ligotti/the narrator makes brief mention of "another style" that would supersede and obliterate all others. In order to do full justice to the story of Nathan (the protagonist whose example story he has been taking through permutations of the three standard styles), Ligotti/the narrator says he "wanted to employ a style that would conjure all the primordial powers of the universe independent of the conventional realities of the Individual, Society, or Art. I aspired toward nothing less than a pure style without style, a style having nothing whatsoever to do with the normal or abnormal, a style magic, timeless, and profound . . . and one of great horror, the horror of a god" (*Songs of a Dead Dreamer* 112). In other words, he was trying to burst the bonds of the written word (which recalls the narrator's thoughts in "Nethescurial") by writing a horror story that presented *pure* horror, the pristine experience in and of itself, on a veritably cosmic-divine level, and that would therefore be able to invade the reader's experience and become, instead of just a story on a page, his or her existential reality. The attempt failed, of course, because it was necessarily founded upon the very unreality (of the world of fiction) that it was attempting to overcome. That is, the whole idea was a categorical impossibility. But the passion behind it was and is real in the minds of both the narrator and Ligotti himself, and also, I think, in the mind of Lovecraft, whose passionate desire to give literary expression to his deepest emotions, and thereby to affect his readers deeply, at least equaled that of his successor.

Speaking of categorical impossibilities, the idea that I have been advancing—that the different form of writing the middle-aged Lovecraft inchoately desired to produce may have been the very form of writing that Ligotti is producing today, and that both may have ultimately longed to write in an impossible godlike style—is of course a categorically unverifiable conjecture. It is also a somewhat outlandish one, and I fear that the very articulation of it may seem extravagant. But for all that, I still feel it is a worthwhile possibility to consider, if only for the way it illuminates the writings of both men.

And having considered them together, as literary soulmates, it is now time to recognize their differences.

IV. Lovecraft and Ligotti, Sui Generis

It should be obvious by now that in stating Lovecraft's authorial ideal as "the use of maximum suggestion and minimal explanation to evoke a sense of supernatural terrors and wonders," Ligotti was stating his own ideal as well.

And this ought to lead us to suspect the objective validity of his judgment. In truth, it is probably the case that his understanding of Lovecraft is too strongly colored by his personal feelings to qualify as objective, and that it is Joshi, the scholar, and not Ligotti, the literary artist, who can validly lay claim to the most technically accurate assessment. For my own part, in poring over Ligotti's essays and interviews, I have gathered the impression that his response to Lovecraft, and in particular his sense of identification with Lovecraft's worldview, has been so intense that it has led him to impute too much of himself to his idol. In other words, he has to a certain extent reimagined Lovecraft in his own image.

A pertinent example of this can be seen in his descriptive analyses of Lovecraft's nightmare vision of reality, which are, in my opinion, entirely Ligottian, but not entirely Lovecraftian. My own reading of Lovecraft has given me the impression that while he was quite serious about the cosmic despair and philosophical concerns that undergird his stories, he did not experience precisely the same kind of existential torture and cosmic-ontological nightmare that characterize Ligotti's fictional world and personal life. Lovecraft, it seems to me, was emotionally and intellectually focused on the horror of "cosmic outsideness," of vast outer spaces and the mind-shattering powers and principles that may hold sway there, and that may occasionally impinge upon human reality and reveal its pathetic fragility. Even a minimal knowledge of his biography leads to the conclusion that this was an thoroughly appropriate focus for him, given his infatuation with, and wide-ranging knowledge of, astronomy in particular and natural science in general. The same personal interests also indicate that his forays into supernatural realism were far from being a waste, since they utilized a definite portion of his knowledge and a side of his character that otherwise would have languished in muteness.

Ligotti, by contrast, seems focused more upon the horror of deep *insideness*, of the dark, twisted, transcendent truths and mysteries that reside within consciousness itself and find their outward expression in scenes and situations of warped perceptions and diseased metaphysics. As with Lovecraft and his own idiosyncratic themes, these themes are characteristically Ligotti's, characteristically Ligottian through and through, and they have grown out of his life. Whereas Lovecraft was passionately interested in astronomy, chemistry, New England history and architecture, and many other subjects that found their ways into his fictional writings, Ligotti's "outside" interests include the literature of pessimism, the composing and playing of music, and the study of religion and spirituality, especially in its mystical or non-dual aspect.[3] Thus the idiosyncrasies of his typical style and themes are as natural and expectable as were Lovecraft's.

Importantly, despite their significant differences, the Ligottian and Lovecraftian brands of horror do exhibit family resemblances. It may even be that they represent opposite poles or complementary opposites on the same continuum, with Lovecraft's outer, transcendent, cosmic focus and Ligotti's inner, immanent, personal one finding their mutual confirmation and fulfillment in each other. But the really important thing to notice is that the distinction between Lovecraft's and Ligotti's respective horrific visions, combined with a recognition of their underlying kinship, helps to answer our original question about Ramsey Campbell's reasons, in his introduction to *Songs of a Dead Dreamer*, for mentioning in the same breath both Ligotti's separateness from and perceptible relationship to Lovecraft.

Another difference that I find between Lovecraft and Ligotti, and one whose significance is even more foundational, is that Lovecraft, as both a human being and an artist, was powerfully shaped by a lifelong experience of *Sehnsucht* (yearning or wistful longing), whereas in Ligotti this quality, while present, is overshadowed or even overpowered by stark, staring horror and a desperate bleakness. Lovecraft's poignant yearning after an experience of absolute beauty can be seen in many of his stories, such as "The Silver Key," where young Randolph Carter, Lovecraft's fictional alter ego, yearns for a return to the reimagined supernal peace and beauty of his childhood world, and also in his letters and essays, where he speaks repeatedly of finding himself overcome by aesthetic rapture and a sense of longing and "adventurous expectancy" at the sight of sunsets, cloudscapes, winding streets, rooftops angled in certain suggestive arrangements, and the like. The following passage from a 1927 letter to Donald Wandrei is typical:

> Sometimes I stumble accidentally on rare combinations of slope, curved street-line, roofs & gables & chimneys, & accessory details of verdure & background, which in the magic of late afternoon assume a mystic majesty and exotic significance beyond the power of words to describe. Absolutely nothing else in life now has the power to move me so much; for in these momentary vistas there seem to open before me bewildering avenues to all the wonders & lovelinesses I have ever sought, & to all those gardens of eld

---

3. An important aspect of Ligotti's psychological preparation for becoming a horror writer that I have not mentioned in this essay is his Roman Catholic upbringing, which he himself has cited as an important influence: "I was a Catholic until I was eighteen years old, when I unloaded all of the doctrines, but almost none of the fearful superstition, of a gothically devout childhood and youth" (Schweitzer 29).

whose memory trembles just beyond the rim of conscious recollection, yet close enough to lend to life all the significance it possesses. (*Selected Letters* 2.125–26)

Or again, from a 1930 letter to Clark Ashton Smith:

My most vivid experiences are efforts to recapture fleeting & tantalising mnemonic fragments expressed in unknown or half-known architectural or landscape vistas, especially in connexion with a sunset. Some instantaneous fragment of a picture will well up suddenly through some chain of subconscious association—the immediate excitant being usually half-irrelevant on the surface—& fill me with a sense of wistful memory & bafflement; with the impression that the scene in question represents something I have seen & visited before under circumstances of superhuman liberation & adventurous expectancy, yet which I have almost completely forgotten, & which is so bewilderingly uncorrelated & unoriented as to be forever inaccessible in the future. (*Selected Letters* 3.197)

Additional examples could be multiplied at length, and all would show, like the above passages, that Lovecraft was gripped by an ingrained and, we might say, "classical" sense of *Sehnsucht*, the "infinite longing that is the essence of romanticism," as E. T. A. Hoffmann famously formulated it. It was precisely this faculty that led him to respond with such intense delight to the mystically charged writings of Lord Dunsany, which exerted an enormous influence on his own subsequent work. Lovecraft's Dunsanian stories can and should be read not only as outflowings of his love for Dunsany's aesthetic vision but as expressions of his own personal sense of infinite longing.

Lovecraft even went so far as to assert that this feeling of longing, this heightened responsiveness to scenes and visions of beauty that seem to hint at a transcendent world of absolute aesthetic fulfillment, is

the impulse which justifies authorship. . . . The time to begin writing is when the events of the world seem to suggest things larger than the world—strangenesses and patterns and rhythms and uniquities of combination which no one ever saw or heard before, but which are so vast and marvellous and beautiful that they absolutely demand proclamation with a fanfare of silver trumpets. Space and time become vitalised with literary significance when they begin to make us subtly homesick for something "out of space, out of time". . . . *To find those other lives, other worlds, and other dreamlands, is the true author's task.* That is what literature is; and if any piece of writing is motivated by anything apart from this mystic and never-finished quest, it is base and unjustified imitation. (*Selected Letters* 2.142–43 [emphasis in original])

The fact that he made all these statements *after* his 1926 conversion (as we might call it) to supernatural realism demonstrates beyond all doubt that the longings and mood-based authorial motivations he experienced during his earlier period were still in full force later on. And this provides still further explanation for why those later, more realistic stories, with their tendency toward narrative over-explicitness and a certain clinical, "scientific" coldness of style, while they may constitute significant literary works in their own right, appeared to him a deviations from his true path and desire.

Ligotti is fully aware of all this, of course. No one who has made even a casual study of Lovecraft's life and works can be unaware of this aspect of his character, and Ligotti has studied him more seriously and extensively than most. He has read Lovecraft's stories, essays, and letters and has seen Lovecraft's repeated claim that his life was made bearable solely by virtue of those transcendent intimations of a supernal beauty. And Ligotti has, I think, responded to this in his own fashion. At the very least, he has recognized that even in a horror story like "The Music of Erich Zann," Lovecraft "captured at least a fragment of the desired object [i.e., the unattainable goal of that burning *Sehnsucht*] and delivered it to his readers" ("Dark Beauty" 84). But as mentioned above, in Ligotti's fictional world this yearning after beauty ends up being utterly subjugated to the experience of cosmic horror. I think it might even be possible to do a chronological study of the appearance and eventual complete submergence or subversion of this impulse in his stories. Early on, in such tales as "Les Fleurs," "The Frolic," "The Chymist," and "The Lost Art of Twilight," one can sense a world of suggestive beauties laced with horrors (or vice versa) being painted in the descriptive passages and in the hints of an alternate realm that borders the normal world: the "blasphemous fairyland" where John Doe frolics with his young victims, the "opulent kingdom of glittering colors and velvety jungle-shapes, a realm of contorted rainbows and twisted auroras" (*Songs of a Dead Dreamer* 12–13, 25) where the narrator of "Les Fleurs" dwells amidst a riotous floral beauty of hideous luxuriance. The emotional center of this subset of tales is summed up in a single sentence in "Vastarien," which itself stands as Ligotti's most singular, unified expression of this sort of longing: "Victor Keirion belonged to that wretched sect of souls who believe that the only value of this world lies in its power—at certain times—to suggest another world" (*Songs of a Dead Dreamer* 263). The very wording, aside from the description of those who are subject to this longing as "wretched," recalls some of the Lovecraft passages quoted above.

But as Ligotti's art progresses, the longing expressed in his stories mutates, until we are presented with such grim spectacles as "The Tsalal," in which protagonist Andrew Maness's longing is described in terms that subvert and transmute the desire for beauty into a desire for Gothic horror and bleakness. Andrew, the story informs us, was conceived as part of a sinister mystical rite that was intended to bring the Tsalal, a god or principle of ultimate darkness, into this world. As "the seed of that one," he will find that throughout his life he "will be drawn to a place that reveals the sign of the Tsalal—an aspect of the unreal, a forlorn glamor in things" (*Noctuary* 93). This attraction takes the form of a longing that still bears certain similarities to Lovecraft's, since it is still based on the desire to see and experience another world—and yet for Andrew Maness, the sights and scenes that evoke the longing, and the fundamental character of the other world that he desires, have nothing whatsoever to do with sunsets or mystical vistas, or indeed with any sort of beauty at all:

> Perhaps he would come upon an abandoned house standing shattered and bent in an isolated landscape—a raw skeleton in a boneyard. But this dilapidated structure would seem to him a temple, a wayside shrine to that dark presence with which he sought union, and also a doorway to the dark world in which it dwelled. Nothing can convey those sensations, the countless nuances of trembling excitement, as he approached such a decomposed edifice whose skewed and ragged outline suggested another order of existence, the truest order of existence, as though such places as this house were only wavering shadows cast down to earth by a distant, unseen realm of entity. (*Noctuary* 83)

For this narrator, such grim and spectral scenes inspire the sense of an imminent, nightmarish transformation being worked upon the world through the agency of his own being, and this in turn "overwhelm[s] him with a black intoxication and suggest[s] his life's goal: to work the great wheel that turns in darkness, and to be broken upon it" (*Noctuary* 83). Obviously, this is light-years from Lovecraft's "vague impressions of adventurous expectancy coupled with elusive memory—impressions that certain vistas, particularly those associated with sunsets, are avenues of approach to spheres or conditions of wholly undefined delights and freedoms which I have known in the past and have a slender possibility of knowing again in the future" (*Selected Letters* 3.243). This contrast, not incidentally, has resulted in dramatic disparities between the two men's fictional representations of longing. One need only compare any of the above-quoted Ligotti passages, or any of a dozen others, to analogous descriptive passages from Lovecraft's dream stories in order to see the difference.[4]

Ligotti has inadvertently given us a clue about how to articulate this particular distinction between Lovecraft and himself. He has written, "Like Erich Zann's 'world of beauty,' Lovecraft's 'lay in some far cosmos of the imagination,' and like that of another artist, it is a 'beauty that hath horror in it'" ("Dark Beauty" 84). For Ligotti himself, however, the order of primacy is reversed: his other-world is a horror that hath beauty in it. It is world of horror first and foremost, with its undeniable, intermittent beauty standing only as an accident or epiphenomenon—and perhaps as a kind of deadly lure. Understanding this, we will not wonder at the fact that his oeuvre contains nothing even remotely resembling Lovecraft's Dunsanian stories. He has never written, or at least never published, anything like Lovecraft's "The Quest of Iranon" or "Celephaïs," the first of which is entirely lacking in horror and the second of which only lightly brushes past it, and both of which take for their primary themes not Gothic darkness but ethereal beauty and bittersweet poignancy.

The thematic progression of Ligotti's fiction away from any sort of expressed longing and toward a zenith, which is to say an emotional nadir, of despair and horror is completed in "The Bungalow House," which portrays

---

4. Consider, for example, the already-quoted passage from Ligotti's "The Tsalal" with the following passage from Lovecraft's *The Dream-Quest of Unknown Kadath*: "Three times Randolph Carter dreamed of the marvellous city, and three times was he snatched away while still he paused on the high terrace above it. All golden and lovely it blazed in the sunset, with walls, temples, colonnades, and arched bridges of veined marble, silver-basined fountains of prismatic spray in broad squares and perfumed gardens, and wide streets marching between delicate trees and blossom-laden urns and ivory statues in gleaming rows; while on steep northward slopes climbed tiers of red roofs and old peaked gables harbouring little lanes of grassy cobbles. It was a fever of the gods; a fanfare of supernal trumpets and a clash of immortal cymbals. Mystery hung about it as clouds about a fabulous unvisited mountain; and as Carter stood breathless and expectant on that balustraded parapet there swept up to him the poignancy and suspense of almost-vanished memory, the pain of lost things, and the maddening need to place again what once had an awesome and momentous place" (*At the Mountains of Madness* 306). The parallels and divergences are equally instructive. Both passages present protagonists who are in the act of surveying and responding to moody architectural scenes. Both are written from the intensity of each authors' genuine emotional and artistic visions. But what a titanic difference there is between their tones and intents! The very magnitude of the difference suggests a fundamental disparity between the respective metaphysical absolutes which the authors are straining to conceive.

the miserable death of the very capacity to yearn. The protagonist of the story, a solitary librarian, becomes infatuated with a series of bizarre audio performance tapes that he discovers at a local art gallery. These tapes contain first-person "dream monologues" narrated by an oddly familiar voice, and the bleak, surreal scenes they describe touch an emotional chord deep within him, causing him to respond with the same feeling of "euphoric hopelessness" described by the taped voice. Expressing a sentiment that rather recalls Ligotti's closing words in his essay "The Consolations of Horror,"[5] the narrator of "The Bungalow House" says he feels comforted by the tapes, since they demonstrate that someone else has shared his most private and powerful insights and emotions. "To think," he says with rhetorical emphasis, "that another person shared my love for the *icy bleakness of things*" (*Nightmare Factory* 523; Ligotti's emphasis).

But by the story's end, he has been emotionally devastated by a personal confrontation with the owner of the anonymous voice, and by a "twist" that reveals a previously unsuspected depth to his own wretchedness. The result is that he has been robbed of that selfsame ability to feel "the intense and highly aesthetic perception of what I call the *icy bleakness of things*" (*Nightmare Factory* 523) that had initially attracted him to the tapes. The story's closing lines explicitly describe the nature of his loss:

> I try to experience the infinite terror and dreariness of a bungalow universe in the way I once did, but it is not the same as it once was. There is no comfort in it, even though the vision and the underlying principles are still the same. . . . More than ever, some sort of new arrangement seems in order, some dramatic and unknown arrangement—anything to find release from this heartbreaking sadness I suffer every minute of the day (and night), this killing sadness that feels as if it will never leave me no matter where I go or what I do or whom I may ever know. (*Nightmare Factory* 532)

This emotional death signals a lasting shift in Ligotti's writing; in his post–"Bungalow House" stories it is difficult, if not impossible, to find evidence of the same yearning, however dark its character by the time of "The Tsalal," that informed much of his earlier work. This leads us to suspect a strong autobiographical component to this thematic arc, and we are confirmed in our

---

5. "This, then, is the ultimate, that is only, consolation [of fictional horror]: simply that someone shares some of your own feelings and has made of these a work of art which you have the insight, sensitivity, and—like it or not—peculiar set of experiences to appreciate" (*The Nightmare Factory* xxi).

suspicions by Ligotti's nonfictional description of his agonized struggles with anhedonia in *The Conspiracy against the Human Race.*[6]

One of the most fundamental elements of any writer's psychological makeup is the central impulse that motivates him to write at all. When we compare Ligotti's expressed motivations with Lovecraft's, we find that this dividing line between them—Lovecraft's golden longing contrasting with Ligotti's gloomy one that eventually dies in desolation—extends all the way inward to that foundational level. We have already seen that Lovecraft said he wrote directly out of his *Sehnsucht,* "to give myself the satisfaction of visualising more clearly and detailedly and stably the vague, elusive, fragmentary impressions of wonder, beauty, and adventurous expectancy" that he derived from various sources. In the same essay, he went on to explain why he wrote the particular kind of story that his readers have come to associate him with, and his words are of paramount significance to our concerns here:

> I choose weird stories because they suit my inclination best—one of my strongest and most persistent wishes being to achieve, momentarily, the illusion of some strange suspension or violation of the galling limitations of time, space, and natural law which forever imprison us and frustrate our curiosity about the infinite cosmic spaces beyond the radius of our sight and analysis. *These stories frequently emphasize the element of horror because fear is our deepest and strongest emotion, and the one which best lends itself to the creation of Nature-defying illusions.* Horror and the unknown or the strange are always closely connected, so that it is hard to create a convincing picture of shattered natural law or cosmic alienage or "outsideness" without laying stress on the emotion of fear. (*Miscellaneous Writings* 113 [emphasis added])

The import of this statement for Lovecraft's role or identity as a horror writer is obvious: he was saying, circa 1933, that he only wrote horror because it was useful for achieving another effect that is not intrinsically horrific. In other words, for him horror was a means, not an end. It was his poignant, wistful longing after transcendent beauty and cosmic freedom that animated his authorial life—and not only that, but his life in general. In the same letter where he described his "vague impressions of adventurous expectancy coupled with elusive memory," he claimed that this intense emotional experience was chief among the reasons why he did not commit suicide—"the reasons, that is, why I still find existence enough of a compensation to atone for its dominantly burthernsome [*sic*] quality" (*Selected Letters* 3.243).

Such an attitude contrasts sharply with the reason, quoted earlier, that Li-

---

6. The reference is to the prepublication draft of the book, mentioned in Note 1 above.

gotti has given for going on with life: "to communicate, in the form of horror stories, the outrage and panic at being alive in the world." He frames this as "following Lovecraft's way," and to a degree he is correct, since the horror Lovecraft expressed in his stories was entirely authentic. But as we have seen, it was not the whole of Lovecraft's subjective reality, nor, by his own account, was it the ultimate end of his creative endeavors. This means it is just one more indication of Ligotti's radical emotional and intellectual appropriation of Lovecraft when he holds up horror as Lovecraft's real message and meaning, and for the most part relegates every other aspect of his life, writings, and character to peripheral status. For Ligotti, horror—the kind he experienced at the age of seventeen in that Lovecraftian epiphany of a meaningless, menacing cosmos— is all that is "really real," and whenever he, Lovecraft, or anybody else departs from living in the full nightmarish intensity of it, this equates with "think[ing] and act[ing] like every other goof and sucker on this planet" (Bee).[7]

So we are left with a kind of paradox or contradiction, in that Ligotti identifies strongly with Lovecraft as a writer and human being and has modeled his own life and writings upon Lovecraft's example, and yet the aesthetic longing that was central to Lovecraft's character and writings, and which comes out most clearly in the early stories Ligotti so greatly admires, is something that Ligotti is forced, by virtue of his own personal vision and experience, to view as peripheral. A likely explanation for this fact is that when Ligotti first discovered Lovecraft and fastened upon his writings as expressions of the emotional and philosophical horror that he was then experiencing, this resulted in his gaining a one-sided understanding. His private predisposition illuminated with stunning intensity an important facet of

---

7. For a general elucidation of this point, see Ligotti's words in *The Conspiracy against the Human Race* (again, the now-vanished original draft) in the section titled "Happiness," where he points out that even Lovecraft, who in his letters wrote about his nervous breakdowns and other personal troubles, as well as about the ultimate futility and miserableness of existence in general, "more often . . . wrote about what a fine time he had on a given day or expatiated on the joys of his travels around the United States and Canada or simply joked around with a correspondent about a wide range of subjects in which he was well-studied." Ligotti closes the section by asserting that "the very idea of happiness [is] an unconscionable delusion conceived by fools or a deplorable rationalization dreamed up by swine." Obviously, he does not think Lovecraft was a fool or a swine, so the implication is that Lovecraft was merely taking a break, as it were, from his real concerns—i.e., he was being just another "goof and sucker"—whenever he distracted himself from the final truth of perpetual, horrified misery.

Lovecraft's vision, but at the same time it relegated equally important facets to secondary status. We may view the overall result as ironic, since the part of Lovecraft's life and work that has hitherto been overlooked by the reading public at large—his longing after beauty—in favor of framing him purely and solely as a horror writer (witness the contents of the 2005 Modern Library collection of Lovecraft's tales, which omit entirely the dream and Dunsanian stories) is also obscured by the overwhelming horrific focus of Ligotti, who is widely recognized as one of Lovecraft's most prominent literary heirs.

V. Conclusion: The Enchanting Nightmare

Having gone on at such length about Ligotti's "appropriation" of Lovecraft, let me now hasten to add that I do not consider his subjective attitude to be at all inappropriate. Far from being a detriment, it is the proper attitude for any artist who comes under the sway of a powerful, life-changing forebear. Indeed, it recalls the response of Lovecraft himself to the writings of Lord Dunsany. Lovecraft first read Dunsany's *A Dreamer's Tales* in 1919. He later described the book's impact by stating that its first paragraph had "arrested me as with an electrick shock, & I had not read two pages before I became a Dunsany devotee for life" (*Selected Letters* 2.328). He felt that Dunsany was saying everything that he, Lovecraft, had hitherto wished to say as an author, and four years later he still claimed a thorough sense of identification with the man: "Dunsany *is myself*. . . . His cosmic realm is the realm in which I live; his distant, emotionless vistas of the beauty of moonlight on quaint and ancient roofs are the vistas I know and cherish" (*Selected Letters* 1.234; Lovecraft's emphasis). Far from injuring or cheapening his work, Lovecraft's love affair with Dunsany served as a catalyst for the crystalization of thoughts, emotions, and a narrative style that were already imminent in his own writing. His felt identification with the man acted as a midwife for his own birth into creative maturity.

I cannot help thinking that Ligotti's position with regard to Lovecraft is analogous. Intellectually, he probably has as balanced an understanding of Lovecraft as any scholar, but this necessarily takes a second place to his emotional response. As an artist, his primary calling is not to pursue the strict scholarly accuracy of a Joshi but to bear witness to what he sees, feels, and knows within the depths of his being. And even though his understanding of Lovecraft is intensely subjective, it is also for that very reason all the more potent. In an artistic or "spiritual" sense, it may even be more accurate than Joshi's, the evidence of which can be seen in the fact, with which we commenced this exploration, that while Ligotti's stories "only resemble Lovecraft's in the most tenuous manner," they almost invariably "evoke Lovecraft's shade" in the minds of his readers. "I hope my stories are in the Lovecraftian tradition," he has said, "in that they may evoke a sense of terror whose source is something nightmarishly unreal, the implications of which are disturbingly weird and, in the magical sense, charming."[8] He has also said, "In my eyes, Lovecraft dreamed the great dream of supernatural literature—to convey with the greatest possible intensity a vision of the universe as a kind of enchanting nightmare" (Ford 32). Whether or not he is technically accurate in this assessment of the deep nature of Lovecraft's artistic vision—and in this particular case I think he is dead-on—his *belief* that this was Lovecraft's dream has led him to produce a priceless body of weird fiction. One likes to think that Lovecraft himself would have been deeply pleased by this showing from his most worthy disciple.

2005

Works Cited

Angerhuber, E. M., and Thomas Wagner. "Disillusionment Can Be Glamorous: An Interview with Thomas Ligotti." In Darrell Schweitzer, ed. *The Thomas Ligotti Reader*. Holicong, PA: Wildside Press, 2003. 53–71.

Ayad, Neddal. "Literature Is Entertainment or It Is Nothing: An Interview with Thomas Ligotti." In Matt Cardin, ed. *Born to Fear: Interviews with Thomas Ligotti*. Burton, MI: Subterranean Press, 2014. 95–116.

Bee, Robert. "Interview with Thomas Ligotti." *Thomas Ligotti Online*. 11 April 2005 (originally published in 1999). www.ligotti.net/showthread.php?t=231.

Bryant, Ed., et al. "Transcript of Chat with Thomas Ligotti on December 3, 1998." *Thomas Ligotti Online*. Accessed 10 December 2020. www.ligotti.net/tlo/flashpointchat.html.

Ford, Carl. "Notes on the Writing of Horror: An Interview with Thomas Ligotti." *Dagon* Nos. 22/23 (September–December 1988): 30–35.

Joshi, S. T. *H. P. Lovecraft: A Life*. West Warwick, RI: Necronomicon Press, 1996.

———. "H. P. Lovecraft." The Scriptorium at *The Modern Word*. Revised 1 June 2000. www.themodernword.com/scriptorium/lovecraft.html. Revision and expansion of an essay originally published in David E. Schultz

---

8. Shawn Ramsey, "A Graveside Chat: Interview with Thomas Ligotti" (1989), quoted in Joshi, "Thomas Ligotti: The Escape from Life" 142.

and S. T. Joshi, ed. *An Epicure of the Terrible: A Centennial Anthology of Essays in Honor of H. P. Lovecraft.* Rutherford, NJ: Fairleigh Dickinson University Press, 1991.

———. "Ligotti in Triplicate." Review of *My Work Is Not Yet Done: Three Tales of Corporate Horror* by Thomas Ligotti. *Necropsy: The Review of Horror Fiction* 6 (Summer 2002). Accessed 1 January 2005. www.lsu.edu/necrofile/ mywork.html.

———. "Thomas Ligotti: The Escape from Life." In Darrell Schweitzer, ed. *The Thomas Ligotti Reader: Essays and Exploration.* Holicong, PA: Wildside Press, 2003. 139–53.

Ligotti, Thomas. *The Conspiracy against the Human Race.* Prepublication manuscript, 2005.

———. "The Dark Beauty of Unheard-Of Horrors." In Darrell Schweitzer, ed. *The Thomas Ligotti Reader.* Holicong, PA: Wildside Press, 2003. 78–84.

———. *Grimscribe: His Lives and Works.* New York: Jove Books, 1994.

———. *The Nightmare Factory.* New York: Carroll & Graff, 1996.

———. *Noctuary.* New York: Carroll & Graff, 1995.

———. *Songs of a Dead Dreamer.* New York: Carroll & Graff, 1991.

Lovecraft, H. P. *At the Mountains of Madness and Other Novels.* Sauk City, WI: Arkham House, 1985.

———. *Dagon and Other Macabre Tales.* Sauk City, WI: Arkham House, 1987.

———. *Miscellaneous Writings.* Ed. S. T. Joshi. Sauk City, WI: Arkham House, 1995.

———. *Selected Letters.* Ed. August Derleth, Donald Wandrei, and James Turner. Sauk City, WI: Arkham House, 1965–76. 5 vols.

Padgett, Jonathan. "Thomas Ligotti FAQ." *Thomas Ligotti Online.* Accessed 24 January 2005. www.ligotti.net/tlo/faq.html

Paul, R. F., and Keith Schurholz. "Triangulating the Daemon: An Interview with Thomas Ligotti." *Esoterra* No. 8 (Winter/Spring 1999): 14–21.

Schweitzer, Darrell. "*Weird Tales* Talks with Thomas Ligotti." In Darrell Schweitzer, ed. *The Thomas Ligotti Reader.* Holicong, PA: Wildside Press, 2003. 23–31.

Wilbanks, David. "10 Questions for Thomas Ligotti." *Page Horrific,* February 2004. Accessed 22 January 2005. www.ligotti.net/showthread.php?t=1248

The Transition from Literary Horror to Existential Nightmare in Thomas Ligotti's "Nethescurial"

Thomas Ligotti's "Nethescurial" may be classed with a half-dozen or so of his tales that deal directly with a theme that, although it is seldom entirely absent from his fiction, he sometimes approaches more obliquely: the theme of transcendent, mystical, ontologically absolute evil. Of particular interest in this story is the way Ligotti augments its emotional power through his use of rich descriptive language and, most importantly, metafictionally flavored multiple framing devices to create the sense of the literary-existential barrier being breached.

"Nethescurial" is framed as a letter or journal written by a man (or perhaps a woman; the sex of the narrator is never specified) who has stumbled across a previously unknown late nineteenth-century manuscript in a library archive. The manuscript relates the story of an ancient religious sect devoted to an evil god, and by the end of "Nethescurial" the narrator discovers that the merely literary horror of the tale in the manuscript has overtaken his own existential reality.

The story is told in three sections. The first, titled "The Idol and the Island," describes the discovery of the manuscript and summarizes its contents in some detail. According to the narrator, the manuscript seems to be a letter, or perhaps a journal entry, written by one Bartholomew Gray (a self-admitted alias) and relating the story of Gray's visit to "an obscure island located at some unspecified northern latitude" at the request of an anthropologist referred to only as Dr. N— (*Grimscribe* 75). When Mr. Gray arrives, he observes that the very structure of the island and its fauna appear to have been twisted or mutated into a sort of nightmarish aspect. Dr. N— reveals to Mr. Gray that he (Dr. N—) has found buried on the island a fragment of an ancient religious idol whose worshippers had apparently held the pantheistic belief that "all created things—appearances to the contrary—are of a single, unified, and transcendent *stuff*, an emanation of a central creative force" (78). The faith of these people was shattered when "one day it was revealed to them, in a manner both obscure and hideous, that the power to which they bowed was essentially evil in character and that their religious mode of pantheism was in truth a kind of *pandemonism*" (79). They coined the name "Nethescurial" to reflect the evil character of the force they served, and then they destroyed their idol and dispersed its fragments to various secret locations around the world. But despite their efforts to destroy the cult, there survived a sect that remained devoted to the service of Nethescurial, and Dr. N— speculates that perhaps he and Mr. Gray are in danger from this very sect. In a plot twist that is expectable (at least according to the narrator who is summarizing this manuscript), it turns out that Mr. Gray is himself one of the surviving servants of Nethescurial and that he has in fact brought with him to the island the other collected fragments of the idol. He takes the last fragment from Dr. N— by force and then sacrifices the unfortunate anthropologist to the god, but later he repents of his evil deed after encountering some "horrific surprises" (80). Finally, he manages to make his escape from the island, throwing the pieces of the idol into the ocean in the process. The manuscript purports to be his own account of the matter.

The narrator of "Nethescurial" casts some aspersions on the literary style of this old manuscript, calling it somewhat incoherent, formulaic, and poorly developed. But then he admits that the central idea of pandemonism is "intriguing," and he reveals within his own psyche and sensibility a certain latent fascination with and responsiveness to the kind of horror described by the story. The section ends with the narrator mentioning in a jocular tone that it is time for him to go to bed.

The second section of the story, titled "Postscript," is dated "Later the same night" (82) and is penned by the narrator while he is still suffering the aftereffects of a horrific nightmare. In the nightmare he had found himself on the isle of Nethescurial, where he witnessed the ritual (and willing) sacrifice of a worshipper to the god. The overwhelming sense of horror and panic that could only be hinted at by the manuscript was communicated to him vividly in the dream. He felt menaced by "an unseen presence, something I could feel was circulating within all things and unifying them in an infinitely extensive body of evil." Perhaps worst of all, he could also feel this evil presence "emerging in myself, growing stronger behind this living face that I am afraid to confront in a mirror" (86). He concludes his remarks with the thought that he will surely be back to normal by morning.

In the third section, titled "The Puppets in the Park" and dated "Some days later, and quite late at night," the narrator notes that his own continuing letter (which of course forms the body of the story) "has mutated into a chronicle of my adventures Nethescurialian" (87). He is awash in horror: unable to take nourishment, and compelled to wear gloves and keep moving because of the nightmarish presence he sees "squirming" and "gushing" inside all things, he has begun to hear an ominous chant sounding from the subconscious minds of everyone with whom he comes in contact. He makes his way to an outdoor park at night, where he stumbles across a puppet show in a clearing. At some point during the show, the puppets freeze and slowly turn to look directly into his eyes. He is standing behind the back row of the audience, and suddenly he notices that the audience members are looking at him as well, all of them turned around on their benches and staring at him "with expressionless faces and dead puppet eyes" (89). He hears a silent chant rising from their subconscious minds, a chant about the omnipresence of a certain evil entity—the same chant, in fact, that appears in the manuscript about the isle of Nethescurial— and he eventually returns home. Once there, he burns the manuscript in his fireplace, but the smoke seems unwilling to rise up the chimney, preferring instead to hang above the smoldering ashes in a cloud of mutating and suggestively horrible shapes. The tale ends with the narrator trying to convince himself that reality is not what he has come to fear, that *"Nethescurial is not the secret name of the creation,"* and finally that "I am not dying in a nightmare" (90–91).

The emotional and psychological impact of this tale is quite profound. As I noted in this essay's introduction, two of the most important factors in generating such a powerful effect, aside from the sheer potency of the story's central theme, are Ligotti's rich descriptive language and his clever use of multiple framing devices. For the first part, Ligotti invests his story from the beginning with an aura of cosmic strangeness when he "quotes" the chant at the beginning of the fictional manuscript: "In the rooms of houses and beyond their walls—beneath dark waters and across moonlit skies—below earth mound and above mountain peak—in northern leaf and southern flower— inside each star and the voids between them—within blood and bone, through all souls and spirits—among the watchful winds of this and the several worlds—behind the faces of the living and the dead" (75). The evocative tone of this passage sets up an expectation of weirdness and profundity that is amply sustained by the rest of the story. Employing a technique borrowed from Poe, Ligotti alternates these poetically toned passages with more mundane ones, such as the narrator's flippant remarks about the inherent weaknesses of horror stories. At the end of the story when the narrator suddenly lapses into florid, adjective-loaded language to speak of his impending personal apocalypse (and perhaps of the universal one?), the effect is truly unnerving:

> See, there is no shape in the fireplace. The smoke is gone, gone up the chimney and out into the sky. And there is nothing in the sky, nothing I can see through the window. There is the moon, of course, high and round. But no shadow falls across the moon, no churning chaos of smoke that chokes

the frail order of the earth, no shifting cloud of nightmares enveloping moons and suns and stars. It is not a squirming, creeping, smearing shape I see upon the moon, not the shape of a great deformed crab scuttling out of the black oceans of infinity and invading the island of the moon, crawling with its innumerable bodies upon all the spinning islands of inky space. That shape is not the cancerous totality of all creatures, not the oozing ichor that flows within all things. *Nethescurial is not the secret name of the creation.* (90)

Of course, Ligotti is working at the same disadvantage that plagues any writer of fiction who wants his or her work to have a real impact on the reader. This disadvantage is nothing more nor less than the simple fact that a story is, by category and definition, just a story. It will never be "real life" in the same sense as the reader's own immediate subjective experience. No matter how powerfully a story may grip a reader's mind or emotions, it is still just a story, still just a bounded narrative that stands outside the circle of the reader's real, living, subjective, first-person experience. It is something with a built-in distance, something that never truly encompasses the one who reads or hears it.

All this is true. And it is also precisely why Ligotti's use of framing devices is so important to "Nethescurial"'s overall effect: because the technique calls attention to the reader's relationship to the ontological world of the story. "Nethescurial" contains four narrative levels. First is the story of the ancient cult of Nethescurial as related by Dr. N—. Second is the story of Dr. N— and "Bartholomew Gray" as penned by the latter. Third is the story of the narrator as told through his letter, which, as mentioned above, makes up the body of "Nethescurial." Fourth is the story of the narrator's letter itself, i.e., the unspoken context of the very story the reader is reading. Each successive level frames the previous ones. Dr. N— tells Mr. Gray the story of the ancient cult; the narrator reads of Dr. N— and Mr. Gray in Gray's manuscript; and the reader encounters the narrator's thoughts in a "letter" that is actually the story itself. This very structure calls attention to the fact of the reader's status as a reader, which in turn lends extra power to Ligotti's tactic of breaching the narrative levels. Level one (the ancient cult) breaches level two (Dr. N— and Mr. Gray) when Mr. Gray turns out to be a member of the cult and murders Dr. N—. This level in turn breaches level three (the narrator) when the narrator is apparently overtaken by the evil god described in the manuscript. If we ask about the breach of the fourth level by the third—that is, of the reader's actual life and world by the story "Nethescurial" itself—we can only say that this of course cannot be accomplished directly, since that would entail the reader's existential world being transformed into the story world. But then, *that is exactly what Ligotti is writing about.* He seems almost to be playing a game with the reader's sense of distance from the horrors of the story.

For example, Ligotti quite deliberately has the unnamed narrator comment on the literary qualities of the newly discovered manuscript, which of course creates a sense of distance between the two (manuscript and narrator). He even has the narrator reflect upon the inability of supernatural literature to effect a real belief on the part of the reader: "The problem," the narrator writes, "is that such supernatural inventions are indeed quite difficult to imagine. So often they fail to materialize in the mind, to take on a mental texture, and thus remain unfelt as anything but an abstract monster of metaphysics—an elegant or awkward schematic that cannot rise from the paper to touch us" (81–82). Ligotti even has the narrator take a kind of comfort in this distance: "Of course, we do need to keep a certain distance from such specters as Nethescurial, but this is usually provided by the medium of words as such, which ensnare all kinds of fantastic creatures before they can tear us body and soul" (82). The trick comes in when, as we have already seen, the narrator's sense of safety with his narrative distance from the manuscript proves to be ill-founded. The analogy between this situation and the reader's own relation to the story, which the reader may only intuit subconsciously (although I am here calling it out for direct recognition—perhaps foolishly? dangerously?), is surely a significant factor in the story's emotional impact.

Joyce Carol Oates, in a comment on H. P. Lovecraft's "The Colour out of Space" in her introduction to the anthology *American Gothic Tales*, notes that the story represents "the wholly obverse vision of American destiny; the repudiation of American-Transcendentalist optimism, in which the individual is somehow divine, or shares in nature's divinity. In the gothic imagination there has been a profound and irrevocable split between mankind and nature in the romantic sense, and a tragic division between what we wish to know and what may be staring us in the face" (7). In "Nethescurial" and other stories, Thomas Ligotti has taken this technique to a new level, in that he posits the *truth* of the Transcendentalist doctrine of ultimate unity, but then raises the question: What if this unity is not blissful, but nightmarish? What if the all-pervading god who is our very self, our own deepest identity, turns out to be a monster? In Ligotti's fictional world, the answer to this question lies all around us and within us. We cannot escape from the nightmare when the nightmare turns out to be our own soul.

2000

Works Cited

Ligotti, Thomas. *Grimscribe: His Lives and Works.* New York: Jove Books, 1994.

Oates, Joyce Carol, ed. *American Gothic Tales.* New York: Plume, 1996.

Liminal Terror and Collective Identity in Thomas Ligotti's "The Shadow at the Bottom of the World"

> But I wanted to witness what could never be
> I wanted to see what could not be seen—
> The moment of consummate disaster
> When puppets turn to face the puppetmaster.
> —Thomas Ligotti, *I Have a Special Plan for This World*

Thomas Ligotti has long been known for the extreme darkness of his philosophical vision, and in this essay I examine this darkness as it relates to his story "The Shadow at the Bottom of the World." Specifically, I explore the ways in which the story uses the motifs of liminal terror and collective identity to achieve the acme of philosophical nightmarishness that has become recognized as the hallmark of Ligotti's work.

Plot Summary

"The Shadow at the Bottom of the World" tells the story of an unspecified rural town that experiences an unnatural prolongation of the autumn season one year. The sights, sounds, and smells of autumn ripen to an almost unbearable pitch, until one night the town's residents see a scarecrow begin to move in a grotesque fashion in a farmer's field on the edge of town. They gather the next day to examine the scarecrow, and when they attack it and remove its outer garments, they discover not the expected wooden frame but "something black and twisted into the form of a man, something that seemed to have come up from the earth and grown over the wooden planks like a dark fungus, consuming the structure" (*Grimscribe* 222). In a vague communal panic, they dig deep into the earth to find the base of the stalk, but no matter how far they dig, they cannot find its end. By the next day the stalk has disappeared—"It's gone back," says the farmer who owns the field, "Gone into the earth like something hiding in its shell" (224)—and in its place there is now a wide and seemingly bottomless pit.

The overripe autumn season continues to linger through the following days and weeks until eventually the townspeople's dreams are affected. "In sleep," they say,

> we were consumed by the feverish life of the earth, cast among a ripe, fairly rotting world of strange growth and transformation. We took a place within a darkly flourishing landscape where even the air was ripened into ruddy hues and everything wore the wrinkled grimace of decay, the mottled complexion of old flesh. The face of the land itself was knotted with so many other faces, ones that were corrupted by vile impulses. Grotesque expressions were molding themselves into the darkish grooves of ancient bark and the whorls of withered leaf; pulpy, misshapen features peered out of damp furrows; and the crisp skin of stalks and dead seeds split into a multitude of crooked smiles. All was a freakish mask painted with russet, rashy colors— colors that bled with a virulent intensity, so rich and vibrant that things trembled with their own ripeness. But despite this gross palpability, there remained something spectral at the heart of these dreams. It moved in shadow, a presence that was in the world of solid forms but not of it. Nor did it belong to any other world that could be named, unless it was to that realm which is suggested to us by an autumn night when fields lay ragged in moonlight and some wild spirit has entered into things, a great aberration sprouting forth from a chasm of moist and fertile shadows, a hollow-eyed howling malignity rising to present itself to the cold emptiness of space and the pale gaze of the moon. (225–26)

Things come to a head one night when two strangers, a woman and a small boy, arrive in town unexpectedly and begin to walk the streets. The townspeople watch from their windows as one of their own named Mr. Marble goes out to meet them. Mr. Marble is an old eccentric, well known to everyone, who all along has seemed to understand much more about what is happening to the town than its other residents are able to grasp. He is a blade sharpener by trade, an "old visionary who sharpened knives and axes and curving scythes" (227), and the spell of the season seems to have overtaken him with an especially virulent intensity. On the night of the visitors' arrival, he reappears from an unexplained absence and begins to stalk the streets with a blade in his hand: "Possessed by the ecstasies of a dark festival, he moved in a trance, bearing in his hand that great ceremonial knife whose keen edge flashed a thousand glittering dreams" (228). The townspeople watch in anticipation as he approaches the visitors to perform the rightful sacrifice that will culminate the energies of this aberrant season. But his hand trembles; he is unable to do it, and the woman and the boy flee. The next morning the townspeople find him face down in the farmer's field, dead of a self-inflicted wound from his own blade. His blood appears to be of the same substance that grew up from the ground and into the scarecrow, and they take the body and throw it into the pit.

Collapsing Categories

From the outset, "The Shadow at the Bottom of the World" abounds in details that invite the reader to analyze it in terms of the motif of liminality. By this term I refer to the idea, so familiar to poststructuralist critics, of a state or category that does not conform to the rigidly defined distinctions of conventional thinking, but instead falls somehow "between" the lines of generally accepted categories. The term "liminal" itself is borrowed from the discipline of anthropology, where many researchers have used it to refer to the status of tribal members during the period of their initiation into full adulthood. Such people are regularly viewed as neither adults nor children for the duration of the initiation ceremony, and as such they "elude or slip through the network of classifications that normally locate states and positions in cultural space" (Turner 95). In a word, they are *liminal* entities.

The significance of this idea for the matter at hand is found in the fact that encounters with liminal phenomena almost always produce a sense of strangeness, uncomfortableness, or uncanniness. This reaction accounts for the fact, noted by structuralist theorist Edmund Leach, that "whenever we make category distinctions within a unified field . . . it is the boundaries that matter; we concentrate our attention on the differences, not the similarities, and this makes us feel that the markers of such boundaries are of special value, 'sacred', 'taboo'" (35). This is the case simply because an encounter with something that falls on the interstices of one's conceptual and cultural "world" tends to remind one of the fact that virtual mountains of phenomena have been, and are being, excluded from one's field of vision by the classificatory grid itself. One realizes that reality itself is much bigger and stranger and more unbounded than one usually perceives it to be, and thus the validity of the grid is called into question. Sociologist Peter Berger argues that "the socially constructed world is, above all, an ordering of experience. A meaningful order, or nomos, is imposed upon the discrete experiences and meanings of individuals" (19). Berger argues further that nomization is every society's most important function. To be separated from the nomizing influence of society, he says, is to be in danger of experiencing a sense of meaninglessness, which in his view is "the nightmare *par excellence*, in which the individual is submerged in a world of disorder, senselessness and madness. Reality and identity are malignantly transformed into meaningless figures of horror. To be in society is to be 'sane' precisely in the sense of being shielded from the ultimate 'insanity' of such anomic terror" (22).

The question at hand, of course, is whether such an experience of anomic terror—which for the purposes of this paper shall be equated with *liminal* terror—is possible without being separated from a societal nomos. Is it possible that hints of this terror may filter into the daylight world of nomic reality through the interstices of the classificatory grid (which in structural terms would be explained as a system of binary opposites) that define the world's parameters? Further, is it possible that *literature* might serve as one such venue for the experience of liminal terror? Literature scholar Scott Carpenter points out that the use of literary techniques that emphasize the fuzzy boundaries between our conceptual categories—that is, techniques that emphasize the *limen*, the threshold between the categories—"traditionally excite[s] the fear and fascination of readers. Thus the intersection of such opposites as living/dead gives rise to ghost stories (phantoms being both animate and inanimate), the blending of human and inhuman gives birth to such figures as Frankenstein's monster, and the intermingling of past and present becomes the stuff of science fiction." He continues with the sociological observation that "historically, elements corresponding to the logic of both/and are regarded by society as exceptional, scandalous, and even monstrous. Often efforts are made to repress or at least to neutralize these representations of 'in-between-ness'" (60).

Quite clearly, the experience of liminal terror can indeed be generated by literature, and this brings us back to Ligotti's "The Shadow at the Bottom of the World." As mentioned above, the story seems almost to invite the reader to analyze it in terms of its use of the motif of liminality, and this gives us a clue about the ways in which the story will attempt to affect its readers. Consider, for example, the second sentence of the first paragraph, in which the narrator says the strange mood of the prolonged autumnal season was evident to everyone, "whether we happened to live in town or somewhere outside its limits" (219). The liminality of the space between town and countryside is a common theme in some anthropological literature. This is a slippery space: where *exactly* does town become country? When you find yourself on the outskirts of a town, how can you know for sure whether you are located inside or outside its limit? Immediately, Ligotti has called attention to this liminal space and has thus begun to invest the story with a mood of liminal terror.

The same issue is brought out even more clearly in the next sentence: "(And traveling between town and countryside was Mr. Marble, who had been studying the seasonal signs far longer and in greater depth than we, disclosing prophecies that no one would credit at the time.)" (219). The liminal space that was referred to only obliquely in the previous sentence is now made explicit. Notice that Mr. Marble's liminal status—he travels "between town and countryside"—is reinforced by the fact that the sentence is enclosed in parentheses. In a way, it can be said that we put mental "parentheses" around all liminal phenomena by relegating them to the periphery of our attention, and so the sentence in which we first meet Mr. Marble has the double effect of situating him in liminal space both in content and in form. This interpretation gains added weight from the fact that the second mention of him in the story, two paragraphs later, is also parenthetical: "But everything upon that land seemed unwilling to support our hunger for revelation, and our congregation was lost in fidgeting bemusement. (With the exception, of course, of Mr. Marble, whose eyes, we recall, were gleaming with illuminations he could not offer us in any words we would understand.)" (221).

In the second paragraph of the story, the narrator describes a field that lies "adjacent to the edge of town" (220), providing yet another invocation of the liminal space between town and countryside. The strange nocturnal dance of the scarecrow represents yet another instance of liminality. What is it about scarecrows that causes many people find them weird and uncanny? Why do scarecrows sometimes appear as prominent figures in weird literature and horror movies? One reason may be that scarecrows are effigies of the human form, and as such they call attention to another basic category distinction, that difference between human and not-human. (On this point the reader is referred to Ligotti's longtime fascination with and literary deployment of dolls and dummies.) On a subconscious level, scarecrows seem to resist being neatly categorized as either completely human, since they are not alive, or completely non-human, since they are vaguely but suggestively shaped like people, and so they provoke a peculiar emotional reaction, namely, the experience of liminal terror. When a scarecrow is portrayed as standing alone in a field on a breezeless night, and then it begins to kick its legs as it raises its face to the moonlit sky, one may easily imagine the heightening of the effect that results.

On the morning after the nocturnal dance of the scarecrow, when the townspeople arrive at the farmer's field, the scene feels strangely dreamlike and murky. It almost seems as if the people are unable to fully wake up: "The sky had hidden itself behind a leaden vault of clouds, depriving us of the crucial element of pure sunlight which we needed to fully burn off the misty dreams of the past night" (221). This passage highlights yet another basic category distinction: the line between waking reality and dreaming reality. In the famous words of the Chinese Taoist sage Chuang Tzu, "Are you a man who dreamed you were a butterfly, or are you now a butterfly dreaming that you are a man?" Strictly speaking, in subjective experience it is impossible to answer this question either way with complete confidence. Equally impossible is the attempt to remember the precise moment when one crosses over from wakefulness into sleep, or vice versa. The very fact that our lives are divided into two realms of consciousness whose blurred boundary make them anything but discrete provides fertile ground for the experience of liminal terror.[1] In "The Shadow at the Bottom of the World," this truth is exploited by the inability of the narrator to wake up fully on the morning following the scarecrow's dance. Henceforth, the narration itself can be understood as taking place in the liminal space between waking and dreaming, and the fact that the story is narrated in the first person means the reader experiences his or her own reading self as being located in the same space.

There is a symmetry with all this in the story's use of liminal periods of time. As with sleep and waking, so with night and day: When exactly does one become the other? Twilight and dawn can both be seen as liminal periods. Significantly, the attack of the townspeople on the scarecrow occurs at twilight, and when they gather back at the field the next morning, it is at the precise moment when "the frigid aurora of dawn appeared over the distant woods" (224).

Near the story's midpoint, the literary cues encouraging the reader to interpret and experience the story in terms of liminal terror begin to increase in scale and potency. When the townspeople begin to have their vivid dreams of "a ripe, fairly rotting world of strange growth and transformation," they are beginning to see the dissolution of all their conceptual and perceptual categories. When the visions from their dreams—the faces and figures visible on walls, the overripe colors of the leaves, etc.—begin to make their appearance in waking reality itself, it is apparent that the "other world" glimpsed in liminal spaces is on the verge of breaking through and overrunning the daylight

---

1. Cf. Berger 42–43 for evocative ruminations on the significance and implications of the fundamental division of human consciousness into the waking and sleeping/dreaming minds: "There are always the 'nightmares' that continue to haunt in the daytime—specifically, with the 'nightmarish' thought that daytime reality may not be what it purports to be, that behind it lurks a totally different reality that may have as much validity, that indeed world and self may ultimately be something quite different from what they are defined to be by the society in which one lives one's daytime existence."

world of conceptual categories. The concluding sentence of this section of the story explicitly describes a liminal presence, an unknown and unknowable something that exists not *in* the categories of our world (or any other) but *between* them, and is thus worth quoting again:

> It moved in shadow, a presence that was in the world of solid forms but not of it. Nor did it belong to any other world that could be named, unless it was that realm which is suggested to us by an autumn night when fields lay ragged in moonlight and some wild spirit has entered into things, a great aberration sprouting forth from a chasm of moist and fertile shadows, a hollow-eyed howling malignity rising to present itself to the cold emptiness of space and the pale gaze of the moon. (225–26)

This is the closest the story gets to describing the nature of the reality that seems to be pressing in upon the daylight "world of solid forms," and the reality so described would seem to correspond in every respect to Berger's description of anomic reality as "a world of disorder, senselessness, and madness" in which "reality and identity are malignantly transformed into meaningless figures of horror."

More than any other single element, the fact that the story is set in an extended autumn season serves to invest it with a sense of liminal strangeness and terror. During the spring and summer, the world is alive. During the winter it is dead. During autumn it is both, and neither. Of course, the boundaries between all seasons are indistinct, but with autumn the sense of strangeness seems to be particularly pronounced. It is no accident that Halloween, the holiday devoted to acknowledging and celebrating the dark side of life, occurs during this season. Ligotti himself speculates about this quintessential mood of autumn in the opening paragraph of the story when he describes the common thread winding its way through all the autumn scenes pictured on all the calendars in the homes of the townspeople:

> On the calendars which hung in so many of our homes, the monthly photograph illustrated the spirit of the numbered days below it: sheaves of cornstalks standing brownish and brittle in a newly harvested field, a narrow house and wide barn in the background, a sky of empty light above, and fiery leafage frolicking about the edges of the scene. But something dark, something abysmal always finds its way into the bland beauty of such pictures, something that usually holds itself in abeyance, some entwining presence that we always know is there. (219)

This "entwining presence" is none other than the liminal strangeness that seems to be more palpable during the autumn months than at any other time of the year. In the very next sentence, the narrator announces this autumn weirdness as the very subject of the story: "And it was exactly this presence that had gone into crisis" (219).[2]

The liminal strangeness of autumn is also accented in this story by the fact that for some reason *autumn won't end*. Winter will not come. The temporal setting becomes more and more strange, more and more liminal, as the leaves that should have fallen long ago remain on the trees, and as the field that should have frozen long ago remains warm. Autumn, to repeat, is already a liminal season. The end of autumn is even more so, and Ligotti prolongs this end until the story seems to take place in a time that nobody has ever known before, a time that is familiar and yet unfamiliar, beautiful yet hideous, flourishing yet decaying. Above all, it is a time that is thoroughly terrifying in its liminality.

The Many in the One

This investigation of the liminal motif in "The Shadow at the Bottom of the World" does not deliver its full reward until we consider it in light of the second motif I have chosen to emphasize; the motif of collective identity. We can see at a glance that the story is told in the first person plural. The pronoun *I* does not appear a single time. Instead, the townspeople seem to narrate the story with a single voice (all emphases in the following quotations are mine):

> The field allowed full view of itself from so many of *our* windows. . . . Soft lights shone through curtained windows along the length of each street, where *our* trim wooden homes seemed as small as dollhouses beneath the dark rustling depths of the season. . . . *Our* speculations were brief and useless. . . . It was not long after this troubling episode that *our* dreams, which formerly had been the merest shadows and glimpses, swelled into full phase. . . . But the truth is that *we* wanted something to happen to them—*we* wanted to see them silenced. Such was *our* desire. (220, 224, 225, 229)

This narrative voice, while relatively rare, is hardly unheard of in the annals of literature, but in this particular story it is unusually important, and we will see that a careful consideration of it will elicit some significant points.

---

2. As one might guess from his deeply emotional description of the season, autumn is Ligotti's favorite time of year, and "The Shadow at the Bottom of the World" is his favorite among his own works for precisely this reason. "Autumn has always held a special magic for me," he has said, "and I tried to put as much of that feeling as I could into this story" (Paul and Schurholz 20).

For instance, consider for a moment the first person plural narrative voice in light of the concept of liminal terror as developed above. Viewed this way, we immediately sense the strangeness of the voice. In concrete reality we never experience a communal voice either objectively or subjectively (the claims of Freudian psychoanalytic theory about repression etc. notwithstanding). In fact, in concrete reality we never experience such a thing as a *group*. Consider, for example, the idea of "fruit." You cannot hold "fruit" in your hand. "Fruit" is a category, a conceptual grouping that is useful for purposes of classification and recognition, but that in truth has no concrete referent. In existential reality you can only hold a specific fruit, an apple, a banana, an orange. The same is true of human groupings. There is no such existential entity as a group, such as—to name one pertinent example—a town. There is real land, there are real houses and streets and streetlamps, there are real individual people, but the grouping of these separate entities into the collective entity known as "town" is a conceptual exercise, and this leads us to view the first person plural narrative voice as something extremely peculiar, something that tends to inspire feelings of liminal terror and strangeness. The collective narrator of "The Shadow at the Bottom of the World" can exist only in mental space. Even if a thousand people were to read the story aloud in unison, they would still add up to a thousand separate voices. At no point could we say that a true collective voice had emerged from the group reading. Ligotti's use of the collective narrator immediately creates an aura of otherworldly strangeness; as we read the story we are placed inside the mind of an entity that is at once entirely familiar (the population of a town) and yet entirely strange (the collective voice of a town).

This point having been established, it becomes most interesting and revealing to note the use of the third person to refer to characters in the story, because such instances serve to sharpen the boundaries of the collective narrator's identity. There are only five people in the story who are referred to in the third person: Mr. Marble, the farmer who owns the field containing the scarecrow, an anonymous townsperson who says "Maybe there'll be some change in the spring" (225) (although this person may still be considered to exist within the boundaries of the collective narrator), and the woman and child who arrive in town unexpectedly. Whenever someone is referred to in the third person, he or she is thereby placed outside the boundary of the "we" who are telling the story. The logic behind these instances seems to make sense. The farmer owns the field from which the black stalk erupts, and the collective narrator wants to distance him/her/itself from the strange manifestation. The farmer is excluded from the boundary of the narrator's collective identity simply by virtue of the fact that he is too closely associated with something the narrator fears. The person who speaks of a possible change in the spring may still be considered a member of the group; perhaps "someone said" may be taken as implying "one of us said." The mother and son are complete outsiders; their very alienage from the narrator seems to bring out the narrator's greatest fear: "Our fear was what they might have known, what they must certainly have discovered, about *us*" (229; Ligotti's emphasis).

But these instances are all overshadowed by the extended treatment of Mr. Marble, who possesses by far the strongest individual identity of any character in the story. He is always referred to in the third person, and interestingly, his distinct individuality seems to be bound up somehow with the fact of his liminal positioning. He is notable because he travels "between town and countryside" both physically and in his thoughts. His deep knowledge makes him opaque: his "eyes, we recall, were gleaming with illuminations he could not offer us in any words we would understand." He is able to "read in the leaves" the activities of that strange liminal presence that is forcing its way into the light. The fact that he sharpens blades for a living only serves to reinforce his individuality and his liminal status: blades *cut*, blades *separate*, just as the sharpness of Mr. Marble's mind slices through, and perhaps widens, the lines or cracks in the world through which the liminal presence is emerging. Importantly, he is the only character in the story to be given a separate name, and the name "Marble" itself suggests the streaking or mottling of separate colors (read: separate conceptual categories) that would occur if the liminal were transposed with the conceptual or the nomic.

Ironically—or perhaps all too expectedly—Mr. Marble's individuality, his ability to see and think on his own apart from the crowd, renders him especially susceptible to invasion and domination by the invading presence. His mental acuity fades as he is drawn further and further into the thrall of the dark presence, until eventually he is entirely under its control, much in the manner of the scarecrow that was invaded by the "thick dark stalk which rose out of the earth and reached into the effigy like a hand into a puppet" (222). Before being taken over by the presence, Mr. Marble unwittingly states his own doom as a cryptic prophecy: "Doesn't have arms, but it knows how to use them. Doesn't have a face, but it knows where to find one" (227). When the strangers arrive in town on the night when the gathering eruption is obviously coming to a head, the liminal has become central. After having been referred to twice in parentheses, after having spent so much time "traveling between town and countryside," Mr. Marble is now at the center of the town and the center of events. In the mind of the collective narrator, by all rights

Mr. Marble ought to kill the visitors. This is the end toward which the entire upsurge of energy has been leading. The proper sacrifice will signal the completion of the strange mutation. The energy has reached a peak and must be discharged.

But at this point the story reveals an even deeper layer, and it is one that further complicates the issue of collective identity vs. individual identity even as it promises a further illumination of the story's use of liminal terror. Even though Mr. Marble's "outsideness," his liminality and individuality, are responsible for opening him up to control by the invading presence, they also endow him with the freedom to choose. When he chooses not to complete the sacrifice, and instead to vent the gathering energy on himself, the true heart of the narrator's identity is revealed by the fact that they want the sacrifice to be completed. They want the outsiders to be killed because "only then would we be sure that they could not tell what they knew. . . . Our fear was what they might have known, what they must certainly have discovered, about *us*."

Which one has truly surrendered self-control to the invading dark presence, Mr. Marble or the narrator? Mr. Marble can still resist. The townspeople cannot, because—and here is the awaited reward—*they realize that the nightmarish reality attempting to break through into their daylit world is none other than their own deepest self*. The dark thing is the root of their own collective identity. It is *they* who have been controlled by the black stalk rising up into the scarecrow "like a hand into a puppet." The very fact that they have been speaking in a collective voice, which, as noted, can occur only in a liminal space, shows that the dark root has been controlling their thoughts and actions all along. Their horror is *self*-horror. They do not want to become self-conscious, to recognize and know the horrible thing that they are.

The Voice of Our Name

Although "The Shadow at the Bottom of the World" was originally published in the sixteenth issue of the small-press horror magazine *Fear*, we can deepen our understanding of its secrets by viewing it as being organically related to Ligotti's second short fiction collection, *Grimscribe: His Lives and Works*, in which it appears as the final piece. This allows us to relate it back to the framing device introduced at the beginning of the book, where an introduction portrays the stories in the collection as tales told by a metaphysical entity that has no name, but that for purposes of the book has decided to call itself Grimscribe. It is also said that his name is the name of everyone, and that "he keeps his name secret, his many names. He hides each one from all the others, so that they will not become lost among themselves. Protecting his life from all his lives, from the memory of so many lives, he hides behind the mask of anonymity" (ix). This could just as well be taken to describe the narrator of "The Shadow at the Bottom of the World," a story that is appropriately the only entry in the final section of the book titled "The Voice of Our [i.e. Grimscribe's] Name." (Other sections are titled "The Voice of the Damned," "The Voice of the Demon," "The Voice of the Dreamer," and "The Voice of the Child.") Considered in light of *Grimscribe* as a whole, this story may be understood as being narrated by Grimscribe itself in the first person, standing out at last from behind the mask of the other characters in whose guises it has appeared (all the stories in the book are told in the first person). If Grimscribe is indeed the name of everyone, then the near transposition of worlds in "The Shadow at the Bottom of the World" represents the near loss of all sanity and identity. The collective identity of the town brings about the horror, because such collectivity is already the beginning of that "backward slide," as Grimscribe calls it, "into that great blackness in which all names [i.e. identities] have their source" (ix).

The narrator's (Grimscribe's) fear of what the visitors might have discovered about it may arise at least in part from the fact that the discovery of the townspeople's secret is also the discovery of the visitors' secret. That is, the madness passes itself on through the recognition of one's own secret self in another. Grimscribe's careful self-deception almost comes unraveled in a horrible birth of self-awareness. When Grimscribe/the townspeople drop Mr. Marble's body into the bottomless pit, its/their motives are obscure. On the one hand, they are still horrified by the black substance that has replaced Mr. Marble's blood, and this shows that they are still horrified at the possible discovery of their own identity. On the other hand, they envy and hate Mr. Marble because he represents the individuality that eludes them. The key to understanding their action lies in the recognition that in a perverse way, they/Grimscribe *wanted* their own destruction to be complete. The murder of the outsiders would have killed the spread of the townspeople's self-knowledge, but it would also have signaled the successful conquest of the daylight world by the darkness and thus brought an end, albeit not a pleasant one, to their, and Grimscribe's, torturous charade. Grimscribe would have met the darkness and discovered it to be his own self, and there would have been no one left to say, or do, or know, or suffer, or fear, or be anything. But since the rightful sacrifice was aborted, Grimscribe must continue the charade, and conscious beings must continue to suffer the ambivalence of simultaneously fearing and longing for ultimate self-knowledge, until at last, in the words of Ligotti's prose poem "Primordial Loathing," "that perfect lid of darkness falls over this world once more" (*Noctuary* 179).

2002

Works Cited

Berger, Peter L. *The Sacred Canopy: Elements of a Sociological Theory of Religion.* Garden City, NY: Doubleday, 1967.

Carpenter, Scott. *Reading Lessons: An Introduction to Theory.* Upper Saddle River, NJ: Prentice-Hall, 2000.

Leach, Edmund. *Culture and Communication: The Logic by Which Symbols are Connected.* Cambridge: Cambridge University Press, 1976.

Ligotti, Thomas. *Grimscribe: His Live and Works.* New York: Jove Books, 1994.

———. *Noctuary.* New York: Carroll & Graf, 1994.

Paul, R. F., and Keith Schurholz. "Triangulating the Daemon: an Interview with Thomas Ligotti." *Esoterra* No. 8 (Winter/Spring 1999): 14–21.

Turner, Victor. *The Ritual Process: Structure and Anti-Structure.* New York: Aldine de Gruyter, 1995.

Icy Bleakness and Killing Sadness: The Desolating Impact of Thomas Ligotti's "The Bungalow House"

Thomas Ligotti's "The Bungalow House" is regularly named as a favorite by many of his readers. It is also a story that enters the reader's psyche and conducts a philosophical and affective work of profound bleakness. Although the same can be said about most, if not all, of Ligotti's work, this particular story accomplishes that act of dark emotional transmission with especial force and finesse. Perhaps this accounts for its popularity. Perhaps this is what his readers are seeking from him. In any event, the focus on bleakness itself, on bleakness as such, is especially pronounced in this story in a way that sets it apart from many of his others.

This is not unrelated to the fact that the word itself, "bleakness," coupled with the word "icy"—as in "icy bleakness"—plays a significant role in the inner life of the story's narrator. Nor is it unrelated to the fact that the story ends with a description of a certain "killing sadness" that has overtaken the narrator as a result of the story's events, and that has become the axis of his conscious existence due to the things he has experienced. Bleakness and sadness are the core of "The Bungalow House," notwithstanding the fact that it also contains elements of a delicious absurd humor.[1] But more than that, the

---

1. Although the story's humorous element lies outside the focus of this essay, interested readers are advised to pay attention to the portion of "The Bungalow House" where the narrator muses on the relative merits of two separate lavatories. I have a distinct memory of Tom telling me at some point in the past that he fairly cackled with laughter as he wrote this scene, because it's so absurd that he couldn't begin to imagine what his readers might think of it. However, I have been unable to locate evidence of this exchange among my records of our correspondence. When I asked him about it recently in preparation for writing this essay, he replied as follows:

story argues that bleakness and sadness are the core of human existence itself, or at least the core of the narrator's, whose private experience is universalized simply by being presented in a work of literary fiction, as is the function, or at least one of them, of all art. Bleakness and sadness. Not horror, as one might expect from coming to "The Bungalow House" with the prior knowledge of Ligotti's classification, and also his active self-identification, as a horror writer. Not horror but killing sadness. Not horror but icy bleakness. This is important.

The Story

"The Bungalow House" takes the form of a first-person narrative told by an unnamed male narrator who works in the Language and Literature department at the main branch of the public library in an unnamed city. This narrator has made a habit of spending his lunch hours at Dahla D. Fine Arts, a shabby little hole-in-the-wall art gallery located not far from the library, and it is here that he encounters "a sort of performance piece in the form of an audiotape" that, as it turns out, is "the first of a series of tape-recorded dream monologues by an unknown artist" (202). These dream monologues mesmerize him with their plotless, oneiric descriptions of bleak, desolate, and eerie settings. The first one, for example, titled *The Bungalow House (Plus Silence)*, describes the interior of a vermin-infested bungalow house at night, where moonlight falls through dusty blinds, dying masses of vermin writhe on threadbare carpet, an array of lamps sits uselessly without lightbulbs, and a powerful, stifling silence seems to muffle countless sounds, including voices. After listening to it along with a second tape titled *The Derelict Factory with a Dirt Floor and Voices*, the narrator becomes obsessed with finding out the identity of the artist behind these works. When he asks Dahla, the gallery owner, if she can arrange a meeting, she acts cagey and demurs. She also appears strangely and secretly amused, as if she is silently mocking him.

I don't recall writing to you about cackling with laughter about the narrator's thoughts on Dahla's lavatory in "The Bungalow House." However, if you remember it that way, it's no doubt true that I said it. Along with both my brothers and my late father, I've been fixated all my life on bathrooms public and private as a site of experiences either comic or painful or both at the same time. To some extent, I think this quirk goes along with my Italian heritage, though that's just an impression. I have the same impression about the Japanese. In *Teatro Grottesco* alone, I think there are at least six stories in which lavatories figure. There's also a restaurant men's room scene in the script for *Crampton* that I wrote to be both comical and creepy. I could go on about this subject, but I think I've made my point and confirmed your recollection. (Thomas Ligotti, email to author, 10 July 2017)

Nevertheless, he does eventually encounter, after a fashion, the artist, through what he thinks is a meeting set up by Dahla, whose real stock in trade, as the narrator informs the reader, is not the selling of crummy pseudo-art but the making of "arrangements" for people: "Whatever someone was eager to try, whatever step someone was willing to take—Dahla could arrange it" (206). The encounter takes place in the early morning darkness of the library before it opens for business. The artist appears as a silent, semi-spectral figure dressed in a long overcoat and a hat that obscures his face, and he proves elusive, as the narrator sees him recede with a sort of gliding motion when approached, eventually to disappear completely in the shadows.

By the time the dramatic climax of "The Bungalow House" arrives, various subtle hints sprinkled throughout the text have conspired to telegraph (perhaps only upon a rereading) the truth of the situation: that the artist is none other than the narrator himself, who is apparently experiencing a dissociative disorder. Or perhaps there is something even weirder going on, some strain of uncanny Doppelgänger mischief. Whichever it is, Dahla delights in laughing cruelly as she destroys his illusion. The narrator himself approached her, she says, with the tapes and asked her to display them as an exhibit in her gallery, and then he ordered her to play along with his self-made charade as he came to her gallery and paid to listen to the tapes as if they had been made by someone else. The narrator does not exactly believe her when she tells him this, but when she shows up dead soon afterward, having choked to death on the plastic arm of a doll shoved down her throat—a plastic arm that may or may not be the same one the narrator stole from her shop earlier in the story—he experiences certain suspicions about his own identity and actions. However, he never really comes to a final reckoning with or realization about himself. In the end he is left with nothing but a plague of the aforementioned killing sadness, which he experiences with overwhelming force, in tandem with a mounting sense of voices speaking in his head: his own, the artist's, and others.

Dreams and Delusions

There are many strands of significance woven together in this tapestry of strangeness and desolation. One is the question of the nature and power of dreams and dreamlike intimations of ultimate things, combined with the question of art and its function and impact. On the metatextual level, this is quite appropriate in light of the fact that a dream was directly involved in Ligotti's writing of "The Bungalow House." The story's first dream monologue is actually a transcription of one of the author's own dreams, which he says he "tried to describe . . . as accurately as possible when I woke up, something I had never done before and haven't done since. Later I developed the transcript of that dream into a story and invented some more dreams to go along with it" (Angerhuber and Wagner 62). He has also explained that, in the context of the story, the "dream monologues were used to characterize the peculiar nature of the main character's psychology" (VanderMeer 235).

To the narrator these taped monologues offer shocking externalizations of his own most secret and deeply felt thoughts, emotions, and painfully worked-out beliefs, reflected back to him by a mysterious, unknown artist. He relates that at the end of the first tape he was

> overcome by a feeling of euphoric hopelessness which passed through my body like a powerful drug and held all my thoughts and all my movements in a dreamy, floating suspension. . . . That feeling of being in a trance while occupying, all alone, the most bleak and pathetic surroundings of an old bungalow house was communicated to me in the most powerful way by the voice on the tape, which described a silent and secluded world where one existed in a state of abject hypnosis. (204, 210)

The tapes speak achingly to a set of subjective conditions, partly affective and partly intellectual, that have come to define the narrator's world. "For as long as I can remember," he announces at one point in the story, "I have had an intense and highly aesthetic experience of what I call the *icy bleakness of things*. At the same time I have felt a great loneliness in this perception" (221; Ligotti's emphasis). It is this loneliness that constitutes his "killing sadness," and in the dream monologue tapes he is confronted, shockingly, with the apparent existence of another person who somehow shares the same perception and sensibility, and who has somehow made from these a work of art that bridges the gulf and speaks directly to the narrator's secret self. Later he reflects on the impact of the first two tapes with a kind of wonder at their singular resonance with his own experience, which indicates the existence of a kindred spirit in the world: "To think that another person shared my love for the *icy bleakness of things*" (214; Ligotti's emphasis). But then, as revealed in the end, this is all delusory and illusory, regardless of whether one opts for a psychological interpretation of the story's events or a more uncanny and/or preternatural one. The narrator has, in some sense, on some level, been caught in a looping, self-referential fiction. There is no real connection with another of like mind and vision. There is just a shadowplay of simulated contact, followed by insupportable grief.

Dreams of Decay

The impact of these things is heightened by Ligotti's evocation of setting. The city where the narrator lives is permeated by an atmosphere of bleakness and desolation that partakes of the decadent and the darkly numinous. Sean Eaton has pointed out that "The Bungalow House" takes place in "a strangely depopulated urban setting" where only three people are mentioned: the narrator, Dahla, and Henry, the night guard at the library. "The narrator interacts with them, responds to what they say," writes Eaton, "but only as a cue ball might interact with the other balls on a pool table—by colliding but not actually connecting with anyone."

This sense of an urban environment devoid of people and human connection is also evoked by the city's physical layout and condition. As the narrator rides home from work on the when that he discovered the first dream tape, he describes how the bus takes him

> past numerous streets lined from end to end with desolate-looking houses, any of which might have been the inspiration for the bungalow house audiotape. . . . [The] streets I saw appeared endless, vanishing from my sight toward an infinity of old houses, many of them derelict houses and a great many of them being dwarfish and desolate-looking houses of the bungalow type. (209–10)

These lines illustrate the story's use of what has been termed the aesthetics of decay, a focus on the aesthetic-philosophical import of deteriorated post-industrial ruins. Chris Brawley has correctly argued that this aesthetic is central to Ligotti's work as a whole, not just as an artistic sensibility but as an entire philosophical worldview that "permeates all his fiction and nonfiction" and "leads to the unique mood or atmosphere his work evokes in the reader" (83, 84), that atmosphere being of the numinous, the uncanny, and the sublime. Detroit, where Ligotti was born, and where he lived and worked for most of his life before relocating to Florida in the early 2000s, has long been associated with the aesthetics of decay and the avant-garde species of photography known as "ruin porn,"[2] and in this regard it is noteworthy that Ligotti has said "The Bungalow House" is "set in my imaginary version of Detroit." Even the vermin in the first dream monologue and thus in the story's dream source, may have been inspired by the author's real-life surroundings in Detroit: He says he "was living in a place with a lot of cockroaches at the time" (Ayad 107).

---

2. On this point, see Brawley 82–83.

However, Ligotti has also indicated that while he has always had a veritable obsession with the settings of his stories, he has generally wanted to avoid
the use of actual place names, the fictionalization of real places, and the creation of detailed fantastic settings. From the start, he says, his authorial desire
was "to set my stories in places as I saw them in my imagination rather than
describing them from personal observation." The result has been that "my
stories are set in my head rather than in any detailed world either real or fantastic" (Ayad 107–8). Therefore, the depopulated city in "The Bungalow
House" with its endless empty streets, its desolate rows of houses, its cavern-
ous library, and its shabby little art gallery owned by Dahla D. is a setting
within the fictive dreamworld of the author himself.

A Dreadful Disillusionment

In the end, it is the narrator's personal isolation in this dark dreamworld of a
city that generates the powerful sense of bleakness and despair that both suf-
fuses "The Bungalow House" and communicates itself to the reader. However, it is not this isolation by itself, but its contrast with the narrator's brief
moment of exhilaration at the thought of having found a kindred spirit, that
really drives it home. "I wanted to believe," the narrator says at a key point in
the story,

> that this artist had escaped the dreams and demons of all *sentiment* in order
> to explore the foul and crummy delights of a universe where everything had
> been reduced to three stark principles: first, that there was nowhere for you
> to go; second that there was nothing for you to do; and third, that there was
> no one for you to know. (214; Ligotti's emphasis)

He goes on to say that while he knows this personal credo or set of principles
is "an illusion like any other," it has "sustained me so long and so well—as
long and as well as any other illusion and perhaps longer, perhaps better"
(214). By the end, however, in his newly half-disillusioned state—only "half"
because it is not clear that he fully understands or accepts what has been happening to him—his former sense of equanimity in holding to these bleak
principles has been shattered. Even the memory of his exhilaration at the
dream monologues is now lost:

> I try to experience the infinite terror and dreariness of a bungalow universe
> in the way I once did, but it is not the same as it once was. There is no com-
> fort in it, even though the vision and the underlying principles are still the
> same. I know in a way I never did before that there is nowhere for me to

go, nothing for me to do, and no one for me to know. . . . More than ever, some sort of new arrangement seems to be in order, some dramatic and unknown arrangement—anything to find release from this heartbreaking sadness I suffer every minute of the day (and night), this killing sadness that feels as if it will never leave me no matter where I go or what I do or whom I may ever know. (225, 226)

Michael Cisco's comments on this dismal denouement effectively unpack core elements of its meaning and significance:

> The voice the narrator hears in these recordings, a new tape each day (the previous ones being destroyed by the gallery owner), is the voice of his own internal muse, the alien voice that speaks through him in his own fever dreams. Time and again in these stories the narrators discover, from unrelated outside sources, the voices and images of their own most chaotic and dimly-glimpsed dreams. This voice is both his and an utterly alien voice. The story ends in a circle, where the deprivation of this voice leads to the sense of bleakness and despair that the narrator seeks in the voice. The feeling he wants from the voice is also there in its absence, but in a different way it seems.

That, then, is the content, crux, and upshot of "The Bungalow House."

There Is No One to Know

However, it is at this point that the story widens in scope to resonate specifically and pointedly with others in Ligotti's oeuvre, and not only that, but with certain aesthetic-philosophical principles that he may personally hold, and not only that, but with the reader's own outlook. The "three stark principles" that serve as the bedrock axioms of the narrator's outlook in "The Bungalow House" are something that Ligotti has returned to elsewhere, as for example in his prose poem *I Have a Special Plan for This World*, where he augments the three principles with a newly added one:

> Then he said to me—he whispered—that my plan was misconceived
> That my special plan for this world was a terrible mistake
> Because, he said—
>   there is nothing to do
>   and there is nowhere to go
>   *there is nothing to be*
>   and there is no one to know
> Your plan is a mistake, he repeated.
> This world is a mistake, I replied. (11 [emphasis added])

He has also incorporated this expanded version into his nonfiction opus *The Conspiracy against the Human Race,* where he lays out his thoughts on the horror of reality itself, and of the human mode of self-awareness that, in his view and personal experience, renders life a nightmare (115–16).

This breach, as it were, between the walled-off fictive dreamworld of "The Bungalow House" and Ligotti's personal philosophical outlook may be taken, with only a little imaginative twist, as a kind of threat to the reader, since it untethers the narrator's icy bleakness and killing sadness from the realm of pure fiction and brings them out into the real world, where they have power to infect and afflict the reader's own outlook. The breaching of narrative boundaries for precisely this kind of effect is not something alien to Ligotti's art,[3] but in this case it represents not so much a technique as a sheer fact. In the relationship between the narrator of "The Bungalow House" and his idealized dream artist, Ligotti has created a metaphor of both his personal relationship to the things that drive him and his authorial relationship to his readers. In both cases, the story argues that any pleasure derived from the sense of a connection with an artist who shares one's vision of things is illusory and destined to die, and not only that, but to leave one worse off in the end.

It is as if this story, first published in 1995, serves as a rejoinder to Ligotti's essay "The Consolations of Horror," first published in 1982 and later used as the introduction to his 1996 omnibus fiction collection *The Nightmare Factory.* In that essay, Ligotti begins by stating, "Horror, at least in its artistic presentations, can be a comfort" (xi). He then proceeds to consider and reject several explanations for this comforting and consoling function of horror in art, before finally offering his own explanation:

> As in any satisfying relationship, the creator of horror and its consumer approach oneness with each other. . . . This, then, is the ultimate, that is only, consolation: simply that someone shares some of your own feelings and has made of these a work of art which you have the insight, sensibility, and—like it or not—peculiar set of experiences to appreciate. (xxi)

And yet, as has been shown above, this idea that it is a consolation to find that someone has shared your feelings and made art from them *is exactly what "The Bungalow House" denies.* In this story, there is no consolation, because there is no connection. Connection is in fact categorically impossible, because there is no other person with whom one could connect. Any sense of another person with whom one shares an affinity of sensibility and worldview is an illusion, and the

---

3. On this point, I refer the reader to "The Transition from Literary Horror to Existential Nightmare in Thomas Ligotti's 'Nethescurial,'" q.v.

knowledge of this kills even the pleasure one formerly felt in contemplating putatively consoling works of art. Instead of consolation, there is only icy bleakness and killing sadness. Instead of connection, there is only a solipsistic hell of "mindless mirrors / Laughing and screaming as they parade about in an endless dream" (to quote from *I Have a Special Plan for This World* [13], two pages after its augmentation of the three stark principles from "The Bungalow House").

And that, ultimately (and arguably), is how and why "The Bungalow House" epitomizes, after a fashion, Ligotti's authorial and aesthetic-philosophical message, meaning, import, and essence. It is how and why it produces such a desolating impact upon the reader's sensibility. There is no solace, it says, either in art or in life, not in this world or any other.[4] In light of this, there is either a paradox, a kind of non sequitur, or else an illustration of some subtle and perhaps inarticulable point on display in the fact that so many people continue to read Ligotti's work and name this particular story among their favorites. "Just to do it, that's all," Ligotti says in "The Consolations of Horror," as a description of what could possibly motivate people to engage in this particular art form, whether as creators or consumers. "Just to see how much unmitigated weirdness, sorrow, desolation, and cosmic anxiety the human heart can take and still have enough heart left over to translate these agonies into artistic forms" (xxi). This may well be as good an explanation as we can hope to receive, both for him and for us.

2018

Works Cited

Angerhuber, E. M., and Thomas Wagner. "Disillusionment Can Be Glamorous: An Interview with Thomas Ligotti." In Matt Cardin, ed. *Born to Fear: Interviews with Thomas Ligotti.* Burton, MI: Subterranean Press, 2014. 59–75. First published at *The Art of Grimscribe*, January 2001, www.angwa.de/Ligotti/interviews/disillusionment_e.htm.

Ayad, Neddal. "Literature Is Entertainment or It Is Nothing: An Interview with Thomas Ligotti." In Matt Cardin, ed. *Born to Fear: Interviews with Thomas Ligotti.* Burton, MI: Subterranean Press, 2014. 95–116. First published at *Fantastic Metropolis*, 31 October 2004. Reprinted at *Thomas Ligotti Online*, 14 August 2005, ligotti.net/showthread.php?t=420

4. I say more about this point in, see the final section of "Thomas Ligotti's Career of Nightmares," q.v.

Brawley, Chris. "The Icy Bleakness of Things: The Aesthetics of Decay in Thomas Ligotti's 'The Bungalow House.'" *Studies in the Fantastic* No. 4 (Winter 2016/Spring 2017): 82–100.

Cisco, Michael. Review of *The Nightmare Factory* by Thomas Ligotti. *Crypt of Cthulhu* No. 96 (1997). Reprinted at *Thomas Ligotti Online*. Last updated 2 May 2013. www.ligotti.net/showthread.php?t=6179.

Eaton, Sean. "Art as Nightmare." *The R'lyeh Tribune*. Last modified 3 August 2015. blog-sototh.blogspot.com/search?q=art+as+nightmare.

Ligotti, Thomas. "The Bungalow House." In *Teatro Grottesco*. London: Virgin Books, 2008. 202–26. First published in *The Urbanite* 5 (1995).

———. "The Consolations of Horror." In *The Nightmare Factory*. New York: Carroll and Graf, 1996. ix–xxi. First published in *Horror Magazine* 13 (1982).

———. *The Conspiracy against the Human Race: A Contrivance of Horror*. New York: Hippocampus Press, 2010.

———. *I Have a Special Plan for This World*. London: Durtro, 2000.

Padgett, Jon. "'The Bungalow House': Commentary." [Interview] *Thomas Ligotti Online*. Last updated 17 May 2004. www.ligotti.net/tlo/ss-bh.html.

VanderMeer, Jeff. "Interview with Thomas Ligotti." In Matt Cardin, ed. *Born to Fear: Interviews with Thomas Ligotti*. Burton, MI: Subterranean Press, 2014. 235–43. First published at *Wonderbook*, October 2013, accessed 4 October 2017, wonderbooknow.com/interviews/thomas-ligotti.

A Formless Shade of Divinity: Chasing Down the Demiurge in Thomas Ligotti's "The Red Tower," *I Have a Special Plan for This World,* and *This Degenerate Little Town*

On the Challenge of Revelatory Texts

In attempting to speak—or, in the present case, write—an illuminating set of words about the three Thomas Ligotti texts at hand, one is confronted immediately by a challenge that stems from the nature of the texts themselves, from the combination of their thematic content with their fundamental intent.

On the first count, each of these texts—the first one presented in the form of a short story, albeit a highly experimental one, and the others in the form of poems or poem cycles—points toward a transcendental reality that lies behind what it posits as the façade of conventional reality.

This in itself is not all that rare or challenging, as the same general theme is encountered in a multitude of weird and cosmic supernatural horror stories, especially those falling into the third of the three streams of horror fiction— moral allegorical, psychological metaphor, and the fantastic—identified by David Hartwell in the introduction to his classic, genre-defining anthology *The Dark Descent.* Third-stream stories, in Hartwell's taxonomic telling, hinge on the sense and/or notion of a certain "ambiguity as to the nature of reality" and the evocation or invocation of a certain "fabulous, formless darkness" (a term that Hartwell borrowed, without acknowledgment, from Yeats [585], who in turn got it from the Irish classical scholar E. R. Dodds [60], who quoted or paraphrased it either from the fourth-century Greek philosopher Proclus or the fourth-century Sophist and historian Eunapius, the latter of whom, as the story goes, was recounting a description of Christianity by his contemporary, the Neoplatonist philosopher Antoninus, as "a fabulous and formless darkness mastering the loveliness of the world"). The primary effect of such stories, said Hartwell, is to leave the reader with "a new perception of the nature of reality" (10). Thus, to repeat, the tendency of some short horror fiction to achieve its effect by hinting at and pointing toward some menacing supernatural/metaphysical/transcendental order of things is not, in itself, rare or challenging. In fact, it is positively conventional, so much so that, as Hartwell noted, it constitutes its own substream or subgenre—or, if we want to accept Douglas E. Winter's classic contention that "horror is not a genre" (182) (as Hartwell himself did), its own sub-mode.

Significantly, the very same theme or idea—that conventional reality is in some sense a façade or construct, or at least a contingent phenomenon, beyond or beneath which lies a truer realm of spiritual and metaphysical verities—forms the very life's blood of most spiritual and religious texts. (Cue the invocation of Lovecraft's penetrating observation that "there is here involved [in the phenomenon of weird supernatural horror fiction] a psychological pattern or tradition as real and as deeply grounded in mental experience as any other pattern or tradition of mankind; coeval with the religious feeling and closely related to many aspects of it" [26].) The sacred texts of the three great Abrahamic religious traditions, for instance—the Tanakh, the New Testament, and the Quran—are all purported to contain or, depending on your theological and hermeneutical persuasion, represent the actual words of an infinite, supernatural, transcendent, supreme, singular God. In the case of the latter, the very textual content itself (but only in the original Arabic) is said to *embody* God's word, God's mind, God's eternal truth, in a literary-spiritual transmission of perfect, unadulterated divine communication. (The same general idea, we may note in passing, also characterizes the beliefs of many fundamentalist-evangelical Protestants about the Authorized or King James Version of the Bible.)

Which brings us back, after a fashion, to the case of Ligotti's "The Red Tower," *I Have a Special Plan for This World*, and *This Degenerate Little Town*. It is, again, the combination of the thematic content of these three texts *with their fundamental intent* that presents the challenge to the would-be expositor or commentator who attempts to discuss them in the aggregate. To cut to the chase, upon starting to read them, one notices immediately that they present themselves and function as more than, and other than, mere works of horror literature. Much like religious texts, these key entries in Ligotti's total body of work convey the sense that they are attempting (as it were) to channel directly to the reader the transcendent reality whose existence they posit. Put differently, they attempt to act as windows, and also, in some sense, as textual instantiations or incarnations of the nightmarish reality toward which they gesture. In this, they are transformative texts—again, more like religious scriptures than mere stories that change the reader's perception of reality. They are texts that work, or try to work, an alteration upon and within the reader's mind, brain, and perception, and in so doing work a veritable ontological change upon the reader him- or herself.[1]

Really, what they call to mind more than anything else is George Clayton Johnson's characterization of Rod Serling's *The Twilight Zone* as a tool, in the form of a television series, for expanding consciousness. "*The Twilight Zone* is a surreal series," said Johnson, who, as a writer of several of the series' classic episodes, knew what he was talking about. "It's saying, 'There is a place beyond that which is known to man.' . . . As we transform ourselves as a culture, [we will use] tools like *The Twilight Zone*, which are consciousness expanders" (Cardin). Johnson, however, viewed this expansion of the viewer's consciousness, this Blakean cleansing of the doors of perception, in a positive and exuberant light, whereas Ligotti, philosophical arch-pessimist and master practitioner of midnight-dark horror fiction that he is, views it as a kind of grim tragedy, notwithstanding what he holds to be the veridical nature of the vision it bestows.

One might say, in other words, that in producing such works of literature, Ligotti is effectively complicit in an act of metaphysical aggression, emotional annihilation, and spiritual destruction that he regards as the very essence of the nightmare that he personally experiences as reality itself, a nightmare that consists not only of a particular metaphysical or ontological set of circumstances but of the dual curse of consciousness-plus-self-awareness within them. These texts seek to work a change upon the reader, to open the reader's mind to a new way of seeing, knowing, and feeling about his or her existence, the cosmic environment in which it plays out, and the foundational ontological reality upon which both of these phenomena, self and cosmos, rest, and from which they derive.

More succinctly, one could say, if one were so inclined, "The Red Tow-

---

1. I say more about the unusually potent impact of Ligotti's fiction on the reader's emotions, intellect, and general sensibility in "Thomas Ligotti's Career of Nightmares," q.v. I say more about the idea that Ligotti's fiction can sometimes reach toward the breaching of the narrative-existential barrier, so that it strives to become something more in the reader's experience than a mere story, in "The Transition from Literary Horror to Existential Nightmare in Thomas Ligotti's 'Nethescurial,'" q.v.

er," *I Have a Special Plan for This World,* and *This Degenerate Little Town* are not so much literary texts that one reads as revelatory experiences that one risks. They are scriptures of a sort, ostensible carriers of a metaphysical truth that seek to transform those who are "sympathetic organisms" (to quote the monstrous eponymous guru in Ligotti's short story "Severini" [*Nightmare Factory* 492]). They speak of a truth—they *reveal* a truth—the very grasping of which can change the one who grasps.

Ironically, they also end up showing that they are utterly unnecessary in this capacity, as it is one of their chief contentions that the selfsame destabilizing, undermining, upending, life-altering revelations can come just as easily to anyone, even to me and to you, at any moment, through any medium, without warning. "I myself have never seen the Red Tower—no one ever has, and possibly no one ever will," says the unidentified narrator of Ligotti's story. "And yet wherever I go people are talking about it. . . . Everything they are saying is about the Red Tower, in one way or another, and about nothing else but the Red Tower. We are all talking and thinking about the Red Tower in our own degenerate way" (*Nightmare Factory* 550). "That day may seem like other days— . . ." says the similarly unidentified narrator of *Special Plan.* "But that day will have no others after" (7). "Who among us," asks the likewise unidentified narrator of *This Degenerate Little Town,*

> has not found himself
> beneath a rotting sky,
> a sky broken and rotting
> from what has been heaved up to it
> during every epoch of this earth,
> this ground that is miles deep
> with the decay of anything
> that has ever lived upon it?
> Who has not travelled
> through twisted streets
> and under the shadow of houses
> even the straightest of which,
> if our eyes could only see it,
> is veering toward the tilt? (16)

In the cosmos of these stories, considered as an informal or accidental triptych, language itself and the events and encounters of daily life form a scripture that can deliver the devastating revelation just as easily as any sacred text.

Mysterious Ways

"The Red Tower" was first published at the final story in Ligotti's 1996 omnibus collection *The Nightmare Factory*, which brought together the contents of his first three fiction collections, *Songs of a Dead Dreamer, Grimscribe,* and *Noctuary,* and added to them a final section of new stories titled "Teatro Grottesco and Other Tales." The decision to place "The Red Tower" at the end was hardly accidental, as the Tower of the title is in fact the collection's eponymous factory of nightmares. The story went on to win the Bram stoker Award for Long Fiction.

As Sean Moreland has noted, "The Red Tower" shares both its title and many of its literary techniques with the 1913 painting of the same name by the Italian proto-surrealist and co-developer of the metaphysical painting movement, Giorgio de Chirico, whose work is generally pervaded and characterized by a dreamlike atmosphere, a manipulation of perspectives to produce irrational and inexplicable results, an equally unsettling use of light and shadow, and a penchant for "reducing ostensibly living forms to atmosphere or architecture." Moreland calls Ligotti's "The Red Tower" his "most explicitly de Chiricoesque contrivance" while pointing out that the artist's influence can also be detected in a great deal of Ligotti's other work ("Maddening Manikins" 117–18). Elsewhere, Moreland has offered an able summary of Ligotti's story that is worth quoting at length:

> More an unnerving prose poem than a plot-driven narrative, it consists of an unnamed first-person narrator's description of a three-story, ruined factory made of crumbling red brick, known as the Red Tower, that stands in an otherwise blank landscape. This factory, operating like an organism, without owners, employees, or even consumers for its products, industriously churns out a wide variety of grotesque "novelty items," until it begins to break down and fade from existence.
>
> This building and its hostile, empty environment, apparently resentful of the factory's novelties, are the story's only major characters, for the reader learns nothing of the narrator beyond that he or she is part of a select group of alienated obsessives who share their "hallucinatory accounts" of the Tower's activities. These accounts inform the narrator's speculation that the factory's environs are attempting to return to a state of total vacancy. The narrator admires the factory's defiant production of absurd artifacts, while anxiously anticipating its inevitable dissolution. ("'The Red Tower'" 552)

Deborah Bridle, in an essay on the "Gothic body" in Ligotti's fiction, observes that in the collective cosmos of his horror stories, virtually everyone is engaged in a perpetual masquerade, an existential and metaphysical puppet show. Everyone exists in "a state of willing hypnosis" that serves as a temporary solace or protection against the horror of reality itself. However, the masquerade itself can often become a source of horror, as when it takes on the form of "the last series of objects produced by the factory in 'The Red Tower'" (Bridle 68–69). These objects are in fact organisms, or rather "hyper-organisms." The story describes them as

> wildly conflicted in their two basic features. On the one hand, they manifested an intense *vitality* in all aspects of their form and function; on the other hand, and simultaneously, they manifested an ineluctable element of *decay* in these same areas. That is to say that each of these hyper-organisms, even as they scintillated with an obscene degree of vital impulses, also, and at the same time, had degeneracy and death written deeply within them. (*Nightmare Factory* 548; Ligotti's emphases)

Bridle notes that these products of the Tower, "alive but decomposing," offer a metatextual "representation of our own condition. They are brought into the world by nameless 'birthing graves,' cast out into an existence where they do not understand their purpose, condemned to live only to finally die" (69).

Michael Cisco augments these considerations with some thoughts on the possible or probable allegorical meaning of this particular story for Ligotti himself, and in particular for his work and identity as a writer:

> Ligotti's story "The Red Tower" is a reflection on the sources of his own fiction. The story has no character other than a nameless narrator, really only a voice saying "I." There is no plot, but only a description of a mysterious red tower, which is continually producing horrific things. This tower does not seem to be inhabited, at least not in any normal sense. There is no reason why it should exist or create horrible things. In a way, the red tower is the imagination of the horror writer. (555)

We may cede the last word to Ligotti himself. In a 2009 interview, it was suggested to him that if "The Red Tower" were to be given a subtitle, a suitable one might be "The Entropy Wars." He responded as follows:

> In the writings of the philosophical essayist E. M. Cioran, who also admitted that he was hopelessly frivolous, this is my favorite sentence: "Nobility is only in the negation of existence, in a smile that surveys annihilated landscapes." In those annihilated landscapes is your entropy, although taken only as far as a picturesque vista of ruin as far as the eye can see rather than into the total derangement of chaos. I have a fantasy in which I patrol the coastal regions of the world before any life emerges from the oceans. And when anything sticks its head up and tries to crawl onto land, I'm there to destroy it—to crush the vitality out of anything that would take evolution

any farther than a hideous life moving about in a black, underwater world. I don't know why my fantasy involves my compromising at all with organic life. Perhaps because it would give me the enjoyment of keeping the rise of humanity at bay, of frustrating the tendency of organisms to become more complex than a fish swimming about and eating other organisms. If there is anything like nobility, I find such nobility in that sort of negation of existence. Happier still, and more satisfying, would be Cioran's annihilated landscapes, with everything torn down and nothing but the dust and debris of what once existed spread out to the horizon, nothing moving and everything like the grey and desolate landscape that surrounds the Red Tower. The horror for me is that there is anything going on in the Red Tower, anything sent out into the world or growing in its depths. But in the blood of each of us is the Red Tower, even if we never see it or know about it. Between the Red Tower and the grey landscape there is forever a struggle going on: Existence versus Nothingness. (Ableev 164–65)

As a kind of coda, it is interesting to compare the original text of "The Red Tower" as it appeared in *The Nightmare Factory* with the slightly revised version that appeared in Ligotti's 2006 collection *Teatro Grottesco* and was reprinted online at *Weird Fiction Review*. One change in particular brings out a shade of meaning or identity for the titular Tower that, while it may have been implicit in the original version, was hardly obvious. "But," says the story's cryptically obscure narrator in both versions, "my own degenerate imagination is most fully captured by the thought of how many of those monstrous novelty goods produced at the Red Tower had been scrupulously and devoutly delivered—solely by way of those endless underground tunnels—to daringly remote places where they would never be found, nor ever could be" (*Teatro Grottesco* 69). In the original version, the paragraph ends there, but in the revised version, a further sentence is added: "Truly, the Red Tower worked in mysterious ways" (*Nightmare Factory* 545). Any alert reader will recognize the embedded allusion to a certain other transcendental entity that is likewise said to work in mysterious ways, and that, like the Red Tower, creates a virtually infinite stream of objects and organisms for reasons that are fundamentally obscure.

So what, exactly, is Ligotti saying with this change? How to parse the relationship of this clarifying revision to his above-described horror at the thought of "anything going on in the Red Tower, anything sent out into the world or growing in its depths," and the eternal struggle between Existence and Nothingness? One could, if one wanted, invoke certain ideas stemming from second-century Gnosticism and its self-consciously blasphemous inversion of apostolic Christianity's fundamental cosmogonic myth and moral cosmology via its (Gnosticism's) counter-mythology of the evil, self-deluded Demiurge or Great Archon, who through his vast conceit and misconception of his own supreme divinity inadvertently imprisoned free spiritual beings—that is, us—in the hell-realm of matter. One could sidle from there into considerations of Schopenhauerian pessimism, of the monstrous Will raging behind the veil of matter, and of certain sympathetically resonant ideas subsisting within the thought realms of Vedanta and Buddhism and having to do with Maya, Brahman, Dukkha, the vast Hindu cycle of cosmic creation and destruction, and the fundamental Eastern desire to find liberation from the wheel of death and rebirth.

One could do all that. However, one might be better off to follow the lead of the Buddha himself, who, when asked questions of a metaphysical nature, was famously said to have "maintained a noble silence." Perhaps that same silence, not from nobility so much as sheer ineffability and a deep, self-acknowledged ignorance—in the same line as that of Socrates and his famous claim that of all the Greeks, he alone knew that he knew nothing—is the only advisable response here.

Laughing and Screaming in an Endless Dream

I Have a Special Plan for This World was first published in 2000 in a limited edition of 125 copies by David Tibet's Durtro Press. Tibet, the founder and long-time beating heart of the British experimental music group Current93, was then and remains now a confirmed fan of Ligotti's work—Ligotti even chose him to deliver his (Ligotti's) acceptance speech for the Bram Stoker Award for Lifetime Achievement in 2020—and *Special Plan* first emerged when Ligotti, who had already written the text, described it to Tibet, who decided he wanted to turn it into a collaborative project. Tibet published the limited-edition book in connection with a compact disc that featured him narrating Ligotti's text, accompanied by an ominous paramusical landscape and interspersed with deeply distorted vocal effusions. The production also featured audio content from a series of mysterious cassette tapes that Ligotti and his colleagues at Gale Research, the educational publisher where he worked as an associate editor for two decades, used to find lying on a park bench outside the Penobscot Building in Detroit.[2]

---

2. Thomas Ligotti, email to author, 6 May 2020. Regarding the specific contents of those tapes, Ligotti has related that they were recordings of "an elderly man reading from various sources, including the local newspaper, the works of Sigmund Freud, and librettos from Gilbert and Sullivan operettas. These readings were often interrupted by mad laughter. Later some of us, including me, saw and heard the guy who

Ligotti's text takes the form of a series of thirteen surreal poems or "discorporeal prose poems," all representing, like the text of "The Red Tower," the darkly unsettling reflections of an unidentified narrator (Burns 107). Dominant themes include the intrinsic and inescapable suffering and despair of mortal, fleshly, embodied life; the dreadfulness of existence itself; the idea of humans as puppets or automatons being controlled by an occult force; the vision of the cosmos as a crummy, creaking, rundown façade that barely conceals a nightmarish horror; and the "special plan" of the title, which seems to have something to do with desiring the unmaking of creation and returning everything to a state of utter non-existence. The exact nature of the plan is never specified, but the narrator hints at it in various ways.

For instance, at the start of the second section, the narrator relates a chance meeting with a shadowy figure—one of many that are encountered in the total dreamscape of the poem cycle—who speaks of having his own special plan. What this figure says indicates that this plan is focused on the idea of annihilating the savage bloody suffering of physical existence and the monstrous drives and appetites that accompany it:

> One needs to have a plan, someone said who was
>> turned away into the shadows
>> and who I had believed was sleeping or dead
> Imagine, he said, all the flesh that is eaten
>> the teeth tearing into it
>> the tongue tasting its savor
>> and the hunger for that taste
> Now take away that flesh, he said
>> take away the teeth and the tongue
>> take away the taste and the hunger
> Take away everything as it is—
> That was my plan, my own special plan for this world (6)

---

was leaving these tapes, which were always placed inside envelopes taken from local banks. ... On the outside of the envelopes this elderly gentleman, who walked around mumbling and laughing to himself, would write strange phrases, which unfortunately I can't recall any longer, as well as the source material from which the reading on the tape was taken. Bungalow Bill, a name given to him by David Tibet, would leave these envelopes on benches along the sidewalks in downtown Detroit, securing the envelopes in place with the weight of several pennies. He was a rather distinguished, professorial looking guy ... and he was most certainly insane" (Angerhuber and Wagner 62–63; second ellipsis is Ligotti's). Interestingly, the same tapes also formed the direct inspiration for the recorded "dream monologues" in Ligotti's short story "The Bungalow House."

The narrator, however, will have none of that, for his plan, he says, extends far beyond a mere removal of things as they are, reaching all the way backward and inward toward the luminous primal darkness that preceded and precedes all things:

> I had heard of such plans, such visions
> And I knew they did not see far enough—
> That what was demanded—in the way of a plan—
> Needed to go beyond tongue and teeth
>   and hunger and flesh
> Beyond the bones and the very dust of bones
>   and the wind that would come
>   to blow the dust away
> And so I began to envision a darkness
> That was long before the dark of night
> And a strangely shining light
> That owed nothing to the light of day (6)

Perhaps it is not surprising, then, that at one point the narrator characterizes his very own plan as the most horrific thing in the entire horror-filled multiverse, calling it "the worst of all / of this world's dreams— / My special plan for the laughter and the screams" (13). And yet, the text is bookended by lines, phrased in incantatory language and repeated verbatim in the first and final sections, that obliquely anticipate a kind of dark bliss that will accompany the plan's eventual accomplishment:

> When everyone you have ever loved is finally gone
> When everything you have ever wanted is finally done with
> When all of your nightmares are for a time obscured
>   as by a shining brainless beacon
>   or a blinding eclipse
> Of the many terrible shapes of this world
> When you are calm and joyful and, finally, entirely alone
> Then, in a great new darkness,
> You will finally execute your special plan (5)

The Hungarian philosopher and social theorist Adam Lovasz observes that *I Have a Special Plan for This World* is "ironically titled," in that the text, in its totality, "seeks to express the very absence of such a plan. Ligotti rejects the notion of a cosmic teleology, a divine blueprint that would integrate atomized, separated moments into itself" (140).

Interestingly, and perhaps contrastingly, Ligotti derived the title of the piece from the Goldberg Mania Questionnaire, a widely used psychological test, developed by the American psychiatrist Ivan Goldberg, that is intended to help diagnose bipolar disorder. One of its questions asks, "Do you have special plans for this world?" Ligotti was apparently so struck by this that he created not just one but two works titled "I Have a Special Plan for This World." The second, unrelated to the one under consideration here by anything except its title, is a corporate horror story that was first published in *My Work Is Not Yet Done* (2002).

In any event, buried in the latter half of *I Have a Special Plan for This World* (the poetic text, not the short story), in section nine, is a set of lines that might validly be thought of as expressing the pure essence of the nightmare ontology that informs and underlies all Ligotti's work:

> I first learned the facts from a lunatic
> In a dark and quiet room that smelled of
> stale time and space
> There are no people—nothing at all like that—
> The human phenomenon is but the sum
> Of densely coiled layers of illusion
> Each of which winds itself upon the supreme insanity
> That there are persons of any kind
>
> When all there can be is mindless mirrors
> Laughing and screaming as they parade about
> in an endless dream

When asked by the narrator, "what it was / That saw itself within those mirrors," the lunatic "only rocked and smiled / Then he laughed and screamed," and the narrator reports seeing in his "black and empty eyes . . . as in a mirror,"

> A formless shade of divinity
> In flight from its stale infinity
> Of time and space and the worst of all
> of this world's dreams—
> My special plan for the laughter and the screams. (13)

In his 2003 book *Rational Mysticism: Dispatches from the Border between Science and Spirituality*, later released in a new edition with the altered subtitle *Spirituality Meets Science in the Search for Enlightenment*, the American science writer John Horgan related his personally transformative experience of taking ayahuasca, as well as the subsequent philosophical quest it put him on. He reported that during his psychedelic episode, after experiencing a number of the conventionally predictable DMT-fueled visual phenomena, he found himself "coming face to face with the ultimate origin and destiny of life." He said he "felt overwhelming, blissful certainty that there is one entity, one consciousness, playing all the parts of this pageant, and there is no end to this creative consciousness, only infinite transformations."

Then, without warning, the bliss toppled over and inverted itself into an experience of nightmarish terror. Horgan's description of the nature and source of that terror, and of his vision of the central core of personal and cosmic reality, may shed light on Ligotti's amorphous divinity and its horrified flight from its own infinitude:

> Why? I kept asking. Why creation? Why something rather than nothing? Finally I found myself alone, a disembodied voice in the darkness, asking, Why? And I realized that there would be, could be, no answer, because only I existed; there was nothing, no one, to answer me. I felt overwhelmed by loneliness, and my ecstatic recognition of the improbability—no, impossibility—of existence mutated into horror. I knew there was no reason for me to be. At any moment I might be swallowed up forever by this infinite darkness enveloping me. I might even bring about my own annihilation simply by imagining it. I created this world, and I could end it, forever. Recoiling from this confrontation with my own awful solitude and omnipotence, I felt myself dissolving, fracturing, fleeing back toward otherness, duality, multiplicity. (25)

Horgan went on to say that in the aftermath of this "nightmarish vision," which he eventually "shaped into a theodicy with gnostic overtones—call it gnosticism light," he realized that he had come to suspect that "God creates not just for companionship or 'fun' but because of His terrified recognition of His own solitude and improbability and even His potential death; God 'forgets' Himself and flees into multiplicity because He cannot bear to confront His plight" (69).

One recalls that Ligotti has told of how he himself experienced a mental-emotional breakdown at the age of seventeen while under the influence of drugs and alcohol, and that this put him in a state of mind that rendered him profoundly receptive to the vision of a bleak, menacing, and monstrous cosmos portrayed in the stories of H. P. Lovecraft, which he discovered soon afterward. Ligotti's particular experience of horror, though, as he would begin to express it decades later in his own stories, might be characterized as the horror of the "deep inside," the horror to be found at the ontological heart of psyche and reality, whereas Lovecraft's might be characterized as the horror of the "deep outside," of the monsters and forces of outer darkness that scratch at the rim of the ordered universe and the walls of conventional human sanity.[3]

In *I Have a Special Plan for This World*, in the image of those "mindless mirrors / Laughing and screaming as they parade about in an endless dream," and of that "formless shade of divinity" fleeing its own infinite isolation—just like Horgan's deity, which lives in terror of its own solitude and flees into multiplicity to escape it—Ligotti has provided perhaps the most potent key to articulating his particular vision of the horror at the center of existence.

The Greatest Secret

This Degenerate Little Town was first published in 2001. Like *Special Plan,* its publication arose through the interaction of Ligotti with Tibet, although again, Ligotti wrote the text independently, without originally intending it as a collaboration (Angerhuber and Wagner 62). Also like *Special Plan,* it consists of a series of shadowy-surreal poems or prose poems, and it was likewise published in a special limited edition by Durtro with a companion audio recording that featured a reading of the poems accompanied by ethereal sounds from Current93. However, the readings this time were performed not by Tibet, but by Ligotti himself.

Content-wise, *This Degenerate Little Town* continues the trend established by (or perhaps only here, in these very reflections, elicited from) "The Nightmare Factory" and *Special Plan* of linking its dark reflections to the question of religion and related matters. This is established in the opening lines of the first of its ten sections:

> The greatest secret,
> which appears in no religious doctrine
> and is found nowhere in the world's
> overburdened library of myths and fables,
> nor receives the slightest mention
> in any philosopher's system
> or scientist's speculation—
> the greatest secret,
> perhaps the only secret,
> is that the universe,

---

3. I discuss the matter of Ligotti's adolescent mental-emotional breakdown and the vision of horror that it revealed in "The Master's Eyes Shining with Secrets: H. P. Lovecraft's Influence on Thomas Ligotti," q.v. On the matter of the contrast between Lovecraft's horror of what is here called the "deep outside" and Ligotti's of what is here called the "deep inside," see the same essay.

> all of creation,
> owes its existence
> to a degenerate little town. (5)

The remainder of the work fleshes out this conceit in greater detail, stating that the "degenerate little town" stands behind everything, lurking beneath "the scenery that surrounds us . . . the landscape of every planet," and that it is "the origin of all things / visible or invisible, / the source of everything that is / or ever can be." The descriptions of "its twisted streets and tilting houses, / its decaying ground and rotting sky," recall aspects of the nightmare land-scape of *Special Plan*, as do, vaguely or implicitly, its repeated references to the sight of "the diseased faces / peeking from grimy windows" (5–6). The text says glimpses of this little town sometimes come to people "who have emerged / from some painful ordeal / of the body or of the mind / and then begun speaking / of how they saw in the distance / an outline of crooked houses / tilting this way and that" (10). The town is also described as a "saving miracle" and perhaps—in a turn of concept and emotion that suddenly recalls and per-haps sheds further light on the nature of Ligotti's "special plan"—

> our last hope,
> the only hope we have
> of killing all the hopes
> we have ever had
> and murdering every mystery
> we have ever cherished,
> so that we may step forth, finally,
> into that great shining kingdom
> of which we have always dreamed. (14–15)

William Burns has called *This Degenerate Little Town* "Ligotti's most concentrated expression of the putrifaction [*sic*] infesting existence" (107). Chris Brawley has declared it the master key to Ligotti's entire oeuvre, the "mythical backdrop of Ligotti's philosophy (and I would argue further, his stories,) and has said, "[It] is easy to analyze any of his stories based on this mythical platform: whether fic-tional or not, people are faced with the reality of death and decay, but instead of deeply knowing this 'truth,' they deny it and create false saviors or paradises which only hide this truth of decay and give them temporary comfort" (88).

In an insightful essay about the veritably salvific—and, as some would view it, paradoxical—power of Ligotti's art to convey healing to those who suffer from psychological and emotional trauma, Dr. Raymond Thoss (a nom de plume drawn from one of Ligotti's stories) has described the way *This De-generate Little Town*, along with another of his David Tibet–related works, helpfully articulates the experience of dissociation:

> For phenomenological descriptions of dissociation, Thomas Ligotti has no peer, and his writings are punctuated with such descriptions of people disconnected from "reality," *dissociated* from "reality." The entirety of the works *In a Foreign Town, In a Foreign Land* and *This Degenerate Little Town* are phenomenological descriptions similar to what my clients suffer who have severe dissociation. Moreover, and attesting to the brilliance of Thomas Ligotti, not only are these works descriptions of what my clients suffer from, but they are descriptions of *why* they suffer from severe dissociation. (231; emphases in original)

In the way of an illuminating connection, one can note that the divinity in Ligotti's *Special Plan* likewise suffers from dissociation, or rather deliberately induces it, in the attempt to escape from itself. This, like the entirety of what has been discussed in these pages, is a clue.

The question is: A clue to what?

And there's the rub.

Mute Fragments in Place of a Conclusion

To sum up:

In *This Degenerate Little Town*, the narrator speaks of "the greatest secret, perhaps the only secret" in the universe, and says it "appears in no religious doctrine" and is not mentioned "in any philosopher's system."

In *I Have a Special Plan for This World*, the narrator writes of a quasi-Gnostic "formless shade of divinity" that is eternally "in flight from its stale infinity."

In "The Red Tower," the narrator depicts a nightmare factory that produces grotesque and hideous novelty items and delivers them by means of subterranean tunnels to the farthest reaches of creation, while existing in a state of everlasting warfare with the gray, featureless landscape around it. This Tower, the narrator says, "works in mysterious ways."

Ligotti grew up as a Catholic. He approached his religion seriously, even obsessively, as "a matter of observance of ritual and private practice without being directed by emotional or spiritual feeling" (*Weird Fiction Review*). By his own account, at the age of eighteen, he "unloaded all of the doctrines, but almost none of the fearful superstition, of a gothically devout childhood and youth" (Schweitzer 29).

In later life, Ligotti became interested in Eastern religion and philosophy. He read the work of Alan Watts, U. G. Krishnamurti, and Douglas Harding, which influenced his authorial work in various ways and on various levels. He practiced meditation at home for more than thirty years (Ableev 157). He spoke once in an interview of his "erstwhile craving for 'enlightenment in darkness.'"[4]

In the final paragraph of "The Red Tower," the narrator says that despite having given a detailed account and description of the Tower and its activities, he has never actually seen it. In fact,

> no one ever has, and possibly no one ever will. And yet wherever I go, people are talking about it. In one way or another they are talking about [its productions]. Everything they are saying is about the Red Tower, in one way or another, and about nothing else but the Red Tower. We are all talking and thinking about the Red Tower in our own degenerate way. I have only recorded what everyone is saying (though they may not know they are saying it), and sometimes what they have seen (though they may not know they have seen it). But still they are always talking, in one deranged way or another, about the Red Tower. I hear them talk of it every day of my life. (*Nightmare Factory* 550)

At one point in *Special Plan,* the narrator says something that calls into question the very act of trying to think about such things, let alone talk about them—or to think or talk about anything at all:

> You can do nothing you are not told to do
> There is no hope for escape from this dream
>   that was never yours
> The words you speak are only its very words
> And you talk like a traitor
> Under its incessant torture (9)

If this dual account of our situation is accurate, then these words, not just Ligotti's but the ones that form the very sentence you are reading right now, as well as whatever train of thought and chain of associations they are currently producing in your head and heart, are not really about what they think they are about. They are not what you and I think they are about. No matter what they seem to say, in reality they are only the words of the dream. They are the incoherent, horrified babbling of a formless shade of divinity in flight from its stale infinity.

They are inadvertent descriptions of the outlines of crooked houses in the distance, tilting this way and that, with diseased and plaster-pale faces

---

4. "Thomas Ligotti's Career of Nightmares," q.v.

peeking out from behind grimy windows.

These words are about the Red Tower and nothing else.

They are in fact its very productions.

As am I.

As are you.

Sometimes, says the narrator of "The Red Tower," the chorus of incessant and inadvertent chatter about the Tower dies down as people begin to speak instead of the Tower's surrounding landscape. "Then," says the narrator, "the voices grow quiet until I can barely hear them as they attempt to communicate with me in choking scraps of post-nightmare trauma" (*Nightmare Factory* 551). In the silence, there eventually arises the sound of the factory beginning its operations yet again.

It is at such times that we will be able to speak again, in unison with the intonations of the Holy Trinity of narratorial voices encountered in these three works, of our special plan for this degenerate little Red Tower.

2020

Works Cited

Ableev, Daniel. "Interview Nonsense with Thomas Ligotti." In Matt Cardin, ed. *Born to Fear: Interviews with Thomas Ligotti.* Burton, MI: Subterranean Press, 2014. 155–74.

Angerhuber, E. M., and Thomas Wagner. "Disillusionment Can Be Glamorous." In Matt Cardin, ed. *Born to Fear: Interviews with Thomas Ligotti.* Burton, MI: Subterranean Press, 2014. 59–75.

Brawley, Chris. "'The Icy Bleakness of Things': The Aesthetics of Decay in Thomas Ligotti's 'The Bungalow House.'" *Studies in the Fantastic* No. 4 (Winter 2016/Spring 2017): 82–100.

Bridle, Deborah. "Visions of the Gothic Body in Thomas Ligotti's Short Stories." *Vastarien* 2, No. 2 (Summer 2019): 55–73.

Burns, William. "Twilight Twilight Nihil Nihil: Thomas Ligotti and the Post-Industrial English Underground." In Darrell Schweitzer, ed. *The Thomas Ligotti Reader.* Holicong, PA: Wildside Press, 2003. 101–10.

Cardin, Matt. "George Clayton Johnson Describes the Reality of 'The Twilight Zone.'" *The Teeming Brain,* 10 January 2013. www.teemingbrain.com/2013/

01/10/george-clayton-johnson-on-the-supernatural-reality-of-the-twilight-zone.

Cisco, Michael. "Ligotti, Thomas." In Matt Cardin, ed. *Horror Literature through History*. Santa Barbara, CA: Greenwood, 2017. 551–56.

Dodds, E. R. *Missing Persons: An Autobiography*. Oxford: Clarendon Press, 1977.

Goldberg, Ivan. "Am I Manic? Quiz." *PsychCentral*. Last modified 11 April 2019. psychcentral.com/quizzes/mania-quiz.

Hartwell, David G., ed. *The Dark Descent*. New York: Tor, 1987.

Horgan, John. *Rational Mysticism: Dispatches from the Border between Science and Spirituality*. Boston: Houghton Mifflin, 2003.

Ligotti, Thomas. *I Have a Special Plan for This World*. London: Durtro, 2000.

———. *The Nightmare Factory*. New York: Carroll & Graf, 1996.

———. *Teatro Grottesco*. London: Durtro, 2006.

———. *This Degenerate Little Town*. London: Durtro, 2001.

Lovasz, Adam. *The System of Absentology in Ontological Philosophy*. Newcastle upon Tyne, UK: Cambridge Scholars Publishing, 2016.

Lovecraft, H. P. *The Annotated Supernatural Horror in Literature*. Ed. S. T. Joshi. New York: Hippocampus Press, 2012.

Moreland, Sean. "Maddening Manikins: The Atmospheric Machines of Poe and Ligotti." *Vastarien* 2, No. 3 (Fall 2019): 109–38.

———. "'The Red Tower': The Universe as a Nightmare Factory." In Matt Cardin, ed. *Horror Literature through History*. Santa Barbara, CA: Greenwood, 2017. 552.

Schweitzer, Darrell. "*Weird Tales* Talks with Thomas Ligotti." In Darrell Schweitzer, ed. *The Thomas Ligotti Reader*. Holicong, PA: Wildside Press, 2003. 23–31.

Thoss, Raymond. "Notes on a Horror." *Vastarien* 1, no. 3 (Spring 2018): 217–38.

Weird Fiction Review. "Thomas Ligotti and the Realm of Nightmares." [Interview] *Weird Fiction Review*. 15 October 2015. weirdfictionreview.com/2015/10/interview-thomas-ligotti-and-the-realm-of-nightmares.

Winter, Douglas E. "The Pathos of Genre." In Ellen Datlow and Terri Windling, ed. *The Year's Best Fantasy and Horror*. New York: St. Martin's Press, 2000. 176–83. Also available at omnimagazine.com/eh/commentary/winter/pages/0799.html.

Yeats, W. B. *Yeats's Poems*. Ed. A. Norman Jeffares. London: Macmillan, 1989.

Introductions

Spookhouses, Catharsis, and Dark Consolations (Introduction to *Horror Literature through History*)

Horror is not only one of the most popular types of literature but one of the oldest. People have always been mesmerized by stories that speak to their deepest fears. But as with all things, this interest is not a cultural constant. Collectively, things come and go in cycles and waves, and beginning with the turn of the twenty-first century, horror began to experience a fierce resurgence after having gone through a cultural downswing during the previous decade.

This was not just a literary matter; in the new century and millennium, horror's chief audience and consumer base, consisting largely of high school-aged and college-aged young people, began eagerly absorbing horror, especially of the supernatural variety, from multiple sources. Along with novels and short fiction collections, there were television, movies, comic books, and video (and other types of) games. It was not that horror had ever actually died, for it is, as many have enjoyed noting, an undying—or perhaps undead—form of art and entertainment. But it had become somewhat sluggish in the 1990s, aided by the flaming out of the great horror publishing boom of the previous decade, and so the revival of the early 2000s constituted a definite and discernible phenomenon. It was also a distinctly diverse one. Weird horror fiction—a form to be defined and discussed in this encyclopedia—entered what some began to call a new golden age. Horror gaming (like other gaming) attained new heights of technological and narrative sophistication. Horror movie subgenres both old (such as exorcism) and new (such as "torture porn" and the found-footage world of movies such as *Paranormal Activity*) became enormously popular and profitable. Armies of zombies began to infest the pages of comic books and the proliferating sea of screens both large and small.

Crucially, in the midst of it all, the various non-literary forms continued

97

to draw deeply on their literary cousins for their basic plots, themes, and ideas. This was always true of horror films, but it is critically important to recognize that it remains true during the present era of exploding new forms and media, when it might be possible for a partaker of these new forms to ignore or forget the literary foundations of the whole phenomenon. Literary horror predates all the other types. It has a vastly longer, and therefore richer and deeper, history. And this is where and why a reference work like the present one comes in: because it serves to illuminate the roots of modern horror, both literary and otherwise, by laying out the field's deep history and evolutionary development.

Why Horror?

But right from the outset, such a project begs an important question: *why horror?* Why do people seek out stories, novels, movies, plays, and games that horrify? It is an old question, and one that has become virtually clichéd from overuse, as many horror novelists and movie directors can testify from years of having been asked some version of it by multiple interviewers, often with an affected attitude of mild amazement or disbelief: "Why horror? Why do you (or how can you) write, direct, imagine, envision, such unpleasant things? Why do you think your readers/viewers flock to them? Why are we insatiably addicted to tales of horror and dread?"

What Is Horror?

In answering this question, one could immediately jump into offering various theories and speculations, but to do this would beg yet another question, one that is usually missed or ignored by those attempting to deal with the "Why?" question, but that is properly prior to it; namely, the question of horror's *definition*. The very word and concept of "horror" is a noun, and also an adjective (as in "horror novel" and "horror movie"), that is too often left uninterrogated. Not by everyone, to be sure, but by a large number of the people who read the books, watch the movies, and play the games labeled as "horror" year in and year out. Many such people, if pressed, would likely say something to the effect that horror has something to do with being scared, and leave it at that. They would assert that "horror" is simply another word for "fear."

But a moment's reflection is enough to disabuse one of that notion. Certainly, horror does involve fear, but simple introspection shows that the word refers to something more than this, to fear *plus* something, fear with an admixture or addition of *something else*. A person may fear losing a job, or facing a tiger, or being mugged or beat up, but this does not mean someone in those positions is experiencing horror. Conversely, one may witness, say, the emotional abuse of a child, or the despoiling of an ecosystem, or the ravaging of a loved one by cancer—things that do not involve the supernatural trappings or operatic violence and gore associated with many books and movies bearing the "horror" label—and yet say in all honesty that one feels *horrified*. What exactly is it, then, about the emotional response to such situations that warrants the use of the "h" word to describe it?

These situations, along with a multitude of additional possible examples, may allow us to triangulate the inner element that makes horror horrifying, and to identify this element as some quality of *wrongness* or *repulsiveness*—physical, metaphysical, moral, or otherwise—that leads one to shrink from someone, something, some event, some idea, a monster, the sight of blood, a situation of gross immorality or injustice, or any number of other things. Horror, it seems, involves an irreducible element of revulsion or abhorrence, centered on a primal gut feeling, often implicit, that something *should not be*, that something is somehow fundamentally *wrong* about a given person, creature, act, event, phenomenon, environment, or situation. (Additionally, and significantly, there is a distinction to be made between horror and *terror*, another word that is of critical importance to the type of art generally labeled "horror" today, and that is addressed in the pages of this encyclopedia.)

In his study of the aesthetics of horror titled *The Philosophy of Horror; or, Paradoxes of the Heart* (1990), the philosopher and film scholar Noël Carroll famously noted the interesting and revealing fact that horror as a genre is named for the chief emotional reaction with which it is concerned, the emotional reaction that we have here called into question. Horror *horrifies:* it sets out to inspire a sense of fear and dread mingled with revulsion. Or, if one follows the lead of Tolstoy and Collingwood and other significant representatives of the expressive theory of art, one might argue that the works of horror that actually achieve the true status of art as such (defined as imaginative works possessing and displaying an intrinsically higher level of quality than "mere" genre or formula fiction, whose purpose is to entertain) do not so much seek to *inspire* horror as to *communicate* a sense of horror that has been experienced by the author. The horror critic and scholar S. T. Joshi, in such books as *The Weird Tale* (1990) and *The Modern Weird Tale* (2001), has advanced the idea that what distinguishes the most important and enduring authors of weird and supernatural horror fiction is their tendency to imbue their work with a consistent vision or worldview. In keeping with this, and regardless of the overall merit of Joshi's specific assertion (which some have disputed), it may well be that one of the distinguishing qualities of the greatest authors in this area is an uncommonly and acutely deep personal sensitivity to the more fearsome, dark, and distressing aspects of life, so that these aspects become a true source of fear, suffering, and, yes, *horror*. Following Tolstoy and Collingwood, one would say that when this quality is present in an individual who possesses (or is possessed by) the inbuilt drive and skill that motivates some people to become writers and artists, it will naturally lead such an individual to tell the rest of us the truth about these dark insights and experiences. And it will empower such a person to use the vehicles of prose fiction, and/or poetry, stage drama, film, television, comic books, or video games to communicate to others an actual experience of horror by recreating it, to some extent, in the reader, viewer, or player.

Interestingly, and as demonstrated repeatedly over the long history of horror literature, this does not necessarily mean that such writers and artists convey their horror in just a single, easily identifiable type of work that can automatically be given a category or genre label. Horror, as has been persuasively argued—perhaps most famously by Douglas E. Winter in his 1998 speech, and later essay, "The Pathos of Genre"—is not really a genre, defined as a type of narrative that has developed recognizable characteristics through repeated use, which can then be used as a kind of formula for producing other, similar works. Rather, it is "a progressive form of fiction, one that evolves to meet the fears and anxieties of its times. . . . [S]ometimes it wears other names, other faces, marking the fragmentation and meltdown of a sudden and ill-conceived thing that many publishers and writers foolishly believed could be called a genre" (182). In other words, horror in art is not a genre but a *mode* that can be employed in any form or genre. Horror has thus had a long and fruitful relationship with, for example, science fiction. And there are also horror Westerns, horror romance novels, religious horror stories, horror thrillers, horror mysteries, and so-called "literary" horror (with "literary" denoting non-genre writing). Being so portable, as it were, horror can spread out into all types of storytelling, and indeed, this is what has been happening with increasing visibility and pervasiveness in the horror renaissance of the early twenty-first century, to the point where the creeping spread of horror throughout the literary and entertainment landscape is one of the defining characteristics of this new era. Horror has become unbound, and its fortunes have become those of literature at large. In this new state of things, horror's reputation has begun to transcend its former questionable status as some darlings of the literary establishment have produced works that could be considered pure horror even though they do not bear the category label. In fact, if these had been published during the great horror boom of the 1980s, they would have been every bit as horrifying as (if not more so than) any 1980s paperback novel with garish Gothic typography and a leering monster on the cover.

Again: Why Horror?

So these, then, are some of the issues involved in identifying and defining horror in life and art. But the question with which we opened still remains: *why* horror? Even having answered—perhaps provisionally, arguably, necessarily incompletely—the question of why some writers write it (because they are themselves subject to a deeper-than-average experience of the horrors of life and consciousness), the question remains as to why readers read it. Fear and loathing are conventionally unpleasant emotions. Why do people seek to be subjected to them?

There are a number of customary answers to this question, many of which have been resorted to repeatedly by the interviewees mentioned above, and all of which carry some merit. For instance, what has sometimes been termed the roller coaster or funhouse theory of horror is surely true to an extent. There is something pleasant, even delightful—so this answer has it—about absorbing fictional stories of darkness, danger, and dread while remaining safe in one's easy chair. There is something purely entertaining and enjoyable about entering an imaginative world of horror, rather like a carnival funhouse ride, in order to enjoy the thrills to be found in such a place. From this point of view, seeking horror in fictional, cinematic, or any other form is no different in principle than seeking an adrenaline rush by reading a thriller or seeking a laugh by watching a comedy. And some people do approach all these things on this very level.

There is also surely something to the more profound theory of horror as catharsis, a position first advanced by Aristotle in his *Poetics* and still invoked more than two thousand years later to explain all kinds of artistic engagements, but especially those of a powerfully stark and unpleasant nature. Aristotle was talking specifically about Greek tragic plays, which brim with grief, betrayal, dark secrets, and unhappy endings, not to mention supernatural horrors and gruesome violence. Such productions, the great philosopher argued, serve to purge viewers of their pent-up emotions of fear and pity in a safely walled-off fictional world, thus preparing them better to deal with the anxieties of real life. One would be foolish and naïve to deny that today's horror fiction (and other forms) may serve this kind of function for some, and perhaps many, people.

But even granting the validity of these views, there is another and deeper answer to be given, and this is where the possible sensitivity of the reader meets up with the sensitivity of the writer who uses imaginative literature to convey his or her personal sense of profound horror at the vicissitudes and strangenesses of life, the world, consciousness, and everything. Perhaps, for some people, the great works of horror provide a deep, visceral, darkly electrifying confirmation of their own most personal and profound experiences and intuitions. After the spookhouse ride has let out, and after the catharsis has come and gone, horror in art, as Thomas Ligotti put it in his essay "The Consolations of Horror," may actually, weirdly, provide some readers with a kind of *comfort* by showing that "someone shares some of your own feelings and has made of these a work of art which you have the insight, sensitivity, and—like it or not—peculiar set of experiences to appreciate" (xi). What's more, horror accomplishes this artistic-alchemical feat not by denying or diminishing the dark, dismal, dreadful, terrifying, and horrifying elements of life, but by *amplifying* them. Never mind the possible therapeutic or other conventionally beneficial results that might be imputed to such a thing; the point, for both writer and reader, is simply to confront, recognize, experience, name, and know horror as such, because it is in fact real. It is part of the human experience. We are, from time to time—and some of us more often than others—haunted by horror. The type of art that bears this name is an expression of this truth, a personal and cultural acknowledgment of and dialogue with it, a means by which we know it, and affirm it, and "stay with" it, instead of denying it and looking away, as is otherwise our wont.

Like all art, horror literature and its associated other forms play out in ways that link up with a host of additional issues: historical, cultural, sociological, ideological, scientific, artistic, philosophical, religious, spiritual, and existential. It is the story of how exactly this has played out over the long span of human history, especially, but not exclusively, since the birth of literary Gothicism in the eighteenth century, with which this encyclopedia is concerned. Whatever the reader's purpose in picking up this work, and whatever the level at which he or she tends to engage personally with horror—as funhouse ride, cathartic tool, or personal consolation—it is hoped that the contents herein will help to clarify and illuminate the history, present, and possible futures of horror in both literary and other forms, while also fostering an enhanced appreciation of the central mystery and core of darkness that lies at the heart of the whole thing. It is in fact this darkness that serves as horror's source of enduring power, and that makes it an undying and undead form of human literary and artistic endeavor.

2017

Works Cited

Carroll, Noël. *The Philosophy of Horror; or, Paradoxes of the Heart.* New York: Routledge, 1990.

Joshi, S. T. *The Modern Weird Tale.* Jefferson, NC: McFarland, 2001.

———. *The Weird Tale.* Austin: University of Texas Press, 1990.

Ligotti, Thomas. *The Nightmare Factory.* New York: Carroll & Graf, 1996.

Winter, Douglas E. "The Pathos of Genre." In Ellen Datlow and Terri Windling, ed. *The Year's Best Fantasy and Horror.* New York: St. Martin's Press, 2000. 176–83. Also available at omnimagazine.com/eh/commentary/winter/pages/0799.html.

Foreword to *Beneath the Surface* by Simon Strantzas

In his seminal horror fiction anthology *The Dark Descent,* speculative fiction editor extraordinaire David Hartwell identified three separate streams or categories into which all horror stories can be classified: moral allegorical, psychological metaphor, and fantastic. He described stories in the third stream as representing or pursuing "a fabulous, formless darkness." Such stories, he says

> have at their center ambiguity as to the nature of reality, and it is this very ambiguity that generates the horrific effects. . . . Third stream stories maintain the pretense of everyday reality only to annihilate it, leaving us with another world entirely, one in which we are disturbingly imprisoned. It is in perceiving the changed reality and its nature that the pleasure and illumination of third stream stories lies, that raises this part of horror fiction above the literary level of most of its generic relations. (10)

I quote this passage from Hartwell's now-classic taxonomy simply to say this: that in *Beneath the Surface,* Simon Strantzas sets out to achieve the very effect Hartwell describes. And he succeeds. For the right kind of reader, meaning one who possesses the peculiar mental-emotional pattern that responds deeply and helplessly to fantastic or weird horror fiction, this book will expand and alter his or her perception of reality in multiple ways, sometimes subtle, sometimes dramatic, for the duration of each story. And just as Hartwell indicates, this alteration produces pleasure and illumination—and horror.

I have spent some time considering how and why Simon's stories succeed so admirably in this way when so many other stories by other writers fail. After much thought, I think I've arrived at an answer. I'll say first what I think the answer is not.

It's not just that Simon writes intelligently, although he certainly does, and this certainly is a major virtue. When he tells a tale that strips away the layers of reality and leaves you staring into a new darkness, he does it deliberately. He knows what he's about. He's smart about the effects he creates, and his deployment of the standard elements of fiction—plotting, characterization, tone, style, and so on—in the service of the delicate stylistic, cognitive, emotional, and philosophical effects sought by fantastic horror fiction is both shrewd and sensitive.

Nor is it just that he knows his chosen genre's history quite well and is therefore able to draw upon it for inspiration while achieving a strikingly original result, although this, too, is definitely present and definitely an asset.

No, beyond those admirable qualities, Simon's success is due to the presence of a unified vision that infuses and underwrites his stories. Simon Strantzas writes in pursuit of a Central Idea. He is gripped by an epic Dark Suspicion about the elemental underpinnings of human existence and reality itself, and his stories are metaphorical explorations and expressions of this Idea, this Suspicion, this Intuition of another order of being that sometimes emerges into view in profoundly troubling, even appalling, ways.

This, at least, is what I gather from reading the contents of *Beneath the Surface,* and I expect that if you pay attention, you will gather much the same. In several of these stories, most notably "A Shadow in God's Eye," Simon lays out his central vision, or at least a part of it, in explicit detail. In others, including "It Runs Beneath the Surface," "The Constant Encroaching of a Tumultuous Sea," "Off the Hook," and my personal favorite, "Behind Glass"—about an office worker who finds himself drawn into a nightmare of dissolving identity—he does not so much explain the vision as illustrate it. In all cases, his authorial choices are informed by that aforementioned intelligence and deep knowledge of the genre in which he is writing and to which he is contributing a valuable body of original work.

The vision behind the stories appears to center on the idea of a dark force that influences and, sometimes, enters into people. And it changes them, or manipulates them, or enlightens them, or destroys them, or sometimes does all these things simultaneously. One story, "A Thing of Love," depicts a weirdly warped relationship between a writer and his muse. The ancient concept of the muse, the personal genius, the daimon or daemon—the external force, entity, and/or intelligence that impinges directly on human consciousness with meanings from a metaphysical and ontological *beyond,* and that inspires writers and artists to produce works that embody these meanings—has become deeply and increasingly significant to me as a writer and a human being over the past couple of decades, and I have noticed that it also evokes a powerful sense of fascination and identification in many others who find themselves drawn to supernatural horror fiction. Judging from "A Thing of Love" and the other contents of Simon's book, I don't think I'm letting my readerly intuition carry me too far astray when I allow myself to speculate that the supervening vision of *Beneath the Surface* may be a dark version of this very concept. I think I detect the shadow of a vast Dark Muse presiding over the goings-on in Simon's fictional universe. I also think this is just as it should be. Tales of "a formless, fabulous darkness" have always tended to emerge as transmissions from beyond the pale. Sometimes this is part of their subject matter itself. Other times it is merely visible in their overall themes and literary effects. Both approaches are on display throughout Simon's book.

And so, in sum, I'm quite pleased to introduce this new ebook edition of *Beneath the Surface*, because the effects, the emotions, the insights, the illuminations, the dark dread and transcendent horror that we're talking about—this entire subgenre of weird, fantastic horror stories—represent a singularly valuable form of fiction, and this book, with its skillful achievement of such things, represents a valuable addition to the genre. I leave you now in Simon's care, with a confident prediction that, if you read these tales with the attention and sensitivity they deserve, you will find yourself becoming acquainted with many murky truths that always lurk just beneath the surface of life, but that always require a sensitive and skilled guide—someone like Simon Strantzas—to bring them briefly into the light, or perhaps to lead us all too briefly into the darkness, where we can collectively contemplate their grim reality and absorb the ineffable lessons they have to teach us.

2015

Works Cited

Hartwell, David G., ed. *The Dark Descent*. New York: Tor, 1987.

Strantzas, Simon. *Beneath the Surface*. 2008. Ebook edition (revised and expanded): Portland, OR: Dark Regions Press, 2015.

Introduction to *The Secret of Ventriloquism* by Jon Padgett

S. T. Joshi has famously argued that the truly great authors of weird fiction have been great precisely because they use their stories as a vehicle for expressing a coherent worldview. I would here like to advance an alternative thesis. I would like to assert that one of the characteristics of great weird fiction, and most especially weird horror—not the sole characteristic, of course, since weird horror is a multifaceted jewel, but a characteristic that is crucial and irreducible in those works of the weird that lodge in the reader's mind with unforgettable force and intensity—is a vivid and distinct authorial *voice*.

Can you imagine Poe's "The Fall of the House of Usher" without the sonorous narrative voice that speaks from the very first page in tones of absolute gloom and abject dread? Can you imagine Lovecraft's "The Music of Erich Zann" minus its voice of detached, dreamlike trepidation tinged with cosmic horror, as generated by the author's distinctive deployment of diction and artistry of prose style? Or Shirley Jackson's *The Haunting of Hill House* without the striking establishment of voice in the classic opening paragraph ("No live organism can continue for long to exist sanely under conditions of absolute reality; even larks and katydids are supposed, by some, to dream . . ."), which then develops over the course of the novel into a sustained tone of mingled dread, loneliness, and melancholy? Or what about Ligotti's "The Last Feast of Harlequin" without its measured tone of fearful discovery foregrounded against an emotional backdrop of desolate inner wintriness, as delivered in the narrative voice of an unnamed social anthropologist investigating a strange clown festival in an American Midwestern town? Each of these stories would be not just diminished but fundamentally altered—neutered, hamstrung, eviscerated—by the removal of its distinctive voice, which, vitally, is not just the narrative voice of the individual story but the voice of the author expressing itself through the environment of that particular work.

107

The point is not, of course, that these writers always maintain the very same voice across multiple works. Poe creates many different narrative voices across the span of his complete oeuvre. But he always, on some level, sounds like Poe. The same is true of Lovecraft, Jackson, Ligotti, and the other great masters of weird and supernatural horror. Their voice is vital to their authorial selves. They don't write in the styleless monotone of much commercial horror fiction. In their works you can hear *them* talking in and through the multitude of voices that make up their respective fictional worlds. It's a special kind of literary art, this creation of a distinctive voice that speaks to the reader in unmistakable tones with a manifest force and singularity of identity.

And it is an art that Jon Padgett possesses in spades. I learned this over a span of years as I was privileged to observe, intermittently and from a distance, the germination and gestation of Jon's authorial self. Eventually he started sending stories that fairly stunned me with the force of their philosophical-emotional impact. I remember first being affected like this by "20 Simple Steps to Ventriloquism," in which—significantly—the narrative itself focuses directly on the nature and power of voice, and of one special, dreadful voice in particular, an "intangible, alien voice twisting through that throat and that mouth, telling us that you have only ever been one of its myriad, crimson arms. . . . Feel that voice that is not a voice bubbling through that mouth that is not a mouth. Let it purge you of your static. Let it fill you with its own static." Presented in the form of a step-by-step guide to learning "the Greater Ventriloquism"—whose practitioners are "acolytes of the Ultimate Ventriloquist . . . catatonics, emptied of illusions of selfhood and identity . . . perfect receivers and transmitters of nothing with nothing to stifle the voice of our perfect suffering"—this is one of the most powerful, unsettling, disturbing, and impactful stories of its kind, or really of any kind, that I have read in the last ten years.

The same current of power winds its way through the other works gathered together here. In these eight striking stories—or, more accurately, six stories plus a one-act play and a guided meditation on experiencing the horror of conscious existence—Jon modulates the voice of his author's self into multiple tones depending on the needs of the piece at hand. In "Organ Void" and "The Infusorium," for example, he calibrates it with galling effectiveness to generate a tone, mood, and worldview of visceral filthiness set in a fictional realm of mounting, horrifying darkness. In "Murmurs of a Voice Foreknown" he applies it successfully to the first-person depiction of the narrator's personal nightmare of childhood persecution and the inner transition that leads this young protagonist to realize his power to outdo his persecutor.

In "The Mindfulness of Horror Practice" (the aforementioned guided meditation), he sounds almost like one of his non-horror influences, the contemporary spiritual writer and teacher Eckhart Tolle, who speaks unfailingly in a gentle voice of detached lucidity and focused self-inquiry—and yet Jon makes this so much his own that the voice guiding the reader toward a state of liberation from, or rather within, the horrors of body, mind, and being itself is recognizable as perhaps the quintessence of the book's other narrative voices. In all this one can, I think, detect traces of Jon's longtime practice of ventriloquism, as he projects his author's voice into each work and makes it speak convincingly through them all, even as it remains, in essence, his own.

I hope and believe that this, the first full-length book by Jon Padgett, will be remembered as an authentically significant debut collection. Along with voice, it also has vision, as may be evident from the lines I have quoted, and Jon's rich elaboration of this vision goes a considerable distance toward establishing a coherent worldview and thus fulfilling the Joshian criterion. "We Greater Ventriloquists are acolytes of the Ultimate Ventriloquist," announces one of his narrators at the end of twenty transformative lessons. "We Greater Ventriloquists are catatonics, emptied of illusions of selfhood and identity. . . . We are active as nature moves us to be: perfect receivers and transmitters of nothing with nothing to stifle the voice of our perfect suffering. Yes, we Greater Ventriloquists speak with the voice of nature making itself suffer." I don't know for sure if "the voice of nature making itself suffer" is actually, ultimately, Jon's own voice. For his sake, I think I hope it isn't. But I do know that it is a voice that lodges in the reader's mind with colossal force and intensity, marking that story and this book as unforgettable.

2016

Of Masks and Mystagogues:
Introduction to *Born to Fear:*
Interviews with Thomas Ligotti

It was in the late 1990s that I first encountered the mystery that is Thomas Ligotti. My initiation thus occurred relatively late, a full decade after Ligotti exploded onto the small-press horror scene. And at that time, among the corridors of the then-young Internet, where people were talking about him in fairly awed tones, strange speculations were flying. Apparently a rumor had arisen some years earlier that the name "Thomas Ligotti" was actually a pseudonym for a group of writers. Poppy Z. Brite had even obliquely invoked its echo in her foreword to the 1996 Ligotti omnibus collection *The Nightmare Factory*, which she began with an evocative question: "Are you out there, Thomas Ligotti?"

There were of course facts and factors working against the rumor. Thomas Ligotti had begun to win genre awards (although he never showed up to accept them in person). Even more pointedly, a small number of interviews with him had appeared in print. If he was a hoax, then he was an incredibly elaborate one. But paradoxically, these interviews sometimes served to cloud the matter still further instead of clarifying it. Ms. Brite actually referenced one of them in her foreword and said that instead of revealing the man behind the mask, the interviews only increased his aura of mystery. "I've never been able to discover anything of substance about you," she wrote, addressing her words directly to Ligotti. "That's the way you seem to want it. Even in the single interview I managed to glean from the wasteland of the small press, you spoke exclusively about the craft of writing. Don't mistake my meaning; there is no one I'd rather read upon the craft. But not a scrap of personal information escaped those lines of print" (ix).

That, as they say, was then. This is now. And two decades later, things have dramatically changed. The turning point occurred right there in the mid-to-late 1990s, just as I was discovering Ligotti and hearing the strange speculations about his possible identity or non-identity. As it turned out, the rumor about his pseudonymous nature was cooked up by Brandon Trenz, Ligotti's friend, screenwriting collaborator, and former coworker at a reference book publisher based out of Detroit. Neither of them had any inkling of just how out-of-hand it would briefly get. But like everything else, its days were numbered, and around the turn of the millennium the man himself—who, much to his own existentially pessimistic chagrin, really did exist—was beginning to emerge from the shadows of his work.

In a nicely resonant reversal on Ms. Brite's experience, it was the interviews he began to give at that time that proved central to this unveiling. After having given just a handful of them in the late '80s and early '90s—some of which, in point of fact, did contain scraps of personal information—he suddenly changed tactics and began to speak to the public more freely and frequently about himself. These public conversations and self-revelations often took the form of philosophical tours de force that were rich with profound, incisive, and bitingly witty observations on and reactions to life, art, writing, literature, and the signal horror of being alive. Over time they all began to cohere into an extensive corpus of their own that we may collectively call, with proper noun caps and a well-deserved tone of gravity, The Ligotti Interviews, whose most choice specimens are herein collected and presented for your personal delectation.

So that's the factual background to the book you're now holding. For another angle on it, I ask you to consider the following analogy: Thomas Ligotti is to his interviews as H. P. Lovecraft is to his letters. To the many readers of Ligotti who are also readers of Lovecraft, the meaning and import of this statement is probably obvious.

S. T. Joshi has argued, quite plausibly I think, that Lovecraft's thousands upon thousands of letters stand as a monumental work in their own right, aside from and in addition to the stories and the major essay ("Supernatural Horror in Literature") for which he is more widely known. Whether or not Joshi is right in his expectation that these letters will one day be generally recognized as a major work is another matter, but as anybody knows who has spent some time reading even the small slice of Lovecraft's total epistolary output that is represented by the five-volume set of his *Selected Letters,* the man himself still lives and breathes in those pages. They are where you can become personally acquainted with the eccentric, brilliant, cranky, erudite, bigoted, kind-hearted, high-strung, witty, contradictory, capacious, lovable person who wrote "The Call of Cthulhu" and *At the Mountains of Madness* and all the rest. Significantly, this creates a mutually enriching resonance with the stories, whose depth and fascination are increased by multiple orders of magnitude when read in light of an acquaintance with their author. The letters in turn gain an added depth and poignancy when read in light of the stories.

It's amusing, and sometimes galling, for those of us who know Lovecraft on both fronts to witness the often caricaturish portraits of his person that are concocted by those who know only the stories and therefore imagine that he was a freak or an occultist or whatever. Even in his own day, his stories tended to generate strange impressions among the readers who strove to imagine their author. I remember once seeing a pencil sketch that a fan or correspondent made of Lovecraft without having met him in person. The sketch was drawn purely from the individual's impressions of Lovecraft as known from his work in *Weird Tales* and so on, and perhaps from his participation in the world of amateur journalism. It showed Lovecraft as a bearded old wizard-like figure, grizzled and forbidding in his mystery, hermitry, and dark knowledge of arcane blasphemies. As I recall, Lovecraft, who was nothing at all like that, found it highly amusing.

Something of the same mystery and misconception still attends the person of Thomas Ligotti. As with Lovecraft, Ligotti's stories generate a certain impression of what their author must be like. Ms. Brite said that if she ever met him in person, she "would expect to meet a slightly dissipated aesthete, sarcastic and decadent and wry, given to odd word-associations, with a taste not just for the macabre but for the truly, nakedly gruesome." She continued with characteristic shrewdness: "But perhaps I would encounter someone else entirely. I suspect I'll never know" (x).

On that count, at least, she was wrong. Today we know for certain that Thomas Ligotti is indeed out there, although almost none of his fervent readers have ever met or are likely to meet him in the flesh. We also know, thanks to his interviews and correspondence, that he is fully as fascinating in his person as the brilliant horror stories that established his reputation and public image. Is it possible for someone to simultaneously deviate from and greatly fulfill a prebaked notion of who they are? Robert M. Price has written that Ligotti is not only someone who frequently invokes the figure of "the mystagogue, the initiator into forbidden knowledge, in almost every short story," but someone who, in doing so, provides "a hint of his own role as a horror writer" (35). There's something of that in Ligotti the interviewee as well. He frequently doesn't answer the way you would expect him to. At times he says far less than the normal rhythm of a conversation would dictate, and at other times far more. As amply hinted at by his stories, he is an authority worth listening to on the subject of weird and supernatural fiction, and also on the subject of literature in general. He is also deeply read in philosophy and religion, and especially in the literature of nihilism and philosophical pessimism. Additionally, he is witty, caustic, sad, tormented, kind, generous, and lots of other things, most of which are on display in the interviews you're about to read.

In short, he has poured a great deal of himself into these public conversations over the years, to the point where, as mentioned, they have emerged as a true creative work in their own right. And that's really what this book is about: bringing the best of these interviews together to connect the dots and reveal the emerging picture. Tom himself already did a little bit of this when he derived portions of his 2010 nonfiction opus *The Conspiracy against the Human Race* from interviews that he had granted several years earlier to Neddal Ayad and me. If you want a useful way to frame or peg this present volume, you could do worse than to view it as a kind of unofficial companion to that book, since in both works the man steps out from behind his fiction-maker's mask and speaks as himself.

Then again, he has also turned the act of being interviewed into a kind of philosophical art form of its own. Where does the fiction maker end and the real man begin? How many masks does he wear? How many layers deep do they go? What ultimately lies behind them all? For that matter, how could we ever know the answers to such questions, or even understand them if they were given to us, multiple mask-wearers and puppet-dancers that we all may ultimately be?

It turns out that Ligotti, the interviewee and conversationalist, is no less a mystagogue than Ligotti, the horror writer.

In closing, I think you will find that the chronological totality of these interviews—four of which appear here in English for the first time—provides a rich feast. In particular, you will find that it offers a striking evolutionary overview of the thinking, reading, living, and suffering that lie behind the still-growing body of supernatural horror fiction flowing from the pen of one of the genre's most important practitioners.

To illustrate the point, and to give you a head start on that dot-connecting process: "I've never been tempted to write anything that was not essentially nightmarish," Tom states in the first of these interviews. "The traditions and conventions of supernatural horror offer everything I need and answer all the sensations and attitudes that are important to me." A quarter century later, in one of the *last* of these interviews, he significantly modifies and darkens the same point:

> Almost everyone who writes or reads horror stories was born to fear. . . . [W]hen I discovered the writings of Lovecraft and Poe, I immediately identified the fear that was the source of their writings and embraced it. Instead of seeking some kind of peace in my life, I aggravated my fear. And I aggravated it further by a seductive dwelling on the most morbid and fearful aspects of existence. I wish I had sought peace instead of fear, but I was not wise enough or insightful enough to do so.

And then, in the very last line of the very last interview, he cuts right across all of the above with a literary and philosophical knife slash: "[Writing] continues to console until practically everything in a person's life has been lost. Words and what they express have the best chance of returning the baneful stare of life."

I think we can be certain that here, at least, it's not a mask speaking but the man himself.

2014

Works Cited

Brite, Poppy Z. "Are You Out There, Thomas Ligotti?" Foreword to *The Nightmare Factory* by Thomas Ligotti. New York: Carroll & Graf, 1996. ix–x.

Price, Robert M. "The Mystagogue, the Gnostic Quest, and the Secret Book." In Darrell Schweitzer, ed. *The Thomas Ligotti Reader*. Holicong, PA: Wildside Press, 2003. 32–37.

Introduction to *Portraits of Ruin* by Joseph S. Pulver, Sr.

Plato once wrote, "But if a man comes to the door of poetry untouched by the madness of the Muses, believing that technique alone will make him a good poet, he and his sane companions never reach perfection, but are utterly eclipsed by the performances of the inspired madman." This is a sentence rich with, and in fact threaded and structured along, a succession of deeply striking and evocative phrases and images: "the door of poetry . . . the madness of the Muses . . . sane companions . . . utterly eclipsed . . . the inspired madman." They are like a collage of implied spiritual-artistic meaning, a chant whose very intonation is at least as important as, and probably more than, its conceptual content. In other words, they *gesture* toward something, some transcendent reality they can't quite articulate. Or at least that's the way I like to take them, regardless of Plato's intentions.

And this, I think—both my fixation on this quotation, which is talismanic for me, and my preferred way of reading it—is one of the main reasons why I find Joe Pulver's *Portraits of Ruin* to be so deeply disquieting. Reading it, I begin to wonder, inadvertently, inexorably, about the name and nature of the particular door that he may have passed through in the pursuit of his art. I wonder about the identity of the particular Muse—dark, wild, daimonic—that may have maddened him. And wondering these things, I'm driven to doubt whether we, his sane companions, can ever really comprehend him, and to suspect that we must instead resign ourselves to having our understanding utterly eclipsed by the performances of this inspired madman.

I've always found "experimental" literature very difficult, notwithstanding the fact that I've produced a couple of pieces of it myself. Apparently, as a fundamental fact of my literary taste and predilection, I'm drawn mostly to conventionally worded writings and traditionally structured narratives. Give me

Lovecraft over Burroughs, Poe over Pynchon, *A Portrait of the Artist as a Young Man* over *Ulysses* (and especially over, God help us, *Finnegans Wake*). As with fiction, so with poetry: I'll take Robert Frost over T. S. Eliot any day, and Lawrence Ferlinghetti just makes my head hurt.

Or actually, this has changed somewhat over the years. It was Robert Anton Wilson, of all people, who cracked open my cosmic-literary egg and initiated me into some of the pleasures and rewards of conventionally unreadable and/or incomprehensible writing. He loved to mix things up in his novels: plain old prose on one page, then stream-of-consciousness gibberish on the next, followed by a scene or two in screenplay format and then a metafictional flourish for good measure. And since I was drawn to him helplessly at age nineteen when I recognized him as one of my natural philosophical mentors, I just rolled with it. I absorbed the lessons he overtly taught and subliminally imparted. All these years later, I find I'm grateful for this education when I approach the Pulver corpus and try to wrap my head around it, or perhaps let it wrap its head around me.

Literature, it turns out, can do a lot more than one might think, especially when it tries not to be literature, or to forget that there is such a thing as restraint by medium, or to burst the bounds of what can actually be communicated via the written word, not just in terms of the concepts being broached but the very form in which they are presented.

Sometimes it is the attempt to say what can't be said, or what can't be said in any form that "makes sense," that says the most.

William Stafford, the United States Poet Laureate from 1970 to 1971, wrote what may be the single most brilliant essay on the art of writing that I've ever been privileged to read. The title is "A Way of Writing," and Stafford uses it to present his philosophy—not abstract but applied, embodied—of the relationship between the authorial act and the writer's very identity, and of the liberatory value writers can find in forgoing a sense of foresight and control by relying on their own innate psychic coherence. "A writer," he tells us,

> is not so much someone who has something to say as he is someone who has found a process that will bring about new things he would not have thought of if he had not started to say them. . . . If I put down something, that thing will help the next thing come, and I'm off. If I let the process go on, things will occur to me that were not at all in my mind when I started. These things, odd or trivial as they may be, are somehow connected. . . . I know that back of my activity there will be the coherence of my self, and that indulgence of my impulses will bring recurrent patterns and meanings again. (17, 18, 19)

I don't know if Joe Pulver has read that essay, but I hope he hasn't. It's neater to think of him practicing something exactly like what Stafford describes without ever having heard of the man, some sort of inner artistic-literary-alchemical act of receptivity or (as we might think of it) "self-theurgy," but perhaps in a more overtly surrealist vein of the André Breton sort than Stafford was wont to embrace. It's neater to think of him sitting down somewhere and loosing his pen or typewriter or word processor in innocence of Stafford's advice, and finding a flood of words and images issuing forth on the page or screen, seeing it all assume a shape that won't make sense to the conscious mind, but that will speak of a deep self, *his* self, with perfect precision.

Or perhaps it's speaking not of him but of that dark-daimonic Muse of his. Then again, perhaps they're the very same thing.

For years I've played a kind of literary game with myself. Before reading any work of fiction, I always turn to the beginning and read the opening lines. Then I skip to the end and read the closing lines. Finally, I pause and mull them over for a moment before diving into the full reading itself. How is the author going to get from point A to point Z? How will those opening words, phrases, sentences, thoughts, images, insights, necessarily have to unfurl and complexify and flow and develop in order to reach the conclusion toward which I know they are headed? Far from ruining the reading experience, I find this practice palpably enhances it.

But alas, it simply *doesn't work* with Joe Pulver's stuff, or at least not in the way I've come to regard as normal and desirable. Consider, for example, the opening story in *Portraits of Ruin*. Its title is "No Healing Prayers," and it bears the dedication "for Gary Myers & Robert Bloch." The colophon page informs me that it was previously published in the anthology *Dead But Dreaming 2* from Miskatonic River Press in 2011. Okay, that's sufficient to establish a surrounding context, and a very compelling one at that, for somebody like me (and, I assume, somebody like you), who is deeply interested and invested in horror fiction, and particularly in the dark philosophical concerns of the branch we call weird or cosmic.

So, having made my mental oblations for the reading act, I turn to the opening lines and find the following:

> Midnight.
> Moonlight.
> Cold.
> The howling sun, far from this place with no hope for tomorrow, running with things that fear what the cold moon brings.

> Captain Jack sits on his front porch. Shotgun on his lap.
> Coffee gone cold.
> Waiting.

Okay. Nice language and darksleek imagery. Very impressionistic, though. I'm aware, yes, that language, especially when artistically deployed, can achieve amazing things when it tries to subvert or explode its own inherent limits. But that's often more of a philosophical conviction than a living reality for me. I still doubt my chops as a reader of experimental stuff. So I know right away that this story may be difficult to get a grasp on. With this in mind, I turn to the closing lines to complete the ritual:

> Coming for bones. Coming for flesh.
> Coming to drink tears and tenderness affirmed and every contour between.
> The corpse-coffin sound of Hell shouting in the trees. Something black in the road.
> "Whatever will be . . . Will be."
> The Piper Man laughs.
> Shotgun leveled. . .
>
> (*Grand Funk Railroad "The Railroad"*)

To borrow that unfortunate and ubiquitous initialism from the culture of social media and digital interconnectedness: WTF? What the hell do *those* lines tell me? In one of my day-job incarnations, I teach remedial reading to community college students, and my practice of thoroughly pre-reading books and stories to gain a sense of their overall contextual contour is something all the textbooks preach: "Get your bearings. Don't just dive into page one, line one. That approach is a surefire route to disaster via incomprehension. Instead, map your mental way to the end before starting, so that what you encounter along the way will make sense because you're fitting it into a bird's-eye map of the total landscape, just like you look at a roadmap before trying to drive to Dallas." Personally, this is something that I've always done intuitively anyway. Nobody had to teach it to me. Now I teach it to others.

And lo! it breaks down and craps out entirely when applied to Joe's work.

But what if we try another item? Maybe one from the middle of the book. Our eyes skim to the midpoint of the table of contents and find "Marks and Scars and Flags." The information at the start of the book lets us know this one is previously unpublished. Okay, here goes. Opening lines:

> Is it real?
> Is it?

These last 6 hours . . .

This pack.

Did she, looking down at her feet and gently smiling—in that crocodile way, really say, "Go. Ask, Alice."?

Did she?

Flip the pages. Closing lines:

> Her smile blurs, releasing cobwebs and corridors.
>
> "Turn." Soft as the saxophone that afternoon, cold, a trumpet that bends the facets of the breast.
>
> Cold.
>
> And someone—someone—has, has opened the gates . . .
>
> *A century in seclusion with the green birds . . . the humors of the lantern as a sedative . . . I've lost my shoes . . .*
>
> *(Deathprod—Reference Frequencies)*

Ah, hell.

One more try. I'll skip to the book's end. The final story, a novella-length piece, is nicely titled: "And this is where I go down into the darkness." It was previously published in *Phantasmagorium* #1, and it bears the dedication "for beelzeBOB & Tom Ligotti, titans BOTH!!!" This is a very promising pedigree indeed. I let the opening lines feed themselves to me:

> *I sat in the Days Between the Years, Darkness whispered to the corpses in the palm of my hand . . . and I planned my escape.*
>
> I am not a learned man. I am an escape artist.
>
> Was when I started.
>
> Poor. Hungry. Inner-city caught, small—walled in, all men are. Here in the grey rain they are. Mired with learning disabilities I took the route I could afford and held the most appeal, or coulda been no option is the only option. The poor care not, an open door is an open door.

Interesting. Still stream-of-consciousness in flavor, but a bit more structured, as if balanced between the poetic-type fragmentary impressionism of the previous stories and something more conventional, more fleshed out along standard lines of narrative development and characterization. I skip to the closing lines:

> Watching the river run . . . looks like little hills rolling along . . . the hills flow . . .
>
> The nightmare of being—head full of false imaginings, the cravings the blundering puppet paints, being handed the scandalous heirloom . . . The surface of the river is graced by soft lights, a trance

and this is where I go down into the darkness

Whoa. This is flat-out breathtaking. And it's followed by some bracketed nods, darkly evocative in their own right, to Ligotti's *The Conspiracy against the Human Race* plus a "bunch of songs by Bruce Springsteen and some by Scott Walker and David Tibet/Current 93," along with acknowledgments and thanks for permission to quote from Ligotti's *Conspiracy* and Robert M. Price's "The Sword of the Stillborn."

Almost in spite of myself, in spite of my pedestrian tendencies as a reader, it's all starting to make sense. Sort of. And the sense it's making is, frankly, dark, dazzling, disturbing, and delicious.

"I know that back of my activity," says William Stafford, "there will be the coherence of my self, and that indulgence of my impulses will bring recurrent patterns and meanings again."

"But," says Plato, "if a man comes to the door of poetry untouched by the madness of the Muses," he will be "utterly eclipsed by the performances of the inspired madman."

Yes, I think I'm catching on, especially when I can also hear the voice of Ray Bradbury chiming in, passing along something that he said Federico Fellini once told him: "Don't tell me what I'm doing. I don't want to know." Bradbury tells us the great filmmaker meant he didn't want to think ahead of time about what he was trying to accomplish, but instead wanted to work in an inspired and ecstatic way, proceeding and producing in the ecstasy of the creative moment, and only afterward try to discover and contemplate the meanings that wanted to emerge from it.

Yes, when it comes to *Portraits of Ruin,* I may indeed be catching on. So the question now becomes: Are you? Because after all, you're about to read the book, and this weird excuse for an introduction by me is supposed to prepare you, or whet your appetite, or do whatever it is that introductions are supposed to do. And my sharing of the process of revelation that I've gone through in grappling with Joe's new literary offspring is the best approach I could think of to prepare you for what awaits you.

But I've probably said too much already, so I'll sum up with this: when a writer simply lets loose the flood of his self, his interiority, his psyche, his soul, and what emerges is so darkly compelling and fascinating that it conveys, even if obliquely, the sense of an imminent and immanent truth, reality, otherworld, something-or-other, whose shape and nature is terrifying and wondrous to behold—when this happens, you stop caring whether it makes conventional sense and simply bask in the glow of something special. Alan

Watts once said the formal concert music scene "came to a final crash" (113) the moment John Cage sat down at a Steinway in full evening dress, opened his musical score, and proceeded to perform a recital composed entirely of rests. And while I certainly don't think literature in general or horror fiction in specific has now crashed to a halt because of *Portraits of Ruin,* I do think something of Watts's meaning attends the publication of this book. Cage was a brilliantly talented and exquisitely trained classical pianist. He could play the traditional classical music game and hold his own with the best of them. But his Muse led him down another path, or rather led him to blaze a trail all his own, and those who understood were deeply enriched. "He was trying to clean our ears of melodic and harmonic prejudices," Watts said (114).

Those who have ears—which Joe is about to clean—let them hear.

The final word can go to Joe himself. Back when he and I were communicating about the possibility of my writing this introduction, he told me, "I never know what to make of my stuff."

This, above all, is what you might want to bear in mind as you turn the page and proceed to immerse yourself in what follows. *The author himself does not know what to make of these writings.* Neither do I. Nor, I daresay, will you. But the very attempt to do so, to "make something" of them—an interpretative activity that the work itself incites because of its native grippingness and stylistic brilliance (that surrealist's flood of unconscious inspiration is channeled, mind you, through a finely honed and tuned set of conscious literary skills, just like Cage's pianistic training)—this very attempt at finding some sort of meaning is, in the end, the point. Because the meaning is really and truly *there.* You can sense it in every line and phrase, grinning darkly at you through the interstices of the words and images. It just happens to be a meaning that you can only "understand" by allowing it to speak to your own deep self, to your—dare I say it?—daimonic Muse.

So don't ask what Joe is doing; that approach only closes it off. Instead, rely on the coherence of your deep self to understand the coherence of his. In learning to do this, to resonate with this book of impossible imaginings presented in improbable forms, you may well find that you're being altered and enlightened in ways that are truly transformative.

After all, only an inspired madman can understand an inspired madman.

2012

Works Cited

Stafford, William. "A Way of Writing." In *Writing the Australian Crawl*. Ann Arbor: University of Michigan Press, 1978. 17–20.

Watts, Alan. *Does It Matter? Essays on Man's Relation to Materiality*. New York: Pantheon Books, 1970.

Gods and Monsters

A Brief History of the Angel and the Demon

I. Introduction: Is There Someone Inside You?

Even a cursory survey of the supernatural horror genre reveals the important role that the angel and the demon have long played in it. From texts such as Dante's *Divine Comedy* (written 1308–21) and Milton's *Paradise Lost* (1667), which straddle the boundary between religious devotional literature and outright fiction, to fictional works such as Matthew Gregory Lewis's *The Monk* (1796) and William Peter Blatty's *The Exorcist* (1971), the demon has provided ongoing fodder for creators of supernatural horror. And while the angel has most often served as a mere foil for the demon and has often been ignored in favor of focusing exclusively on demonic horrors, it has still made its presence known. *Paradise Lost,* for example, begins with a dramatic narration of the fall of Lucifer and his fellow angels from heaven and their subsequent transformation or transition into demons. More recently, in the 1990s and early 2000s, American popular culture portrayed the angel in a context of supernatural horror in the *Prophecy* movie franchise, which flouted modern Western conventions by abandoning the cute, cozy angels of Victorian art and the greeting-card industry to return to a more ancient and traditional portrayal of angels as powerful, terrifying beings.

Nor are these figures influential merely within the confines of the supernatural horror as such. In 1973 the cinematic adaptation of *The Exorcist,* directed by William Friedkin—fresh from his success with *The French Connection*—became a sensation among audiences and was subsequently recognized as the first true "blockbuster," predating the likes of *Jaws* and *Star Wars.* It was nominated for ten Academy Awards, including Best Picture and Best Director, and won two of them. Its earnings made it one of the top grossing films at the U.S. box office that year, and since then it has steadily remained in and around the top ten highest-grossing films of all time both domestically and internationally. Upon its first release, it ignited a national conversation about theological matters within the United States, just as its author (William Peter Blatty, who wrote the screenplay from his novel) had hoped it would do, and spurred many fear-based conversions and reconversions to Christianity.

Angels have shared a similar widespread influence. Director Frank Capra's *It's a Wonderful Life*, which begins and ends with angels, received only a middling response from audiences and critics when it was first released in 1946 (although it was nominated for five Academy Awards). Then in 1974 a copyright lapse due to a clerical error placed the film in the public domain. When television stations around the country began to take advantage of the opportunity to run the film free of royalty charges, a new generation of viewers rediscovered and fell in love with it, thus transforming it into a widely beloved "holiday classic" and making the supporting character of Clarence the most famous cinematic angel of them all.

During the 1980s and 1990s, angels became a bona fide national obsession in the U.S. A slew of television programs (*Highway to Heaven*, *Touched by an Angel*), movies (*Angels in the Outfield*, *City of Angels*), and best-selling books (*A Book of Angels*, *Ask Your Angels*, *Where Angels Walk*) reflected and catered to a rising fascination with the idea of winged heavenly guardians and messengers. In 1994 the NBC television network aired a two-hour primetime special titled *Angels: The Mysterious Messengers*. That same year, PBS ran a well-received documentary titled *In Search of Angels*. A 1993 *Time* magazine cover story about the angel craze included a survey indicating that 69 percent of Americans claimed to believe in angels, while nearly half believed they were attended by a personal guardian angel. *Newsweek*, which ran its own angel-themed cover story the same week the *Time* issue appeared, reported that the angel craze appeared to be rooted in a very real spiritual craving: "It may be kitsch, but there's more to the current angel obsession than the Hallmarking of America. Like the search for extraterrestrials, the belief in angels implies that we are not alone in the universe—that someone up there likes me" (quoted in Nickell 152–53).

Not incidentally, this sentiment closely echoed Blatty's expressed motivation for writing *The Exorcist*. As he has explained in numerous interviews and also in his 2001 memoir *If There Were Demons, Then Perhaps There Were Angels: William Peter Blatty's Story of* The Exorcist, when he was a junior at Georgetown University in 1949, he encountered a *Washington Post* story about a fourteen-year-old boy in Mount Rainier, Maryland, who had undergone an exorcism under the official sanction of the church. Blatty had long been concerned about the spiritual direction of modern Western society—*The Exorcist,* let it be noted, was published in the immediate wake of the 1960s "death of God" movement and during the tumultuous Vietnam era—and in the account of this boy and his apparent demonic affliction, Blatty thought he could discern "tangible evidence of transcendence." Two decades later he fictionalized the story in his famous novel. But it was a fiction with a serious existential purpose; as he later explained, in his view the reality of demons serves as a kind of apologetic proof for the existence of God, because "if there were demons, there were angels and probably a God and a life everlasting" (Whitehead). A bit later, in 1999, Blatty invoked a version of the same idea to account for the millennial resurgence of supernaturally themed films such as *The Sixth Sense, Stir of Echoes, The Blair Witch Project,* and *Stigmata:* "One of the prime allures of the supernatural thriller is that there is a world of spirit and that death doesn't mean our final destiny is oblivion" (Bonin). In this, he echoed the twentieth-century theologian Paul Tillich, as quoted by Victoria Nelson in *The Secret Life of Puppets,* her exploration of the mystical/gnostic psychological and spiritual "underside" of modern popular entertainment:

> Lacking an allowable connection with the transcendent [in our Western intellectual culture where the religious impulse is deemed unacceptable], we have substituted an obsessive, unconscious focus on the negative dimensions of the denied experience. In popular Western entertainments through the end of the twentieth century, the supernatural translated mostly as terror and monsters enjoyably consumed. But as Paul Tillich profoundly remarked, "Wherever the demonic appears, there the question of its correlate, the divine, will also be raised." (19)

In the early 1970s, it seemed the Roman Catholic Church, or at least the Pope, agreed with at least the first half of Blatty's demon-angel apologetic. In November 1972, Pope Paul VI delivered an address to a General Audience in which he expressed his concern over what he viewed as demonic influences at work in the world: "Evil is not merely an absence of something but an active force, a living, spiritual being that is perverted and that perverts others. It is a terrible reality, mysterious and frightening. . . . Many passages in the Gospel show us that we are dealing not just with one Devil, but with many." These statements ignited a debate both inside and outside the church and embarrassed many priests whose outlook was more in tune with the secularized and demythologized tenor of the time than with what they viewed as the mythological belief system of pre-Enlightenment Christianity. But the international phenomenon that was *The Exorcist* demonstrated that the Roman

pontiff spoke not only for himself but for an enormous public that either believed as he did or, at the very least, suspected or wanted to believe in the literal existence of a transcendent spiritual reality. The fact that the pope's
remarks were bookended, temporally speaking, by the 1971 publication of
Blatty's novel and the 1973 release of the movie makes it difficult to avoid
speculating that all three statements—the novel, the movie, and Paul VI's
speech—were expressions of a proliferating cultural phenomenon that also
encompassed the aforementioned angel craze. This was and still is a phenomenon whose central, guiding obsession is invoked by the character of the psychiatrist in *The Exorcist* when he asks a hypnotized girl the most
psychologically and spiritually potent question of all: "Is there someone inside
you?"

All this brings the argument back to the matter at hand. It will be the task
of this essay to explore the ancient origins of the iconic Angel and Demon
(henceforth referred to as proper nouns) in folklore, history, religion, literature, philosophy, psychology, and art. The overall purpose will be to demonstrate how and why a knowledge of the deep history of these ubiquitous
horror icons dramatically illuminates their frequent appearances in works of
supernatural horror. Such an investigation will also, inevitably, illuminate
widespread popular religious conceptions, which are often poorly demarcated—if indeed they are demarcated at all—from the images presented in
popular entertainment.

To preview what will be explained in detail, supernatural horror as it has
developed in the West has generally employed the concepts and iconography
of Christian theology in dealing with demons and angels. The stereotypical
images of the Angel and Demon have their roots in old Christian, pre-
Christian, and extra-Christian ideas. They result from a fusion or synthesis of
concepts and images that occurred throughout Europe and the Middle East
during the Hellenistic and Roman periods. This fusion arose out of the rich
cross-fertilization of various ancient currents of thought extending back into
history and prehistory, and it was finalized and codified for the modern West
by a few significant literary works during the Middle Ages and the Renaissance. The overall picture is rich and complex, but the rewards of grasping
it—the benefits of seeing, understanding, and appreciating more of what is
going on beneath the surface as one observes the Angel and Demon striding
through the outpourings of the supernatural horror genre—are significant.

II. The Prehistory of the Demon

Introduction: What's in a Name?

A fruitful place to begin is with an unpacking of the word "demon," since this will preview the broad outlines of the story as a whole. The figure of the Demon originally derived from the minor evil spirits common to all religions and mythologies of the Middle East, as processed through Jewish theology and the Greek belief in spirits called *daimones* (pronounced "DY-mon-ez"). The name "demon" itself indicates the use of the old Greek idea by Hellenistic and later writers and religious thinkers who were most responsible for helping to codify this category during the first few centuries before and after the beginning of the Common Era. The English word "demon" comes from the Latin *daemon*, which itself came from the Greek *daimon*. "Demon" is technically a neutral word that refers to any spirit, whether good or evil, that is neither divine nor mortal but inhabits the intermediate realm between gods and humans. Thus, even angels belong to the general class of beings known as demons. But in common usage, owing to habits established between roughly 200 B.C.E. and 200 C.E., "demon" has come to refer solely to the evil members of the category.

Demonism or daimonism itself, meaning especially the nexus of religious attitudes and practices built around the experience of *deisidaimonia* or "demon dread" that flourished briefly in Greece during the sixth and fifth centuries B.C.E., was much subdued in the wake of the philosophical golden age of Socrates, Plato, and Aristotle (the fifth and fourth centuries B.C.E.). For several centuries after this philosophical flowering, a number of influential Greek skeptics and rationalists made it their mission to debunk what they regarded as old superstitions. Meanwhile, a vital Jewish demonology, heavily influenced by Zoroastrian beliefs, was thriving and producing an extensive literature. Then, during the Hellenistic period—from roughly the late fourth century B.C.E. to the dawn of the Common Era—the love of all things mystical and occult that proliferated among writers, intellectuals, and occultists served to inflame the old daimonic beliefs once again. The categorizing and labeling of spirits became a popular pastime, and the Hellenistic thinkers took the plethora of evil spirits that were ubiquitous throughout their richly syncretistic culture, including the evil variety of the Greek daimons called *kakodaimones*, and also the spiritual hierarchies of the Middle Eastern and Jewish demonologies, and lumped them together under the category of daimons—eventually to be known as demons—thus creating the earliest recognizable version of the iconic Demon of supernatural horror.

As indicated by this highly compressed account, three of the most important currents of thought that went into forming the Demon were, first, the beliefs and ideas about spirits that saturated the Middle East from the earliest antiquity; second, the angels and demons of ancient Judaism; and third, the Greek idea of *daimones*.

Demons of the Ancient Middle East

As described by E. V. Walter in his essay "Demons and Disenchantment," the Greek word *deisidaimonia* refers to "a certain dimension of sacromagical, numinous experience" (19) that formed an authentic religious tradition in the ancient world. In addition to playing an important part in ancient Greece, this sacred experience of demon dread "constituted the central element of the religious experience of the most ancient civilization we know from historical records: the Sumerian-Babylonian-Assyrian people. It also appeared in ancient Egypt, which was cheerful, optimistic, and much less demon-ridden than the Mesopotamian civilization" (20). This assertion is entirely in keeping with the established historical fact that by the dawn of recorded history, circa 4000 B.C.E., the two great centers of early civilization, Mesopotamia and Egypt, both possessed well-developed demonologies. It is here that the oldest ancestors of the Demon can be observed in nascent form.

The early inhabitants of Mesopotamia believed their daily lives were saturated with evil spirits. If one had a headache, it was caused by a demon. If one broke a pot or got into a quarrel with a neighbor, it was because of a demon. Even such an intimate experience as dreaming was under the control of these beings, with nightmares and night terrors being caused by such beings as *rabisu* and *lilitu*, both of whom later appeared in Hebrew mythology and folklore (the latter as the "night-hag," lilith).

Owing to its later appearance in Blatty's *The Exorcist*, the ancient Mesopotamian demon *Pazuzu* is of special interest to followers of supernatural horror. Often pictured as a vaguely man-shaped figure with a monstrous head, the wings of an eagle, the tail of a scorpion, and the talons or claws of an eagle or lion, Pazuzu was believed to bring famine and plague and was famously associated with the southwest wind. It was this demon that Blatty referenced when he set out to build a suitably horrifying and awe-inspiring backstory to explain the origin of the demon that possessed young Regan in his novel.

In addition to this rather loose body of folkloric belief, the Mesopotamians also possessed a larger body of systematic "official" theology that featured its own demonic beings. Most famously, the Babylonian state religion that was centered around the creation epic known as *Enuma Elish* featured a horde of monstrous demons that had been birthed by Tiamat, the primeval chaos dragon, in an effort to eradicate her own children. These included such figures as the dragon, the sphinx, the scorpion-man, and monstrous serpents whose bodies were filled with venom instead of blood. After the war was over and Tiamat had been defeated by her children, humankind was created from the blood of Tiamat's consort, the serpentine Kingu. So in Babylonian belief there was something of the primally demonic in the most basic substance of human life—"a recognition perhaps of the daemonic, rebellious element in human nature" (Gray 35).

To the west in Egypt, the overall situation was very similar, with many demons both mundane and exalted playing a significant part in the lives of everyone from the Pharaoh on down to the lowest peasant. As in Mesopotamia, most of these beings were associated with the everyday phenomena of childbirth, illness, weather, and so on. Also as in Mesopotamia, they were often depicted as animal-human hybrids, when they were depicted at all. In the more codified realm of "official" Egyptian theology, the god Set displayed a few typically demonic elements in his evil nature.

The most colorful and systematic arm of Egyptian demonology was set in the afterlife. As described in the famed *Book of the Dead*, after physical death, a person's spirit was required to pass through multiple gates guarded by various beings on the way to judgment by the supreme god Osiris. Many of the beings encountered during this afterlife journey were demonic, in the generalized sense of being monstrous supernatural entities.

Among the ancient Arab and Semitic peoples in general, the spirits known as *djinn* were widely known and feared. Before they were somewhat tamed and softened by being adopted into Islamic folklore, where some of them were transformed into beautiful and benevolent spirits, djinn were known among the Arabs for being purely malicious. It was this fearsome background that would be exploited thousands of years later, in the late twentieth and early twenty-first centuries, by the makers of the low-budget *Wishmaster* series of horror films (to be discussed later). In their original folkloric form, djinn were born of fire and able to metamorphose into any shape they wished, and they lived and roamed in wild and desert places. Much later they became widely known in the West due to the appearance of a djinnee (the singular of djinn) in the story of Aladdin and his lamp in the *Arabian Nights*. It was this story that created the image of the djinn as wish-granting spirits who reside in oil lamps.

Not incidentally, the term "djinnee" displays an obvious phonetic similarity to the English word "genie," which is the more commonly known term for these spirits among English-speaking cultures. "Genie" itself derives from the Latin word *genius*, which in Hellenistic Rome referred to spirits in general, and which became the direct inheritor of the meanings associated with the Greek *daimon*. The etymological relationships among all these words and their referent spirits are tangled and uncertain, but in the end this only makes them all the more fascinating and potent.

The greatest spur toward the incorporation of the Middle Eastern demons into later Christian and Christianized beliefs was the rise of new religious movements that reframed the old beliefs and subjected the various indigenous spirits to new interpretations, thus laying the groundwork for the later Judeo-Christian demonologies and angelologies. In Mesopotamia this occurred most famously during the sixth century B.C.E., under the influence of Zoroastrianism in Persia. When Zoroaster introduced the dualism of Ahura Mazda as the one true god who was opposed by the evil god Angra Mainyu or Ahriman, the stage was set for all the native deities and demons to be demoted and divided according to their allegiances. Zoroaster "found it impossible to throw overboard all the deities his people had been honoring for generations, so he declared that some of them were good spirits, or 'bounteous immortals,' while the rest were condemned as demons. None disappeared" (Hahn and Beneš 16). Thus, when all was said and done, the Zoroastrian hierarchy of spirits was colorfully extensive, with multiple levels of beings lined up in descending orders of power and influence. Ahriman boasted an impressive army of demons, known as devas, to serve him and work his will, including such powerful beings as Aeshma, the demon of wrath and fury, and Azhi Dahaka, the demon of lies and deceit, whose body was so full of lizards, scorpions, and other vile creatures that if he were cut open they would overrun the earth. A horde of lesser demons were associated with such common negative attitudes and emotions as jealousy, arrogance, and sloth.

Jewish Demons

Of all the ancient Middle Eastern peoples, the Jews were the most directly important to the formation of Christianity. Naturally, this importance extended to their ideas about demons and angels as well. The Jewish contribution was much more significant to the formation of the latter than the former, but this does not mean it contributed nothing at all to the Demon.

Unlike its later and, to modern peoples, more familiar forms, Judaism up until the second or third century preceding the Common Era lacked the idea of "fallen angels" that wage war against the one God. Instead, Jewish beliefs about evil spirits remained more on a folkloric level and took two general forms. For the first, evil spirits were conceived as coming directly from Yahweh and remaining totally under his control. This can be seen in 1 Samuel 16, which tells how King Saul was plagued by a spirit sent from Yahweh: "Now the Spirit of the LORD departed from Saul, and an evil spirit from the LORD tormented him. And Saul's servants said to him, 'Behold now, an evil spirit from God is tormenting you'" (vv. 14–15). The servants looked for someone to play music in order to soothe Saul and eventually alighted upon David, who successfully drove the spirit away: "And whenever the evil spirit from God was upon Saul, David took the lyre and played it with his hand; so Saul was refreshed, and was well, and the evil spirit departed from him" (v. 23). So this type of evil spirit was related in a way to the Jewish idea of angels, since it came as a kind of messenger from Yahweh. This is in keeping with the ancient Jewish idea that Yahweh's omnipotence meant he was the ultimate source of all things, both good and bad.

The other view arose from beliefs about evil spirits that were incorporated into Judaism from the Jews' Mesopotamian neighbors. It was here, more than in the previous view, that Jewish beliefs about evil spirits proper came into their own. According to the *Jewish Encyclopedia*, "Jewish demonology can at no time be viewed as the outcome of an antecedent Hebrew belief" (Hirsch et al.). Similarly, rabbi and scholar Ronald H. Isaacs observed that the Jews, who were "surrounded by animistic notions of primitive people," ended up "absorb[ing] some of these [and] develop[ing] a variety of legends of their own concerning evil spirits that wield destructive powers over human beings" (91). In such cases, the Jews always reinterpreted the nature and status of these foreign spirits according to a strict Yahwistic monotheism. Sometimes this meant foreign spirits were scorned as being illusory, as in Deuteronomy 32:17, which contains a chastisement for people who "sacrificed to demons [*shedim*, from the Babylonian spirit *shedu*], which were no gods, to gods they had never known, to new gods that had come in of late, whom your fathers had never dreaded." The passage makes it clear that the author believed the worshippers of the *shedim* were worshipping mere figments of their imagination.

At other times, in other contexts, the Jews thought of evil spirits as real but inferior powers. This became the norm after the sixth century B.C.E. influx of the Chaldean religious ideas, and it is crucial to note that this Zoroastrian influence not only gave the Jews many of their evil spirits but also many of their good ones, eventually resulting in their famous division between the kingdom of God and that of the Devil. "It was," says the *Jewish Encyclopedia*, "the primitive demonology of Babylonia which peopled the world of the Jews with beings of a semi-celestial and semi-infernal nature. Only afterward did the division of the world between Ahriman and Ormuzd [a.k.a. Ahura Mazda] in the Mazdean system give rise to the Jewish division of life between the kingdom of heaven and the kingdom of evil" (Hirsch et al.).

In a distinct but related vein, a significant factor in the rise of Jewish beliefs about demons was the First Book of Enoch. This text, which is usually dated to the second or third century B.C.E., was foundational to the formation of both Christian and Jewish beliefs about "fallen angels." It was rejected for inclusion within the official Jewish and Christian canons, and even from inclusion in the Christian apocrypha, thus relegating it to the realm of the pseudepigrapha or "doubtful writings" whose authenticity is severely questioned or rejected. Nevertheless, its influence was widespread; nearly all the early church fathers quoted from it, and it even ended up making an appearance in the New Testament itself (see the quotation from it in Jude 14–15). Since the main focus of First Enoch is angels, including those who rebelled against God, more will be said about it in the section on the Angel below.

The upshot is that the ancient Jewish, Egyptian, and Mesopotamian (primarily Chaldean) beliefs about demons provided a basic content and structure for the formation of the Demon. It remained for the Greek notion of the *daimon* to provide the overarching concept that would synthesize these various elements into a coherent, unified portrait.

The Greek Daimones

Although most educated modern people are familiar with the Olympian gods and goddesses of classical Greek mythology, decidedly fewer are aware that long before the Greeks developed their beliefs about the humanlike gods of Olympus, they believed in vague and mysterious spirits called *daimones* that exerted a ubiquitous influence over people and events. Using the alternative form "daemon" to refer to these spirits, E. R. Dodds writes in his classic *The Greeks and the Irrational* that the "daemonic, as distinct from the divine, has at all periods played a large part in Greek popular belief (and still does)" (40). Indeed, as psychologist Stephen A. Diamond points out, while some classical scholars maintain that Greek writers such as Homer, Hesiod, and Plato used *daimon* as a synonym for *theos* (god), others "point to a definite distinction between these terms. The term 'daimon' referred to something indeterminate, invisible, incorporeal, amorphous, and unknown, whereas 'theos' was the *personification* of a god, such as Zeus or Apollo" (66).

If we are to believe classical scholar Reginald Barrow, modern ignorance of the daimons must be counted among the many ironies of history; Barrow argues provocatively that belief in these beings was so powerful, important, and prevalent that it actually formed a kind of underground mainstream in ancient Greek religion:

> Because the daemons have left few memorials of themselves in architecture and literature, their importance tends to be overlooked. . . . They are omnipresent and all-powerful, they are embedded deep in the religious memories of the peoples, for they go back to days long before the days of Greek philosophy and religion. The cults of the Greek states, recognised and officially sanctioned, were only one-tenth of the iceberg; the rest, the submerged nine-tenths, were the daemons. (90–91)

Like so many religious beliefs throughout history, the idea of the *daimones* took many different and sometimes contradictory forms. In the beginning they were conceived as abstract forces in the neuter gender. Hesiod and others described them as "invisible and wrapped in mist" (Dietrich 95). Much farther back, Mycenaean and Minoan daimons, in a period ranging from 3000 to 1100 B.C.E., were regarded as servants or attendants to deities and were pictured in the form of animal-human hybrids, much like their Egyptian and Mesopotamian analogues. Barrow offers a concise summary of the evolution of beliefs about these daimons over half a millennium, and also, again, of their vaguely shadowy and underground nature as they lurked perpetually in the background of orthodox Greek religious thought:

> [The] histories of Greek religion or philosophy do not usually say much, if anything, about daemons. Though the idea occurs as early as Homer, it plays little or no part in recognized cults; for it had no mythology of its own; rather it attached itself to existing beliefs. In philosophy it lurks in the background from Thales, to whom "the universe is alive and full of daemons," through Heraclitus and Xenophanes, to Plato and his pupil Xenocrates, who elaborated it in detail. . . . In Hesiod the daemons are the souls of heroes or past ages now kindly to men; in Aeschylus the dead become daemons; in Theognis and Menander the daemon is the guardian angel of the individual man and sometimes a family. (86)

In their most ancient forms, the daimons were neither good nor evil, or rather were potentially both. In Homer's time, around the eighth century B.C.E., people commonly believed that daimons caused all human ailments, but they also believed they could cure disease and give blessings such as health and happiness. Several centuries later the Hellenistic Greeks developed the more concrete categories of *eudaimones* (good daimons) and *kakodaimones* (evil daimons).

Arguably the most famous description or definition of daimons and the daimonic comes from a "canonical" source: Plato's *Symposium,* wherein Plato had the old wise woman Diotima describe the daimonic realm as a kind of bridge or intermediary between the human and divine worlds:

All that is daemonic lies between the mortal and the immortal. Its functions are to interpret to men communications from the gods—commandments and favours from the gods in return for men's attentions—and to convey prayers and offerings from men to the gods. Being thus between men and gods the daemon fills up the gap and so acts as a link joining up the whole. Through it as intermediary pass all forms of divination and sorcery. God does not mix with man; the daemonic is the agency through which intercourse and converse take place between men and gods, whether in waking visions or in dreams. (Quoted in Dodds, *Pagan and Christian* 86–87)

It is also Plato who provided probably the most familiar example of specific daimonic influence when he wrote of Socrates' famous *daimonion* (the neuter adjectival form of *daimon,* which is either male or female). This has often been translated into English as the "sign" that Socrates claimed had visited him frequently since childhood in the form of an audible voice that warned him whenever he was about to commit an error.

Socrates's experience of daimonic communication highlights what is, in fact, the most significant aspect of the matter: the Greeks understood their daimons to have not only an objective but a subjective existence. That is, they believed the daimons were objectively real presences that made themselves known through their influence upon and within the human psyche. This tension between the objective and subjective seems to have existed on a kind of continuum. On the one hand were the more typically animistic conceptions of daimons, which associated them with particular places, natural occurrences, circumstances, or souls of the dead. On the other hand were the more subtle, psychologically oriented conceptions that gained preeminence over time and that regarded the daimons as inner influences upon human thoughts and emotions, and even as arbiters, keepers, conductors, and emblems of individual character and destiny. This second type of understanding can be seen in the fact that the characters in Homer's *Iliad* and *Odyssey,* which were probably composed around the eighth century B.C.E., and which represent an inherited oral tradition extending several centuries earlier, attributed many of the events of their lives—not only outer, physical events but also, and especially, inner psychological ones such as moods, emotions, sudden insights, and bursts of motivation to say or do something or to refrain from speaking or acting—to the influence of daimons. Although Homer's characters seemed to take this idea relatively lightly—"[W]e get the impression," writes Dodds, "that they do not always mean it very seriously"—in the three centuries between Homer's epics and Aeschylus' *Oresteia* "the daemons seem to draw closer: they grow more persistent, more insidious, more sinister" (*Greeks and the Irrational* 41).

By "sinister," Dodds may have meant not that the daimons came to be regarded as predominantly evil but that they came to be progressively more entangled with human interiority, and also that they became progressively more mysterious and autonomous. He calls attention to the fact that many Greek writers after Homer drew a connection between the daimons and "those irrational impulses which arise in a man against his will to tempt him," and he says that "behind [this] lies the old Homeric feeling that these things are not truly part of the self; since they are endowed with a life and energy of their own, and so can force a man, as it were from the outside, into conduct foreign to him" (*Greeks and the Irrational* 41).

The twentieth century existential psychologist Rollo May, who resurrected the concept of the daimon and the daimonic for use in modern depth psychotherapy, gave definitive statement to this idea of strange internal influence in his book *Love and Will:* "The daimonic is any natural function which has the power to take over the whole person. Sex and eros, anger and rage, and the craving for power are examples. The daimonic can be either creative or destructive and is normally both" (123). Although May wrote about the daimonic in metaphorical terms, his description is still effective for giving an impression of what it must have felt like to the ancients when they found themselves thinking, feeling, saying, and doing things that were outside their voluntary control. Modern peoples are of course still quite familiar with this experience (although we generally frame its causes and significance quite differently), and so we can reasonably imagine that ancient peoples must have been all the more awed and disturbed when popular belief attributed these involuntary behaviors to the influence of the mysterious mediators of divine reality. In more dramatic cases of daimonic influence, the internal power might take control completely: "When this power goes awry," May wrote, "and one element usurps control over the total personality, we have 'daimon possession,' the traditional name through history for psychosis" (123).

It was Plato (again) who gave definitive voice to this newly developing view of the daimonic as primarily an inner force. He closed his most famous work, the *Republic,* with the "myth of Er," which teaches that prior to being born, each human being voluntarily chooses his or her own daimon, understood in this case to be a combination of guardian angel, spiritual double, and life pattern. The daimon accompanies an individual throughout life and constantly recalls him or her to the pre-chosen plan. It guides a person inevitably to evince a certain character, make certain choices, feel certain predilections, and encounter certain experiences, all in the service of fulfilling the fate chosen beforehand. Thus it is that the Greek word *eudaimonia,* which in later times came to mean "happiness" or "well-being," in its earliest sense literally meant "having a good daimon." A person with a good daimon was happy and blessed, while a person with a bad daimon was inevitably miserable. The pre-Socratic philosopher Heraclitus encapsulated this idea in a cryptic statement that has puzzled and fascinated scholars for the past twenty-five hundred years: *ethos anthropoi daimon*. The statement translates literally as "a man's character is his daimon," but nobody knows for certain what Heraclitus really meant to convey with it, although various translations and glosses have been offered, as listed by James Hillman in his modern book of daimonic psychology, *The Soul's Code:* "Man's character is his Genius. A man's character is his guardian divinity. A man's character is his fate. Character is fate. A man's character is the immortal and potentially divine portion of him. Character for man is destiny" (256–57).

The bottom line is that it is impossible to overemphasize the prevalence and significance of beliefs about daimons to the ancient world, and especially to ancient popular understandings of human selfhood and its relation to the divine. For Greek culture, including its underground tradition of daimonism, was destined to become the common coinage, as it were, of the entire ancient world. When first Alexander and then the Romans succeeded in exporting all things Greek to the farthest corners of their respective empires, the resulting cultural matrix was rife with daimons in the Greek mold. According to Dodds, although the *Symposium*'s "precise definition of the vague terms 'daemon' and 'daemonios' was something of a novelty in Plato's day," by "the second century after Christ it was the expression of a truism. Virtually everyone, pagan, Jewish, Christian or Gnostic, believed in the existence of these beings and in their function as mediators, whether he called them daemons or angels or aions or simply 'spirits'" (*Pagan and Christian* 37–38).

As indicated by this quotation and much of the foregoing, the idea of daimons contained elements of both the Demon and the Angel of the later supernatural horror genre. Thus, before moving on to trace the formation of the Demon itself from all these currents, it is necessary to fill in the backstory of the Angel.

III. The Prehistory of the Angel

Introduction: What's in a Name?

The word "angel" derives from the Latin *angelus,* which derives from the Greek *angelos*. In the Septuagint (the ancient Greek translation of the Jewish scriptures from the third century B.C.E.), *angelos* is used to translate the Hebrew *mal'ak*. Both *angelos* and *mal'ak* mean "messenger" and can refer either to a supernatural spirit or to a human being who delivers divine communication to other humans. An example of a person being referred to as an angel in this sense can be found in the New Testament in Galatians 4:14 when Paul reminds the Christians at Galatia that when he first brought the gospel to them, they received and treated him "as an angel [*angelos*] of God." In later history the word came to refer exclusively to the supernatural type of messenger.

Dreadful and Awesome: Biblical Angels

The first mention in the Bible of the supernatural type of angel is found in the Old Testament, in Genesis, when God stations angels called *cherubim* at the entrance to the Garden of Eden to keep Adam and Eve from returning after they have been expelled. After that, supernatural angels appear frequently throughout the Hebrew scriptures to announce God's will, to save and direct God's people, and often to mete out God's wrath.

Significantly, biblical angels were portrayed as awesome and even terrifying beings that directly represented and, in a manner that is never precisely explained, *embodied* the awesome, terrifying God they served. Thus, in the Book of Judges when an angel of Yahweh appears to Manoah's wife to tell her that she will have a son, she describes it to her husband by saying, "A man of God came to me, and his countenance was like the countenance of the angel of God, very terrible" (Judges 13:6), with "terrible" meaning something akin to "dreadfully awesome." Later, when the same angel appears again to both of them, its true nature becomes clear when they burn a sacrificial animal and "the angel of the LORD ascended in the flame of the altar while Manoah and his wife looked on" (13:20). In a response typical of such scenes, both husband and wife fall on their faces to the ground, and Manoah says to his wife, "We shall surely die, for we have seen God" (13:22). To see an angel of God was in some sense to see God himself, and as everybody knew (since it had been stated to Moses on Mount Sinai and reiterated many times elsewhere), no one could see God and live.

This "terrible" aspect of angels is also visible in their many destructive actions. A prime example is found in the story of the destruction of Sodom and Gomorrah. Three angels, looking like men—or actually two angels; one of the visitors is later revealed to be Yahweh himself—appear to Abraham to announce the imminent destruction of these cities because of their notorious wickedness. Then the (two) angels depart to escort Abraham's nephew Lot and his family out of Sodom to safety, after which "the LORD rained on Sodom and Gomorrah brimstone and fire from the LORD out of heaven" (Genesis 19:24). Equally famous, and an example in which an angel took a direct part in administering a terrible punishment, is the story of the final plague that Yahweh brought against Egypt when he sent his Angel of Death to kill all the first-born males of the Egyptians (Exodus 11–12). Likewise in Isaiah 37:36, Yahweh intervenes with his death angel in order to help Jerusalem when it is besieged by the Assyrians: "And the angel of the LORD went forth, and slew a hundred and eighty-five thousand in the camp of the Assyrians; and when men arose early in the morning, behold, these were all dead bodies."

Other Angelic Influences: Pseudoepigraphal, Zoroastrian, Egyptian, Greek

The idea not only of angels that were fearsome, but of angels that were positively monstrous, was advanced by the First Book of Enoch. The text describes a band of two hundred angels, called "the Watchers" in the earliest English translation (from 1912), which, led by powerful beings named Semjaza and Azazel, rebelled against God by marrying human women and teaching them various secrets of herb lore, metallurgy, magical enchantments, astronomy, meteorology, and other subjects that were forbidden for humans to know. The children born of these forbidden unions were giants with appetites so ravenous that they devoured everything on earth, including humans, and finally turned to eating one another. As a punishment, God chained the angels in dark places of the earth and left them to await the Final Judgment, at which point they would be cast into fire. But the giants lived on and eventually produced evil spirits. On the other end of matters, among the angels who remained faithful to God were Michael, Uriel, Raphael, and Gabriel, who heard mankind crying out in anguish and ended up helping them.

As the title implies, First Enoch purports to have been written by Enoch, the grandfather of Noah, who learned of all these matters in a series of visions. Even though First Enoch was probably written in the second or third century B.C.E., the story itself, along with its antecedent influences, extends much further back into history. In the Jewish scriptures the basic idea of humans intermarrying with angels goes all the way back to Genesis with its bizarre story of the Nephilim, which were born when "the sons of God saw that the daughters of men were fair; and they took to wife such of them as they chose. . . . The Nephilim were on the earth in those days, and also afterward, when the sons of God came in to the daughters of men, and they bore children to them. These were the mighty men that were of old, the men of renown" (6:2, 4). Immediately after this, the text moves to describing God's disgust with humankind's wickedness and his plan to wipe everything out with water while saving a remnant through Noah and his family. This indicates a connection to First Enoch, since the story of Noah and the flood appears there as well, and as in the Genesis version, the flood is sent by God to wipe the earth clean of wickedness. The ubiquitous Persian influence is also quite evident in First Enoch: a pre-Zoroastrian Persian myth tells of demons that corrupted the earth and married mortal women.

As mentioned earlier, the practice of ranking angels into types and hierarchies was absorbed into Judaism from Zoroastrianism. Many Jews lived in close contact with the Persian religion in the sixth century B.C.E. during the period of the Babylonian captivity. The cultural cross-fertilization that naturally occurred had the dual effect of, on the one hand, cementing the Israelite religion of the post-exilic period into the first true Judaism, and on the other hand, giving the Jews various new theological ideas to incorporate into their religion. The elaborate angelologies of later Judaism and Christianity were one of the most colorful results.

In Zoroastrian theology, the Wise Lord Ahura Mazda was served by his immortal sons and daughters, the Amesha Spentas or "bounteous immortals," each of whom represented a facet of the divine nature or an aspect of that nature in which humans could share (truth, devotion, and wholeness). He also had in his employ lesser beings called Yazatas or "worshipful ones," who were mortal, and who engaged with humans in a more personal, protective fashion than was possible for the exalted Wise Lord himself. The Amesha Spentas thus corresponded in very important ways to the archangels, and the Yazatas to the guardian angels, that later populated the Christian cosmos.

In Egypt a similar influence was set in motion by Pharaoh Amenhotep IV, more widely known today as Akhenaten or Akhenaton, who radically reformed Egyptian religion in the 14th century B.C.E. by instating a monotheistic form of sun worship. Under the new solar monotheism, the gods of traditional belief were not eradicated, which would have been culturally impossible, but were instead demoted to the status of lesser spirits thus rendering them "angels in the making" (Hahn and Beneš 14). Even after Akhenaton's death, when his reforms failed and subsequent Pharaohs returned Egypt to more traditional forms of religion, the revised status of many gods persisted.

Additionally, the Egyptian belief in multiple souls that compose the human self may have contributed to the development of the guardian angel. Although the precise meaning of the soul called the *ka* is now impossible to determine, the *ka* may have functioned as a kind of spiritual "double" that accompanied a person through life. This is hinted at by the fact that Egyptian art sometimes represents the *ka* as a duplicate of the individual. While some scholars believe this indicates the ancient Egyptians thought of the *ka* in much the same way that moderns sometimes speak of a person's "life force," the idea and imagery also resonate with later beliefs about a guardian angel that accompanies each person from birth to death. Clearly, this also corresponds significantly to the Greek idea of the daimon.

From Monstrous to Beautiful: The Angel's Appearance

Greece and Egypt also shared another correspondence that proved significant, and in fact decisive, for the development of the Angel by providing the pattern for its visual appearance. Although Jewish angels were sometimes conceived as having, or at least appearing in, human form, just as often they took on a monstrous appearance that was drawn directly from Sumerian or Babylonian mythology. Cherubim, for instance, were thought of as hybrids of human and animal characteristics, sometimes with multiple faces and eyes, always with multiple feathered wings. Another type of Jewish heavenly being, the seraphim, may have been conceived as winged, fiery serpents (the Hebrew word *seraph* can mean both "burning ones" and "serpents"). Obviously, these images were not the ones adopted for portraying the Angel of supernatural horror. Instead, the Angel received its look from ancient Egypt by way of Greece.

Isis, the Egyptian queen of the gods, was the object of a major cult that venerated her as the goddess of magic. Both she and her sister Nephthys were depicted in the form of human women with feathery wings sprouting from their sides or backs. Via the deep logic of cultural inheritance, the Greeks later imported this same imagery and attached it to Nike and Eros, the winged daimons of victory and love, respectively, whose attractive human bodies with feathery white wings sprouting from their shoulders—or perhaps replacing their arms, as in the famous Hellenistic statue of Nike known as The Winged Victory of Samothrace—are well known. It was these figures, and not the monstrous Jewish angels, that served as the specific template for the iconic Angel's appearance, which coalesced around the first century C.E.

The fact that the Angel in a Judeo-Christian context had its visual appearance drawn from a Hellenic source may be attributable to the old tradition of Jewish iconoclasm, which originated in the Decalogue with the second commandment's injunction against making idols or images of the divine. As a result of this theologically central commandment, the Jewish visual tradition simply was not as developed as that of Greece, whose stronger tradition therefore won out. The effect of the winged Jewish cherubim and seraphim on the appearance of the Angel was thus felt only at a remove, and it arrived in Christian angelic iconography only by being processed through the intermediaries of Nike and Eros in the same way that the more influential Isis had been.

IV. The Demon from the First Century to the Present Day

If we bear in mind Dodds's assertion that by the end of the second century C.E., almost everybody in the ancient world believed in daimons in some form, and if we put this together with all the information just considered, the rise of the Demon as understood by Christianity and the later Western supernatural horror tradition is an easy phenomenon to grasp. The Septuagint, as already noted, had used the Greek word *angelos* to translate the Hebrew *mal'ak,* both referring to supernatural (or sometimes human) messengers from God. Equally significant was the fact that the Septuagint used the Greek *daimon* or *daimonion* to translate the various Hebrew words for idols, alien gods, and the like, while *theos* was reserved for referring to the one God. Thus the "bible" used by many first-century Jews, including Jesus and his disciples, had already made these terminological distinctions. The New Testament documents were likewise written in the same Greek as the Septuagint, Koine Greek, which had become the common language of Israel by the first century. These terminological conventions for referring to angelic and demonic beings were therefore retained in the Christian scriptures.

This meant that the rich trove of concepts and connotations associated with the Greek daimons was now attached to the Jewish understanding of the spiritual world, which, as evidenced by First Enoch and other Jewish apocalyptic and apocryphal works, was already heavily influenced by ancient Middle Eastern beliefs with their cosmic dualism. Thus the moral ambivalence and the dual sense of demonic dread and spiritual inspiration or exaltation that were inherent in the concept of the daimon became divided, with half the associations attaching themselves to the idea of the Angel and half to the Demon. The fact that the word *daimon* itself was retained to refer only to the evil or negative half of the cosmic dualism entailed the demise and, in the eyes of some observers both modern and ancient, degradation of the word's original meaning. "Around the rise of Christianity," writes Diamond, "the old daimons started to disappear, their Janus-like nature torn asunder. 'Evil' and 'good' were neatly divided, and the daimons, now isolated from their positive pole, eventually took on the negative meaning and identity of what we today term demons" (71).

Thus arose the demons and "unclean spirits" of the New Testament period, which, with their usurpation of people's personalities and their desire to inflict moral and physical harm, embodied the most violently negative aspect of the old daimonic understanding, the "daimon possession" that Rollo May equated with psychosis. In the gospels Jesus is frequently shown casting out demons that cause their hosts to rage and foam at the mouth, with the most famous story being the encounter with the Gerasene demoniac. Matthew, Mark, and Luke all contain the story, although Matthew's version differs from the other two in that it says the incident occurred in the land of the Gadarenes (instead of Gerasenes) and that there were two possessed men instead of one. Mark's version is the most detailed:

> And when [Jesus] had come out of the boat, there met him out of the tombs a man with an unclean spirit, who lived among the tombs; and no one could bind him any more, even with a chain; for he had often been bound with fetters and chains, but the chains he wrenched apart, and the fetters he broke in pieces; and no one had the strength to subdue him. Night and day among the tombs and on the mountains he was always crying out, and bruising himself with stones. And when he saw Jesus from afar, he ran and worshiped him; and crying out with a loud voice, he said, "What have you to do with me, Jesus, Son of the Most High God? I adjure you by God, do not torment me." For he had said to him, "Come out of the man, you unclean spirit!" And Jesus asked him, "What is your name?" He replied, "My name is Legion; for we are many." (5:2–9)

In his nearly identical version, Luke clarifies the meaning of "we are many" by changing it to a line of third-person narration: "for many demons had entered him" (8:30). In all three versions, as well as in the numerous other stories of possession and exorcism in the New Testament, the very nature of the accounts both revealed and helped to solidify the prevailing understanding of what a demon actually was. In all cases the possessing demons grievously hurt—psychologically, physically, or both—the possessed individuals and those around them, and in all cases they were subject to the authority of the one God as channeled through or incarnated in Jesus, and sometimes through his deputized disciples. Roughly two thousand years later, the same general understanding was still in place when Blatty quoted from Luke's version of the Gerasene demoniac story at the beginning of *The Exorcist* and from Mark's version at the start of the sequel novel, *Legion*.

The newly born Christian world was of course not the only place whence the new ideas came together to form the Demon. Other writers in other traditions continued to turn the spiritual earth, with such writers as Philo of Alexandria, himself a Hellenized Jew, and Josephus, the famous first-century Jewish historian, and also the entire roster of early church fathers in the first few centuries after the birth of Christ, contributing to the developing Christian demonology. In all cases, demons were conceived in a manner influenced by a combination of Chaldean/Jewish apocalyptic beliefs and a now-mutated form of Greek daimonism. For the Chaldean/Jewish part, demons were conceived as angelic beings who had rebelled against the one God and were now devoted to making war against Him and his world. For the Greek part, this demonic war was seen as being conducted not solely, nor even primarily, on an objective, external plane, but on an internal one. The battle was conducted within and for the sake of people's souls. "The change," writes Wolfgang M. Zucker, "from a divine 'daimon' to a devilish demon made out of the 'daimon' a superstitious mythological concept. The predilection of Hellenistic writers for the mysterious and the supernatural made it possible that the inner voice of the rational sage of Athens became in the course of time something like a personal servant ghost, a *Spiritus familiaris*" (39). In the hands of the influential men who created a comprehensive Christian theology in the first few centuries after Christ—Clement of Alexandria, Origen, Iranaeus, Justin Martyr, Augustine, and others—this inner voice-cum-personal ghost was transformed into the voice of temptation, whispered directly into one's mind by demons who delighted in drawing people away from Christ and the Father.

As it had been for the ancient Mesopotamians, so for these post-Hellenistic peoples the world was positively teeming with demons. There was no shortage of these evil spirits because every spirit that was not aligned with the one God as part of His heavenly host was by definition a demon. In virtually all cases, this meant foreign gods were held to be demonic spirits that had deceived entire nations, and this inevitably led to an outburst of iconoclastic idol-smashing after Christianity became the official religion of the Roman Empire under Constantine in the fourth century. It was widely believed among Christians that all the old idols, including those depicting the deities of traditional Greco-Roman paganism, were inhabited by demons, and so they took to persecuting pagan temples and statues. According to many accounts, Constantine himself joined in the destruction by ordering and participating in the sacking of several temples and, as the story goes, torturing the resident priests to death. The Eastern Roman emperor Theodosius II added fuel to the fire by declaring officially in 423 that Gentile religion was definitively and exclusively nothing more than demon worship. The iconoclastic fury reached Athens shortly afterward, where according to some accounts the Parthenon itself, the ancient and widely venerated temple of Athena located on the Acropolis, was sacked and defaced. But although their images and residences in non-Christian temples could be attacked, the demons themselves persisted.

At this point it is possible to "press the fast forward" button, as it were, in this account of the iconic Demon's history, for once the concept of the Demon was firmly established in the Hellenistic and early Christian mind, it continued in much the same form for a very long time, with only a few substantial alterations and/or additions over the centuries.

Between the consolidation of Christian political power in the first few centuries C.E. and the turn of the first millennium, beliefs about demons remained steady and largely unchanged. The basic idea that had arisen during the Hellenistic period proved to be remarkably resilient, so that any new developments, such as the rise of a popular lore about monks and saints who were tempted and tormented by demons (beginning with St. Anthony in the early second century), or the ongoing attempts of prominent figures such as Augustine to define, classify, and account for demons, did not so much alter or add to the concept as make use of it. It was not until the high Middle Ages, from approximately 1000 to 1300, that several new developments helped finalize the Demon's emergence.

One of these was the adoption at the Fourth Lateran Council, convened by Pope Innocent III at Rome in 1215, of a resolution that firmly defined demons as fallen angels and definitively distinguished them as *daemones* as distinct from their leader, *diabolus*, the Devil himself. This resolution, adopted along with many others in response to the pressures surrounding the Crusades and the need to confront heretical movements both inside and outside the church, established for the first time the familiar modern idea of "the devil and his angels" as official Catholic orthodoxy. It was an idea that creators of supernatural horror stories would use extensively in later centuries.

It is probably no coincidence that the Italian poet Dante's famous *Inferno*, the first installment of his *Divine Comedy*, was published in 1314, almost exactly a century after the Fourth Lateran Council. Dante's depiction of a multilayered hell populated by dreadful demons, many drawn from classical pagan mythology, who spent eternity tormenting a multitude of sinners via hideous and often ironically appropriate punishments, made direct use of the Church's official demonology. It was also Dante who in effect finalized the Gothic visual imagery that has come to be associated with demons and hell ever since. His depiction of demons with leathery bat-like wings, long tails, claws, and monstrous faces, and his descriptions of what goes on in hell, such as the famous episode where demons use sharp hooks to keep sinners submerged in boiling tar in the same way a chef might keep chunks of meat submerged in boiling water, inspired countless visual artists, first in Italy and then throughout Europe. Dante did not so much invent the Demon's appearance as make use of pre-existing trends and materials; it is instructive to note that many of the features he chose had a history extending all the way back to the Middle Eastern demons of ancient history and prehistory (recall Pazuzu with his perverted man-shaped form adorned with claws, tail, and monstrously distorted visage). But he certainly assembled them into the definitive portrait, thus creating a literary and imaginative experience that was equivalent to being led on a guided tour through a horrifying nightmare.

The period of the High Middle Ages was also important to the Demon because of the sometimes obsessive fear of witches that gripped many Christians. Helen P. Trimpi writes that the

> history of the idea of witchcraft in the Christian period is mainly the history of the application by the Church of Judaic-Christian demonology to non-Christian—hence idolatrous—religious impulses among the baptized. Wherever a surviving or revived impulse came to the attention of Church writers they dealt with it in terms derived from biblical statements about witches, sorcerers, the Serpent, Satan, Leviathan, and evil spirits in the Old Testament and the Hebrew Apocrypha, and from references to Satan and evil demons in the New Testament. ("Demonology")

The interaction between beliefs about demons and beliefs about witchcraft culminated in the so-called "witch craze" that engulfed Europe during the thirteenth through seventeenth centuries, and also in the infamous witch trials and executions at Salem Village, Massachusetts, in 1692. Much of this mania was inspired by the ideas of the great scholastic theologian Thomas Aquinas, who wrote extensively about demons in his magnum opus, *Summa Theologica* (*Summary of Theology,* written from 1266 to 1273). Aquinas argued, among other things, that demons can and do assault humans sexually. For example, the female demons known as *Succubi* might assault human men and save their semen, which the male demons known as *Incubi* might then use to impregnate women, thus begetting children in an unnatural way. This idea drew upon ancient stories from various cultures, including the ones already discussed in this essay, about sexual assaults upon humans by supernatural forces. During the Middle Ages and the following centuries, under the influence of scholastic theology and its further developments, this idea would become one of the centerpieces of the witch craze; it was extended and elaborated upon in the most famous of the witch-hunt manuals, *Malleus Maleficarum* [The Hammer of the Witches] (1486).

The cataloguing and categorizing of demons continued apace as well, with Dr. Johann Weyer declaring in his *De Prestigiis Daemonum* (*The Illusions of the Demons,* 1568) that there presently existed no fewer than 2,665,866,746,664 demons of all ranks and types. Perhaps it was his attention to this subject, and the keen attention to demons and demonology paid by Sigismund Feyerabend (*Theatrum Diabolorum* [Theatre of the Devils], 1587) and other followers of the new Protestant reformation, that induced the Catholic church in 1614 to issue its famous instructions concerning the exorcism of demons in chapter XII of the *Rituale Romanum*. Forever afterward in the supernatural horror genre, the Catholic Church's guide to exorcism in the *Roman Ritual* would remain the gold standard for judging how such procedures should be depicted.

In an interesting bit of timing, one of the most famous cases of demonic possession in history occurred just two decades after the Church's publication of its exorcism ritual. Father Jean-Joseph Surin, a Jesuit who served as an exorcist for the nuns at Loudun, France, when they experienced an outbreak of possession, himself became possessed by a demon of lust (or so the story goes) that tormented him for many years. Three centuries later, Aldous Huxley told the story in *The Devils of Loudun* (1952), which itself became the basis for director Ken Russell's 1971 film, *The Devils*.

The fifteenth through the seventeenth centuries were also a golden age for Demon-inspired artwork, with such luminaries of Hieronymus Bosch, Pieter Bruegel the Elder, Sandro Botticelli, Jean Duvet, and Albrecht Dürer offering their visual interpretations of everything from the demonic temptations of famous saints, to the demons tormenting the damned in Dante's underworld, to the demonic hordes let loose to plague the world in the biblical Book of Revelation. Coming somewhat on the heels of this, and coming to the matter from the vantage point of an Englishman who was a contemporary of the Italian Renaissance, was John Milton, whose *Paradise Lost* (1667) ranks on a level with Dante's *Inferno* as a profound influence upon cultural views of the Demon and, importantly, of Satan himself. Milton's magnum opus displays clear evidence of having been influenced by First Enoch, or at least of having been influenced indirectly by that text's absorption into Christian demonology and angelology; the story of Milton's angels, both those who have fallen and those who have remained loyal to God, is very similar to the story in First Enoch and even features some of the same characters, such as Uriel, Raphael, and Azazel. Milton may have written this work, as he famously put it, to "justify the ways of God to man," but what he largely accomplished was to present a sympathetic Satan whose vibrant interiority fascinated subsequent generations of Christians. And although, as already discussed, the idea of demons as fallen angels had a very long pedigree by Milton's day and was already established as Roman Catholic doctrine, Milton may be credited with raising popular awareness of it to such a pitch that it was cemented permanently in the forefront of Christian demonological thought. Not surprisingly, Milton's demonic imagery became a favorite subject for many artists, just as Dante's had done.

With *Paradise Lost*, the final refinement of the iconic Demon was put in place. In the centuries to come, the primary vehicle for a continued focus on the Demon would shift increasingly from overtly religious texts to the literary genre that emerged with the birth of the Romantic movement and its offshoot, the Gothic horror story. The Demon was now a unified entity that had coalesced from numerous sources and that would as a result display numerous aspects of its diverse history in the supernatural stories to come.

V. The Angel from the First Century to the Present Day

As with its prehistory, the history of the Angel from its formation in Hellenistic times to the present day is largely a complement to the history of the Demon. The framers of the demonic hordes and hierarchies created the angelic hosts and hierarchies at the same time, under the influence of the same Chaldean-inspired Jewish theology and from the aspects of the Greek daimons who had not been allotted to the Demon. But this meant the nature of the Angel as not just an objective entity but an inner spiritual reality was emphasized in a distinctly different manner than that of the Demon.

In the New Testament writings, angels were cast largely in the mold of their fearsome ancient Jewish progenitors. As in the Jewish scriptures, angels were central to God's interactions with humans. In the Old Testament, angels had attended the callings of prophets and effected the birth of the nation of Israel via Jacob's nocturnal wrestling match; in the New Testament they herald the birth of Christ and also, in the end, help to effect the destruction of the sin-corrupted world order.

In Luke's gospel the angel Gabriel appears to the Levitical priest Zechariah to announce the birth of Christ's herald, John the Baptist, and "Zechariah was troubled when he saw him, and fear fell upon him" (Luke 1:12). Shortly afterward, the same angel appears to Mary to announce that she will be made pregnant by the power of the Holy Spirit, and she is "greatly troubled" by his greeting (1:29). On the night Christ is finally born, an unnamed angel appears to lowly shepherds to announce the joyous news, and the shepherds are terrified: "And an angel of the Lord appeared to them, and the glory of the Lord shone around them, and they were filled with fear" (2:9). In Matthew's gospel with its alternative birth narrative, an angel appears three times to Jesus' human father, Joseph, with specific instructions about actions he should take (e.g., "Rise, take the child and his mother, and flee to Egypt, and remain there till I tell you; for Herod is about to search for the child, to destroy him" [2:13]). After Jesus's crucifixion and interment, an angel descends upon the rock rolled over the entrance to the tomb, whereupon the guards (either Roman soldiers or Jewish temple guards) who have been posted there are literally overcome by terror: "And behold, there was a great earthquake; for an angel of the Lord descended from heaven and came and rolled back the stone, and sat upon it. His appearance was like lightning, and his raiment white as snow. And for fear of him the guards trembled and became like dead men" (28:2–4). In all three synoptic gospels, the women who go to anoint Jesus's corpse with oil are seized with great fear when they find an empty tomb and are confronted by an angel or angels who announce his resurrection. The terrifying quality of these appearances is reinforced by the first words a New Testament angel, like its Old Testament forebears, is typically obliged to speak before it can deliver its message: "Do not be afraid!" Given the famous destructive capabilities these angels display in the New Testament's culminating text, the Book of Revelation, wherein God employs them to unleash hideous wars, plagues, and other assorted punishments upon the earth, the fear expressed by those who receive a visit from the Angel under more subdued circumstances is understandable.

As for the cataloguing of the angelic host, it was well underway by the close of the New Testament period. *The Testament of Solomon,* a Jewish pseudoepigraphical text that spoke primarily of demons, also spoke of angels by way of naming which ones should be called upon to counter and put down specific demons. Probably the most significant angelology of the period was created by the fifth-century mystical theologian Pseudo-Dionysius the Areopagite, who in his *Celestial Hierarchy* adapted the Neoplatonism of Plotinus and Proclus to establish a hierarchy of angels in three "triads"—for the first, Seraphim, Cherubim, and Thrones; for the second, Dominions, Virtues, and Powers; for the third, Principalities, Archangels, and Angels—which greatly influenced later medieval scholastic theologians.

The Neoplatonists, it should be recalled, represented a deeply mystical interpretation of Greek Platonic philosophy, and for this reason their "take" on the Angel had a more mystical character than those of a more typically Judaic or New Testament cast. As already explained, the Demon had inherited the negative, destructive aspect of the Greek daimons associated with daimonic/demonic possession, wherein a person was overtaken by a violent force that welled up from within the psyche. The angelic counterpart to this was the attaching to the Angel of the other half of the old daimonic concept, the half that was framed more in terms of what might today be called a "higher self." Plotinus, the second-century philosopher who was the first of the great Neoplatonists, expressed this when he described the individual daimon not as "an anthropomorphic daemon, but an inner psychological principle, viz: the level above that on which we consciously live, and so is both within us and yet transcendent" (Wallis 71). The same idea entered into the Latin concept of the *genius,* understood as a guiding and/or guardian spirit attached to each person, which gained wide currency throughout the Roman world when it was used to translate the Greek *daimon* (and which, as the reader will recall, bears an obscure etymological relationship to the ancient Middle Eastern *djinnee*). Instead of tempting or possessing a person, the psychologized or spiritualized Angel that was associated with these concepts called upon people to realize of their own free will their highest and deepest spiritual potential.

Thus was born an interesting division in the figure of the Angel. Considered as hierarchies of objectively existing beings, the early angelologies clearly reflected their origins in the theology of Zoroastrianism, Hellenistic Judaism, and so on. But considered as descriptions of inner spiritual and psychological states and forces, the same angelologies clearly reflected their origins in the more mystically oriented Neoplatonic and Gnostic practice of theurgy, or the divinizing of matter and the self by "drawing down" the divine into it. In the long historical view, this practice doubtlessly derived from the more mystical and angelic aspects of the Greek daimons, which were in turn at least partly derived from the older Hermetic mystery religion of ancient Egypt that was evidenced in such representative concepts as the previously mentioned *ka* self.

The history of the Angel on down to the modern day evinces these exoteric and esoteric dual understandings. Although the division of duties was never absolute, the more objectively oriented or "mythological" understanding naturally tended to be the province of the exoteric, orthodox Christianity, while the other, more psychological understanding was the province not only of the mystical orders of the Church, which frequently threatened to burst the bounds of orthodoxy with their free-form spiritual theologizing, but also of all-out esotericism and occultism. While such figures as Augustine, Aquinas, Dante, and Milton devoted their energies to elaborating ever more refined ideas and images of what might be called the objective Angel, various adherents and teachers of the esoteric tradition that was influenced by Neoplatonism, Gnosticism, Kabbalism, and Hermetism (revived and revised as Hermeticism in the fifteenth and following centuries) were elaborating ever more refined ideas and instructions for how to realize the subtle, inner angelic realm in actual personal experience. This second tradition reached an apex of sorts during the fifteenth through the eighteenth centuries—roughly the same period when the final touches were being applied to the iconic Demon— when, among others, Cornelius Agrippa (1486–1535), Paracelsus (1493– 1541), John Dee (1527–1606), Cagliostro (1743–1795), and Emanuel Swedenborg (1688–1772) pursued occult studies involving aspects of angel magic and the divinizing of the self through communion with its higher guardian spirit or spirits. The same practice has continued into the modern era, where it still survives in the form of various rituals, such as those taught by the Hermetic Order of the Golden Dawn, for contacting the "Holy Guardian Angel," understood as both a higher self and a transcendent entity.

Swedenborg, who claimed to converse regularly with angels face to face, wrote that "angels are wholly men in form, having faces, eyes, ears, bodies, arms, hands, and feet" (Hirsch 115–16). This is much in line with the general tenor of angelic artwork from the period. As already noted, the visual template for the Angel had been provided by the Greek deities Nike and Eros. Thus we can see that the human-looking angels with whom Swedenborg conversed were inheritors of a basic visual concept that proved as remarkably resilient as the theological one. Chester Comstock writes in "Angel Images in Art History" that the pattern provided by Nike and Eros remained "the historic and classical basis for Christian angel iconography used from the 1st century A.D. until modern times, having changed little over the last 2600 years." Byzantine Christianity made particularly vital contributions to the concretizing and proliferating of Christian angelic art during the fourth and fifth centuries, after which the famous variations introduced during the medieval and Renaissance periods were more matters of individual artistic style than of real substance.

A final bit of duality to enter into the figure of the Angel is found in this very area of artistic representation. On the one hand, the image continued in its original majestic form down through the Middle Ages and into the Renaissance, arguably culminating in the paintings of the Dominican monk Fra Angelico ("the angelic friar," 1400?–1455), for whom angels were a favorite subject. C. S. Lewis voiced a widely held sentiment when he wrote that "Fra Angelico's angels carry in their face and gesture the peace and authority of Heaven" (7). Television critic John J. O'Connor noted that it was these same Renaissance-style angels that were "culled from art masterpieces" to populate NBC's *Angels: The Mysterious Messengers*. This was in 1994, so obviously the type of angelic representation in question has survived all the way to the modern day.

But in the same breath when he was praising angels in the tradition of Fra Angelico and other, similar artists, Lewis also voiced a widely noted observation about a different artistic trend that produced a decidedly different sort of angel, stating that "in the plastic arts these symbols [i.e., representations of angels] have steadily degenerated" (7). The specific degeneration he referred to was the steady birth of the cuddlier, cuter angel that has carved out a distinctive niche for itself in Western popular consciousness and is most associated with the work of Fra Angelico's near-contemporary Raphael (1483–1520), who portrayed angels as fat, naked babies adorned with candied white wings. These are matched by yet another diluted version of the angel in the form of the pale feminine figure that arose to populate the art world during the nineteenth century. A few prominent figures such as William Blake may have labored to maintain a more transcendently serious vision of the angel, but the shape of the future was clear, and it was neutered and insipid.

Emily Hahn, in her interesting little book *Breath of God: A Book about Angels, Demons, Familiars, Elementals, and Spirits,* links these changes to an impulse that arose with the advent of the Christian religion itself:

> Taking stock of itself, the new Christianity made a change in all this [i.e., the fearsome angels of Middle Eastern religion]. The type of angel desired and needed by Christians, it became increasingly evident, was not the sort of Being the Jews had been satisfied with, so the authorities, viz., historians and illustrators, evolved a new concept of angel which, though we cannot all claim to love it, at least does not send us rushing off in screaming flight if we happen to encounter it in dreams. (53)

For Hahn, all Christian angels, even those of the Middle Ages, represent a kind of devolution of power. "[I]f we are to believe the medieval painters," she writes,

> all was sweetness and light before the birth of Jesus. After He made His appearance, the manger must have been full of the soft rustle of cherub wings, as little angels—*not* griffins or sphinxes, but amoretti—hovered over the crib, peering down lovingly at the Babe, between the ears of donkeys and the horns of cattle—two horns per animal, no more. Something new in religion came in with Jesus: prettiness, innocence, call it what you will. The Nightmare Angel's sway was over. (58)

Obviously, Hahn was taking poetic license with history when she wrote that. The change did not occur immediately with the advent of Christianity. But occur it did, so that today, two millennia after the birth of Christ, Mark Edmundson can accurately observe in his *Nightmare on Main Street* that "America's current angels are fluffy creatures, flown off the fronts of greeting cards," and that they compare unfavorably to the original biblical angels, which are "beings of another order: an encounter with an angel transforms life—puts one on a harder, higher path" (86).

Lewis, for his part, brought the issue to a head and also summarized the history of this degeneration in his typically inimitable way:

> Later [i.e., in the wake of Fra Angelico's angels] come the chubby infantile nudes of Raphael; finally the soft, slim, girlish, and consolatory angels of nineteenth century art, shapes so feminine that they avoid being voluptuous only by their total insipidity—the frigid houris of a teatable paradise. They are a pernicious symbol. In Scripture the visitation of an angel is always alarming; it has to begin by saying "Fear not." The Victorian angel looks as if it were going to say, "There, there." (7)

One can only wish Lewis were still around to comment on the angel-oriented advertising campaign mounted by the American lingerie company Victoria's Secret in the early 2000s, which featured images of nearly nude female models decked out with large, white, feathery wings. This enormously profitable mockery of the Angel both underscored the figure's cultural prevalence and one-upped the "pernicious symbol" of Victorian art by presenting a figure that managed to appear exceedingly voluptuous and artistically insipid all at once.

Although the details lie outside the scope of this essay, it might be noted that in addition to playing a major role in the founding of Christianity—and also, in one of its earlier versions, the founding of Judaism—the Angel played a major role in the creation of two other Western religions: Islam, when the angel Gabriel began to speak to a humble Arab camel driver named Muhammad in the early seventh century; and Mormonism, when the angel Moroni visited a poor, uneducated American teenager named Joseph Smith in 1823 and told him where to find buried golden plates containing a secret scripture written in "reformed Egyptian." The wide-ranging results of these two angelic interventions are matters of global significance. Who knows but that the iconic Angel may return to found other religions in the future?

VI. The Angel and the Demon in Supernatural Horror Fiction and Film

This, then, is the origin of the Angel and the Demon. The modern icons are inheritors of a vastly rich and ancient trove of meanings, and when they appear in works of supernatural horror they generally display one or more facets of their varied natures, a knowledge of which can greatly enhance the reader's understanding and enjoyment. A highly selective survey of several classic—and in some cases, less than classic—texts will be sufficient to establish the point.

By way of setting a context, it is prudent to recognize that from its beginnings in the Gothic literary movement of the late eighteenth and early nineteenth centuries, supernatural horror has consistently made the Demon a more frequent focus than the Angel, which has remained more active in the province of religion and spirituality proper. In fact, the Angel as a major focus of fictional supernatural horror did not really see much use at all until the late twentieth century. Perhaps this is due in part to the Angel's aforementioned artistic degeneration. In the nineteenth century, right about the time the Angel was finding itself trapped in the bodies of chubby babies and doe-eyed androgynes, the supernatural horror story was just getting off the ground, and many of these stories made prominent use of the Demon, which, unlike the angel, had retained its ancient horrific nature intact and was thus ready for immediate casting in stories of supernatural horror. Interestingly, in its literary guise the Demon has remained very much in touch with its ancient cultural background, while in its cinematic guise, as discussed below, it has often been severed from this mooring and allowed to roam free as a nearly contextless monster.

Three Primary Aspects of the Demon

The idea, mentioned above, of multiple "facets" or "aspects" provides a useful conceptual tool for clarifying the Demon's various appearances in stories of the supernatural. The coherent, unified Demon that was hammered into existence over the course of millennia still displays a number of distinct aspects owing to its multifarious origin, and supernatural stories may be classified according to which of these they emphasize. In general, three such aspects are identifiable: the *Demon as fallen angel* (the Miltonic Demon), the *Demon as moral tempter,* and what might be called the *Demon as afflicting presence.* This last aspect takes one of several forms ranging from physical and/or psychological harassment, to internal daimonic-type influence, to full-blown demonic possession.

The Demon as Fallen Angel and Moral Tempter: The Monk *and* Faust

One of the most celebrated (and notorious) Gothic novels, Matthew Gregory Lewis's *The Monk* (1796), represents the first major use of the Demon in the nascent supernatural horror genre. Published only twenty-two years after

Horace Walpole's overwrought medievalesque fantasy *The Castle of Otranto* invented the Gothic novel, *The Monk* caused a scandal and a sensation. A quick survey of its content indicates why.

Set in Madrid in the time of the Inquisition, *The Monk* tells the story of a Capuchin monk named Ambrosio who is renowned for, and also far too arrogantly proud of, his ironclad moral virtue. This virtue is corrupted when he falls in lust with a woman named Matilda, who is later revealed as a demon, and whose enticements lead him into acts of intense debauchery and violence. The theology of the book, and thus the nature of the Demon it envisages, is entirely orthodox, with a few faint rumblings of occultism thrown in for good measure, as is typical of such literature from the period. Demons in the book are framed as fallen angels with Lucifer as their king. They can be "called up" via occult rituals, as Matilda first describes and then later demonstrates to Ambrosio, who ends up signing a contract with Lucifer and suffering a hideous punishment in the end. Although the salacious and gruesome nature of the book aroused such spectacular controversy and condemnation, especially from the Catholic church, that the author's reputation was threatened, it is clear that *The Monk* and its demonology are entirely grounded in a traditional morality, since the novel "plays off" this morality at every turn in order to wring the maximum amount of moral-aesthetic horror from its story and subject matter. So this first prominent use of the Demon in a work of supernatural horror emphasizes both the moral and the Miltonic aspect of the Demon. A movie version starring Franco Nero and scripted by renowned surrealist filmmaker Luis Buñuel appeared almost two hundred years later, in 1973, and did not significantly alter the story's presentation of the demon.

Goethe's *Faust,* whose Part One was published in 1808, is of course not generally labeled a horror story as such, although Goethe himself was prominent in the Romantic movement that spawned the horror genre. But Goethe's rendering of the ancient story of the great magician who sells his soul to the Devil or a demon is of such major importance that it really must be mentioned. It has become known as the definitive version of the story, surpassing and virtually supplanting Christopher Marlowe's *The Tragical History of Doctor Faustus* (1604) in popular literary memory. As in *The Monk,* the view of the Demon here is utterly in line with the Roman Catholic and Miltonic concept established in the thirteenth through the seventeenth centuries, although Goethe with his eclectic political, theological, philosophical, scientific, and mystical concerns put the concept to decidedly wider use. The demon Mephistopheles who offers his diabolical bargain to the eponymous protagonist was portrayed in medieval and Renaissance Christian legends as a powerful angel who had been the second to fall from heaven after Lucifer. In Goethe's story, Mephistopheles makes reference to his own fallen status a number of times, and the play's "Prologue in Heaven" further signals and cements the deployment of the iconic theology by presenting the archangels Michael, Gabriel, and Raphael praising God in heaven, followed by Mephistopheles making a wager with God about Faust, in a scene modeled directly on the interaction between Satan and Yahweh in the Book of Job. In Part Two of the play, published in 1832, Mephistopheles meets with various mythological creatures and takes on the appearance of the monstrous Phorkyas, thus bringing to prominence the Demon's ancient association with the whole multitude of non-Christian gods and spirits. All in all, the play ranks as one of the most significant works in the history of demonic literature.

The Demon as Afflicting Presence: "Green Tea," "The Horla," and "Casting the Runes"

By the middle and late nineteenth century, the supernatural horror story had come fully into its own and begun to produce authors and works that would later constitute a canon. Many of them made use of the Demon, as in the spate of stories in which the Demon was active as a psychologically and physically afflicting presence. These include J. Sheridan Le Fanu's "Green Tea" (1872), Guy de Maupassant's "The Horla" (1887), and M. R. James's "Casting the Runes" (1894), which are all recognized as classics of the genre.

"Green Tea" (1872) offers a fascinating take on the theme by depicting the plight of one Reverend Mr. Jennings, who is driven to suicide by either a mental breakdown or an excess of supernatural sight that has enabled him to see a demon, in the shape of a monkey, pursuing him everywhere. It even jumps on his Bible as he attempts to preach. But the creature is invisible to everyone else. Le Fanu uses the opportunity provided by his basic plot idea to offer some fascinating spiritual and metaphysical speculations, as when he has the narrator translate a few lines from Swedenborg's *Arcana Coelestia* that illuminate the possible nature of Mr. Jennings's afflicting presence:

> When man's interior sight is opened, which is that of his spirit, then there appear the things of another life, which cannot possibly be made visible to the bodily sight. . . . There are with every man at least two evil spirits. . . . The evil spirits associated with man are, indeed, from the hells, but when with man they are not then in hell, but are taken out thence. The place where they then are, is in the midst between heaven and hell, and is called the world of spirits. (Wise and Fraser 377)

This "world of spirits" corresponds, of course, to what Plato and other ancient Greeks called the daimonic realm. The story's basic conceit is that Mr. Jennings may have accidentally had his "interior sight opened," thus attracting the malevolent attention of the little demon that is attached to him.

Maupassant's "The Horla" and James's "Casting the Runes" present similar tales of men plagued by demons, and like "Green Tea," they demonstrate their awareness of the background and context of such a theme. The protagonist of "The Horla" suffers from attacks by an invisible creature that are so purely horrifying, he is eventually driven to kill himself. But before his end, he realizes that the entity attacking him is a representative of an entire race that is intent upon wresting control of the earth from humankind. The Horla, he comes to understand, is the entity that throughout history "was feared by primitive man; whom disquieted priests exorcised; whom sorcerers evoked on dark nights, without having seen him appear, to whom the imagination of the transient masters of the world lent all the monstrous or graceful forms of gnomes, spirits, genii, fairies and familiar spirits" (Wise and Fraser 466). In other words, the thing attacking the narrator is the original source and template for all the evil spirits that mankind has ever conceived. For the reader who is aware of the deep background of hideous hosts and hordes encoded in the idea of the iconic Demon, the story's conceit is all the more effective and impressive.

In James's "Casting the Runes," a man named Edward Dunning is similarly plagued by an invisible demon who is unleashed upon him by a resentful occultist. In the end the occultist himself is apparently done in by his own evil. The entire story, as well as its famous cinematic adaptation, *Night of the Demon*, a.k.a. *Curse of the Demon* (1957; see below), demonstrates an awareness of the subject's rich background, thus repaying and playing upon the informed reader's existing knowledge of such things. This is unsurprising, since James was a professional academic, specifically a medieval scholar, whose interest in the Demon extended far beyond the writing of horror stories: He studied medieval and ancient demonology in earnest and applied his powers to translating ancient works, producing, for example, a translation of *The Testament of Solomon*.

The Demon and the Cult of Genius

In addition to considering the Demon's appearances in supernatural horror fiction during the genre's early years, we will find it instructive to look back briefly to the early nineteenth century, to the height of the Romantic period, and observe that the trope of the Demon as afflicting presence appears most prominently not in works of supernatural horror at all, but in works of philosophy and literary theory that explore the Romantic concept of "genius."

All the great Romantics—Goethe, Rousseau, Shelley, Byron, Blake, Coleridge—as well as their philosophical heirs in the Transcendentalist and anti-transcendentalist movements (Emerson, Thoreau, Poe, Hawthorne, Melville) devoted a great deal of attention and many thousands of words to analyzing, celebrating, and even deifying the creative impulse that lead people such as themselves to produce art and literature.

In the Romantic view, creative inspiration became likened to a demon, or rather a daemon, or rather a genius in a modified classical Roman mode, so that these individuals with their overheated personalities and obsessive creative manias were framed as being influenced and inspired by a type of higher power. Additionally, Goethe, E. T. A. Hoffmann, and others wrote much about the idea of the "demonic" man who is controlled by a deeply obsessive force that leads him always to strive in quasi-Promethean fashion for *more* in all things. So this was an alternate mode by which aspects of the Demon remained visible in the cultural consciousness of the period. Naturally, it made itself known in reams of poetry and fiction, many of which did not mention it directly but instead manifested its spirit (as in the case of Mary Shelley's *Frankenstein* with its Promethean and daimonically driven title character).

Other Literary Demons

Many additional and notable depictions of the Demon occurred throughout the nineteenth and twentieth centuries as the supernatural horror genre expanded and gained an identity. Many of these were associated with the popular wave of novels and stories that explored the ever-popular "deal with the devil" motif, of which Charles Robert Maturin's *Melmoth the Wanderer* (1820) is a notable example. Even skeptical works such as Sir Walter Scott's *Letters on Demonology and Witchcraft* (1830), which surveyed the long history of both subjects and offered a decidedly anti-supernatural explanation of both, evinced the strong popular interest in such matters by becoming bestsellers. Nor was this interest confined to Great Britain and Western Europe; the great Russian poet Lermontov's best-known work was a long poem titled *The Demon* (1842), which he worked on for most of his life, much like Goethe and his decades-long infatuation with *Faust*. Although Lermontov devoted much of his poem's thematic energy not to depictions of demonic matters as such but to ruminations on the idiosyncratic connotations of the word "demon" that were peculiar to Russian culture, his story of an angel that becomes a demon by being exiled from paradise, after which it wanders the earth in misery, makes obvious use of tropes typical to the Demon of supernatural horror fiction. The poem was later adapted as an opera by Anton Rubinstein in 1871, which was in turn adapted as a silent film in 1911.

During the early and mid-twentieth century, one of the Demon's most popular hangouts was the colorful world of pulp fiction. *Weird Tales*, perhaps the most famous of the early pulp magazines devoted to fantasy, science fiction, and horror, published a number of stories by various authors that made use of demonic tropes and themes. Although the majority of these were forgettable hackwork, a number of truly talented authors for *Weird Tales* contributed memorably to the Demon's development. Robert Bloch, for example, created a gripping story in "Yours Truly, Jack the Ripper" (1943), which posited that Jack the Ripper was a sorcerer who achieved immortality by offering sacrifices to evil demons, and that he had survived down to the present day through his power to possess people's minds and bodies. The idea was potent enough that Bloch later reworked it for a teleplay for *Star Trek* in the 1960s.

Another prominent *Weird Tales* writer who advanced the Demon's literary evolution was H. P. Lovecraft. In various loosely interlinked stories, Lovecraft developed an eldritch demonology that went on to evolve still further after his death, via the contributions of other writers to his mythos, into a pervasive pop-cultural phenomenon. Lovecraft himself was a brilliant, self-educated polymath who, by following the thread of the diverse subjects that interested him—astronomy, chemistry, the philosophy of science, ancient history, antiquarianism, the sociology of religion, supernatural horror literature, and more—and by extracting from each the essence of what fascinated him about it, succeeded in creating a novel mythology involving a strikingly new type of demon in the form of monstrous alien godlike creatures whose existence and nature destabilize human sanity and undermine the human race's sense of cosmic security. Since this type of demon, represented most famously by Cthulhu, does not have much to do with the iconic Demon of Western religious history, it largely lies outside the scope of this essay. But it worth pausing to note that Lovecraft's alternative demonology has gained new force and momentum in recent years by inspiring an ever-growing number of writers, filmmakers, composers, and game designers to extend and expound upon his themes. It is a measure of his genius as a literary visionary that in his quest to evoke cosmic horror he deliberately—and successfully—stepped off the beaten path of Western theological and spiritual concepts and used the very horror of anomie, of cosmic "outsideness," to achieve his yearned-for aesthetic effect.

The mid-twentieth century saw the publication of various notable works involving the Demon. Not all of them were associated with the supernatural horror genre. C. S. Lewis's *The Screwtape Letters* (1942), for example, with its witty fictional presentation of the advice and instruction given by a senior demon to a lower demon in the fine art of tempting humans, offers an effective and influential take on the Demon-as-moral-tempter. More specifically in a fantastic fictional vein, L. Ron Hubbard's novel *Fear* (1957) tells an interesting story about an anthropologist who, after publishing a monograph in which he dismisses belief in demons as primitive delusions, finds himself under apparent attack by demons in search of revenge. In the late 1960s, Ira Levin's *Rosemary's Baby* (1967) and director Roman Polanski's film adaptation (1968) both made a stir with their tale of a young housewife in modern-day Manhattan finding that her husband has conspired with a satanic cult to impregnate her with the devil's child. In tandem with the "death of God" movement that was then making waves across the American and British cultural landscapes—and that was explicitly referenced in Polanski's film—*Rosemary's Baby* may be credited with laying the groundwork for the literary and cinematic phenomenon that was *The Exorcist* in the 1970s.

The Demon as Bestseller: The Exorcist *and What Followed*

E. V. Walter has characterized *The Exorcist* as a representation of "the ambiguity of Roman Catholic culture in the throes of disenchantment after Vatican II" (20). In the 1960s and 1970s, it was not just Roman Catholic culture but Western culture at large that was suffering such a disenchantment, and Blatty's 1971 novel and its 1973 film counterpart landed right in the middle of this. In retrospect, it seems impossible to separate the two presentations of the story (novel and film), so intertwined have they become in cultural memory. Walter hit upon the key to the electrifying power of both when he wrote that the film version "exploits the deisidaimonia of a disenchanted public" (20). *The Exorcist* demonstrated that a visceral portrayal of the Demon in its most horrific guise, as the afflicting presence that possesses a person's body and personality, was capable of wrenching the emotions of a confused modern populace in a way that nobody would have predicted, but that had been quite familiar to people in former historical eras. The unhappy priest Damien Karras, who in the story examines the possession case and subjects it to intense medical scrutiny before proceeding to explore supernatural explanations, served effectively as a stand-in for a spiritually skeptical but existentially fearful American (and also international) public. The story seemed all the more horrifying to that public because it posited that a vile supernatural presence, like a revenant of a mythological age thought long dead, could enter the body of an innocent young girl. As already noted, in an attempt to build a suitably fearsome back story, Blatty turned to ancient Mesopotamian mythology and framed the demon that possessed young Regan MacNeil as Pazuzu.

Along with its exploration of the possession theme, *The Exorcist* also played upon the Demon's aspect as fallen angel in its depiction of the confrontation between Pazuzu and the aged Roman Catholic exorcist Father Merrin. The performance of the exorcism rite from Chapter XII of the Roman Ritual formed the substance of the story's latter half, and with the various adjurations in the name of Christ and the traditional names and identifications hurled at the demon, the novel and film left no doubt about the nature and status of the spirit.

The explosive impact of *The Exorcist* changed the face of popular entertainment. In the literary world, for instance, it helped to launch the pop horror fiction boom that reached its apex in the works of Stephen King in the 1980s. Many of these books and stories featured the Demon in some form or other. Some of the best of them evinced a real awareness of the figure's deep history and achieved their emotional and philosophical effect partly by considering the implications of this history in a modern-day setting. One such story was Harlan Ellison's "The Whimper of Whipped Dogs" (1974). Ellison was inspired by the notorious case of Kitty Genovese, who in 1964 was stabbed to death outside her apartment building in Queens while dozens of her neighbors watched and/or listened without attempting to help or call the police. (Or at least this is how the incident was memorialized in popular memory thanks to an article in the *New York Times*. The article's veracity has since been called into question.) Ellison's fictionalized version used a similar murder as the jumping-off point for a story positing the existence of a malevolent supernatural force at work in the heat and grime of New York, a demonic god that is the true spiritual source of human depravity and violence in the modern urban milieu: "A new God, an ancient God come again with the eyes and hunger of a child, a deranged blood God of fog and street violence. A God who needed worshippers and offered the choices or death as a victim or life as an eternal witness to the deaths of other chosen victims. A God to fit the times, a God of streets and people" (129). The fact that Ellison was fully aware of the wider and deeper psychological and philosophical implications of his story, as opposed to merely offering it for entertainment, can be seen in the epigraph he placed at the end of it, a meditation on violence and the daimonic from Rollo May's *Love and Will*.

Among the post-*Exorcist* wave of works featuring the Demon, the Christian supernatural thrillers of Frank Peretti deserve special notice, both because of their popularity and because of their link to a major cultural current not yet considered. As mentioned, *The Exorcist* entered American public consciousness during a period of religious and more generalized cultural confusion. Then, in the late 1970s, the cultural scale tipped sharply, though not universally, in the direction of conservatism, which, in combination with the resurgent popularity of religious fundamentalism, engendered a renaissance of literalistic supernatural Christian belief. This soon found an outlet in the new field of Christian popular fiction, in which Frank Peretti became one of the first giants. His novels *This Present Darkness* (1986) and its sequel *Piercing the Darkness* (1988) depicted the literal reality of Demons warring with Angels in the American heartland. Peretti's demonology and angelology were entirely Miltonic and Dantesque, as were his descriptions of the figures themselves. *This Present Darkness* describes one demon as being "like a high-strung little gargoyle, his hide a slimy, bottomless black, his body thin and spiderlike: half humanoid, half animal, totally demon" (36). Others are enormous saurian beings of immense power. In expression of an idea common to the type of theology these books represent, many demons are named after specific sins or negative emotions, such as the demons Complacency, Deceit, and Lust, whose functions are obvious. Additionally, in these novels full-blown demon possession, complete with the requisite writhing, guttural speech, and so on, results when people dabble with dastardly New Age beliefs.

Clearly, all three aspects of the Demon are exhibited here: fallen angel, moral tempter, and afflicting presence in its three variations. From a viewpoint informed by the Demon's history, what seems most fascinating about these novels is that they employ the streamlined, generic prose and narrative style typical of modern thriller fiction in order to expound a theology that might be dubbed "Milton-lite." What is more, they do so quite effectively given their peculiar ideological and stylistic constraints, and given the willingness of the reader to surrender to their simplistic worldview.

Another best-selling post-*Exorcist* novelist who has made intelligent use of the Demon is Anne Rice. The fifth book in her Vampire Chronicles, *Memnoch the Devil* (1995), presents one of the most extensive demonological explorations in modern popular fiction when the vampire Lestat is given a guided tour of hell and heaven, along with a thorough explanation of the spiritual cosmology of the universe, by a being named Memnoch, who presents himself as the Devil in his fallen-angel form. Another series by Rice, The Chronicles of the Mayfair Witches, tells the history of a family that has been plagued for centuries by a demon named Lasher. Rice's novel *Servant of the Bones* (1998) tells the story of Azriel, an educated Jew in ancient Babylon who is transformed into a spirit that survives into modern times. In all these books, Rice's use of the Demon consistently demonstrates a knowledge of the figure's history and prehistory.

Brian Keene's debut novel *The Rising* (2003) and its sequel *City of the Dead*

(2005) also demonstrate a contextual awareness of the Demon and feature a storyline that combines the afflicting aspect of the Demon with another supernatural icon, the zombie (a fusion that he may have derived from the Evil Dead film series, mentioned below). Keene explicitly links his demons to the iconic Demon by referencing various evil spirits of ancient Hebrew and other mythologies; in *The Rising*, a demon named Ob (whose name is taken from a spirit mentioned in the Old Testament) tells a human, "We are your masters. Demons, your kind called us. Djinn. Monsters. We are the source of your legends—the reason you still fear the dark" (31–32).

The Demon in Movies and Other Media

The 1890s saw the birth of the movies, and the Demon got involved in the new industry right from the start. The great early French director George Méliès became famous for his short films featuring fantastic subjects and plenty of trick photography. The spirit world was an obvious treasure trove to draw upon for such entertainments, and many of Méliès's films, such as *Le Cabinet de Mephistopheles* (The Laboratory of Mephistopheles, 1897) and *La Cavern maudite* (The Cave of the Demons, 1898), featured devils and demons, mostly in the "trickster" or tempter mode, all displaying stereotypical physical traits. Before the silent era was over, the Demon would also appear in such productions as director Giovanni Vitrotti's 1911 adaptation of the Russian poet Lermontov's *The Demon* (mentioned earlier), numerous versions of Dante's *Inferno*, director Paul Wegener's 1920 remake of his own earlier film *The Golem*, and director Benjamin Christensen's enigmatic *Häxan* (1922), also known as *Witchcraft through the Ages*. This last film with its odd early cinematic chronicling of the history of witchcraft and its depiction of classically bestial demons drawn from medieval iconography, which perform and preside over numerous acts of depravity, would continue to excite interest and consternation for decades to come. Like *The Monk, Häxan* reconfirmed the association of the Demon with things rejected and taboo; it was banned outside its home country of Sweden for many decades after its initial release.

The year 1957 saw the release of *Night of the Demon*, director Jacques Tourneur's superlative cinematic adaptation of M. R. James's "Casting the Runes." Released in America under the title *Curse of the Demon*, the film deservedly became a classic. As in the short story, the Demon here appears in its guise as an afflicting presence that harasses its victims both physically and psychologically. The controversy involving Tourneur's supposed dispute with the film's producer over whether an actual demon should be shown onscreen, as opposed to letting the interpretation of the movie's supernatural-seeming events remain more murky, is as famous as the film itself. Whatever the truth of the matter, the film that was released indeed featured an explicit "head-on" depiction of the title demon. Although Tourneur may ultimately have been correct that the narrative's final interpretation would have been better left ambiguous, the visual design of the creature showed an admirable grasp of the iconic Demon's historical and artistic grandeur; its creator reportedly worked with an eye to reproducing the sort of nightmarish figures seen in medieval woodcuts (and also depicted thirty-five years earlier in *Häxan*).

The Demon also appeared frequently in the comic book industry, as in Marvel Comics's *Ghost Rider* and DC Comics's *The Demon*, always with the traditional iconography intact and the traditional theology at least referenced. The enigmatic character of John Constantine, created by the now-legendary comic book writer and magickal practitioner Alan Moore, encountered the Demon in various guises as he strode through a number of titles in the booming comics industry of the 1980s, 1990s, and 2000s. Eventually, Constantine gained his own comic book series, *Hellblazer,* which was loosely adapted as the 2005 film *Constantine*. In the movie, the eclectic spiritual world of the comic book was simplified into a watered-down Roman Catholic dualism that involved demons of an entirely traditional cast warring against equally traditional angels, with humans employed as pawns. Thus, the film emphasized the Demon's fallen angel and afflicting presence aspects, with a few instances of demonic possession thrown in for good measure.

Constantine was only one in the flood of Demon-inspired movies that followed *The Exorcist,* and an interesting bifurcation soon became evident in this cinematic outpouring. On the one hand were movies that, like *The Exorcist* and *Constantine*, framed demons in relation to their ancient cultural and religious history. On the other hand were the aforementioned movies that severed demons from this historical mooring and gave them a new kind of life.

A particularly interesting example of the former type—not because of cinematic quality (which it lacks) but because of sheer concept—is *Wishmaster* (1997), which kicked off a series of low-budget, gore-laden movies that attempted with some success to wring horror from the old Middle Eastern *djinn*. Although the first entry in the series degenerated into camp humor by the end, as did its sequels, the series still represents an interesting attempt to locate ancient demonic horror in a modern context. Its "take" on the *djinn* invokes the Demon's role as an afflicting and, in a sense, a possessing spirit, since in the film world these spirits are able to force people to act against their will. The first movie's explanation of the horrific nature of the *djinn*, as told to the protagonist by an anthropology professor, is worth quoting: "Forget what our culture has made of the *djinn*. Forget Barbara Eden. Forget Robin Williams. To the peoples of ancient Arabia, a *djinn* [*sic*] was neither cute nor funny. It was something else entirely. It was the face of fear itself."

The Post-Modern Demon

Departing from such films as *Wishmaster, The Exorcist,* and *Constantine* was the new type of demon that came on the scene when certain filmmakers in the late twentieth century decided to ignore tradition and cut the iconic Demon free from its past associations with Christian cosmology and theology. Examples of this type could be multiplied *ad nauseam,* since it became popular in the low-budget and direct-to-video markets that, in the 1980s, began churning out a seemingly endless stream of B-grade and Z-grade horror flicks made by filmmakers with various degrees of talent and skill. But the two series that did it best are the Evil Dead trilogy, consisting of *The Evil Dead* (1981), *Evil Dead II: Dead by Dawn* (1987), and *Army of Darkness* (1993), and the Demons trilogy, consisting of *Demons* (1985), *Demons 2* (1986), and *La Chiesa* (1989). The demons in both series are portrayed as spirits that commandeer people's bodies and personalities and turn them into vicious killing machines. The violence is copious and explicit, and the demons' behavior is standardized: possessed people roar in guttural voices, foam at the mouth, writhe, rend, claw, shriek, and tear. They are the human—or perhaps inhuman, given their tendency to transform the human body in monstrous ways—embodiment of pure ferality, of an insatiable lust for wanton, bloody destruction.

What indicates that these demons have been cut loose from their mooring in the iconic Demon is the general hastiness and thinness of the explanations offered for them. In *The Evil Dead* the demons are raised by the reading aloud of passages from a book titled after Lovecraft's fictional book of black magic, the Necronomicon, which in the movie is said to be of Sumerian origin. The demons are thus, perhaps, of the ancient Sumerian variety. But this explanation is quickly downplayed or ignored in favor of moving the action forward with scenes of intense, savage violence. It is almost as if the explanation is a mere perfunctory nod to the more sustained and detailed ones explored in other films. Similarly, in *Demons* the demons are "explained" by a faux quotation from Nostradamus that prophesies "the coming of the time of the demons" and warns that these creatures "will make cemeteries their cathedrals and the cities your tombs." The film offers nothing else by way of explaining what the demons are supposed to be or where they are supposed to come from.

Although it would be all too easy to interpret this omission as a liability and to label it the result of lazy or inept writing and directing, it is in fact possible to see it as a strength, and to interpret it as a new and effective angle on the iconic Demon in its afflicting aspect. *Demons* makes this clear when it reveals that it is actually a kind of existentialist cinematic parable. The basic plot involves members of a movie audience who find themselves trapped in a nightmarish scenario when a movie about demons ruptures the boundary between cinematic reality and existential reality. People in the audience begin transforming into demons and killing everyone around them. Eventually the panicked crowd concludes that since the movie caused the crisis, maybe shutting it off will stop the killing. But when they storm the projection booth, they find that it is completely automated, without a projectionist running the film. This leads to the startled realization, "But that means—nobody's ever been here!"

The point seems to be that the demon plague is playing out automatically, without any oversight or direction by an intelligent force. It is simply a spontaneous occurrence, without explanation. The demons have no reason, no history, no background in anything like the long history that lies behind the iconic Demon. Seeing this, one can recognize that these unmoored demons represent an alternative answer to Blatty's and Friedkin's challenge from the 1970s.

What if God died but the Demon survived? What if there were evil but no good to counterbalance it? What if there were indeed demons, but this in no wise entailed the existence of Blatty's "angels, God, and a life everlasting"? This seems to be the philosophy or theology implicit in the postmodern demon (as it might be called).

Still, a more careful look at the behavior of this demon shows that it is not entirely divorced from its iconic cousin. The postmodern demon may not be linked by a shared theological background, but it is linked by the behaviors listed above. All that frothing, snarling, and screaming is familiar from Regan's behavior in *The Exorcist,* and also from the countless cases of demonic possession documented throughout history. By the Middle Ages, these behaviors were standardized and catalogued, and all are visible in the postmodern demon, which thus seems to represent the phenomenon of possession divorced from the possibility of exorcism. The postmodern demon is not a fallen angel that can be commanded in the name of Christ or driven away by any version of the iconic Angel. Instead, it is an unaccountable spirit of viciousness that arrives for no reason and cannot be driven away. As such, it may be taken as a kind of apotheosis of the iconic Demon as the afflicting, possessing presence.

So in effect, tales of the postmodern demon represent an alternative strand sprouting from the pop cultural tradition begun by *The Exorcist,* but they pursue different philosophical tangent. At the time of this writing, both streams remain strong. Movies about the postmodern Demon continue to proliferate, even as one of the most prominent of the post-*Exorcist* films is *The Exorcism of Emily Rose* (2005), which was based on the true case of a young German college student named Anneliese Michel who reportedly became possessed and, after several months of grueling Roman Catholic exorcism ceremonies, died in 1976. Even as the postmodern demon continues to rampage across movie and television screens in its orgy of theologically ungrounded violence, *The Exorcism of Emily Rose* presents almost the exact same spiritual message that Blatty had hoped to convey with his novel: that the horror of the demonic harbors the seeds of its own redemption, since it directly entails its opposite in the saving grace of God.

The Demon, it seems, is ever the subtle trickster.

The Angel on Walkabout

A representative history of the Angel in supernatural horror for the purpose of demonstrating its illuminating power is much quicker to relate, for the simple reason that there is less of it to deal with. As mentioned earlier, the Angel's near-exclusion from the supernatural horror genre as a serious object of attention may have been due, at least in part, to the artistic coma into which it had fallen. For well over a century, the Angel was far more associated in popular consciousness with saccharine ideas of peace and rose-filled gardens than with serious matters of supernaturalism. For most serious dealings with the Angel, one had to look not to supernatural fiction and film but to actual religion. A few serious literary works did mention or otherwise deal with angels, such as Anatole France's *The Revolt of the Angels* (1914), Jonathan Daniels's *Clash of Angels* (1930), and John Cowper Powys's *Lucifer* (1956). But many of these, while they often referenced the traditional Miltonic theology, also employed the angel in the service of a separate agenda. France's novel, for example, was a satire in favor of freethought; it depicted an angel that becomes an atheist after being exposed to theological literature.

One notable angel in a work of supernatural horror fiction can be found in Thomas Ligotti's 1991 story "Mrs. Rinaldi's Angel," which offers a unique take on the figure. It tells of a young boy whose mother takes him to a local sage-like woman named Mrs. Rinaldi for help in curing his nightmares. Mrs. Rinaldi takes the boy to a back room in her house and performs a strange ritual intended to free him entirely from all dreaming. Dreams, she tells him, "are parasites—maggots of the mind and soul, feeding on the mind and soul as ordinary maggots feed on the body" (56). Then she produces a curious box that, when opened, emits a shining white light couched in a misty vapor. After the conclusion of the ritual, the boy returns home and seems cured for a time, but then his dreams return, and he finds himself unaccountably drawn to embrace them. His mother takes him back to Mrs. Rinaldi, and they find her strangely transformed and withered. "You let my angel be poisoned by the dreams you could not deny," she tells the boy. "It *was* an angel, did you know that? It was pure of all thinking and pure of all dreaming. And you are the one who made it think and dream and now it is dying, but as a demon" (64). This seems to mean that the angel contained in the box was associated with absolute formlessness and freedom from matter, just as ancient Gnostic theology held that the material world is an evil trap, the creation of a bungling or malevolent demiurge, while the truly divine realm is one of pure spirit. Whatever the interpretation, Ligotti's story represents a singularly interesting use of the Angel in supernatural horror fiction, not least because it strips the layers of its historically syncretic nature and reimagines it as something else entirely.

During its vacation from supernatural horror, the Angel was quite prominent in the Hollywood studio system, where it found its way into many movies during the 1940s and 1950s. It appeared in various guises in such movies as *A Guy Named Joe* (1944; remade in 1989 as *Always*), *It's a Wonderful Life* (1946), *The Bishop's Wife* (1947), *Heaven Only Knows* (1947), and *Angels in the Outfield* (1951; remade in 1994). In 1956 Cecil B. DeMille's bloated but entertaining Bible epic *The Ten Commandments* presented a surprisingly frightening angel of death that arrived in the form of a sentient mist to claim all the firstborn Egyptians. But this was an aberration. By the 1970s, when audiences were reportedly vomiting, fainting, and fleeing theatres where *The Exorcist* was playing, the Angel was still confined to light entertaining fare such as *Heaven Can Wait* (1978). In 1987 German director Wim Wenders's *Der Himmel über Berlin* (*Wings of Desire*, remade by Hollywood as *City of Angels* in 1998) gave a truly interesting portrayal of angels that watch over the human denizens of a modern city and envy their earthly existence. But this was still a far cry from supernatural horror.

Wenders's film, however, arrived near the end of the supernaturally fearsome Angel's long coma. Already in 1983, Blatty had given readers an interesting bit of angelic speculation in *Legion*, his sequel to *The Exorcist*, wherein he offered a sweeping solution to the age-old "problem of evil" by suggesting that humans are all fragments of the original angelic being, Lucifer, who fell from heaven, and that we are all therefore involved in a collective, ongoing attempt to be reunited with God. This did not constitute an actual use of the Angel as an object of fear, but it did involve the Angel in a horror novel.

Oddly, Blatty omitted this concept entirely from the film version, titled *The Exorcist III* (1990), which he not only wrote but directed. It remained for another Christian author, not a Catholic but a Protestant, to effect the Angel's full resurrection as a fearsome presence.

Return of the Warrior Angel

It was Frank Peretti's supernatural thriller novels of the 1980s that were largely responsible for reviving the Miltonic Angel as a fierce heavenly warrior. Near the beginning of *This Present Darkness*, Peretti depicts two men visiting the small Midwestern town of Ashton. Soon after their arrival, these strangers are revealed as more than human:

> And now the two men were brilliantly white, their former clothing transfigured by garments that seemed to burn with intensity. Their faces were bronzed and glowing, their eyes shone like fire, and each man wore a glistening golden belt from which hung a flashing sword. ... [T]hen, like a gracefully spreading canopy, silken, shimmering, nearly transparent membranes began to unfurl from their backs and shoulders and rise to meet and overlap above their heads, gently undulating in a spiritual wind. (13)

Reading this description is like witnessing the resurrection from the dead of the pre-Victorian, non-Raphaelite Angel that had warred against the Demon in the service of God for centuries. The novel's later intricate and overheated descriptions of spiritual and aerial battles between sword-wielding Angels and Demons is an equally welcome sight, regardless of its comic-bookish gaudiness.

Of course, the warrior Angel could not stay confined to the world of evangelical Christian thriller/horror fiction. Hollywood, for example, got involved in the early 2000s when it portrayed classical warrior angels in supernatural thrillers and fantasies such as *Constantine* and *Frailty* (2001). Moreover, the warrior was joined in popular entertainment by its more fearsome cousin, also newly resurrected from its long sleep.

Return of the Nightmare Angel

Given the popularity of the "Milton-lite" phenomenon Peretti helped to create with his novels, and given the ongoing popularity of the horror genre, it was just a matter of time before a purely horrific angel appeared. The venue where this rare modern creature finally reared its head was *The Prophecy* (1995), a film written and directed by Gregory Widen and featuring a fascinating premise: unbeknownst to humans, there is presently a supernatural war being waged, not between angels and demons, but between angels and other angels. This is a second war, described only in an extra "lost" chapter of the Book of

Revelation, that came after the original war in heaven that resulted in the expulsion of Lucifer and his followers. The archangel Gabriel, jealous of God's love for humans, whom he (Gabriel) refers to as "talking monkeys," is spearheading an effort among the angels to return things to the way they were when humans were secondary and God loved angels the most.

The whole concept is Miltonic through and through, even with its peculiar "twist," and the film's considerable artistic success is principally due to careful writing and a deeply realized, deeply fascinating concept. Widen truly understands the horror inherent in the ancient, iconic Angel before whom men and women traditionally fainted and fell to their knees. One of *The Prophecy*'s protagonists, a former candidate for Catholic priesthood, describes the nature of this Angel in words as effective as any: "Did you ever notice how in the Bible whenever God needed to punish someone or make an example, or whenever God needed a killing, he sent an angel? Did you ever wonder what a creature like that must be like? A whole existence spent praising your God, but always with one wing dipped in blood. Would you ever really want to see an angel?" This point is reinforced later in a scene featuring the film's villain, the archangel Gabriel, played to the hilt by Christopher Walken in a memorably creepy performance. In a brief speech that distantly but definitely recalls Yahweh's upbraiding of Job, Gabriel describes his own nature to a horrified human who has dared to question him: "I'm an angel. I kill first-borns while their mamas watch. I turn cities into salt. I even, when I feel like it, rip the souls from little girls. And from now till kingdom come, the only thing you can count on in your existence is never understanding why."

The Prophecy spawned sequels—three of them at the time of this writing—that became progressively more mired in their own "cool factor." It seems the temptation to use Widen's ideas simply as an excuse for presenting attractive actors running around and fighting each other against a backdrop of shadowy, Gothic imagery and choral music was too much for lesser filmmakers to resist. The third installment in the series, which came two years after the stupendous success of *The Matrix* (1998), even featured some *Matrix*-type wire fu. But even in these progressively degenerated outings, the power of Widen's original concept, and thus the power of the iconic Nightmare Angel, occasionally shone through.

This was especially visible in *The Prophecy II* (1998), which surprised by providing the single most powerful visual depiction of an Angel and its emotional impact in modern American cinema. Presaging the scene, a young woman encounters a man who is actually an angel, and his first words to her echo the words spoken so often by biblical angels when they make an appearance to affrighted humans: "Don't be afraid." Later, she doubts him when he tells her of his true identity. The scene takes place in a cathedral, and the film depicts the angel's self-unveiling via its shadow projected on the wall and on the woman herself: enormous wings unfurl from his back, and his stature increases. The woman's reaction is the quintessence of angelic dread: her eyes widen in an expression of mingled wonder and terror, her hand rises to her mouth, and then her head drops as she falls to the floor sobbing, unable to bear the sight any longer. It is major moment in the Angel's sojourn through supernatural horror.

A 1998 episode of *The X-Files* titled "All Souls" helped draw further attention to the now-reawakened Nightmare by looking even further back into history, to the period before the iconic Angel had been finalized, and drawing upon the Jewish seraphim. A seraph is actually depicted in the episode—although its visual appearance is more related to descriptions of the cherubim—and serves as a source of horror with its multiple wings and four faces (human, lion, bull, eagle), imagery drawn from the biblical Book of Ezekiel.

The year 1998 also saw the release of director Gregory Hoblit's *Fallen,* which likewise contributed to the modern revival of the Angel's fearsomeness. The film is structured as a police procedural thriller in which two detectives try to fathom how someone can be murdering people in the exact mode of a notorious serial killer who was recently executed. As it turns out, the original killer was possessed by the angel Azazel, who migrated to another body after the killer's death. The police procedural aspect of the film is thus paralleled by a spiritual one, in which the head detective on the case moves from skepticism to belief in Azazel and the world of angels, and then tries to figure out how such a being can be stopped when, as quickly becomes apparent, Azazel can migrate instantaneously from person to person through the simple medium of physical touch, temporarily displacing the human personality and assuming control of the body. A character in *Fallen* offers the protagonist a succinct statement of the film's central angelology, which, to those who are aware of the cultural backgrounds traced in this essay, makes an obvious play on the daimonic origins of both the Angel and the Demon while couching the whole in a quasi-orthodox Christian theological framework: "There are certain phenomena which can only be explained if there is a God and if there are angels. And there are. They exist. Some of these angels were cast down, and a few of the fallen were punished by being deprived of form. They can only survive in the bodies of others. It's inside of us, inside of human beings, that their vengeance is played out."

Although *Fallen* could easily have been discussed in the section of this essay dealing with the Demon, its inclusion here seems appropriate given the angelic emphasis of the above comments. However, if we consider the film's Azazel as a demon, then it is clear that the film emphasizes both the iconic Demon's fallen angel aspect and its possession aspect. Azazel is familiar from The First Book of Enoch, *Paradise Lost,* and a host of other literary and occult works from history. Its inclusion in *Fallen* is only one of many reasons why the film's relative lack of impact among critics and audiences is unfortunate. *Fallen* is a significant work that will perhaps one day be valued for its merits.

VII. Conclusion: The Daimonic Zeitgeist from 1971 to the Twenty-First Century and Beyond

In 1999 the Roman Catholic Church revised its exorcism rite to bring it more into line with modern knowledge about mental illness. In 2000 reports surfaced of Pope John Paul II's involvement in the exorcism of a demon from a young girl. Both events occurred on the heels of the North American angel craze. Obviously, something had changed in the thirty years since William Peter Blatty had seen in the Maryland possession case an opportunity to write an apologetic in fictional form that would address the rising secularist tide in America. When he conceived and wrote *The Exorcist,* he could not have known that America was on the verge of a revival of religious sentiment that would rival the various Great Awakenings of its national history.

By the dawn of the twenty-first century, Christianity had not only survived but thrived, and not always in traditional ways. There had long been a modest segment of the publishing world devoted to selling "Christian fiction," but nothing had ever approached the popularity of the Left Behind series of apocalyptic fundamentalist Protestant novels by Tim LaHaye and Jerry Jenkins, which were selling hundreds of millions of copies and may even have been influencing U.S. policy decisions via the influence of their literalistic Christian eschatology on the thinking of President George W. Bush, himself a conservative Christian. Victoria Nelson has argued that "in certain ways popular entertainments more than high art act as a kind of a modern sub-Zeitgeist that is constantly engaging in a low-level discourse on intellectually forbidden subjects—philosophy's disavowed avant-garde, as it were" (18). This would imply that if one wants to find out what is currently being rejected by a culture's dominant, respectable, above-board philosophy, one should look to that culture's popular entertainments.

That is what the bulk of this essay has been devoted to doing. The proliferating popular Demonology and now Angelology of modern culture would seem to bear out the rest of Nelson's assertion, alluded to in this essay's introduction:

> Because the religious impulse is profoundly unacceptable to the dominant Western intellectual culture, it has been obliged to sneak in this back door, where our guard is down. Thus our true contemporary secular pantheon of unacknowledged deities resides in mass entertainments, and it is a demonology, ranging from the "serial killers" in various embodied and disembodied forms to vampires and werewolves and a stereotypical Devil. (18)

Not to mention an iconic Angel and Demon, sculpted into recognizable archetypes over the course of millennia and now active not only in popular books and movies but also in music, computer games, and elsewhere. Armed with a knowledge of the origin, history, and deep nature of these two icons of supernatural horror, the modern reader can better understand, appreciate, and enjoy them in their frequent appearances.

What's more, this ability may have wider implications. The introduction to this essay stated that Blatty's *The Exorcist* is purely a work of fiction, while *Paradise Lost* and the *Inferno* are partly devotional literature. In light of the manifest trajectory of Western cultural and pop cultural history from 1971 to the early years of the twenty-first century—a trajectory that amply confirms Nelson's observation about the modern West's demonological (or daimonological) sub-Zeitgeist—a hard distinction between fiction and religion now seems difficult to maintain. Amid this stew of repressed religious motivations, it is possible that the books, films, and other works that constitute the supernatural horror genre may serve as serious religious texts in their own right. It remains for the future to reveal how narrow the gap will become between fictive enjoyment and real-world conviction, and how much the deep meanings of the Angel and the Demon may continue to contribute to the modern individual's psychological and spiritual self-understanding.

2006

Works Cited

Barrow, R. H. *Plutarch and His Times*. Bloomington, IN: Indiana University Press, 1967.

Bonin, Liane. "Devil's Advocate." *The Exorcist Tribute Zone*. Accessed 15 April 2006. www.the-exorcist.co.uk/Devil.htm. Originally published at *Entertainment Weekly Online*, 9 November 1999.

Comstock, Chester. "Angel Images in Art History: An Angelic Journey through Time." *ARTsales.com.* 2003. Accessed 25 April 2006. www.artsales. com/ARTistory/angelic_journey/index.html. Also published in *Sculptural Pursuit* (Spring 2003).

Diamond, Stephen A. *Anger, Madness, and the Daimonic: The Psychological Genesis of Violence, Evil, and Creativity.* Albany: State University of New York Press, 1996.

Dietrich, B. C. *Tradition in the Greek Religion.* Berlin: Walter de Gruyter, 1986.

Dodds, E. R. *The Greeks and the Irrational.* Berkeley: University of California Press, 1959.

————. *Pagan and Christian in an Age of Anxiety: Some Aspects of Religious Experience from Marcus Aurelius to Constantine.* Cambridge: Cambridge University Press, 1965.

Edmundson, Mark. *Nightmare on Main Street: Angels, Sadomasochism, and the Culture of Gothic.* Cambridge, MA: Harvard University Press, 1997.

Ellison, Harlan. "The Whimper of Whipped Dogs." In David G. Hartwell, ed. *The Dark Descent.* New York: Tor, 1987. 118–31.

The Encyclopedia Americana, s.v. "Angel" and "Demonology." International ed. 1996.

Fallen. Gregory Hobbit, dir. 1998. Turner Home Entertainment, 1998. DVD.

Golden, Christopher, Stephen R. Bissette, and Thomas E. Sniegoski. *The Monster Book.* New York: Pocket Books, 2000.

Gray, John. *Near Eastern Mythology.* Rev. ed. New York: Peter Bedrick Books, 1985.

Hahn, Emily, and Barton Lidice Beneš. *Breath of God: A Book about Angels, Demons, Familiars, Elementals, and Spirits.* Garden City, NY: Doubleday, 1971.

Hillman, James. *The Soul's Code: In Search of Character and Calling.* New York: Random House, 1996.

Hirsch, Edward. *The Demon and the Angel: Searching for the Source of Artistic Inspiration.* Orlando, FL: Harcourt, 2002.

Hirsch, Emile G.; Gottheil, Richard; Kohler, Kaufmann; and Broydé, Isaac. "Demonology." *Jewish Encyclopedia.* Accessed 15 April 2006. www.jewish encyclopedia.com/view.jsp?artid=245&letter=D. Originally published in *Jewish Encyclopedia,* 12 vols., 1901–06.

Isaacs, Ronald H. *Ascending Jacob's Ladder: Jewish Views of Angels, Demons, and Evil Spirits.* Northvale, NJ: Jason Aronson, 1998.

Keene, Brian. *The Rising.* North Webster, IN: Delirium Books, 2003.

Lewis, C. S. *The Screwtape Letters*. 1942. New York: Simon & Schuster, 1996.

Ligotti, Thomas. *Noctuary*. New York: Carroll & Graf, 1994.

May, Rollo. *Love and Will*. New York: W. W. Norton, 1969.

Nelson, Victoria. *The Secret Life of Puppets*. Cambridge, MA: Harvard University Press, 2001.

Nickell, Joe. *Entities: Angels, Spirits, Demons, and Other Beings*. Amherst, NY: Prometheus Books, 1995.

O'Connor, John J. "Critic's Notebook: TV's Infatuation with the Mystical." *New York Times*. 30 June 1994. www.nytimes.com/1994/06/30/arts/critic-s-notebook-tv-s-infatuation-with-the-mystical.html.

Paul VI, Pope. "Confronting the Devil's Power." Address to a General Audience, 15 November 1972. Accessed 15 April 2006. www.ewtn.com/catholicism/library/confronting-the-devils-power-8986.

Peretti, Frank E. *This Present Darkness*. Wheaton, IL: Crossway Books, 1986.

The Prophecy. Gregory Widen, dir. 1995. Dimension Home Video, 1999. DVD.

Rice, Anne. *Servant of the Bones*. New York: Alfred A. Knopf, 1996.

Trimpi, Helen P. "Demonology." In Philip P. Wiener, ed. *The Dictionary of the History of Ideas*. New York: Charles Scribner's Sons, 1973–74. 4 vols. Online at etext.virginia.edu/cgi-local/ DHI/dhi.cgi?id=dv1-79. Accessed 22 April 2006.

———. "Witchcraft." In Philip P. Wiener, ed. *The Dictionary of the History of Ideas*. New York: Charles Scribner's Sons, 1973–74. 4 vols. Online at etext.virginia.edu/cgi-local/DHI/dhi.cgi?id=dv4-71#. Accessed 22 April 2006.

Wallis, R. T. *Neoplatonism*. London: Duckworth, 1972.

Walter, E. V. "Demons and Disenchantment." In Alan M. Olson, ed. *Disguises of the Demonic*. New York: Association Press, 1975. 17–30.

Whitehead, John W. "Who's Afraid of the Exorcist?" *Gadfly Online*. October 1998. Accessed 7 March 2006. www.gadflyonline.com/home/archive/October98/archive-exorcist.html

Wise, Herbert A., and Phyllis Fraser, ed. *Great Tales of Terror and the Supernatural*. New York: Modern Library, 1944.

Wishmaster. Robert Kurtzman, dir. 1997. Live Entertainment, 1998. DVD.

Zucker, Wolfgang M. "The Demonic: From Aeschylus to Tillich." *Theology Today* 6, No. 1 (April 1969): 34–50.

Works Consulted

Allen, Thomas B. *Possessed: The True Story of an Exorcism.* New York: Bantam Books, 1994.

Buckland, Raymond. *The Witch Book: The Encyclopedia of Witchcraft, Wicca, and Neo-paganism.* Canton, MI: Visible Ink Press, 2002.

Davies, T. Witton. *Magic, Divination, and Demonolatry among the Hebrews and Their Neighbors.* New York: KTAV Publishing House, 1969.

Guiley, Rosemary Ellen. *Harper's Encyclopedia of Mystical and Paranormal Experience.* Edison, NJ: Castle Books, 1991.

———. *The Encyclopedia of Witches & Witchcraft.* 2nd ed. New York: Facts on File, 1999.

Harpur, Patrick. *Daimonic Reality: A Field Guide to the Otherworld.* Ravensdale, WA: Pine Winds Press, 2003.

Mäyrä, Frans Ilkka. *Demonic Texts and Textual Demons: The Demonic Tradition, the Self, and Popular Fiction.* Tampere, Finland: Tampere University Press, 1999.

Nataf, André. *Dictionary of the Occult.* Ware, UK: Wordsworth Editions, 1994.

Price, Robert. "Demons." In S. T. Joshi and Stefan Dziemianowicz, ed. *Supernatural Literature of the World: An Encyclopedia.* Westport, CT: Greenwood Press, 2005.

Rosenberg, Donna. *World Mythology: An Anthology of the Great Myths and Epics.* Lincolnwood, IL: National Textbook Co., 1989.

Stableford, Brian. "Angels." In by S. T. Joshi and Stefan Dziemianowicz, ed. *Supernatural Literature of the World: An Encyclopedia.* Westport, CT: Greenwood Press, 2005.

Loathsome Objects:
George Romero's Living Dead Films as Contemplative Tools

[Note: I wrote this paper in 1999 and then revisited, revised, and updated itin 2002–2003, when Romero had made only three Living Dead films and appeared highly unlikely to make any more, despite long rumors of a fourth one in development. Ironically, that fourth one appeared only a few years later—a full twenty years after the third—and was quickly followed by two more quasi-sequels. I've given absolutely no thought to how these later films might impact my argument and exploration of the Romero zombie universe in this essay, but I suspect they wouldn't alter it or add to it in any substantial way.]

When it came to close-up, hard-focus revulsion, nothing could beat the movies.
—Theodore Roszak, *Flicker*

Approaching death and death itself, the dissolution of the physical form, is always a great opportunity for spiritual realization.
—Eckhart Tolle, *The Power of Now*

Remember death; think much of death; think how it will be on a death bed.
—"Commonplace Book of Joseph Green," 1696

I. Introduction: Night of the Living Critics

Most critical analyses of director George Romero's celebrated zombie trilogy—*Night of the Living Dead* (1968), *Dawn of the Dead* (1978), and *Day of the*

Dead (1985)—have focused, quite rightly, on the subtext of social criticism that winds its way through the series. Film scholar Gregory Waller, for example, has said of *Night of the Living Dead* that it "offers a thoroughgoing critique of American institutions and values. It depicts the failure of the nuclear family, the private home, the teenage couple, and the resourceful individual hero; and it reveals the flaws inherent in the media, local and federal government agencies, and the entire mechanism of civil defense" ("Introduction" 258). J. Hoberman and Jonathan Rosenbaum call it "a brilliant, open-ended metaphor for topical anxieties" and describe it as "not only an instant horror classic, but a remarkable vision of the late sixties—offering the most literal possible depiction of America devouring itself" (125). Of the second film, critics have universally observed that it represents a satire on the rampant consumerist greed of 1970s America. One reviewer went to far as to praise it as "a thoughtful social commentary that may be deservingly compared to *Taxi Driver*" (Taylor). As for *Day of the Dead,* Robin Wood identifies its central metaphor as the idea that "science and militarism [are] male-dominated, masculinist institutions threatening to destroy life on the planet" ("What Lies Beneath?"). Examples of sociocritical readings and analyses of these films could be multiplied almost indefinitely. Even a Unitarian Universalist preacher has gotten in on the act by referencing these movies in a sermon (see Erhardt)—not to join the chorus of preachers who condemn horror movies, but to enlist Romero's aid in criticizing the rampant real-life violence endemic to Western culture at the turn of the third millennium.

In keeping with contemporary academia's emphasis on methodological multivalence, I do not intend to argue against or detract from this body of work.[1] Rather, I intend to shift the focus a bit and concentrate on a less well-

---

1. It would, however, be tempting to do so. "Romero and his backers," write Hoberman and Rosenbaum, "have often remarked that [*Night of the Living Dead's*] social implications weren't consciously sought after, but were discovered only by later critics" (124). Journalist and film critic Tom Mes remarks that "*Night* has been analyzed to the point of dissection by film critics, resulting in the 'discovery' of the most ridiculous and far-fetched subtexts. People have read meaning into the film's use of black and white, the grainy look of the film stock (an accident because the lab had to switch to cheaper stock), the use of effects and the anonymous masses of the zombies." The real reasons for so many of the movie's "brilliant innovations," says Mes, were simply budget constraints. (The story reminds one of Orson Welles's and cinematographer Greg Toland's legendary cinematic-artistic innovations in *Citizen Kane,* which were likewise driven to a significant extent by budget considerations.) In the case of casting Duane Jones, a black actor, in the lead role of

explored aspect of Romero's famous trilogy, namely, its spiritual aspect. But I will explore this by way of and in tandem with an examination of its high gore content. In a nutshell, I will argue that the viewer who chooses to do so may use the promptings toward body horror and spiritual horror presented by the Living Dead films as tools for exploring a particular existential spiritual understanding, one that recognizes in the mortality of flesh and the ego-self a revelation of the indestructible center of inviolable awareness that constitutes each person's most fundamental identity. The net result will be to establish that Romero's zombie trilogy can be seen and used as a tool to enhance the clarity of non-dual spiritual realization.[2]

The paper's first three parts tackle the gore issue. In the first of them, I explore the gory violence that is widely recognized as the visual hallmark of the modern horror film in general, and I consider the ways in which these films generate a sense of horror through their portrayal of a body that defies conscious control. In fleshing out this idea, I refer to Julia Kristeva's theory of the abject and discuss the ways in which cinematic assaults on the body's integrity attack the human sense of personal identity. In parts two and three, I focus specifically on Romero's zombie films in order to demonstrate how they attack the viewer's sense of a stable identity and thus generate horror through their portrayal of animated corpses—which are, after all, *bodies* of a particular type—and especially through their characterization of these corpses as cannibals, as bodies that eat other bodies of the same kind. With help from food theory as established by Roland Barthes, Anna Meigs, and others, I contend that cannibalism destabilizes one's sense of identity by presenting a literalistic metaphor of the self becoming the other, and also by reducing the body with its generally stable form and healthy integrity to a mass of disconnected tissues and organs.

Ben (on which also see Hoberman and Rosenbaum), the decision rested on the fact that Jones was simply the best actor the producers could get with their budget. In other words, race had nothing to do with it. Even when the films' social commentary became overt and intentional, as in *Dawn of the Dead*, some critics insisted on offering patently far-fetched interpretations, such as when Robin Wood read homosexual implications into the relationship between two male characters and claimed the "true nature of the relationship can be tacitly acknowledged only after Roger's death, in the symbolic orgasm of the spurting of a champagne bottle over his grave" (*Hollywood from Vietnam to Reagan* 120).

2. For a book-length exploration of the religious aspects of Romero's zombie films, published several years after I wrote this essay (and approaching the matter from a significantly different angle), see Kim Paffenroth's *Gospel of the Living Dead: George Romero's Visions of Hell on Earth*.

In part four, I turn to an exploration of the spiritual or religious theme that permeates Romero's zombie films alongside the gore. Of particular interest is the fact that this theme receives progressively greater prominence as the trilogy progresses, moving from the muted and implicit spirituality of *Night*, to the brief but direct mention of spiritual matters in *Dawn*, to the full-frontal apocalypticism of *Day*.

In the fifth and sixth parts, I tie together the previous sections' explorations of body horror and apocalyptic spirituality to show how these themes work in tandem to generate a bleak and nihilistic cinematic experience in which the human self is portrayed as a helpless, groundless phantom lost in a vortex of bloody flesh. But more than this, in the paper's final section I argue that instead of inducing utter despair, this emergent realization represents an opportunity for the reader to experience a kind of epiphany regarding his or her selfhood and its relationship to the body.

II. Flesh Becomes Meat: The Perishable Body

"Violent pastimes are nothing new," writes Jonathan Lake Crane, "but there has never been anything quite as violent and massively popular as the contemporary horror film" (1). The truth of this assertion is by now beyond argument. Violence is one of the defining aspects of the contemporary horror film—direct, visceral, vividly portrayed violence. Referring specifically to American horror films of the 1970s—that is, horror films produced in the immediate wake of *Night of the Living Dead*, the film from which the modern era of the genre is commonly dated—Jack Sargeant writes, "These films stand apart from previous generations of horror movies, because of their narrative focus on the bruised and torn flesh of the body as the text on which terror becomes inscribed." There is no longer a looking away as in, to name one famous example, director Tod Browning's *Dracula* (1931), where the eponymous villain's death by stake occurs offscreen. The Hammer horror films of the 1950s gave movie audiences their first glimpse of the stake actually entering the vampire's chest. Since 1968, the chest has been laid open and the viscera exposed for all to see. In the words of Cynthia Freeland,

> It would be hard to discuss the modern horror film without talking about scenes in these films (or their many imitators) of over-the-top, ever-escalating graphic violence and gore (or "FX" [effects] as the fans say). It is common to witness gross bodily dismemberments, piles of internal organs, numerous corpses in stages of decay, headless bodies, knives or chain saws slashing away at flesh, and general orgies of mayhem. In these films, flesh

becomes meat, the inside becomes outside, blood pours out, skin is stripped off, viscera exposed, heads detached. People die in any number of creatively disgusting ways. (242)

One of the most significant subtextual messages conveyed by this gory violence is that our bodies are *fragile* and are thus in constant danger of being injured or corrupted. An important corollary of this recognition, as noted by Anne Jerslev, is that human identity itself is fragile, since the body, which is so fundamental in setting the boundaries of the human sense of self, refuses to retain its integrity. "Generally speaking," Jerslev writes,

> the splatter movie's mutilated body is fragile. Its skin is thin as parchment and thus cannot function as a bodily armour symbolizing and demarcating the subject at the same time. It is a body without firm outlines; on the contrary, it is constantly transforming from one shape into another, as its unreliable innards all of a sudden break through the skin to start a life of their own.

This vivid image of innards assuming "a life of their own" highlights another key aspect of the way the modern horror film serves to disturb its viewers through its depiction of the body: in these films, the body is often *out of control.* In another essay ("Awakening from the Nightmare: The Horror Film as a Tool for Transcendence," published in 2000–2001 at the now-defunct website *Imaginary Worlds*), I have argued that people are horrified by the sight of gore, whether fictional or actual, because we—and by "we" I mean specifically the children of Western culture—are accustomed to regarding our bodies not with an attitude of identity but with an attitude of ownership. In this regard, we would do well to remember what philosopher and cultural critic Theodore Roszak said in *Where the Wasteland Ends* about the "anti-organic fanaticism" of Western culture, by which he meant an ingrained attitude of fastidiousness toward our organic natures that tends to lead Westerners to "cringe from anything as oozy as the inside of our body" (96). Roszak said the body "has become for us an alien object located Out There, the mere receptacle of our true and irrevocable identity. That identity is ultimately felt to reside at a point inside the body . . . inside the head . . . somewhere just behind the eyes and between the ears" (93; Roszak's ellipses). This antiseptic and cozy attitude comes under merciless assault in the modern horror film, which, as Philip Brophy puts it, "tends to play not so much on the broad fear of Death, but more precisely on the fear of one's own body, of how one controls and relates to it" ("Horrality" 280). In the words of Sargeant, "These films emphasize a brutal estrangement envisioned through the loss of control over the body, which becomes both unwitting source and victim to the horror."

Film scholars have been quick to pick up on this fact and have frequently referenced Julia Kristeva's famous theory of abjection to aid in analyzing the horror film. Crane summarizes Kristeva as follows: "The abject are those objects, oftentimes bodily detritus, that desecrate our narcissistic mirage of self by effacing the boundary between myself and that which is not 'I.' The abject provides proof that our idealized portraits of pristine flesh and whole egos are, unfortunately, nothing more than brittle fantasies" (30).

Roszak, in a perceptive comment on the types of things that tend to horrify us, lists a number of elements that commonly play into discussions of abjection (although he does not use that term):

> Consider for a moment: since we were children, what have we been taught to regard as the quintessential image of loathing and disgust? What is it our horror literature and science fiction haul in whenever they seek to make our skin crawl? Anything alive, mindless, and gooey . . . anything sloppy, slobbering, liquescent, smelly, slimy, gurgling, putrescent, mushy, grubby . . . things amoeboid or fungoid that stick and cling, that creep and seep and grow . . . things that have the feel or spit or shit, snot or piss, sweat or pus or blood . . . In a word, anything *organic*, and as messy as birth, death, and decay. (96; Roszak's emphasis and ellipses)

It is, then, our very organicity, the fact of our fleshly existence, that horrifies us, for this carnal part of us lies outside our ability to manage or control and thus reminds us that we are not exclusively ethereal egos ensconced in positions of invulnerability and dominion. Our bodies in their entirety therefore constitute one of the major instances of the abject.

The modern horror film excels at playing upon this horror reaction. Jerslev goes so far as to say that all such films may be understood as different representations of "the fantasy of abjection":

> The abundance of fragmented bodies in the new horror film and the flow of filth issuing from the body's inner parts in images of blood and bowels, of the dissolution of differences between the subject and object— represented, for example, in the often occurring theme of cannibalism in the genre—of the dissolution of differences between inside and outside represented by an abundance of symbolizations of the womb; all these genre defining, or splatter film subgenre defining, images can be understood as different representations of the fantasy of abjection. This is one of the reasons, I will contend, why these films are so sickening and yet so fascinating. Because signifiers of abjection affect a basic condition of subjectivity, the

complicated, profoundly ambiguous experience of a yearning for, and yet the dread of, fusion as well as separation.

In view of our ultimate topic here, which, to recall, is a spiritual reading of Romero's zombie trilogy, it is of no small importance that Kristeva identifies the ultimate object of abjection as the *corpse*. The corpse, she emphasizes, is a body without a soul, i.e., a body with the entire contents of the personal identity emptied out. In contrast to the "normal" state of things in which the ego constantly "casts off" unwanted products, both mental and physical, in order to retain its sense of walled-in security, for a corpse it is the ego itself that has been cast off. In Kristeva's clever formulation, "It is no longer I who expel. 'I' is expelled" (4). Film scholar Barbara Creed picks up on this when she points out that "the horror film abounds in images of abjection, foremost of which is the corpse, whole and mutilated, followed by an array of bodily wastes such as blood, vomit, saliva, sweat, tears and putrefying flesh" (66). Jerslev becomes even more specific when she points out that in Romero's zombie films, the disgusting appearances of the zombies, combined with their cannibalistic appetites, "are . . . nauseating because they insistently *construct the entire body as an abject*. Thus they point toward subjectivity as a fragile illusion" (emphasis in original).

It is here that we may narrow our focus and turn toward the specific figure of the zombie, and more specifically toward the zombie as portrayed by Romero. For the zombie in Romero's Living Dead films is nothing more nor less than an animated, shambling corpse that roams the world seeking to devour the flesh of the living. As such, it assaults the viewer's sense of integrity as a stable subject in the most shocking possible fashion by presenting a literal embodiment of corpse-horror.

III. The Dead Walk

The general plot of the Living Dead films is pretty much universal public knowledge at this point, but the details are worth recounting. In the first film, *Night of the Living Dead,* for reasons that ultimately remain obscure, the bodies of the recently deceased begin to come to life and lumber through the countryside of the eastern United States in search of warm human flesh to devour. To make matters worse, the condition is communicable: if someone is bitten by a zombie and remains sufficiently intact to be mobile, he or she will soon rise to become one of them. The majority of the plot centers around seven people who barricade themselves inside a rural farmhouse and try to ride out the crisis during a single night of horror. In the end, they all die—the last of them, ironically, from a bullet shot by a sheriff's deputy who mistakes this final survivor for one of the zombies.

Dawn of the Dead follows a similar plotline but moves the story further ahead in the timeline of the zombie apocalypse. The societal order that seemed to have been restored at the end of the first film is now nowhere apparent. SWAT teams battle zombies in low-income tenements while drunken rednecks with rifles pick off zombies in open fields for the sheer fun of it; in the background, television pundits argue over the meaning of and proper response to the crisis. The action centers on four people—two SWAT team members, a helicopter pilot, and a television station employee—who escape from the chaos in a helicopter and hole up in an abandoned shopping mall, where they wall themselves off and revel in a kind of consumerist paradise while the zombies shuffle forlornly around the other parts of the mall. The film concludes with a marauding gang of bikers putting an end to this dubious idyll, after which only two of the main characters escape alive (again via the helicopter), the other two having succumbed to the zombie plague.

Day of the Dead takes place still further into this imagined future, at a time when, as far as the characters and the viewer can tell, only a dozen humans are left alive. These unhappy survivors reside in an underground military bunker where three of them—scientists—spend their time conducting experiments on the zombies to see if there is any way to reverse the zombification process or domesticate those who have already succumbed. The other survivors consist of a helicopter pilot, a radio operator, and several soldiers. As in the first two films, the human characters spend most of their time arguing and even physically threatening one another (thus raising the question of whether the human race is morally superior to the zombies) while the zombies press inward, both literally and figuratively, at the perimeter of their world. It ends with nearly everybody dying in spectacularly violent ways, some at the hands of their fellow humans, others at the hands (and in the jaws) of the zombies, which eventually overrun the compound. Only three of them—a scientist, the pilot, and the radio operator—escape the carnage by flying away to a tropical island where they will presumably spend the rest of their days enjoying perpetual safety, sunlight, and solitude.

One notices immediately that all the major elements of body horror are featured prominently in these films. Consider, for instance, the issue of bodily control. S. S. Prawer has described the zombie or living dead motif as being founded on "the fear that when the brain has ceased to function and the heart has ceased to beat, the tissues of the body might still be able to go on performing purposive and destructive actions" (75). In keeping with this,

Mikita Brottman places a loss of bodily control at the top of the list of taboos whose violation creates a sense of horror in *Night of the Living Dead:*

> The first taboo to be broken is that of bodily control. The zombies stumble and drool in their clumsy quest for human flesh, often with intestines spilling out or broken limbs dangling. Brains splatter against the walls; zombies collapse groaning to the ground. The human body—even your own body—is out of control, and you're no longer able to understand or relate to it.

Sargeant points out that Romero zeroes in on this fear by showing the breakage that occurs in relationships when someone becomes a zombie: "The zombies were once friends and relatives. In each of Romero's zombie films there is a sequence in which one of the protagonists undergoes the zombification process." In other words, anyone, even your dearest loved ones—even you—may be transformed into one of these flesh-eating monsters despite all possible exertions of willpower to resist it. The prospect is disturbing and provocative, and is made even more so by the fact that the motif of rebellious bodies moves on to newer heights of fancy as the trilogy, not to mention the zombie subgenre in general, progresses. Robert Hood, writing about Romero's seminal influence on the cinematic portrayal of zombies, notes a direct link between Romero's innovations and the common motif in later zombie movies of individual body parts retaining animation. "In the end," he says, "even bits of zombies—arms, heads and, in the case of [director Peter] Jackson's *Braindead,* stomach and intestines—are able to maintain a 'life' of their own. This is the human body—our material being—engaging in a sheer act of rebellion."

Rose London has written that the zombie "represents our ancient fear that a necromancer will resurrect our body for his purposes" (98). In commenting on London's assertion, Prawer notes that "gifted film-makers have been able to use the conventions [of the horror film] as a kind of grid against which to draw their own rather different picture—as something to be at once alluded to and subverted" (69). Thus it is that Romero, who is definitely a gifted filmmaker, compounds and alters the conventional horror of zombies by instead representing his version as being essentially purposeless and free-roaming. "In Romero's film," writes Prawer, "the dead have no zombie-master to direct them, and they are raised, not by voodoo, but rather by an (unexplained) scientific accident" (68). Tom Mes amplifies:

> In all previous films dealing with zombies, these creatures had been innocent people, revived and controlled by their powerful master to do his evil bidding. More often than not, the zombies were actually used not as weap-

ons but as a work force, providing cheap labour for a rich tycoon. . . . This was the blueprint on which these films were based, finding its source in voodoo mythology. *Night of the Living Dead* dispensed with all of this. In a radical break with tradition, and seeing the full potential of using living dead in a horror film, Romero made zombies pure evil, out to eat the flesh of the living and controlled by nothing but their own instinct.

Romero's zombies are thus true corpses, empty shells, simply the reanimated dead, and not tools being used for some outside purpose. As such, they assault the viewer's sense of identity by presenting him or her with the threatening sight of that "ultimate in abjection." "The first vision of death is physical," says an article at Monstrous.com, an online resource devoted to cataloguing information about monsters of all kinds. "Therefore, to confront a zombie is to be reminded of our own mortality. . . . The zombie is the embodiment of the insatiable tyranny of mortality, its rotting face and shuffling implacability represents [*sic*] a potent symbol for the horror of death" ("Zombie Symbolism"). R. H. W. Dillard offers a classic analysis of *Night of the Living Dead* in his book *Horror Films,* where he reminds the reader of the ancient "fear of the dead and particularly of the known dead, of dead kindred." He quotes a passage from Anthony Masters's *The Natural History of the Vampire* that speaks of the meticulous rituals that have traditionally surrounded the burial, as well as the warding off, of the recently dead, and he claims that Romero's film "is almost a reenactment of these rituals in reverse. The unburied recent dead stalk the landscape seeking the flesh of the living. . . . The ancient fear is unleashed on the characters in the film and on the audience with a force that only savage violence can repel" (57, 58). In a bit of poetic symmetry that reverses Dillard's point about the effect of these films but still highlights the corpse horror they embody, Bryan Stone writes that the "assaults on the human body heralded by George Romero's *Night of the Living Dead* . . . provide the new body language, the iconography, the communal rituals, if you will, for disposing of bodies that had been quietly kept out of sight, removed hygienically from the public eye, whose decaying flesh had been covered with leftover sacred deodorants but never buried." Whichever way one views the living dead trilogy—as representing a reversal of traditional corpse-burial rituals or as a new symbolic version of them—the fact remains that the films confront the viewer with the sight of the corpse, the ultimate abject, the empty shell of the body, returning to animation (but not to life in the commonly accepted sense) and behaving in overtly menacing ways.

This brings us to yet another of Romero's innovations: Not only did he confront audiences with animated corpses, but he introduced another motif into the zombie film by presenting his zombies as cannibals, and it is this, even more than those confrontational corpses, that plays masterfully upon the primal fear of losing one's identity.

IV. The Dead Eat

In the modern horror film, said Cynthia Freeland, "flesh becomes meat." Nowhere is this more literally the case than in films about cannibalism. Film critic Lew Brighton even referred to *Night of the Living Dead* and its progeny, such as *The Texas Chainsaw Massacre*—another horror film dealing with cannibalism—as "meat movies" (cited in Dillard 57). Walter Kendrick has remarked that the financial success of *Night of the Living Dead* "seemed to mark a turning point in horror by displaying not only severed limbs and spilled innards, but also cannibal zombies munching them" (250). By 1968, zombies were already an established presence in the world of the horror film. Indeed, as Hood notes, "Cinematic animated corpses have been a source of fascination ever since the earliest days of film," with movies such as *White Zombie* (1932) and *I Walked with a Zombie* (1943) now generally regarded as classics. But in the words of Mikita Brottman, "What's special about Romero's zombies . . . is their cannibalistic appetite. Romero is almost entirely responsible for the now-familiar incarnation of the zombie as ghoulish cannibal, as bloodthirsty anthropophage who adds to his numbers by feeding on living human flesh."

The significance of this fact for the argument at hand emerges when we pause to consider the act of eating itself, and to acknowledge that food of any kind serves more than just a nutritional function. Roland Barthes, in his essay "Toward a Psychosociology of Contemporary Food Consumption," asks the question, "What is food?" He answers that in addition to being "a collection of products that can be used for statistical or nutritional studies," food "is also, and at the same time, a system of communication, a body of images, a protocol of usages, situations, and behavior. . . . [F]ood sums up and transmits a situation; it constitutes an information; it signifies. . . . One could say that an entire 'world' (social environment) is present in and signified by food" (21, 23). In other words, food is a cultural sign, a system of communication, and the act of choosing and eating certain foods, as well as the *manner* in which ones chooses and eats them, expresses values and meanings. We may thus ask ourselves: what is the meaning or message expressed by the act of cannibalism?

An answer comes from synthesizing the ideas of three separate authors.

First, we see that anthropologist Anna Meigs has called attention to what is perhaps the most unique aspect of food: "Food has a distinctive feature, one that sets it off from the rest of material culture: it is ingested, it is eaten, it goes inside." Moreover, food's social nature—the fact that it is commonly prepared by one person for another to eat—makes it "a particularly apt vehicle for symbolizing and expressing ideas about the relationship of self and other" (105–5).

Next, we may recall Jerslev's contention that "the dissolution of differences between the subject and object . . . between inside and outside" is frequently represented in the horror genre via the motif of cannibalism. Jerslev expands this point by asserting that cannibalism "signifies the ultimate dissolution of even the mere thought of distinguishing between the body's interior and exterior. Cannibalism denies the skin of the other as a border; it disorganizes distinctions, and the differences separating 'I' from 'you.'"

Finally, we consider Anne Marie Oleson combination of Meigs's and Jerslev's positions, which gives a definitive statement to the matter:

> The question of the boundary between the One and the Other is raised with eating and with the meal. Eating presupposes a clear distinction between the subject eating and the object being eaten, but the *act* of eating abolishes the distinction. The subject incorporates the object, the object stays in the subject and mixes with it, thereby obliterating the subject/object distinction.
>
> Food and meals in art can basically be seen as metaphors for drawing and crossing boundaries. So can cannibalism. But cannibalism makes a difference. Taking part in a meal means eating *of* the same but not *the* same, and in particular—not eating one another. You do not eat the person you are eating with. . . .
>
> I believe that cannibalism . . . theorize[s] that the boundary between the "inside" and the "outside," between the One and the Other, is not stable, not natural, not "God-given," and that—in a conceptual sense—it never has been. (Oleson's emphases)

The meaning of cannibalism as a cultural sign is thus apparent: cannibalism signifies the fragility of the self, its permeability and susceptibility to being fused with the other. It is a potent metaphor for the breakdown of the stable subject, for it shows the subject, as represented by its externalized manifestation in the physical body, being consumed by another of the same kind.

Oleson also points out a further fact that assumes great importance in our current investigation: "It is natural to eat but it is civilized (or cultural) to take part in a meal, because in the process you refrain from eating one another. Thus cannibalism metaphorizes the breakdown of civilization, the dissolution of culture into nature." Romero explicitly works this theme into his trilogy by framing his zombies as representations of the human animal reduced to its most primal level. These creatures, as he repeatedly tells us through the dialogue he puts in the mouths of his characters, are simply human beings, minus all the cultural and civilized trappings.

The picture that emerges from such a portrayal is not pretty. Waller calls Romero's zombies "diseased, instinct-driven automatons" and contrasts them with another undead creature, the suave and cultured Dracula. In doing so, he finds zombies all the more horrible for their animal-like behavior. "The major distinction," he writes,

> between the living dead and the vampires . . . is, of course, the fact that the creatures in *Night of the Living Dead* eat warm human flesh, a fact that Romero graphically records and never allows us to forget. The feeding habits of the living dead have nothing in common with the sexually charged, mutually pleasurable act of bloodsucking. . . . Romero's living dead tear at their food and devour it like starving animals to whom all of existence is only a matter of hunting food and eating. (*The Living and the Unead* 280, 276)

Romero's zombies, then, eat for no purpose. They eat simply to eat. Jerslev contrasts the ideas of anthropologist Peggy Reeves Sanday, who detects a religious, cosmogonic purpose in ritual tribal cannibalism, with Romero's portrayal of the act, and draws a grim conclusion:

> With Romero, the zombies are not just primitive cannibals: they are inhuman, cannibalistic machines. . . . Contrary to Sanday's interpretation of cannibalism one cannot say that there is a religious subtext to the zombies' cannibalism, that flesh thus transforms into spirit, or that the cannibalistic incorporation aims at preserving the souls and the power of the dead. One cannot talk about regeneration or cannibalism symbolizing the drama of constituting subjectivity. In Romero's zombie trilogy there is, contrary to Sanday's conceptualization of cannibalism, only excessive gluttony controlled by nothing but pure instinct. Thus, the zombies represent the human reduced to mere bestiality.

That this idea is borne out in the actual films themselves is easy to verify. In *Dawn of the Dead*, in a famous line of dialogue, a commentator on television describes the zombies as "pure, motorized instinct." Another frustrated commentator says, "They kill for one reason: they kill for food. They *eat* their victims. . . . That's what keeps them going." But in fact, as we discover in *Day of the Dead*—the last and by far the most reflective of the three films (to the point of talkiness, some would say)—the flesh the zombies consume does *not* keep them going. It apparently does nothing for them at all, other than to satisfy their instinctual urge to consume. In a key scene, Sarah, the scientist who later escapes to the tropical island with her two friends, finds the leader of the scientific team, a researcher named Logan (known more commonly to everyone else, even to his fellow scientists, as "Frankenstein"), working in his laboratory with a zombie strapped to a table. He has opened the creature's abdomen and severed all the vital connections, and yet the creature still retains animation. Moreover, it is still hungry, as Logan demonstrates by placing his hand near its mouth. The creature snaps at Logan's fingers with its teeth, prompting Logan to exclaim to Sarah with excitement, "You see, it *wants* me! It wants food, but it has no stomach. It can take no nourishment from what it ingests. It's working on *instinct*, Sarah—deep, dark, primordial instinct."

Logan then turns to a chalkboard covered with diagrams and labels indicating a study of the human brain, and continues his lecture: "Decomposition occurs first in the frontal lobes, the neo-cortex, and next in the limbic system, the middle brain. But the core, the core is the last thing to be attacked by the decay. It's the R-complex, Sarah, that central bit of prehistoric jelly that we inherited from the reptiles." The obvious implication is that these monsters represent what we humans really are at our most fundamental level, behind our forebrains and beneath our cultural veneers. When stripped to this primal level, we are nothing but murderous, cannibalistic eating machines, and our drive to ingest human flesh is all the more horrific because it is thoroughly pointless.

This identification of the zombies with living humans is first articulated in *Dawn of the Dead* when Fran, one of the lead characters, stands watching the zombies mill around the shopping mall and suddenly feels compelled to ask, "What the hell *are* they?" to which Peter replies matter-of-factly, "They're us, that's all." This theme receives only passing mention in *Dawn,* although it receives significant graphic reinforcement via the scenes of the zombies stumbling through the mall accompanied by the voiceover comments of "experts" on television who make it clear that the zombies are pathetic, low-grade parodies of full human beings. But it comes to the fore in *Day.* Some time after the above-described laboratory scene, *Day* shows another scientist trying to convince one of the captured zombies to eat military-issued "beef treats." The creature refuses, preferring human flesh instead. Logan then appears on the scene and offers the requisite philosophical justification for his attempts to re-enculturate the zombies, claiming that even though they do not eat for nourishment, it is still necessary to satisfy their urge. "You see, Sarah," he says, echoing his earlier point, "*they are us*. They are the extensions of us. They are the same animal, simply functioning less perfectly."

To sum up: the cannibalism in Romero's zombie trilogy attacks the viewer's sense of secure subjecthood in two ways. First, it depicts a literal breach of the barrier between self and other as self *becomes* other by means of physical ingestion. Second, it graphically illustrates the dissolution of culture into nature by framing the zombies as the embodiment of humankind's primitive urges. Dillard states it well when he writes that "the characters in *Night of the Living Dead* [and by extension in the other two films of the trilogy] lose all identity—they become food, or walking dead flesh, or simply fuel for a fire" (112).

There is yet a third way in which the cannibalism motif attacks the viewer's sense of self. By the simple fact of showing the human body broken, torn, and opened up for its insides to be revealed, the cannibalistic violence in the zombie trilogy reduces the body from a sleek and whole object possessing an innate, healthy integrity to a mass of disconnected organs and tissues. Recall Freeland's words: "It is common to witness gross bodily dismemberments, piles of internal organs, numerous corpses in stages of decay, headless bodies, knives or chain saws slashing away at flesh, and general orgies of mayhem. In these films, flesh becomes meat, the inside becomes outside, blood pours out, skin is stripped off, viscera exposed, heads detached" (242). What Freeland is talking about is nothing less than a literal deconstruction of the body into its constituent parts. Jerslev uses the fascinating and appropriate term "organ body" to describe this deconstructed body, and she writes at great length about its nature and meaning. The organ body, she says, is

> a body without skin—metaphorically as well as literally—a non-organized amorphous mass of biological matter without gender distinction, a body that discloses interior substances for which there is, so to speak, nothing exterior. . . . When [the zombies] skin a human being and tear out the bowels, the image frames disclose the gory interior normally hidden beneath the armour of the skin. The killing is not the end in itself, it is a means of getting under the victims' skin. In the scenes where the zombies kill the human beings, Romero is thus staging the idea of the body as disconnected organs and pure soft parts.
>
> [Because late twentieth-century Western culture placed such great emphasis on the body] as the signifier of the well-defined, psychologically delimited, self-conscious subject, then the organ body represents the destruction of this very idea of the subject. The organ body signifies the amorphous, the floating, an abject without boundaries, the place that has turned inside out and is turning subject into object.

In other words, by deconstructing the body, these films deconstruct the subject as well, the personal identity whose perceived nature is inextricably linked to notions of the body's perceived health and wholeness.[3]

In view of a segue to discussing the religious or spiritual dimension of Romero's zombie trilogy, we will do well to note that in Jerslev's opinion, the cannibalism in these films, more than merely reducing human bodies to lumps of organic materials, represents a veritable transformation. "Violence," she writes, "is not an end in itself" in these movies, "but a means of staging metamorphosis. . . . By means of the disgusting images of zombies killing and tearing people apart to eat them, it becomes very clear that the living human beings are nothing but meat to the zombies, and thus they metamorphose in front of our eyes into muscles, bones, and gory intestines." It is significant in this regard that Marina Warner, in an article about the pervasive Western cultural fascination with zombies, says that whereas zombies "used to be primarily victims of voodoo masters," today the word zombie "has become an existential term . . . a deathly modern variation on the age-old theme of metamorphosis." She is speaking about the idea of metamorphosis as a fundamental transformation of the self, as found in, for example, theories and doctrines of soul transmigration. And while she is thinking primarily in sociocritical terms when she mentions *Night of the Living Dead* as a significant movie in this regard, her point is equally applicable to our discussion of the metamorphosis of the human body in the zombie film from an integrated whole into a steaming, bloody pile of disconnected parts.

Brophy, for his part, seems to find something almost religious about this metamorphic portrayal of humanity's visceral organic nature:

> Forget the wonders of modern science and advanced technology—we are more overwhelmed by our very gizzards! The screen body in contemporary horror is thus a true place of physicality: a fountain of fascination, a bounty of bodily contact. If there is any mysticism left in the genre, it is that our own insides constitute a fifth dimension; an unknowable world, an incomprehensible darkness. ("The Body Horrible")

If Brophy is right about the mystical potentialities inherent in the act of contemplating our innards, if he is correct in believing that the interior of the body constitutes a remaining repository of mysticism in the horror genre,

---

3. The fact that it has been common in the West both to define the self according to the image of the body, as Jerslev contends, and also to be horrified by the fact of existing as a body at all, as Roszak has argued, merely highlights the ambiguous relationship between body and self in Western consciousness.

then surely we are justified speculating about the way the gory violence of the horror film interacts with other, more direct expressions of spirituality.

V. "He Visited a Curse on Us": The Spiritual Angle

There are several possible angles from which to investigate the spiritual aspect of the Living Dead trilogy. Of these, a number have been well explored. For instance, there is the widely noted fact that traditional religious values and rituals are portrayed as useless, or even as a positive danger, in *Night of the Living Dead*. For instance, the character of Barbara insists on kneeling in prayer at her father's grave at the start of the film, despite her brother Johnny's cynical impatience. When Johnny is killed by a zombie and Barbara escapes to the nearby farmhouse, it seems that her faith is going to be rewarded and Johnny's impiety punished. But nothing of the sort takes place. "Johnny's suffering," writes Crane, "is very limited when compared to that which Barbara must endure" (12). She spends most of the film locked up in a catatonic stupor, and when she finally emerges from this state near the conclusion to help fight off the zombie horde, she is dragged out of the house to her doom by none other than Johnny, who has returned from the dead to claim her. In the words of Waller, Barbara is "clearly the character who most fully believes in the values of tradition and religion," but her "faith only seems to make her awakening to her dilemma that much more rude and catastrophic" (283).

Night also highlights the fact that traditional emotional attachments to the bodies of dead loved ones must be relinquished in the name of safety. "No, you're right," says a medical doctor when a news anchor points out that cremation, the recommended course of immediate action to take with all dead bodies during the crisis, does not allow time for funerals. "It doesn't give them time to make funeral arrangements. The bodies must be carried to the street and burned. They must be burned immediately. Soak them with gasoline and burn them. The bereaved will just have to forego the dubious comforts that a funeral service will give. They're just dead flesh, and dangerous." As it was with Barbara, so it is here. Dutiful observance of religious rituals will not offer protection, and it may actually lead to harm. The same theme carries over into *Dawn*, where television commentators offer similar warnings to a largely unreceptive audience.

In addition to the trilogy's attack on the efficacy of traditional religious observances, there is the further fact that these films deal explicitly with many of the images of abjection that we studied earlier. Creed observes that "various sub-genres of the horror film seem to correspond to religious categories of abjection" and points out that "cannibalism, a religious abomination, is central to the 'meat' movie," in whose company she names *Night of the Living Dead.* "The corpse as abomination," she writes, "becomes the abject of ghoul and zombie movies" (67).

However, these intertwined themes—images of abjection and the uselessness of traditional religion—are only two possible angles from which the religious or spiritual aspect of the trilogy might be discussed. For my own purposes, I want to take a different tack by focusing specifically on two speeches delivered by two different characters, one in *Dawn* and one in *Day,* that in my view constitute the spiritual heart of all three films. Both speeches offer spiritual interpretations of the meaning of the zombie plague, and they linger in the viewer's memory long after other possible explanations have faded.

It is important to note beforehand that these speeches have such lasting impact largely because the films in the Living Dead series deliberately subvert the various explanations offered by scientists and other authority figures to account for the phenomenon of the dead returning to a semblance of life. In *Night of the Living Dead,* the only explanation offered for the zombie plague is the possible influence of a strange radiation that has accompanied a space probe recently returned from Venus. But this explanation, as Waller notes, is superfluous, since "to assert that 'mysterious radiation' in some unexplained way causes the dead to roam the land in search of human flesh is finally little better than no explanation at all (especially since this is a quasi-official explanation and therefore likely in *Night of the Living Dead* to be a lie, distortion, or cover-up)" (276). Waller's parenthetical comment refers to the fact that in these films, institutionalized authority is invariably portrayed in a dismal light. The sheriff and his men in *Night of the Living Dead* are brutal and incompetent; as mentioned earlier, one of them kills Ben, the protagonist, when he and his posse mistake Ben for a zombie. In *Dawn,* one of the SWAT team members goes on a racist rampage in a Puerto Rican tenement and starts shooting residents indiscriminately. The general manager of a television station insists on keeping an outdated list of rescue stations scrolling across the bottom of the screen because it attracts viewers. In *Day* the military men are all brutal, vulgar, racist, and sexist, and their commander, Captain Rhodes, is a bona fide sociopath. The head of the scientific team, Dr. Logan—"Frankenstein"—is dangerously unbalanced, as we learn when we discover that his re-enculturation experiments on the zombies are motivated primarily by his repressed and pathological hatred for his parents. A lack of trust in official explanations from authority figures is thus well founded within the world of these films, leaving an open door for a more spiritually oriented explanation to recommend itself.

As it turns out, this is exactly what happens. The first character to offer a spiritual explanation is Peter in *Dawn of the Dead*. We might note to begin with that Peter shares the name of one of the biblical apostles, and that Saint Peter himself delivered a brief apocalyptic message in the second of the two New Testament letters attributed to him, and also a famous quasi-apocalyptic speech in the Book of Acts after he and the other apostles had been infused with the Holy Spirit.[4] Appropriately, *Dawn*'s Peter delivers an explanation of the zombie plague that is short, apocalyptic, and to the point. Immediately after telling Fran that the zombies "are us, that's all," he muses, almost to himself, "There's no more room in hell." When Fran's boyfriend, Stephen, asks him what he means, Peter replies, "Something my granddaddy used to tell us. You know Makumba?" When Stephen shakes his head, Peter explains: "Voodoo. Granddad was a priest in Trinidad. He used to tell us, 'When there's no more room in hell, the dead will walk the earth.'"

This line has become a favorite among fans of the film. Although it is brief and receives no further comment, it offers a poetically powerful explanation for the reason behind the zombie plague, and one that obviously goes well beyond hackneyed science fiction explanations such as "radiation from outer space." If we take Peter's statement as a valid account of things, then we find that when we contemplate the zombies lumbering around a shopping mall or tearing a person to pieces or gnawing on human entrails, we are really contemplating the physical reality of hell itself. The zombies are hell's overflow; they are bringing hell itself to earth. Hood calls Peter's words "the best explanation (though it is a non-explanation) for the 'living dead' phenomenon." It is a non-explanation because it is merely asserted without clarification or evidence to back it up, but it is the best explanation because it carries such a powerful emotional charge. It simply feels like the best explanation for a horrifically apocalyptic situation.

Or at least it feels this way until the character of John delivers an even longer and more weighty apocalyptic speech in *Day of the Dead*. John, too, shares the name of a biblical apostle, and it is appropriate that Saint John is

---

4. See 2 Peter 3:1–13, especially verse 11: "But the day of the Lord will come like a thief. The heavens will disappear with a roar; the elements will be destroyed by fire, and the earth and everything in it will be laid bare." See also Acts 2:14–21, especially vv. 17–21, where Peter quotes the Hebrew prophet Joel's prophecy about the apocalyptic "Day of the Lord" being preceded by various dramatic and fearsome celestial signs.

perhaps best known as the purported author of that supreme Christian apocalyptic text, the Book of Revelation. Romero, incidentally, almost seems to want us to notice the shared name. *Day of the Dead* begins with four characters—John, Billy, Sarah, and Miguel—flying over Fort Myers, Florida, in search of human survivors. Sarah says she wants to set down to use the megaphone. Billy, hearing this plan, utters his favorite curse—"Jesus, Mary, and Joseph!"—and is cut off by Sarah, who clips the end of this biblical triad of names by saying, "Take us down, John."

John delivers his speech on an outer edge of the underground bunker where the surviving humans dwell. Whereas the others prefer to live in the relative safety of the actual compound, John and Billy have made their home out in the cave, where they have decorated a trailer home to look like a tropical paradise. It is in the open area behind this trailer, in a "back yard" adorned with lawn chairs and umbrella tables, that John gives Sarah his own speculative explanation for the zombie plague. First, he holds up a book that he has been reading, and he says,

> Hey, you know what all they keep down here in this cave? Man, they got the books and the records of the top five hundred companies. They got the defense department budget down here, and they got the negative for all your favorite movies. They got microfilm with tax return and newspaper stories. They got immigration records and census records, and they got official accounts of all the wars and plane crashes and volcano eruptions and earthquakes and fires and floods, and all the other disasters that interrupted the flow of things in the good old U.S. of A.[5]

With these words, John effectively establishes the military bunker as a microcosm of modern civilization. Everything that existed in the upper world still exists down here, but in condensed form. John's subsequent words may thus be interpreted as a diagnosis of human civilization itself. He goes on to tell Sarah that all this obsessive record keeping is a waste of time, since nobody will ever have the chance to see the records, and that the bunker with its treasure trove of civilization's recorded lore is nothing but "a great big, fourteen mile tombstone, with an epitaph on it that nobody gonna bother to read." In light of this, he asks, what good can Sarah and the other scientists possibly do with their "whole new set of graphs and charts and things"?

Sarah listens with a weary and glazed expression, as if his words are hurt-

---

5. Non-standard grammar and syntax in John's dialogue are due to the fact that, as written by Romero, he is Jamaican and speaks English with a subtle hint of Jamaican patois.

ing her, but she remains silent as he forges on toward the heart of what he has to say. "I'm gonna tell you what else," he says. "Yeah, I'm gonna tell you what else: you ain't ever gonna figure it out, just like they never figured out why the stars are where they're at. It ain't mankind's job to figure that stuff out. So what you're doing is a waste of time, Sarah. And time is all we got left, you know." We may validly take these words as the ultimate statement of the futility of all attempts to explain the zombie plague. In comparing such attempts to the age-old quest to figure out "why the stars are where they're at," John is asserting that the reason for the zombie plague is, and will always remain, as mysterious and incomprehensible as the reason for the existence of the universe at all. The question of the plague's true meaning resides on a level with all those other questions of ultimate meaning and purpose that categorically elude human understanding. In this portion of his speech, John offers a compact version of what the previous films have already provided; that is, he clears the air of possible rational explanations, thus opening the way for his listeners, both Sarah and the viewer, to experience the deepest possible emotional impact from his forthcoming spiritual explanation.

After speculating briefly that the few people still alive might be able to restart human civilization on a better footing—a civilization founded on the chief imperative *not* to dig out the records of the previous one—John offers his own explanation for the catastrophe, in words that echo and amplify Peter's speech:

> Hey, you want to put some kind of explanation down here before you leave? Here's one as good as any you're likely to find: We been punished by the creator. He visited a curse on us, so we might get a look at what hell was like. Maybe he didn't want to see us blow ourselves up and put a big hole in his sky. Maybe he just wanted to show us he was still the boss man. Maybe he figure we was getting too big for our britches, trying to figure his shit out.

The three possible explanations that John offers here at the end of his speech—that God did not want to see the human race destroy the earth, that God wanted to reassert his authority, and that God wanted to punish humans for seeking forbidden knowledge—are all subordinate to his central statement that the zombie plague is God's doing, that it is a curse directly caused by God's intervention, and that the ultimate point, whatever the secondary reasons, is to give humans a glimpse of what hell is like. Thus, this final movie in the zombie trilogy casts a retroactive religious reading back over the other two.

Waller, writing of *Night of the Living Dead*, states the matter well:

Romero emphasizes . . . the utter lack of supernatural assistance for man.
. . . As Romero will insist much more completely in *Dawn of the Dead* [than
in *Night*], there is no hope of being rescued by outside agencies. In *Night of
the Living Dead*, no God, father, or president, no military, scientific, political,
or religious form of authority guarantees or in any way promotes the surviv-
al of the living. (283–84, 290)

If this point is emphasized even more completely in *Dawn* than *Night*, then it
receives its definitive statement in *Day*, both in the fact of John's speech and
in the fact that the humans in this film are, so far as we know, the last living
people on earth. There are no others left to help, and God will certainly not
do it, as he may have caused the zombie plague in the first place.

And so we arrive at the heart of the trilogy's spiritual message: humans
are bereft, with no outside agencies left to aid us, and we must face this
nightmarish world of ravenous walking corpses without the possibility of redemption, without the possibility of being saved. Even John, the trilogy's
arch-diagnostician of spiritual meaning, contents himself with merely explicating the (possible) spiritual dimension of the zombie plague without offering
any kind of hope that it might eventually end. As we have seen, his recommended course of action is simply to flee from the whole mess and seek a life
of private enjoyment on a remote island.[6] "Meaning," Hood writes, "can now
only come through the struggle to remain human (and all that that means),
not through the possibility of success." Writing of the trilogy's first film, but
making a point that applies equally to all three, Sargeant says, "*Night of the Living Dead* should, were it a conventional horror film, have recalled the mythic
themes of danger and salvation, but there is no end to the path here, no
promised escape and, most importantly, no cavalry racing to the rescue. A
bloody death is the only possible outcome."

The situation recalls Roszak's diagnosis of the post-industrial era as the
first period in human history in which spiritual alienation has been divorced
from the possibility of anything better. "Until our own time," he writes, "al-

---

6. Incidentally, John first displays this attitude early on, within the first ten minutes of
the film, long before he gives his apocalyptic speech. As he and Sarah walk away
from the helicopter after the opening scene's scouting expedition, he tells her that he
thinks the ongoing project to study the zombies is "bullshit" and "crazy." She asks
him if he has a better idea, and he responds by telling her his plan to fly away to an
island "and spend what time we got left soaking up some sunshine." She fixes him
with a steely gaze and mutters with incredulous anger, "You could do that, couldn't
you? Even with all this going on, you could do that without a second thought." To
which he replies, "Shit, I could do that even if all this wasn't going on."

ienation has always stood in the shadow of salvation; it has been the falling rhythm of the soul's full cycle. It carried with it implications of transcendence. Ours is the first culture so totally secularized that we descend into the nihilist state without the conviction, without the experienced awareness that any other exists" (449). The world of the Living Dead trilogy is similarly dreadful, for there is no real escape or salvation to be had. Even the escape to a tropical island at the end of *Day* still resides in the shadow of ultimate failure and death, and God—to repeat—who is the ultimate power in charge of the whole universe, to whom one might otherwise expect to turn for solace, has proved to be the causative supernatural force behind the whole nightmarish scenario.

Roszak, not incidentally, was writing about the post-industrial world in terms of the classical Gnostic motif of the fallenness of the cosmos, and it is here that our exploration curls back upon itself and touches its own earlier parts. For the Gnostics viewed the material world, and thus the life of bodily existence itself, as a nightmare. The typical Gnostic attitude toward the physical body was one of terror and loathing, since in the Gnostic view it is the body with its manifold desires, needs, and impulses that chains one's true spiritual self to this world of darkness (i.e., the world of matter, the cosmos) and endarkens what would otherwise be a clear spiritual perception. In the eyes of the Gnostic, there is no lower hell than physical existence.

Recalling this, one cannot help recalling as well the horror of the body that occupied our attention earlier, when we saw that the Living Dead films attack the sense of secure subjecthood in four ways via their attacks upon the body: first, by depicting the body as an animated corpse, an organic nightmare that is out of control; second, by portraying a symbolic breach of the subject-object barrier via the literal act of one body consuming another in an act of cannibalism; third, by portraying these cannibalistic eating-machines as nothing more nor less than the human animal reduced to its most fundamental level of operation; and fourth, by transforming the body from a sleek and whole entity into a mass of bloody, disconnected parts. In this current section of the essay, I have argued that the overriding spiritual message of the Living Dead trilogy, established via Peter's and John's speeches, is that humans have no grounds for holding to a hope in some kind of supernatural deliverance or redemption, that there is no escape from this world of suffering into another, better world, and that the zombies are a literal depiction of the nature of hell.

Putting this all together, we arrive at a reading of the Living Dead films as a kind of Gnostic nightmare in which the world of flesh is solely about consuming and being consumed. The human self is always in process of being threatened by awful intrusions upon its sanctity and integrity, and there is no possibility of anyone's ever being saved or finding any solace in the midst of it all, because there is no ultimate metaphysical ground for the human self or for human hope. Organic, embodied life is a horror—the gory iconography of the films makes this abundantly clear—and the subjective, internal aspect of life has no footing, no firm ground, on which to rest and resist the horror of its fleshly connection. God has been revealed as an Old Testament–type deity who, like Yahweh, zealously punishes those who violate the limits he has set. There is no possibility of escape. It begins to look as if the final interpretative resting point has turned out to be an attitude of absolute nihilism and hopelessness.

VI. The Missing Rainbow: Theism's Inadequacy

This is not, however, the *necessary* end of the matter. When faced with the inescapability of this inferno of flesh as depicted in the Living Dead films, one does not have to accept endless horror as the final result. There are other options. For example, one might instead make a deliberate effort of awareness to reconsider one's presuppositions and check for a possible error. This seems a sensible enough move in a situation where there is nothing left to lose.

Something that becomes immediately evident upon reconsideration, something that the reader may have already noticed, is that John's theistic explanation of the zombie plague does not sit entirely well with the horrific hopelessness of the trilogy's overall tenor. If God has indeed brought about the zombie plague as an act of divine punishment, then what is the punitive, which is to say, *corrective* purpose of his act? Instead of appearing on earth as a kind of warning sign combined with a global housecleaning, the zombie plague has led to a total destruction of life and civilization. The motive behind such an act would appear to be not corrective but vindictive. The God who would bring about such a wholesale cataclysm would seem to be a sort of demonic version of the deistic clockmaker-God who sets the universe in motion and then absents himself eternally from its goings-on.

Still another thought occurs: is there not something unreasonable about positing the very *existence* of such a god who unleashes a horrific punishment in response to human transgressions and then has nothing further to do with the situation? Upon reflection, it begins to seem as if John's religious reading of the zombie plague, while it may be poetically evocative, and while it may be useful in its emphasis on the spiritual aspect of events, is fundamentally misguided, since the apocalypse portrayed in the Living Dead films inherently lacks anything that would recommend itself to a theistic interpretation. Rather, such an apocalypse seems much more in line with what Charles Derry has described as the horror of "Armageddon-movies" in which cataclysmic events are played out *in the absence of a divine cause:*

> There seems to be a strong relationship between these films and many of the stories in the Bible; for instance, the many plagues sent out to express the wrath of God, or even more dramatically the most archetypal story in the Bible: the flood. Take God away from the flood, and you have a true horror-of-Armageddon movie: suddenly, out of the sky, it begins to rain. What was previously considered a normal aspect of nature turns abnormal when the rain starts acting unlike rain and refuses to stop. The rain attacks and kills everyone; only Noah and his family manage to survive the existential test by working hard to hold tightly to their floating house. Ultimately, a rainbow appears as congratulations and in promise that the existential horror has come to an end. The pattern is exactly like that of *The Birds,* only Hitchcock refuses us the satisfaction of the horror-releasing rainbow. (50)

We can see that not only in tone but also in basic content Derry's words fit startlingly well with what occurs in the Living Dead films. Suddenly, the dead start returning to life and attacking the living. What was previously considered a normal aspect of nature (death) turns abnormal when the dead start acting unlike the dead and refuse to stop. The dead attack and kill everyone; only a tiny group of survivors, three in all, survive in the end by escaping to an island (their "floating house," perhaps?). And in perfect contradistinction to the biblical flood story, no "horror-releasing rainbow" appears in the heavens to congratulate these survivors and assure them that the horror is over. Indeed, it seems that the events of these films lend themselves more easily to interpretation in non-theistic terms, and that we must therefore revise our previous reading. But we do not want to dispense entirely with the spiritual angle, since it has proved to be so very useful. The question thus becomes one of finding a religious or spiritual angle that will make for a better fit with the films and that will address their intolerable hopelessness and horror, which, as Derry has pointed out, are increased by the absence of divine control.

VII. Leaning Eastward: The Contemplation of Foulness

The first thing to note is that John's religious interpretation of the zombie plague is overtly Western. Western religions are characterized chiefly by the fact that they are theistic, and more specifically, monotheistic. To reject theism is to reject out-of-hand the mainstream of Western religion. The same cannot be said of Eastern religions, however, which run the gamut from semi-theism to polytheism to atheism to agnosticism, but which contain nary a trace of the monotheistic emphasis that lies at the heart of their Western counterparts.

One of the things the Western tradition has always tended to reject—at least in its mainstream, orthodox manifestations—is the idea of *hopelessness.* To name one obvious example, the extreme pessimism of the biblical book of Ecclesiastes, which contains as piercing a statement of existential despair as can be found anywhere in world literature, stands in vivid contrast to the progressive historical hope of the Jews for a post-mortem resurrection to eternal life instead of a gloomy eternity spent in Sheol. Even within Ecclesiastes itself, one can find expressed a considerable number of conventionally pious and hopeful ideas, which many Bible scholars take to be later interpolations intended to mitigate the book's central message of despair. It is as if Jewish thought is constitutionally unable to rest with the idea of real, utter hopelessness. Additional examples of this attitude at work in Western religion are easy to come by. We may think of the Jewish hope for a messiah, and the way the Christian tradition has preached that this hope was fulfilled in the person of Jesus of Nazareth. Christianity itself is founded upon an attitude of hope for salvation and immortality based upon Jesus' crucifixion and resurrection. Generally speaking, in the eyes of these paired religious traditions and in Western religion as a whole, an attitude of hopelessness is something to be avoided, resisted, remedied, or otherwise denied.

This contrasts sharply with the explicit approach of some of the Eastern spiritual traditions that actively *embrace* hopelessness, and it is here that we may begin to explore the effectiveness of Eastern religious thought in offering a satisfying spiritual reading of the Living Dead films. One thinks first and foremost in this regard of Buddhism, and of the first of the Buddha's four noble truths, which teaches that "all life is suffering" or, interpreted differently, "all life is impermanence." To the Buddhist, the idea of "impermanence" refers to the realization that everything in life is fleeting, that there is no firm ground upon which to base one's sense of security, meaning, or identity. The entire phenomenal world, which for the Buddhist includes not only his or her own physical body but also his or her psyche, is constantly shifting, changing, evolving. There is no enduring "essence" to any of it. This truth is the foundation and starting point of Buddhist practice, which takes the form of a rigorous repertoire of psychophysical exercises designed to increase one's experiential realization of this and the other noble truths.

So in a very real sense, the starting point of Buddhist practice is a piercing realization of the fact of existential *hopelessness*. Pema Chödrön, the popular contemporary Tibetan Buddhist nun, teacher, and author, has written with clarity about the meaning and value of impermanence and the hopelessness is engenders. "Death and hopelessness," she writes, "provide proper motivation—proper motivation for living an insightful, compassionate life." She says the "experience of complete hopelessness, of completely giving up hope" is

> an important point. This is the beginning of the beginning. Without giving up hope—that there's somewhere better to be, that there's someone better to be—we will never relax with where we are or who we are. . . . When we talk about hopelessness and death, we're talking about facing the facts. No escapism. . . . If we totally experience hopelessness, giving up all hope of alternatives to the present moment, we can have a joyful relationship with our lives, an honest, direct relationship, one that no longer ignores the reality of impermanence and death. (42, 37, 43)

Obviously, this contrasts sharply with the Western attitude described above. Chödrön draws a connection between hope and theism on the one hand and hopelessness and nontheism on the other. Theism, she says, is too often based on a wish for a cosmic "babysitter," someone or something that one can latch onto with an attitude of hopefulness. From the non-theistic perspective, abandoning hope is an act of affirmation, since it liberates one to deal with reality as it is instead of wasting one's energy pining after sugar-coated illusions. Chödrön also points out that, thanks to the Buddha's articulation of the first noble truth, suffering can be separated from guilt. "The first noble truth of the Buddha," she writes, "is that when we feel suffering, it doesn't mean that something is wrong. What a relief. Finally somebody told the truth. Suffering is part of life, and we don't have to feel it's happening because we personally made the wrong move" (39). We recall that according to John in *Day of the Dead*, the characters in the Living Dead films suffer because of their own actions. The zombie plague is or may be a punishment from God for what people have done. But as we now see, John was speaking from a set of theistic assumptions that we have reason to regard as dubious in the world of these films. If his interpretation is fundamentally erroneous, then perhaps there is another way of interpreting suffering that has nothing to do with moral culpability and everything to do with the hopelessness inherent in the truth of impermanence.

The decision to turn to Buddhism looks all the more promising when we look into the classical Buddhist tradition and find much interesting material dealing with death and decay, which (as if this even needs to be reiterated) are topics of central importance in the Living Dead films as well. Consider, for example, the Theravada text titled *The Book of Protection,* "the most widely known Pali book in Sri Lanka" (Thera). In this text, which purports to be an anthology of teachings by the Buddha himself, in the section titled *Girimananda Sutta,* the Buddha is said to have been approached by Ananda and asked to visit Girimananda, who was gravely ill from a disease. The Buddha thereupon gave Ananda a list of "ten contemplations" to recite to Girimananda, saying, "Should you, Ananda, visit the monk Girimananda and recite to him the ten contemplations, then that monk Girimananda having heard them, will be immediately cured of his disease" (Thera).

These ten contemplations center almost entirely around the idea of impermanence, both physical and spiritual, and aim to engender an attitude of detachment in those who practice them, "detachment" being traditionally understood as an attitude of complete openness to the present moment, whatever may arise in it. One who has cultivated this attitude neither clings to nor rejects anything, for such a person has realized deeply the truth of impermanence, and in so doing has transcended the former sense of being bound or trapped by life in the body and the phenomenal realm. What is notable in the context of our current study is the explicit physicality, one might even say the goriness, of two of the contemplations the Buddha gives to Girimananda. The third one, titled "contemplation of foulness," is explained by the Buddha as follows:

> And what, Ananda, is contemplation of foulness? Herein, Ananda, a monk contemplates this body upwards from the soles of the feet, downwards from the top of the hair, enclosed in skin, as being full of many impurities. In this body there are head-hairs, body-hairs, nails, teeth, skin, flesh, sinews, bones, marrow, kidneys, heart, liver, pleura, spleen, lungs, intestines, intestinal tract, stomach, feces, bile, phlegm, pus, blood, sweat, fat, tears, grease, saliva, nasal mucous, synovium (oil lubricating the joints), and urine. Thus he dwells contemplating foulness in this body. This, Ananda, is called contemplation of foulness. (Thera)

The point of this exercise, as mentioned above, is to achieve an attitude of detachment. By directing attention specifically to the "foulness" of the body, to the very fact of its organic sliminess—to Roszak's "things amoeboid or fungoid that stick and cling, that creep and seep and grow . . . things that have the feel or spit or shit, snot or piss, sweat or pus or blood"—the aspirant learns not to identify with the body, not to be bound by a sense of loathing at its seeming horridness.

Similarly, the fourth contemplation, called "contemplation of disadvantage (or danger)," focuses upon the various diseases to which the body is susceptible:

> What, Ananda, is contemplation of disadvantage (danger)? Herein, Ananda, a monk having gone to the forest, or to the foot of a tree, or to a lonely place, contemplates thus: "Many are the sufferings, many are the disadvantages (dangers) of this body since diverse diseases are engendered in this body, such as the following: Eye-disease, ear-disease, nose-disease, tongue-disease, body-disease, headache, mumps, mouth-disease, tooth-ache, cough, asthma, catarrh, heart-burn, fever, stomach ailment, fainting, dysentery, swelling, gripes, leprosy, boils." (Thera)

The list goes on for quite a while longer, naming a plethora of different diseases and illnesses, and as with the contemplation of foulness, one can see, especially in context with the tenor of the other eight contemplations (e.g., contemplation of impermanence, contemplation of *anatta* [no-soul], contemplation of detachment, contemplation of distaste for the whole world), that the point of the whole is to teach an attitude of detachment or aloofness, an attitude of freedom from dependence on the body and the rest of the physical world. As the story goes, the treatment worked for Girimananda: "Thereupon the Venerable Ananda, having learned these ten contemplations from the Blessed One, visited the Venerable Girimananda, and recited to him the ten contemplations. When the Venerable Girimananda had heard them, his affliction was immediately cured. He recovered from that affliction, and thus disappeared the affliction of the Venerable Girimananda."

Lest the uninformed reader think this story is only a quaint part of an obscure (to most Westerners) scripture, it is important to point out that the attitude expressed in it and the recommended list of contemplations has a real-life counterpart in actual Buddhist practice. Buddhism as a whole speaks of forty traditional "meditation themes," ten of which are grouped together under the heading of "foul" or "loathsome" objects. *All these ten objects are human corpses in various states of injury and decay.* They include the bloated corpse, the livid corpse, the festering corpse, the corpse cut open, the gnawed corpse, the scattered corpse, the hacked corpse, the bloody corpse, the worm-ridden corpse, and the skeleton. For centuries many Buddhists have engaged in the practice of meditating on actual corpses to achieve a sense of disidentification from the impermanence of the body, and Buddhist literature is rife with descriptions of the meditative struggles of various advanced masters as they have deliberately contemplated or imagined corpses in various of the above-

named ten states, and have succeeded in conquering their delusional attach-
ment to the body as the linchpin of their sense of selfhood.

The point of dwelling on all this is, as indicated above, to demonstrate
that a sense of utter, inescapable despair in the face of the combined spiritual-
horrific and organic-horrific messages of the Living Dead trilogy is not the
only possible reaction. It is possible—not necessary, but possible—to take
an entirely different approach, one based on a Buddhist agnostic-
contemplative outlook instead of a biblical monotheistic one, and to use these
films as contemplative tools similar to those used by Buddhists in their corpse
meditations. For as we have seen, every one of the ten types of corpses described in Buddhism's list of "loathsome things" is present in the Living
Dead films. And although the same could be said of many other entries the
zombie subgenre, Romero's hold the distinction of presenting a powerful
spiritual message, as indicated by John in the final film. Just as the Buddha's
recommended list of contemplations combines meditations on the foulness
and vulnerability of the body with meditations on the impermanence of the
human self, so do the films of Romero's Living Dead trilogy combine extreme body horror with extreme spiritual horror, such that the two are inex-
tricable. The violent abuse and deconstruction of the body in these films also
heralds the violent abuse and deconstruction of the human self, and this self
is shown via the trilogy's spiritual emphasis to be utterly without ground or
hope in any possible transcendent spiritual realm. This two-pronged nature of
the trilogy's thematic impact, one prong consisting of or emerging from the
trilogy's graphic gore, and the other from its spiritual focus, thus results in a
situation where the choice to view these films in contemplative terms, that is,
to direct one's attention deliberately to the graphic violence with the intention
of allowing the depiction of corpse horror to loosen one's identification from
the body, seems entirely warranted.

The effects of such an exercise will surely be limited and will vary according to the will, intentions, and concentrative power of each individual viewer.
But in general, if one wonders what the result of such a contemplative exercise might be, one might look for answers in the spiritual literature that makes
mention of the contemplation of death and corpses. In the modern era there
is, for instance, the story told by the Danish-born writer Janwillem van de
Wetering at the end of his book *A Glimpse of Nothingness: Experiences in an
American Zen Community:*

> A Chinese allegory tells how a monk sets off on a long pilgrimage to find
> the Buddha. He spends years and years on his quest and finally he comes to
> the country where the Buddha lives.

He crosses a river, it is a wide river, and he looks about him while the boatman rows him across.

There is a corpse floating on the water and it is coming closer.

The monk looks. The corpse is so close he can touch it. He recognizes the corpse, it is his own.

The monk loses all self-control and wails.

There he floats, dead.

Nothing remains.

Anything he has ever been, ever learned, ever owned, floats past him, still and without life, moved by the slow current of the wide river.

It is the first moment of his liberation. (180)

More recently, there are the words of bestselling author and spiritual teacher Eckhart Tolle, who has written at some length about the power and value of death, and about the value of contemplating one's own death as a spiritual exercise:

One of the most powerful spiritual exercises is to meditate deeply on the mortality of physical forms, including your own. This is called: die before you die. Go into it deeply. Your physical form is dissolving, is no more. Then a moment comes when all mind-forms or thoughts also die. Yet *you* are still there—the divine presence that you are. Radiant, fully awake. Nothing that was real ever died, only names, forms, illusions. (165; Tolle's emphasis)

Both Tolle, who represents no specific tradition but whose teaching draws on Hindu Vedanta, Buddhism, and Christian mysticism, and van de Wetering, representing Zen Buddhism, along with the entire tradition of Buddhism in general, are getting at a similar, if not the same, point: neither the physical reality of the body nor the psychological ego associated with it represent one's truest, deepest identity. And contemplating death, especially one's own, helps to verify and reinforce this fact.

VIII. Conclusion: The Transmutation of Horror

When it comes to the films we have been examining, we may say that to view them in this way—as tools for aiding in this contemplation of physical and psychological mortality—is to experience them exactly as we have described them in this paper, with all their hopelessness, all their gore and violence, all the horror of abjection that attends the sight of animated corpses, still active with full, emotionally penetrating effect, *and yet* to experience at the same time a veritably alchemical transmutation of the horror and hopelessness into something else, something that may approach a genuine epiphany about the nature of one's true self. Viewing the many acts of savagery and cannibalism on the screen—which, as we have argued, affect the viewer emotionally and psychologically with a message about the vulnerability, instability, and ultimate fragility of the human subject, and which might well lead the viewer to a Gnostic loathing of the flesh while simultaneously denying him the possibility of salvation in some transcendent world of pure spirit—we now see that, when understood from a "higher" or "deeper" perspective, the self that can be injured, deconstructed, or destroyed through such acts is not one's true self at all. Only the ego, which is linked to the physical body, has been affected by such events.

In fact, our reading of the films with the intent to elicit, understand, and experience to the greatest possible extent their combination of body horror and spiritual horror has been nothing other than an intellectualized instance of this very contemplation, since it is the ego in its intellectual and emotional obsessiveness that has engaged in the reading and experienced the horror. Coming away from this, we realize that we have *benefited* from the experience, since we have come to recognize more clearly the difference between the ephemeral, illusory ego that commonly masquerades as our true self and the enduring empty center of awareness that always precedes and lies behind the extensional existence of the ego and the body. To quote Tolle a final time: "Only the ego dies. . . . The end of illusion—that's all that death is. It is painful only as long as you cling to illusion" (188, 121).

1999; 2002–2003

Works Cited

Barthes, Roland. "Toward as Psychosociology of Contemporary Food Consumption." In Carole Counihan and Penny Van Esterik, ed. *Food and Culture: A Reader*. New York: Routledge, 1997. 20–27.

Brophy, Philip. "The Body Horrible: Some Notions, Some Points, Some Examples." *Interventions* 21/22 (1988). Also available online at www.philipbrophy. com/projects/bodyhorrible/essay.html.

———. "Horrality: The Textuality of Contemporary Horror Films." In Ken Gelder, ed., *The Horror Reader*. London: Routledge, 2000. 276–84.

Brottman, Mikita. "Supernatural Cannibals." Excerpt from Mikita Brottman, *Meat Is Murder: Cannibal Films and Culture*, new ed. London: Creation Books, 2001. Accessed 23 November 2002. www.creationbooks.com/ text-meat.html.

Chödrön, Pema. *When Things Fall Apart: Heart Advice for Difficult Times*. Boulder, CO: Shambala Publications, 1997.

Crane, Jonathan Lake. *Terror and Everyday Life: Singular Moments in the History of the Horror Film*. Thousand Oaks, CA: SAGE Publications, 1994.

Creed, Barbara. "Kristeva, Femininity, and Abjection." In Ken Gelder, ed. *The Horror Reader*. London: Routledge, 2000. 64–70.

Derry, Charles. *Dark Dreams*. Cranbury, NJ: A. S. Barnes & Co., 1977.

Dillard, R. H. W. *Horror Films*. New York: Monarch Press, 1976.

Erhardt, Rev. Dr. Richard. "Vampires and Other Plagues." *South Nassau Unitarian Universalist Congregation* (29 October 2000). Accessed 16 November 2002. members.aol.com/snuuc/snuuc/Sermons/vampire_and_other_plagues. htm.

Freeland, Cynthia A. *The Naked and the Undead: Evil and the Appeal of Horror*. Boulder, CO: Westview Press, 2000.

Hoberman, J., and Jonathan Rosenbaum. *Midnight Movies*. New York: Harper & Row, 1983.

Hood, Robert. "Nights of the Celluloid Dead: A History of the Zombie Film." *Tabula Rasa*. Accessed 12 November 2002. www.tabula-rasa.info/Horror/ZombieFilms1.html.

Jerslev, Anne. "The Horror Film, the Body, and the Youth Audience." *Young: Nordic Journal of Youth Research* 2, No. 3 (1994). www.alli.fi/nyri/young/1994-3/artikkelJerslev3-94.htm (accessed 16 November 2002).

Kendrick, Walter. *The Thrill of Fear: 250 Years of Scary Entertainment*. New York: Grove Weidenfeld, 1991.

Kristeva, Julia. *Powers of Horror: An Essay on Abjection*. Tr. Leon S. Roudiez. New York: Columbia University Press, 1982.

London, Rose. *Zombie: The Living Dead*. New York: Bounty Books, 1986.

Meigs, Anna. "Food as a Cultural Construction." In Carole Counihan and Penny Van Esterik, ed. *Food and Culture: A Reader*. New York: Routledge, 1997. 95–106.

Mes, Tom. "The End Is Nigh! (And It Starts in Pittsburgh): George Romero's Living Dead Trilogy." *Project A: Cultfilm and Lifestyle e-zine*. Accessed 16 November 2002. www.projecta.net/george1.htm.

Olesen, Anne Marie. "Cannibalism and the Serial Killer as Metaphors for Transgression." *p.o.v.: A Danish Journal of Film Studies* 4 (December 1997). Accessed 16 November 2002. pov.imv.au.dk/Issue_04/section_2/artc2A.html

Prawer, S. S. *Caligari's Children: The Film as Tale of Terror.* Oxford: Oxford University Press, 1980.

Roszak, Theodore. *Where the Wasteland Ends: Politics and Transcendence in Postindustrial Society.* Berkeley, CA: Celestial Arts, 1989.

Sanday, Peggy Reeves. *Divine Hunger: Cannibalism as a Cultural System.* Cambridge: Cambridge University Press, 1986.

Sargeant, Jack. "The Baying of Pigs: Reflections on the New American Horror Movie." *Senses of Cinema* 15 (July–August 2001). Accessed 29 March 2005. www.sensesofcinema.com/contents/festivals/01/15/biff_nightmare.html.

Stone, Bryan. "The Sanctification of Fear: Images of the Religious in Horror Films." *Journal of Religion and Film* 5, No. 2 (October 2001). Accessed 29 March 2005. www.unomaha.edu/ ~wwwjrf/sanctifi.htm.

Taylor, Rumsey. Review of *Dawn of the Dead. 24 Frames Per Second.* Accessed 16 November 2002. www.24framespersecond.com/reactions/films_d/dawndead .html.

Thera, Piyadassi, tr. *The Book of Protection. Access to Insight: Readings in Theravada Buddhism.* 1999. Accessed 4 November 2003. www.accesstoinsight.org/ lib/bps/misc/protection.html.

Tolle, Eckhart. *The Power of Now: A Guide to Spiritual Enlightenment.* Vancouver, BC: Namaste Publishing, 1997.

van de Wetering, Janwillem. *The Empty Mirror: Experiences in a Japanese Zen Monastery.* New York: Ballantine Books, 1988.

Waller, Gregory. "Introduction to *American Horrors.*" In Ken Gelder, ed. *The Horror Reader.* London: Routledge, 2000. 256–64.

———. *The Living and the Undead.* Urbana: University of Illinois Press, 1986.

Warner, Marina. "The Devil Inside." *Guardian* (2 November 2002). books.guardian.co.uk/reviews/politicsphilosophyandsociety/0,6121,824 095,00.htm.

Wood, Robin. *Hollywood from Vietnam to Reagan.* New York: Columbia University Press, 1986.

———. "What Lies Beneath?" *Senses of Cinema* 15 (July–August 2001). Accessed 29 March 2005. www.sensesofcinema.com/2001/freuds-worst-nightmares-psychoanalysis-and-the-horror-film/horror_beneath/

"Zombie Symbolism." *Monstrous.* Accessed 16 November 2002. death.monstrous. com/zombie_symbolism.htm.

Works Consulted

Bourassa, Eric. "The End Is Near!!! The Non-Regenerative Apocalyptic Horror Film." *HorrorTheory*. Accessed 1 December 2002. www.horrortheory.com/articles/bourassa_1.html.

Grant, Barry Keith, ed. *Planks of Reason: Essays on the Horror Film*. Metuchen, NJ: Scarecrow Press, 1984.

Grant, Barry K. "Prolegomena to a Contextualistic Genre Criticism." Accessed 16 November 2002. www.sunyit.edu/~harrell/Pepper/pep_grant.htm.

Humphrey, Clark. "Food for Thought on Cannibal Movies: Bite Me." 1996. Accessed 16 November 2002. www.miscmedia.com/1996/01/31/cannibal-movies/

Huss, Roy, and T. J. Ross, ed. *Focus on the Horror Film*. Englewood Cliffs, NJ: Prentice-Hall, 1972.

Jonas, Hans. *The Gnostic Religion: The Message of the Alien God and the Beginnings of Christianity*. 2nd ed. Boston: Beacon Press, 1991.

Lavery, David. "The Horror Film and the Horror of Film." Accessed 16 November 2002. www.mtsu.edu/~dlavery/Writing/The%20Horror%20Film%20and%20the%20Horror%20of%20Film.htm. Originally published in *Film Criticism* 7 (1983): 47–55.

Merritt, Greg. *Celluloid Mavericks: The History of American Independent Film*. New York: Thunder's Mouth Press, 2000.

Religion and Vampires

I. Introduction: An Intrinsically Religious Monster

For a ready indication of the profound interconnectedness between the subject of religion and the subject of vampires, one has only to look to the fact that four of the towering figures in the field of vampire studies have also been formidable presences in the field of religion.

The first of these, Augustin Calmet (1672–1757), was a renowned French Benedictine abbot and theologian who may have ranked as the eighteenth century's pre-eminent Catholic biblical scholar. He is best remembered for having written a masterful treatise on vampires—*Traité sur les apparitions des esprits, et sur les vampires*... (Paris, 1746), translated into English in 1850 as *The Phantom World*—in response to the vampire hysteria that swept across Central and Eastern Europe in the 1720s and 1730s.

The second, Montague Summers (1880–1948), was a colorful British eccentric who achieved the reputation of being the world's greatest vampire scholar for his books *The Vampire: His Kith and Kin* (1928) and *The Vampire in Europe* (1929). He also claimed to be a Roman Catholic priest, although this was almost certainly a pose that he employed to enhance his mystique as a vampire expert. But he was, in fact, an ordained deacon in the Church of England (according to Father Brocard Sewell in his memoir of Summers) and thus formally bore the Christian title "reverend." In any event, Raymond T. McNally, in his 1974 anthology of vampirana, *A Clutch of Vampires* (published by the New York Graphic Society), drew an overt connection between Calmet's and Summers's religious credentials and their canonical status in the field of vampire studies by identifying them as "the only major researchers in this field" and referring to them in the book's dedication as "holy fathers in the Christian faith and the spiritual fathers of all latter-day vampirologists" (9, 5).

The second, Antoine Faivre (b. 1934), was called out as "the father of contemporary vampire studies" by the Italian sociologist of religion Massimo

Introvigne in his 2001 essay titled, appropriately enough, "Antoine Faivre: Father of Contemporary Vampire Studies." Introvigne asserted that Faivre, an eminent French scholar of religion and esotericism, "opened up and established the field of vampire studies as an independent and relevant academic discipline" with his *Les Vampires: Essai historique, critique et littéraire* by "proving that the vampire controversy was historically significant as the last great European theological and philosophical discussion of magic" (610).

The fourth figure, J. Gordon Melton, is a prominent American scholar of religious studies who, in addition to founding the Institute for the Study of American Religion and creating *Melton's Encyclopedia of American Religions*—which has gone through multiple editions and is widely regarded as the standard general reference work in its field—is also a leading authority on vampires whose scholarly areas of specialization include parapsychology and the occult. His 1994 opus *The Vampire Book: The Encyclopedia of the Undead* is arguably the most comprehensive English-language reference work in the field of vampire studies, and he has also published a comprehensive bibliography of vampires in folklore, history, literature, film, and television. In 1997 he collaborated with Introvigne and literary scholar Elizabeth Miller—one of the leading authorities on Bram Stoker's *Dracula* and the founding editor of the *Journal of Dracula Studies*—to organize a vampire conference in Los Angeles for scholars of the field.

This coming-together of vampires with prominent scholarly and sometimes ecclesiastical authority serves to underscore a significant fact: that vampires are intimately bound up with religion, to the point where beliefs about them are sometimes indistinguishable from religious belief as such. It is not an overstatement to say that vampires, with their inherent invocation of fundamental human questions and fears, stand as intrinsically *religious monsters*. And this means that even though a person need not be a clergyman or religion scholar in order to understand vampires, no understanding of them can be complete or even adequate without taking into account their religious aspects.

II. The Vampire as Religious Focal Point

The vampire's religious connections extend all the way back to its murky origins. Various theories have been advanced to explain these origins, but all are linked by the fact that they identify religion, often in a primal but still recognizable form, as a principal factor. Summers, for instance, attributed the matter to beliefs held by primitive peoples about the relationship between the body and the soul. Devendra P. Varma focused on certain vampire-like deities among the ancient Hindu pantheon, the stories of which were brought to

Europe by Arab traders. According to the entry on vampirism in the *Dictionary of Literary Themes and Motifs,* while it may be impossible to pinpoint the origin of vampires definitively, a good place to look is the Tibetan and Egyptian books of the dead, which specify the necessity of elaborate burial rituals, without which the dead will plague the living.

Even in the many cases where scholars have posited non-religious factors such as catalepsy and premature burial as the material cause of vampiric belief, the outcome has still been a cultural figure that draws heavily on a given people's stockpile of religious stories about souls, gods, demons, and the afterlife. Thus, regardless of the impossibility of positively identifying their most ancient origins, vampires manifestly entered human culture through the channel of the human religious sensibility, and therefore they arrived as creatures laden with religious connotations, which in turn served to further solidify the cultural image of the creature itself along religious lines.

III. Blood of My Blood: The Christian Connection

Nowhere was this self-reinforcing relationship more visible than in the vampire's relationship with Christianity. In the first century C.E., the vampiric element of this new religion was implicit from the start, as seen in the centrality of its blood motif. The anonymous author of "The Vampire Archetype," a Jungian exploration of the vampire's spiritual-psychological meanings, neatly summarizes this deep-rooted connection: "Blood stands for life, and blood is also the archetypal symbol of the soul (life energy). Therefore blood is a central symbol in many religions, including the Christian. The central image of all vampire lore is blood."

The early church fathers recognized the danger inherent in their religion's sanguinary emphasis—the danger that it would encourage Christians to revert to paganism, which was rife with its own blood motifs, including those found in folk-level vampire-type beliefs—but they could not escape it, since the developing body of Christian tradition and scripture proclaimed that Christ had commanded his disciples at the Last Supper to take the wine as his blood. More than a millennium after that foundational event, when medieval theologians and clergymen sought a popular explanation of the theology of transubstantiation, they may or may not have been aware of the irony in their choice to employ folk vampire beliefs as a kind of spiritual shorthand. The church had by this time co-opted vampires from their previous folk existence and reinterpreted them as minions of the Christian devil, so it was an easy enough analogy to draw: just as a vampire takes a sinner's very spirit into itself by drinking his blood, so also can a righteous Christian by drinking Christ's blood take the divine spirit into himself.

In addition to this doctrinal use, the Roman Catholic Church made political use of vampires in the seventeenth century when it was seeking to expand its reach eastward through the Balkans. Upon encountering religious resistance from Muslims and Greek Orthodox Christians, the church manipulated a widespread fear by proclaiming that all people buried on officially unconsecrated ground would rise again as vampires. It also reserved for itself the official authority to identify and dispatch vampires through the agency of its priestly representatives wielding their divinely empowered weapons.

The Greek Orthodox Church, for its part, was equally responsible for inflaming vampire-associated fears during the same period through its overuse of excommunication. This contributed to the swelling vampire mania by playing into Eastern European fears about the vampiric qualities of incorruptible corpses, since excommunication was accompanied by the curse "and the earth will not receive your body." In other words, every instance of excommunication produced a new potential vampire. The practice was so widespread and so prone to agitating vampire fears that some scholars have mistakenly identified the Greek Church as the original source of vampires.

Not coincidentally, the very geographical region where the confrontation between Western and Eastern Christianity occurred went on to become the "imaginative whirlpool" referred to by Bram Stoker in *Dracula:* the mythic-magnetic nexus in Eastern Europe, centered on Transylvania, where "every known superstition in the world is gathered," including, especially, the world's most completely developed folk beliefs about vampires.

IV. Amplifying the Vampire: Spiritualism and Gothic Entertainment

By the end of the eighteenth century, popular belief in vampires among Eastern Europeans had been largely subdued thanks to the vigorous efforts of civic authorities and the educated classes, not to mention Calmet, who, unlike his contemporary clerical fellows, wrote not to provoke fears about vampires but to discredit them. But vampires, as Introvigne notes, "never stay dead long" (610), and their resurrection took place along two separate lines, both of which underscored their inherent religious nature.

The more minor but still noteworthy of these lines involved Theosophy and, more generally, spiritualism, both of which emerged as extremely popular movements all across Europe and North America in the late nineteenth and early twentieth centuries. Helena Petrovna Blavatsky, the founder and figurehead of the theosophical movement, wrote at length about vampires in her first major work, *Isis Unveiled* (1877). Her associate in Theosophy, Colonel Henry Steel Olcott, wrote an essay titled "The Vampire" for an issue of the *Theosophist* in 1891. Both treated the subject as something "real," but they modified it in the direction of a spiritual or astral vampirism, advancing the idea that vampires are the spirits of the dead that prey upon the blood or the life force of the living. The idea gained considerable popularity among like-minded readers, and vampires remained creatures of interest for decades afterwards among theosophical and spiritualist circles.

The other and more momentous development occurred when the mostly successful expulsion of vampires from governmental reports, theological treatises, and popular belief resulted in their migrating in the late eighteenth century to the realm of popular entertainment. In poetry, short fiction, novels, and the theater, the folk idea of the vampire was transformed for the first time into a coherent figure, possessing a set of standardized characteristics, that could be properly referred to with the definite article: not "vampires" or "a vampire" but "*the* vampire." Fused with the newborn images of the Gothic villain and the Byronic hero, the vampire achieved an iconic form that, to date, appears truly immortal.

In its new literary guise, the vampire was, if anything, even more associated with religious symbolism than it had been in its previous folkloric existence. The narrative needs of fiction demanded confrontation and high drama, and authors seized upon the vampire's religious connections to construct a literary universe where vampires, framed as minions or channels of supernatural (usually Christian-satanic) evil, stalked and stormed through the stock settings of the Gothic genre, which often included the requisite dark religious surroundings of shadowy cemeteries, gloomy churches, and so on. These vampires were often challenged by heroes wielding divinely empowered weapons and/or possessing special religious knowledge of occult matters, including knowledge of the best ways to defeat vampires. "The presence and function of Christianity and the clergy," writes M. M. Carlson, "assume a very important role in vampire literature, greater by far than their role in the later folklore of the vampire." The fact that, as Carlson notes, this development was "a reflection of contemporary European religious values, and not a motif taken from folklore" (30), where vampires were more customarily dispatched by extra-Christian means, indicates that the move to literature served to amplify the vampire's religious nature in a way previously unseen.

Carlson offers a further observation that is key to understanding the nature and significance of this amplification:

> In this new environment the character of the vampire gradually underwent a psychological probing—impossible in his folklore environment—which elucidated the meaning of his character in a new and exciting way. Literature examined, more explicitly and from a wide variety of viewpoints, the nature of the evil locked within the figure of the vampire, and adapted that figure to suit the needs and understandings of the authors who generated it and the reading public it served. (31)

Importantly, in examining "the nature of the evil locked within the figure of the vampire," the authors who created the new subgenre of vampire fiction found much having to do with religion and spirituality, as evinced most famously by the nature of Stoker's Dracula. Leonard Wolf has observed that Stoker "designed *Dracula* to be read as a Christian allegory. . . . The struggle is not merely between good guys and a supremely bad man, but between high-minded Christians and a minion of the devil" (x, xi). The evidence of this is seen in the novel's prominent use of Christian symbols as weapons against vampires, and in Stoker's overt use of biblical and biblical-sounding language in key passages (e.g., Renfield's maniacal insistence that "The blood is the life!"; Dracula's crypto-biblical announcement to Mina Harker that she is now "flesh of my flesh and blood of my blood"). And there is, of course, the name Dracula itself, which Stoker took from his studies of the fifteenth-century Wallachian ruler Vlad III, and which associates the character with the mythic dragon of John's Apocalypse, since *dracula* in Romanian means "son of the dragon" or "son of the devil."

V. The Vampire as Divine Revelation

Additional evidence of Dracula's Satanic or, perhaps more accurately, anti-Christian nature is seen in various subtler shadings of characterization that Stoker built into him, and a thoughtful inquiry into this very subject as it applies not only to Dracula but to vampire fiction in general serves to recontextualize the Christian elements within a vastly more expansive realm of spiritual meanings.

Timothy K. Beal, yet another scholar of religion, wrote of this realm in his 2002 study *Religion and Its Monsters*, where he noted that the character of Dracula "is by no means reducible to the diabolical. At several points [in the novel], in fact, he is described in distinctly biblical terms that suggest a certain divine semblance" (125). In other words, Dracula, and by implication other literary vampires, may serve as an avatar not only of the Christian Devil but of divinity in general. The very nature of the vampire may cause it to stand as a theophany, a manifestation the divine.

More specifically, and following the clue provided by the dragon connection, tales of the literary vampire may serve as re-enactments of the primal myth of the chaos dragon, a figure that appears in its earliest recorded form as Tiamat. To the ancient Babylonians in the second millennium B.C.E., Tiamat represented the state of uncreated chaos that existed before the cosmic order was established. The conflict with her solar-deity son Marduk, who slew her and created the world from her split carcass, served as the template for all the later tales of dragons and their slayers. According to Ronald Foust, the stock elements and attributes of the literary vampire—"its power, its chthonic characteristics, its ritualized manner of dying—are the necessary results of the requirements of the archetypal story, that of the dragon-battle, that lies at the heart of all Gothic fiction." The reader of such tales therefore "experiences what may be called crypto-religious emotions in his purely imaginative encounter with the numinosity—the power, the mystery, the awesomeness—of the vampire" (81–83).

Such a recognition adds all the more fascination to the fact that the makers of the legendary first cinematic adaptation of *Dracula*, 1922's *Nosferatu*, deliberately incorporated the idea of the vampire as a theophany into their film. As recounted by Beal, *Nosferatu*'s German producers, Albin Grau and Enrico Dieckman, wanted to use monster movies as avenues for religious reflection. To this end, they adopted such tactics as naming their Berlin-based production company Prana-Film (drawing the word *prana* from Hinduism, where it refers to the cosmic and human life spirit) and choosing for their company logo the Chinese tai chi disc (the yin/yang symbol). The result, in Beal's words, is that Count Orlok, *Nosferatu*'s thinly disguised version of Count Dracula, emerges as "an icon of monstrous divinity" (148).

VI. The Vampire as Spiritual Figurehead

Dracula's transition from novel to screen launched a movement that continued for the remainder of the twentieth century and showed no signs of letting up by the early years of the twenty-first. In the United States and Europe, vampire movies joined vampire literature in making prolific and even profligate use of the iconic vampire, and in the majority of these instances religion played a major role, usually in the standard form of Christian symbols and talismans appearing as defenses and weapons against the vampire. But beyond such conventionalisms, a number of movies explored subtler connections between the vampire and religion. In *Dracula 2000* (2000), for instance, the title character was revealed not only as the first vampire but as a reincarnation of Judas Iscariot, a conceit the filmmakers employed to explain the inability of vampires to abide Christian symbols, which evoke Judas's emotional agony. *John Carpenter's Vampires* (1998) similarly advanced the idea that the Christian Church was actively involved in the creation of the original vampire, this time by means of a botched exorcism in which a demon was trapped in the body of a fourteenth-century priest. Such plot devices must be considered remarkably astute in light of the real-world history of Christianity's involvement with vampires. The apex of this historical awareness in vampire cinema may have been reached in *Bram Stoker's Dracula* (1992), which depicted the fifteenth-century Romanian ruler Vlad Dracula being cursed with a vampiric existence after he renounced Christ and desecrated his own chapel when he returned home from war to find that his wife, having received a mistaken report of his death, had committed suicide and was therefore being denied proper burial in typical—and historically authentic—Eastern Orthodox fashion.

Alongside the movies, vampire literature also continued to develop, and the deep connection between the vampire and religion was reconfirmed in particularly interesting fashion in both the work and the life of the most popular vampire novelist of the twentieth century. Beginning with *Interview with the Vampire* in 1976 and continuing through *Blood Canticle* in 2003, the American author Anne Rice created an alternate world populated by immortal vampires whose existences are marked by agonizing moral dilemmas and existential uncertainties.[1] Unsurprisingly, religious themes abounded, and the vampire Lestat, the series' protagonist, eventually emerged as a kind of stand-in for Rice herself, who was experiencing a decades-long personal spiritual crisis. In 2002 she surrendered to a full-blown reconversion experience to Roman Catholicism and turned to writing novelizations of the life of Christ. She later explained in an August 2007 open letter to her readers that she originally chose to write about vampires because she saw in them "the perfect metaphor for the outcast in all of us, the alienated one in all of us, the one who feels lost in a world seemingly without God." Obviously, her choice of the vampire as the proper symbolic vehicle for her spiritual exploration underscores the figure's innate religious connections.

So, too, does the striking subcultural effect of Rice's novels. The Vampire Chronicles almost single-handedly launched the North American Goth-vampire subculture that arose in their wake. David Keyworth, one of the

---

1. 2021 update: Rice later wrote three additional novels for the series, published in 2014, 2016, and 2018.

many scholarly writers who have devoted attention to this movement, offered a sociological description of the extensive network of organizations and individuals in the United States and elsewhere that, beginning in the 1980s, adopted the vampire as its defining spiritual icon. Members of these groups pretend or in some cases truly believe they are vampires. Some are role-players. Others are bona fide blood fetishists. Many have created their own vampire-centered metaphysical mythology and branded themselves in religious terms. Such people represent, in Keyworth's words, "a socio-religious movement [that] has become well entrenched in contemporary culture" (368).

The ironic nature of these developments is immediately evident to the informed observer. From its birth via the human religious sensibility, the vampire's arc has taken it through a folklore-level existence as a monster shaped by institutional religious pressures, and thence through a codification in popular entertainment as an iconic nexus of supernatural dread, and thence to a circumstance in which these very entertainments have spawned a subculture that fashions the vampire into an object of religious belief. The significance of this latest evolutionary development, and also of much having to do with the vampire's religious nature, can be seen in the fact that Keyworth's paper appeared in 2002 in a professional scholarly publication, the *Journal of Contemporary Religion*.

VII. Conclusion: The Supernatural Problem of the Vampire

Douglas Cowan, yet another scholar of religion, expresses the cumulative upshot of this essay's thesis with remarkable concision: "Because the supernatural problem of the vampire is tied to the mystery of death, our fear of dying badly, and what happens to us once we have died, religion remains a central concern of vampire tales" (130). As established by the entirety of what has been said here, the effect Cowan describes is not confined to the telling of fictional tales. Rather, it is something that has entered deeply into the actual religious beliefs, fears, and hopes of individuals and entire civilizations throughout human history. The vampire's legendary immortality thus emerges not only as a cause but as a result of its intimate entwinement with the deepest concerns of human life. People will no doubt continue to find new ways of drawing new meanings out of this archetypal figure. But even as the vampire continues to metamorphose into an endless variety of cultural shapes, religion will remain one of its fundamental components, and the human spiritual impulse will continue to use the vampire as a lens through which to focus itself.

2010

Works Cited

Beal, Timothy K. *Religion and Its Monsters*. New York: Routledge, 2002.

Carlson, M. M. "What Stoker Saw: An Introduction to the History of the Literary Vampire." *Folklore Forum* 10, No. 2 (Fall 1977): 26–32.

Cowan, Douglas. *Sacred Terror: Religion and Horror on the Silver Screen*. Waco, TX: Baylor University Press, 2008.

Foust, Ronald. "Rite of Passage: The Vampire Tale as Cosmogonic Myth." In William Coyle, ed. *Aspects of Fantasy: Selected Essays from the Second International Conference on the Fantastic in Literature and Film*. Westport, CT: Greenwood Press, 1986. 73–89.

Introvigne, Massimo. "Antoine Faivre: Father of Contemporary Vampire Studies." In Richard Caron, Joscelyn Godwin, Wouter J. Hanegraaff, and Jean-Louis Viellard-Baron, ed. *Esotérisme, gnoses et imaginaire symbolique: Mélanges offerts à Antoine Faivre*. Leuven, Belgium: Peeters, 2001. 595–610.

Keyworth, David. "The Socio-Religious Beliefs and Nature of the Contemporary Vampire Subculture." *Journal of Contemporary Religion* 17, No. 3 (2002): 355–70.

McNally, Raymond T. *A Clutch of Vampires*. New York: Bell Publishing Co., 1974.

Rice, Anne. "Essay on Earlier Works." *Anne Rice: The Official Site*. 15 August 2007. www.annerice.com/Bookshelf-EarlierWorks.html.

"The Vampire Archetype." *Vampire*. 17 June 2010. thewebofnarcissism.blogspot.com/2010/06/vampire-archetype_17.html.

Wolf, Leonard. "Returning to Dracula." Introduction to *Dracula* by Bram Stoker. New York: Signet Classic, 1992. i–xii.

Works Consulted

Cavallaro, Dani. *Gothic Vision: Three Centuries of Horror, Terror and Fear*. London: Continuum International Publishing, 2002.

Day, Peter, ed., *Vampires: Myths and Metaphors of Enduring Evil*. Amsterdam: Rudopi, 2006.

Garry, Jane, and Hasan N. El-Shamy, ed. *Archetypes and Motifs in Folklore and Literature: A Handbook*. Armonk, NY: M. E. Sharpe, 2005.

Green, Gary. "Vampirism." In Jean-Charles Seigneuret, ed. *Dictionary of Literary Themes and Motifs*. Westport, CT: Greenwood Press, 1988. 1373–83.

Herbert, Stephen C. "Dracula as Metaphor for Human Evil." *Journal of Religion and Psychical Research* 27, No. 2 (April 2004): 62–71.

Joshi, S. T., and Stefan Dziemianowicz, ed. *Supernatural Literature of the World: An Encyclopedia*. Westport, CT: Greenwood Press, 2005. 3 vols.

Keyworth, G. David. "Was the Vampire of the Eighteenth-Century a Unique Type of Undead-Corpse?" *Folklore* 117 (December 2006): 241–60.

Masters, Anthony. *The Natural History of the Vampire*. New York: G. P. Putnam's Sons, 1972.

McDonald, Beth E. *The Vampire as Numinous Experience: Spiritual Journals with the Undead in British and American Literature*. Jefferson, NC: McFarland, 2004.

Moore, Russell D. "The Red Cross of Jesus: On Rediscovering the Lifeblood of the Church." *Touchstone: A Journal of Mere Christianity* (March 2007): 24–27.

Twitchell, James B. *Dreadful Pleasures: An Anatomy of Modern Horror*. Oxford: Oxford University Press, 1988.

———. *The Living Dead: A Study of the Vampire in Romantic Literature*. Durham, NC: Duke University Press, 1981.

"Vampire Culture." In Gary Laderman and Luis León, ed. *Religion and America Cultures: An Encyclopedia of Traditions, Diversity and Popular Expressions*. Santa Barbara, CA: ABC-CLIO, 2003. 279–83.

Varnado, S. L. *Haunted Presence: The Numinous in Gothic Fiction*. Tuscaloosa: University of Alabama Press, 1987.

Zanger, Jules. "Metaphor into Metonymy: The Vampire Next Door." In Joan Gordon and Veronica Hollander, ed. *Blood Read: The Vampire as Metaphor in Contemporary Culture*. Philadelphia: University of Pennsylvania Press, 1997. 17–26.

Those Sorrows Which Are Sent to Wean Us from the Earth: The Failed Quest for Enlightenment in Mary Shelley's *Frankenstein*

I. Introduction: A Mythically Potent Text

Frankenstein has stood for nearly two centuries as one of the most mythically potent texts in world literature. As I have read and reread Ms. Shelley's iconic novel over the years—some twenty times in all, since I used to read it cover-to-cover each year with multiple classrooms full of high school students—the one theme that has come to dominate my thoughts is the quest for psychic or spiritual wholeness that weaves its way symbolically through the narrative. In this essay, I draw out this theme to find out what it can tell us about ourselves and the world we have created.

First, I consider the insights of the many critics and scholars who have seen in the characters of Victor Frankenstein and his unhappy creation a distinct portrayal of psychic doubling, with each character representing the other's complementary opposite. Next, I turn to the writings of Theodore Roszak and Huston Smith, who help to clarify both the nature of Frankenstein's self-alienation via his passionate scientistic monomania and the corresponding opposite nature of the monster he brings to life. I argue that Victor and the monster may be read as symbols of the alienation of intellect from visionary power that Roszak and Smith view as endemic to Western scientific culture. Finally, I draw out the wider cultural and civilizational implications of this alienative dichotomy by arguing that the novel offers more than a mere warning about the dangers of divorcing intellect from what I shall be calling the human psyche's "visionary powers." With its pointed and despairing denial of the drive for psychic reintegration that it leads the reader to desire so keenly, *Frankenstein* delivers both a profoundly dire diagnosis of Western civilization's current condition and a starkly pessimistic prognosis for its long-term future.

II. Victor and the Monster as a Split Self

In *The Gothic Tradition in Fiction,* Elizabeth MacAndrew gives a concise statement of the idea that is my starting point: "The monster Frankenstein creates is his spiritual mirror image" (101). This reading of the novel's central riddle has long been accepted by many scholars, to the point where it has become a largely unquestioned maxim in the field of *Frankenstein* studies.[1] The idea of "doubles" or Doppelgängers was already an established convention in Romantic literature by the time Mary Shelley wrote *Frankenstein.* It was previously employed by, for example, James Hogg in *Confessions of a Justified Sinner,* E. T. A. Hoffman in "The Doubles," and Mary's father, William Godwin, in *Caleb Williams.* According to Martin Tropp, however, it would be a mistake to view Mary's use of the theme as a simple act of literary repetition: "The Doppelgänger theme in *Frankenstein* is more than the reworking of a literary tradition or the expression of Mary Shelley's personal conflicts; it is an integral part of the mythic statement of the novel, an insight that helps keep *Frankenstein* alive" (47–48). Nora Crook points out that more than one critic has said Frankenstein may well be "*the* novel . . . about doubling, shadow selves, split personalities" (59; Oates's emphasis).

Furthermore, some have contended that by having Victor's double come into being via human agency, instead of as an unmediated eruption from the unconscious in the manner of most Doppelgängers stories, Mary put a new and significant spin on the old theme. In the words of Joyce Carol Oates, the monster is a "'modern' species of shadow or *Doppelgänger,*" because it is "*deliberately created by man's ingenuity* and not a mere supernatural being or fairy-tale remnant." Whereas Doppelgängers, shadow selves, and so on have traditionally had supernatural origins, emerging spontaneously "from unacknowledged recesses of the human spirit," Frankenstein's monster is "a manufactured nemesis," one with a pointedly "natural" origin (548; Oates's emphasis). Terri Paul says the entire novel can be read as "an examination of [Victor's] interior

---

1. On this point see David Ketterer: "Although *Frankenstein* is far from being an overt allegory, there appears to be a growing consensus among critics that, from a certain point of view, the monster should be regarded as Frankenstein's double, 'something out of self' in the monster's phrase. This insight was first recorded by Muriel Spark in 1951 and subsequently amplified by others" (56).

universe and the way science enables him to objectify, give a physical reality to, the product of his imagination" (50). Christopher Small gives definitive statement to this line of thought:

> The Monster is not a ghost. He is not a genie or a spirit summoned by magic from the deep; at the same time he issues, like these, from the imagination. He is manifestly a product, or aspect, of his maker's psyche: *he is a psychic phenomenon given objective, or "actual" existence.* A Doppelganger of "real flesh and blood" is not unknown, of course, in other fictions, nor is the idea of a man created "by other means than Nature has hitherto provided," the creation of Prometheus being the archetype. But Frankenstein is "the modern Prometheus": the profound effect achieved by Mary lay in showing the Monster as the product of modern science; made, not by enchantment, i.e., directly by the unconscious, an "imaginary" being, but through a process of scientific discovery, i.e., the imagination objectified. (214–15; Small's emphasis)

I will return later to this point about the importance of Victor's double having been created through the agency of science, for it contains an important clue to the nature of Victor's self-alienation and the nature of his monster.

The character of the symbolic relationship between Victor and the monster has been subject to varying interpretations. Some critics have opted for an explicitly psychoanalytic approach, as in the case of Rosemary Jackson, who has analyzed the monster, and also the wider realm of the "double" motif in general, in terms of Freudian and Lacanian psychology. "At the heart of . . . all fantasies," Jackson writes, "is the problem of identity, a problem given particular prominence in tales of the double." She says such "tales of the double" are fueled by a desire to reverse the alienation process that humans experience in their early development ("Narcissism" 45). Jackson makes a compelling case for viewing Frankenstein's monster as representing both "a displaced desire [on the part of Victor] to be at one with the mother again and through her to reattain that primary narcissism of undifferentiated existence," and "a fantastic example of the idea of '*le corps morcelé*,' the body in pieces," as elaborated in Lacan's theory of the mirror stage of infant psychological development ("Narcissism" 48, 49). In fact, says Jackson, the driving force behind the novel's entire narrative is "a strong desire to be unified with this 'other' side. The monster *is* Frankenstein's lost selves, pieces of himself from which he has been severed, and with which he seeks re-unification" (*Fantasy* 100; Jackson's emphasis). In a roughly similar vein, Bruce Kawin regards the monster as Victor's "poetic and linguistic side with which, as a compulsive scientist, he is out of touch." Kawin also sees in the monster the personification of Victor's "inner child," his "child nature" (195–96), with the monster's destructiveness dramatizing what happens when Victor fails to sufficiently love and honor part of himself. Like Jackson with her speculations about the implicit desire for overcoming alienation, Kawin writes that "the quest of Frankenstein's life is, or ought to be, to 'reown the projection' (in Gestalt terms), to take the monster back into himself" (196).

Along the same lines, but in contrast to Kawin's rather soft-edged picture of the monster as Victor's "poetic and linguistic side" or "inner child," Robert Wexelblatt has contended that "the monster can be understood as a representation of the 'monstrous' side of Victor Frankenstein" (110). If understood in a strictly Freudian since, this amounts to probably the simplest and cleanest of all these readings. It portrays the monster as a kind of id-on-the-rampage and implies a significant duality in human nature, with light and goodness on one side, opposed by darkness and evil on the other. Wexelblatt takes this explicitly Freudian tack when he claims that Victor, representing the ego, is involved in a kind of tug-of-war between the censoring impulse of the superego, represented by Victor's fiancée Elizabeth, and the "buried and forbidden" impulses of the id, as represented by the monster (109). Paul makes similar use of the basic Freudian rubric when she calls the monster "the dark side of the scientist's soul. . . . Frankenstein's unconscious raging out of control" (60, 58). She says the monster's very existence reveals an intrinsic, conflicted duality in human nature, with the novel's central thematic-dramatic tension hinging on the conflict between mind and body, conscious and unconscious, reason and emotion.

An interesting combination of the preceding views, and one that seems more subtle and nuanced than any bald assertion that the monster represents only the evil in Victor, can be seen in MacAndrew's analysis. "The monster is Frankenstein's double," she says, "representing not the evil side of Frankenstein only, but his whole complex spiritual state" (103). In analyzing Frankenstein as "a Sentimental character lured into Faustian wrongdoing," MacAndrew advances the notion that

> Mary Shelley was more interested in maintaining the idea of the basic goodness of human nature, than in portraying a split personality. So Frankenstein does not split into good and evil parts. He suffers because he has become a monster. The sensitive, virtuous being that he was remains within him, half aware of its own monstrosity and helpless to change it. (103–4)

This interfaces with the views of José Monleon, who reads Victor and the monster as "all part of a single unit standing in a precarious equilibrium" (48), a unit in which good and evil are so thoroughly intermingled that it is difficult to discern their dividing line. MacAndrew agrees and offers some further insight: "Victor is not simply good-gone-bad. Mary Shelley makes him a despairing human being by symbolically projecting the evil in him onto the monstrous exterior of his creation" (100). Small brings out the clearly Jungian implications of such a reading when he asserts that the monster is, quite simply, the projection of Frankenstein's shadow (293).

The point is established: Victor Frankenstein and his creation may be understood as dual aspects of a single self. When Victor created his monster, it was not a mere act of objective mechanical animation. In some obscure way, he projected a part of his own psyche into the creature, making the subsequent conflict between the two of them stand as an externalized and literalized representation of a conflict within his own soul. But this very "answer" to the riddle of *Frankenstein* raises another important question: what exactly was it in Victor's psychology that made him, as a scientist devoted to reason and rationality, susceptible to such a catastrophic case of self-alienation?

III. Alienation, Objectivity, and Power-Knowledge: Exposing the Roots of Scientism

"Long before the demonic possibilities of science had become clear for all to see, it was a Romantic novelist who foresaw the career of Dr. Frankenstein— and so gave us the richest (and darkest) literary myth the culture of science has produced" (Roszak 279). So wrote the prominent culture critic and American counterculture spokesperson Theodore Roszak in 1972. By the mid-1990s, Roszak's conviction that the story of Frankenstein was scientific culture's richest literary myth had intensified to the point that he would call it the central myth of Western culture itself.[2] This was already implicit in his

---

2. See the statement to this effect on the back cover flap of Roszak's novel *The Memoirs of Elizabeth Frankenstein* (1995). In the years since Roszak's groundbreaking work in *The Making of Counterculture* (1969) and *Where the Wasteland Ends,* the exploration of the Frankenstein myth and its place in Western scientific culture has emerged as a central part of Roszak's life work, in conjunction with his radical ecological concerns. See, for example, one of his most recent books at the time of this writing, *The Gendered Atom* (1999), in which he "examine[s] the science of today through a close, insightful reading of Mary Shelley's *Frankenstein* and feminist psychology," and of which he has said, "It seemed to me that, in a certain sense, [Mary Shelley] was the first feminist psychologist, that she had an insight into science, which had no precedent, nobody had ever seen things this way before, recognizing the underlying sexual politics of modern science. That seemed to me so important

book *Where the Wasteland Ends,* from which the above quotation comes. In that book, Roszak advanced a radical critique of the Western scientific-technocratic worldview and the urban-industrial society it has created. His argument centered on the contention that this worldview is based on a psychology of "single vision" (a term borrowed from Sir Isaac Newton) that alienates the human intellect from its organic substratum and results in a similarly and equally alienated society and culture.

The heart of Roszak's position is found in his analysis of modern Western science, which he regarded as being founded on a fallacious and ultimately pathological notion of objectivity. "Every society," he wrote, "claims a portion of the private psyche for its own, a piece of our mind from which it fashions an orthodox consciousness adapted to what Freud called the Reality Principle. In Freud's view, the Reality Principle was the result of a latent activity called 'reality testing,' the purpose of which was to fix the frontier between objective and subjective" (74).

As a thoroughgoing nineteenth-century positivist, Freud considered the realm of the objective to be constituted by "nature as defined by science, the *real* external world of empirical fact and mechanistic determination" (74; Roszak's emphasis). So conceived, the idea of objective reality creates a division in the total experience of being human. The human sense of identity contracts into an "In Here" that "is ultimately felt to reside at a point inside the body . . . inside the head . . . somewhere just behind the eyes and between the ears," while everything else, including the body, is felt to be "out there." The result is a stupendous experience of self-alienation as "the body itself has become for us an alien object located Out There, the mere receptacle of our true and irrevocable identity" (93; ; Roszak's ellipses). The problem with this, Roszak said, was that Freud and those who shared his viewpoint "never wished to face squarely . . . the fact that the line we draw between the world Out There and the world In Here must be predicated on metaphysical assumptions that cannot themselves be subjected to scientific proof" (75). In Roszak's reading, objectivity as conceived by Freud and the entire nineteenth-century scientific materialist ethos is not really objective at all. Instead, it merely represents the selection of one set of elements out of the totality of human subjective experience upon which to concentrate the bulk of one's attention and energy.

This gives rise to two questions. First, why would someone want to per-

---

an insight as part of feminist psychology, that I decided to start with her and thread my understanding of western science along the lines of this classic, gothic fable" ("Puritanical Physics").

form such an exercise of consciousness? Second, what loss is suffered, if any, by the act of delimiting one's sense of identity like this? To answer the first of these, Roszak embarked on an intensive analysis of the history of the psychology of science, tracing the specific origin of the objectivizing impulse back to the early seventeenth century and the person of Sir Francis Bacon. In Bacon, said Roszak,

> we find the moral, aesthetic, and psychic raw materials of the scientific worldview. They are all there in his writing—the bright hopes and humanitarian intentions, obscurely mingled with hidden forces of dehumanization. . . . More than any other figure in the western tradition, it was Bacon, writing in the first generation of the scientific revolution, who foreshadowed— but ironically, unintentionally—the bleakest aspects of scientized culture: the malaise of spirit, the nightmare of environmental collapse, and the technocratic *machine à gouverner* [governing machine]. They brew and swirl darkly in his rich sensibility, elemental motifs within a primordial chaos. (145–46)

The key to understanding Bacon's motivation, according to Roszak, is to recognize that the man desired nothing so much as power over nature. In the context of the Western tradition's ancient quest for such power—a quest whose earliest inspiration can be seen in the Biblical injunction for humans to subdue the earth and have dominion over it (Gen. 1:26–28)—Bacon arrived a method of *knowing* that would enable people to attain this goal to a greater extent and with greater efficiency than anyone had previously thought possible. This method was, of course, the scientific method, as elaborated in Bacon's *Novum Organum* and elsewhere. Bacon and his disciples had discovered the great secret of what Roszak calls "power-knowledge": "Break faith with the environment, establish between yourself and it the alienative dichotomy called objectivity, and you will surely gain power. Then nothing—no sense of fellowship or personal intimacy or strong belonging—will bar your access to the delicate mysteries of man and nature. Nothing will inhibit your ability to manipulate and exploit" (168).

Roszak said Bacon's genius was to recognize that there is a certain type of knowledge "that grows incrementally and systematically over time" as the result of deliberate mental activity instead of lucky accident or chance. The chief value of this knowledge is that it will enable us to assert power over the natural world. In fact, in the Baconian view, the very fact that such knowledge confers power over nature is what verifies it as *true*. Bacon's sole criterion of truth was a purely operational and pragmatic one. The "great Baconian dictum," Roszak said, is "that in a true natural philosophy 'human knowledge and human power meet in one.'" There is no distinction at all between truth and utility (149).

To repeat: according to Roszak, the motivation for establishing the "alienative dichotomy" of the subjective In Here and the objective Out There is simply the desire for "power-knowledge" over the world. Read this way, the history of Western culture subsequent to Bacon is a history of increasing human alienation from self and world as technical expertise grows ever more stupendous through the application of the scientific method to all areas of life. Roszak pointed out that Bacon wanted his *novum organum* to apply "'not only to natural sciences but to *all* sciences' (specifically including ethics and politics)" and to result in the discovery of axiomatic truths "that apply to ethics, physics, mathematics, theology, medicine" (147; Roszak's emphasis). The result is the culture that we see around us today, where human beings are routinely quantified in a multitude of ways, and where the very existence of anything like "the self" or "consciousness" as *sui generis* phenomena has been seriously questioned by some of the most respected philosophers and scientists.

This brings us around to the second question raised earlier: what loss is incurred by the decision to view and live in the world in this way? Why is it that the closing decades of the twentieth century saw the widespread grip of a "devouring sense of alienation from nature and one's fellow man—and from one's own essential self" that had become "the endemic anguish of advanced industrial societies" (168)? Roszak's answer is that this crisis stems directly from the epistemological stance that lies at the very foundation of the scientific worldview:

> What is there about the knowledge of scientists that makes it so peculiarly capable of distillation and accumulation? The answer is, *the product of scientific thought has been purged of its personal characteristics.* As the Baconian ideal would have it, science is not some one person's feeling or opinion. Rather, it derives from a kind of knowing that has eliminated all elements of the knower's personality—taste or feeling, moral disposition or aesthetic temperament. (154 [emphasis in original])

In other words, what is lost in the decision to contract one's sense of identity into the subjective world of In Here, from where one can witness the objective world of Out There without the taint of error-prone human presence distorting one's view, is precisely that human presence itself. We lose our very selves when we attempt to see the world as if we had no place in it. Scientific knowing, says Roszak, "seeks a neutral eye, an impersonal eye . . . in effect, the eyes of the dead wherein reality is reflected without emotional distortion" (156; Roszak's emphasis).

As for the specific nature of the human presence that we lose in this way, Roszak calls it our "visionary powers," our ancient sense of the "Old Gnosis" by which we felt at home in the universe. "The psychic distance that separates the scientist's objectified uniformity of nature from the Oneness of the Old Gnosis is immense," he writes. "It is the distance separating St. Francis from Albert Camus' Stranger. Existentially speaking, it is all the difference between the life of one who is at home in the universe and the life of one who feels himself to be a cosmic freak" (400). Ironically, it is from the very people who have lived most intensely within the grip of this ancient visionary power—artists, musicians, poets, scientists in the old alchemical tradition such as Goethe—that "our science inherits the concept of cosmos, the meaningful whole" (398) that is psychically sundered through the myth of objective consciousness.

At this point it might be added tangentially, but not incidentally, that this subtle complicity between the old science and the new—the intellectual, reductionist, rational new science living off the visionary capital of the alchemical, Hermetic, mystical old science—is fully visible in the pages of *Frankenstein*, where it appears in the form of Victor's struggle to choose between two competing views of the universe. The first view is that of the ancient alchemists, whose epic quest for "immortality and power," as described in the writings of Cornelius Agrippa, Albertus Magnus, and Paracelsus, grips a youthful Victor with powerful visions of deep mysteries laid bare and provides him with the first external confirmation of his seemingly inborn desire to learn "the secrets of heaven and earth" (Shelley 43). But he soon finds his interests divided between the visionary alchemical view and the more practically minded view of "modern natural philosophy."

Victor explains this to Captain Walton in the story's outermost frame narrative, describing his loss of inspiration and motivation when he learned at the University of Ingolstadt that modern science had given up the grand visions of the alchemists in favor of more prosaic goals:

> I had not been content with the results promised by modern professors of natural science. . . . I had a contempt for the uses of modern natural philosophy. It was very different, when the masters of the science sought immortality and power; such views, although futile, were grand: but now the scene was changed. The ambition of the enquirer seemed to limit itself to the annihilation of those visions on which my interest in science was chiefly founded. I was required to exchange chimeras of boundless grandeur for realities of little worth. (50)

Victor goes on to explain that it wasn't until he heard a brilliant lecture delivered by Professor Waldman, who went on to become his mentor, that he regained his passion. Waldman explained that the new science, despite appearances to the contrary, contains seeds of the same grand vision that drove the old. While it may seem, said Waldman, that the new scientists have "hands . . . only made to dabble in dirt, and . . . eyes to pore over the microscope or crucible," they have actually

> performed miracles. They penetrate into the recesses of nature, and show how she works in her hiding places. They ascend to the heavens: they have discovered how the blood circulates, and the nature of the air we breathe. They have acquired new and almost unlimited powers; they can command the thunders of heaven, mimic the earthquake, and even mock the invisible world with its own shadows. (51)

Immediately upon hearing these words, young Victor felt a veritable engine of passion start churning inside him, and, in a moment of Baconian hubris, he asserted with renewed fervor that he would go on to achieve "more, far more . . . [T]reading in the steps already marked, I will pioneer a new way, explore unknown powers, and unfold to the world the deepest mysteries of creation" (51). In these words, one hears clear echoes of Bacon's famous boast that he would "put nature on the rack" (quoted in Smith 114) and force it to reveal its deepest secrets.

Obviously, this development set Victor on the road to the creation of his monster, and it thus orients us back into a consideration of the novel itself. But before returning there to examine Victor and his creature in light of Roszak's concept of the alienation inherent in the epistemology of modern science, let us pause and take a moment to examine more fully the content of what we lose when we experience the self-alienation that comes from trying to control nature through forced "objectivity."

IV. The Wisdom We Have Lost in Knowledge

The reader will recall that Roszak designated the desire for power over the natural world as the primary motivation that led Bacon and his followers to formulate an epistemology that would rigorously remove all vestiges of the human subject from the perceived external world of nature. Roszak wrote *Where the Wasteland Ends* in 1972, and his argument, while still compelling today (at least in my opinion), might sound suspiciously "sixties-ish" to some readers and therefore not worthy of consideration. Such readers would do well to recognize that the same type of argument has been made, and is still being made, quite forcibly by many contemporary thinkers who agree that modern science has led to a breakdown of culture. One of the most vocal, visible, and respected such persons is Huston Smith, the scholar and philosopher of religion whose career longevity—his most well-known book, *The World's Religions*, originally titled *The Religions of Man*, was first published in 1958 and is still one of the most widely used college textbooks on comparative religion—seems to be exceeded only by his prolificity.

Like Roszak, Smith views the modern science-and-technology dominated culture as pathological, and he attributes our arrival in such a predicament to the same "single vision" that Roszak quoted from Blake (although Smith does not use this term). "The most pertinent way to characterize the modern ethos briefly," Smith says, "is to say that it is a blend of naturalism and control." He sees this ethos as proceeding from three related factors: a Promethean motivation, a Promethean epistemology, and a naturalistic metaphysics. The Promethean motivation is our will to power over nature. The Promethean epistemology is the Baconian way of knowing that is based on empiricism or the scientific method. The naturalistic metaphysics is "the view that (a) nothing that lacks a material component exists, and (b) in what does exist the physical component has the final say" (76–78, 132). In passing, the reader might note that Smith's characterization of the modern West's overweening motivation and epistemology as "Promethean" may be seen as constituting a superficial reference to Frankenstein, "the modern Prometheus." This recognition is not at all arbitrary in light of Roszak's claims about the centrality of the Frankenstein myth to western culture.

Smith ties all this into a neat package when he identifies four steps that lead to a given culture's understanding of what it means to be human:

> We begin with *motivations*. Nothing is more uncompromising about ourselves than that we are creatures that want. . . . These wants give rise to *epistemologies*. From the welter of impressions and surmises that course through our streams of consciousness we register, firm up, and take to be true those that stay in place and support us like stepping stones in getting us where we want to go. . . . Epistemologies in turn produce *ontologies*—they create world views. In the case in question, the epistemology we fashioned to enlarge our cognitive bite into the natural world produced an ontology that made nature central. . . . Finally, ontologies generate *anthropologies*. Man being by definition a part of reality, his nature must obviously conform to what reality is. So a naturalistic world view produces, perforce, a humanistic view of man, "humanistic" being used here as adjective not for the humanities but for a specific doctrine that makes embodied man, man's measure. (102–3; Smith's emphasis)

When we apply this Smithian rubric to the issue at hand, we discover the following: what we *want* (power over nature) leads us to formulate a way of asking questions and seeing the world (empiricism, the scientific method) that in turn filters out some information and lets other information through, thus producing a worldview (scientific naturalism) that contains a picture of what it means to be a human being (an alienated intellect).[3]

We have already seen that Roszak believes the scientific worldview excludes by its very nature a crucial part of human reality. Smith agrees, and he goes on to designate some of the specific areas that he sees as falling outside the scope of scientific knowing. There are four things, he says, that "science cannot get its hands on": intrinsic and normative values, purposes, ultimate and existential meanings, and quality. For the first, Smith explains, "science can deal with instrumental values, but not intrinsic ones. It can tell us that smoking damages health, but whether health is better than somatic gratification it cannot adjudicate. Again, it can determine what people *do* like, but not what they should like. Opinion polls and market research are sciences, but there cannot be a science of the *summum bonum*."

Second, science may recognize that human beings and other animals act as if they were purposeful, but by its own principles it must reduce these apparent purposes to behavioristic explanations. Smith quotes Bacon in this regard: "Teleological explanations in science are the province of theology, not science." He also quotes Jacques Monod, the twentieth-century biochemist and Nobel laureate, who has stated unequivocally that "the cornerstone of scientific method is . . . the *systematic* denial that 'true' knowledge can be got at by interpreting phenomena in terms of final causes—that is to say, of 'purposes.'" In other words, says Smith, explanations of nature that are framed in terms of "purpose" are anthropomorphic, "and anthropomorphic explanations are the opposite of scientific ones."

Third, science cannot handle ultimate and existential meanings. Ultimate meanings are those that refer to questions about "the meaning of it all," the meaning of life and reality. Existential meanings are ones that specify the import of any given information for the individual person. The thing is, nothing in modern science intrinsically compels anyone to find anything particularly

---

3. It might be of interest here to note Smith's characterization of what might constitute this process in the *other* direction, fueled by what he calls "the perennial philosophy" and what Roszak would call the "Old Gnosis": motivation: participation; epistemology: intuitive discernment; ontology: transcendence; anthropology: fulfillment (144).

meaningful in these senses. Science "is powerless to force the human mind to find its discoveries meaning*ful*."

Fourth, science cannot say anything about quality, which "is fundamental, for it is their qualitative components that make values, meanings, and purposes important. But qualities, being subjective, barely lend themselves to even the minimum requirement of science—objectivity—let alone submit to quantification." As an example, Smith points out the absurdity of trying to quantify the quality of *happiness:* "Euphrometers have been attempted, but without success, for two pains do not add up to one that is twice as painful, and half a happiness makes no sense" (111–12; Smith's emphases).

The upshot of all this is plain to see. By its most basic principles, Smith says, science excludes the values, meanings, purposes, and qualities that make life worth living. As he vividly puts it, "an epistemology that aims relentlessly at control rules out the possibility of transcendence in principle" (134). Regarding the quality of transcendence, he says something is transcendent when it is "superior to us by every measure of value we know and some that elude us." This quality has direct epistemological implications, since "to expect a transcendental object to appear on a viewing screen wired by an epistemology that is set for control would be tantamount to expecting color to appear on a television screen that was built for black and white" (114). On this point, one might helpfully paraphrase Eliot by saying that ultimately Smith is agreeing with Eliot's famous line about "the wisdom lost in knowledge." In our search for greater knowledge, fueled by a desire to gain control over nature, we have lost the wisdom that is what makes life worth living and knowledge worth having. Where is the wisdom we have lost in knowledge? It is located in the cast-off part of the human psyche, in the visionary aspect, the purposeful, valuing, qualitative part that sees the world in terms of meaning. In other words, the part that modern science does not want to recognize or deal with.

Here is where the thought of Smith meets most intimately with that of Roszak, and where I take my cue to return to a direct examination of *Franken-stein* and see what I can draw from it in light of the above discussion. Both Smith and Roszak agree that the "relentless objectivity" or "single vision" of the modern scientific mindset omits from view the most valuable parts of the world and of human nature. Smith designates these items as values, purposes, meanings, and quality. Roszak simply calls them the "visionary powers" of the human race. Either way, if we agree that Victor Frankenstein was possessed by the scientistic monomania of single vision or relentless objectivity (a point that will be substantiated below), then we can now see the enormous load of psychic baggage that went into the creation of his double. The *disjecta membra* of Victor Frankenstein's soul include all those things that fall outside the ken of the contracted self of the scientific world view, all those meanings and qualities and visionary powers upon whose recovery in the life of Western culture Smith and Roszak have set their sights.

V. Intellect Versus Visionary Powers

At this point, half of my argument concerns Victor Frankenstein and half concerns the monster. Regarding Victor, I am advocating the idea that he may be viewed as a symbol of the alienated intellect of scientific single vision, as described by Roszak and Smith. We can now see that Victor's progress toward alienation and the ultimate splitting of himself into complementary halves can be analyzed in terms of Smith's four-step process of motivation, epistemology, ontology, anthropology. Victor's motivation is the Baconian lust for power over nature. Although many have analyzed his motivation in terms of the desire for knowledge, it clear that for Victor, this desire is subordinate to his will to power. We see this especially as his education progresses. Tropp brings this out in his comment about the grand speech by Professor Waldman that converts Victor into an ardent proselyte of the new science: "Even though he begins by attacking the pretensions of the medieval alchemists, it soon becomes clear that Waldman is promising, if not the same secrets, the same power" (61). Under Waldman's tutelage, Victor moves on from making boasts about discovering nature's secrets to boasting that he will conquer death. "Life and death," he says, "appeared to me ideal bounds, which I should first break through, and pour a torrent of light into our dark world. . . . Pursuing these reflections, I thought, that if I could bestow animation upon lifeless matter, I might in process of time (although I now found it impossible) renew life where death had apparently devoted the body to corruption" (55).

With his motivation being power, Victor chooses as his epistemology the approach of modern scientific method. Valdine Clemens writes that Victor's "fascination with and subsequent rejection of alchemical studies calls attention to the rupture between the medieval and modern worlds, a break that is signaled by the scorn Bacon expressed for medieval magic and alchemy and their lack of attention to empirical reality" (92). As we have seen, Bacon's scorn for the Old Gnosis led him to formulate the scientific method as a means of removing from view all vestiges of the error-prone human subject. While Mary Shelley never explicitly refers to the scientific method in her novel, it is clear that Victor's choice of the new science over the old must involve his adoption of the new scientific way of interrogating nature by putting it "on the rack."

Armed with the scientific method and a will to power over nature, Victor soon arrives, as Smith could have predicted, at an ontology of naturalism. This is seen most clearly in his total lack of responsiveness to the horrors of the "charnel-houses" he is forced to haunt in the course of his research. He explains that he was already disinclined from superstition by his upbringing— "In my education my father had taken the greatest precautions that my mind should be impressed with no supernatural horrors" (53)—but it is clear that his attitude also stems from his monomania. When he relates the story of his abortive attempt to create a female and recalls the feelings that gripped him during the creation of the original monster, he says, "During my first experiment, a kind of enthusiastic frenzy had blinded me to the horror of my employment; my mind was intently fixed on the consummation of my labour, and my eyes were shut to the horror of my proceedings" (139). As a result, he came to view nature through what Roszak vividly referred to as "a dead man's eyes" (142). Victor tells Walton that as he went about the work of collecting the materials to make his creature, the conventional grimness and eeriness of the environments he was forced to work in did not affect him in the least: "Darkness had no effect upon my fancy; and a churchyard was to me merely the receptacle of bodies deprived of life, which, from being the seat of beauty and strength, had become food for the worm" (53). He even admits that in his efforts to learn the secret of bestowing life, he resorted to the torture of living animals: "My limbs now tremble, and my eyes swim with the remembrance; but then a resistless, almost frantic, impulse, urged me forward; I seemed to have lost all soul or sensation but for this one pursuit" (56). Tropp underscores the stark attitude of scientific naturalism that characterized Victor's outlook at this point:

> In describing the events leading to the creation of the Monster, Mrs. Shelley shows . . . her preoccupation with the reflection of the motives of the creator in the things he creates. On this level, the Monster is symbolic of the mechanistic attitude behind man's new technology; its construction out of the parts of dead corpses is a logical extension of the reductionist equation of living things with inorganic matter. (63)

The result of all this is that, as Roszak and Smith would have predicted, Victor becomes alienated from himself as his sense of identity contracts into the stunted "In Here" of the dichotomous modern scientific consciousness. Paul writes that Victor lived "too much in his mind and not enough in the world. . . . Frankenstein is a character curiously lacking in physical substance and vitality. He is all mind and no body." As in Roszak's analysis, Paul recognizes that this decision to identify purely with the intellect leads Victor to an experience of alienation not only from himself, but from other people and from the natural world as well: "Frankenstein is an alienated figure, cut off from his own humanity as well as that of the people around him. . . . [He] is alienated from society and human companionship. . . . Because he lives almost exclusively in the mind, Frankenstein is alienated from nature" (52–54). Maggie Kilgour, in a discussion of the figure of the scientist in Romantic thought generally and *Frankenstein* especially, states that scientific knowledge, far from healing alienation and isolation, actually exacerbates such things. Such knowledge "sets subject over object as victor over victim." In fact, Kilgour says the epitome of "the alienated autonomous individual, the loner *par excellence,*" is none other than the figure of the scientist, "a cerebral questor who, in his laboratory (the new castle that in films becomes the central image for *Frankenstein*) has to detach himself not only from the objects of his analysis but from all relationships" (195).

In *Frankenstein,* the relationships that are severed by this alienation include everyone and everything Victor has ever held dear. He loses, for instance, the joy he formerly felt in his relationship with nature and the consolation he formerly gained from the enjoyment of art, literature, and science. In his youth, he says, "if I was ever overcome by *ennui,* the sight of what is beautiful in nature, or the study of what is excellent and sublime in the productions of man, could always interest my heart, and communicate elasticity to my spirit" (136). But the pursuit of his goal destroys this peaceful sense of harmony. During the exceptionally beautiful summer season that unfolds around him while he is engrossed in his project of creation, he is psychically unable to pay attention either to nature or other people (56). After the deed is done and he falls into a black despair, he finds that he is now lost within himself: "I shunned the face of man, all sound of joy or complacency was torture to me; solitude was my only consolation—deep, dark, deathlike solitude." He is even unable to accept the affection Elizabeth offers him as she tries to comfort him (83, 85–86). Later, when he is about to undertake the creation of a female, the crisis is increased. "I saw an insurmountable barrier placed between me and my fellow men," he says. The only one who is able to surmount the barrier is Victor's dear friend Henry Clerval, in whom Victor says he "saw the image of my former self" (135). But Clerval ends up murdered by the monster, and Victor's complete isolation is sealed. Let us recall what Roszak said about the secret of power-knowledge: "Break faith with the environment, establish between yourself and it the alienative dichotomy called objectivity, and you will surely gain power. Then nothing—no sense of fellowship or personal intimacy or strong belonging—will bar your access to the delicate mysteries of man and nature. Nothing will inhibit your ability to manipulate and exploit" (168). Now, having accepted the Baconian bargain of power in exchange for breaking faith with the environment, Victor discovers the shattering result: that he has become "a blasted tree . . . a miserable spectacle of wretched humanity, pitiable to others, intolerable to myself" (136).

And what of the monster? If Victor is embodied intellect, miserable in his self-imposed exile from the rest of the universe, then what components are active in his unhappy creation? What characterizes the monster's consciousness and nature? Earlier, I mentioned the significance of the fact that the monster is not a spontaneous eruption from the unconscious but the product of rational scientific experimentation. We are now in a position to see why this is so important. Victor, let it be repeated, is embodied intellect, the "In Here" of scientific knowing. As his double, the monster is his complementary opposite, which means that *the monster serves as nothing other than the repository for all Victor's discarded visionary powers* as elaborated by Smith and Roszak.

The importance of seeing the monster not simply as Victor's "dark side" but as the literal embodiment of what MacAndrew characterized as Victor's "whole complex spiritual state" is now apparent. As complements, the two halves of Victor's psyche are indeed different from each other, but the monster is far from being a creature of unadulterated evil. I have already quoted Kawin's contention that the monster is Victor's "poetic and linguistic side." Other readers have similarly noticed the monster's visionary nature, or at least the fact that he is not all monstrous and evil. David Ketterer writes, "The usual conclusion, that the monster represents the destructive and diabolical nature of Frankenstein's overweaning [*sic*] intellectual ambition does not square with the actual presentation of the monster as a noble savage, an innocent more sinned against than sinning" (57). Wexelblatt, who, as I noted earlier, called the monster the representation of Victor's monstrous side, has also applied the Nietzschean categories of Apollonian and Dionysian to the matter, saying that the monster represents Dionysus, human nature's passionate aspect as opposed to its rational Apollonian aspect. Recall that for Nietzsche, despite the fact that Apollo was the god of art and music, it was Dionysus who represented the creative energies—the visionary aspects of life—that constitute the vitality of an individual or a culture.

Another important avenue of insight opens up when we consider the *gendered* aspect of the unconscious mind. Crook reminds us that "feminist criticism of the last twenty-five years has directed attention to *Frankenstein* as 'female gothic,' revealing a specifically *female* unconscious" (59; Crook's emphasis). In the novel, the unconscious is of course represented by the monster, and this de facto characterization of him as feminine falls right in line with the decision to view him as symbolizing humanity's visionary aspect, for one of the most important qualities of these visionary powers is that they are categorically feminine, as understood by Roszak, Smith, and countless others. These "dark" energies are the earthy, "irrational" wisdom of the Mother Goddess as opposed to the light-filled, cerebral, rational knowledge of the Father God. They are the soft, yielding fluidity of the feminine Yin as opposed to the hard unyieldingness of the masculine Yang. And while it may seem strange to equate the monster with both Nietzsche's ecstatic Dionysus and the softness of femininity, we may call to mind two things that explain the connection: first, that the "irrational" exuberance of Dionysus corresponds to the "irrational" emotion and intuition of the feminine; and second, that such seeming contradictions are inherent in the nature of visionary wisdom, which, so it is said, transcends the traditional wisdom of "either-or."

It is easy to see this union of opposites in Mary Shelley's portrayal of the monster, who is capable of both exceptional tenderness and exceptional cruelty. He is transported to the heights of ecstatic philosophical contemplation by reading Plutarch and Milton, and he is sunk to the depths of satanic rage by his utter exclusion from the world of human affections. He unhesitatingly plunges into a river to rescue a drowning girl, but then he later mercilessly strangles Victor's younger brother William. He sets himself the goal of destroying Victor by destroying all that Victor loves, but then he leaves food behind to keep Victor alive, and in the end he weeps over Victor's corpse. By his nature as the visionary aspect of Victor's soul, the monster is susceptible to all these contradictory behaviors if he is not properly recognized and honored.

In commenting on the spiritual alienation of the modern West, Roszak notes this connection between, on the one hand, the denial, exclusion, suppression, or otherwise neglect of the visionary powers, and, on the other hand, the way they express themselves: "Let us be honest enough to confront our culture in its entirety and ask: is it merely coincidence that, in the midst of so much technological mastery and economic abundance, our art and thought continue to project a nihilistic imagery unparalleled in human history? Are we to believe there is not a connection between these facts?" (370). The visionary powers will have their say whether or not they are consciously honored. If they are repressed or cut off via the decision to view the world from a position of Baconian "objectivity," they will appear as murderous monsters.

As noted earlier, Small designates the monster as Victor's "shadow" in the Jungian sense, and we can take this as the ultimate word on the matter. Tropp quotes a Jungian psychologist's description of the shadow as containing not just "bad" aspects of the personality but good ones, "normal instincts and creative qualities" (48). For Jung, the shadow was a function of psychological wholeness. While the shadow may appear threatening and evil to the ego that creates it by repressing qualities in the self that are perceived as undesirable—just as the monster appears hideous and evil in the eyes of Victor and a society that does not want to contend with the inevitable alienative aspect of scientific naturalism's and materialism's psychology and anthropology—in fact the shadow is the complement of the ego, without which the ego has no solidity or ultimate sense of meaning. Likewise, for Victor there can be no sense of wholeness without the reincorporation of his visionary aspect into himself. Lacking that, he remains a blasted tree, and with this recognition we come to the final point of my argument.

VI. Frankenstein *as Nihilistic Parable*

I have analyzed *Frankenstein* as the story of the eponymous protagonist's seduction by the lure of the will to power over nature, resulting in his experiencing a split with his visionary side and creating a separate autonomous being who embodies this repressed and rejected aspect of his self. Roszak has called Frankenstein the central myth of Western culture. Smith has identified the ethos of the modern West as being founded on Promethean principles. If these assessments are accurate, then it is surely reasonable to view Victor and the monster as representing fundamental forces at work not just in Mary Shelley's novel but in Western culture itself. "For a thousand people familiar with the story of Victor creating his monster from selected cadaver spares and endowing them with new life," writes Brian Aldiss, "only to shrink back in horror from his own creation, not one will have read Mary Shelley's original novel. This suggests something of the power of infiltration of *this first great myth of the industrial age*" (23; emphasis added). Small declares that "*Frankenstein* lives on, in popular imagination, detached from its origins, as part of the folklore of modern man" (14). Jackson observes that the novel "has become one of the central myths of post-Romantic culture, both through literary and film texts" (*Fantasy* 101). Victor Frankenstein himself is "a near-allegorical figure," writes Oates, who calls the novel itself "a parable for our time, an enduring prophecy" (552, 553). In short, the story of Victor Frankenstein and his monster has burst the bonds of its original genre (the Gothic novel) to become a text of world-historical importance that says something about human life. A canonical Gothic parable, we might call it.

But what, exactly, does this "enduring prophecy" prophesy? If a parable is construed as a story with a metaphorical meaning, often a moral one, then what is the deep parabolic meaning of *Frankenstein?*

In the terms that I have drawn in this paper, *Frankenstein* is a parable about the failure of the Romantic quest for enlightenment in an age of scientific rationality. Stated another way, it is about the demonic power of science to prevent the fulfillment of the eternal spiritual quest. For there can be no doubt, I think, that the ultimate message of the novel is one of despair. When Victor dies in the arctic waste, a ruined and despairing man; and when the monster weeps over his body, lamenting both the death of his creator and his own final transition from benevolent spirit to murderous fiend; and when the monster then vanishes "in darkness and distance" into the arctic night to immolate himself, there is no redemption to be had for anybody.

Recall that Crook identified *Frankenstein* as possibly the arch-novel about doubles and shadow selves. Then recall Jackson's assertion that the novel is driven by "a strong desire to be unified with this 'other' side. The monster *is* Frankenstein's lost selves, pieces of himself from which he has been severed, and with which he seeks re-unification." To generate this very desire, says Jackson, is the whole function of doubles, so that "Frankenstein, as a subject, is driven by a desire for unity with another, by a desire for his life to have absolute significance" (*Fantasy* 108). Kawin, invoking Gestalt psychology, says Victor's proper quest is "to 'reown the projection' . . . to take the monster back into himself" (196). Employing a psychological scheme that sees the human psyche as divided into three selves (the "higher self," "conscious self," and "basic self"), with Victor representing the conscious self and the monster the basic self, Kawin calls the novel "a parable of the conscious self's absolute need for the basic self and of the tragedy that attends an irresponsible rejection of the innocent, creative, poetic, angry, emotional, sexual, hungry, and vulnerable being inside even the most disciplined person." Mary Shelley's "underlying vision," says Kawin, is "the drive toward personal wholeness, of the integration of creativity and compassion, industry and spirit" (197–99).

Let us further note that the theme of doubles and their quest for wholeness in reunion is quite ancient. In *Man and His Symbols,* Jung delineated four cycles of the hero myth, the last of which involves twins who are united in the mother's womb, separated at birth, and then embark on a life mission to be reunited with each other in order to form a whole being (103, 106). There is thus a pre-existing mythic pattern that leads us to desire the reunification of Victor with his creature.

So all these factors—*Frankenstein*'s specific narrative and intrinsic logic, the inner psychological core and meaning of tales of the double, and an ancient mythic pattern at work in the human psyche—work together to make us crave a resolution of the Victor/Monster split by having them come together again. But in the face of all this longing, which is simply the longing to attain spiritual wholeness, the novel denies us any fulfillment. Victor "never successfully reconciles these opposing forces within himself and becomes an integrated man" (Paul 58). In the words of Oates, *Frankenstein* emerges as "a remarkably acute diagnosis of the lethal nature of *denial*—denial of responsibility for one's actions, denial of the shadow-self locked within consciousness" (553; Oates's emphasis). Jackson, employing her Freudian/Lacanian analytical grid, says the novel "suggests that there can be no satisfactory resolution of the conflict between the Ideal ego and the fragmented, protean selves outside its formation. It is an open-ended work, leaving in tension various parts of the psyche" ("Narcissism" 51). She says that with its mythic centrality in post-Romantic culture, *Frankenstein* "lies behind modern fantasy, as an influence and inspiration, but also as in index of the *loss* registered through the fantastic" (*Fantasy* 101; Jackson's emphasis).

This sense of loss is devastating. The narrative "shows us a gradual tearing away of all other relationships, ties, affections, until, in the midst of frigid and inhuman landscapes, the two sides pursue each other in a frantic fable of revenge and the ultimate disintegration of personality" (Wexelblatt 110). As a parable of the West's centuries-long journey through the psychic and physical landscape of alienated spiritual vision, this disintegration of personality is not just personal but cultural. On this level, Mary Shelley seems to be telling us that the rift between intellect and visionary self that the scientific mindset has opened up can never be healed. As the wife of Percy Shelley and the compatriot of Byron and others, Mary lived right in the heart of English Romanticism. She knew as well as anybody the desire for spiritual enlightenment that glowed like a hot coal at the center of the Romantic sensibility. Byron with his poems about transcending the world of sense and matter and finding a realm of pure beauty; Shelley with his Platonic idealism; Wordsworth with his conviction that we are all born "trailing clouds of immortality"; and especially Blake with his visionary ideas about "the marriage of heaven and hell"—all these and more formed the central part of the intellectual and spiritual milieu in which Mary Shelley lived and wrote. In the midst of it all, the blatantly nihilistic message of *Frankenstein* is all the more apparent, and all the more appalling. Roger Shattuck has described the novel as a "remarkable fiction that flies in the face of the Romantic and utopian themes that spawned it." Victor's ruin, he says, is "no Fortunate Fall. No one can redeem the destruction Frankenstein has left behind him" (98, 99). Oates writes that as the novel nears its conclusion, it starts to seem like a kind of "antiromance, a merciless critique of Romantic attitudes" (552). True, the attitudes she specifically names are not utopian or spiritual but are instead "sorrow, misery, self-loathing, despair, paralysis." But she is speaking of these qualities in Victor's character. And in the scheme I am proposing here, where Victor symbolizes the alienated intellect of the modern West, a critique of these attitudes amounts to a critique of the vestigial remnants in Victor's personality of the Romantic longing for transcendence that he betrayed.

In a strong statement of the general position that I am advancing about the function of *Frankenstein,* Jackson quotes Robert Hume as saying, "Almost schematically, Mary Shelley's novel reverses and denies the Romantic quest for gnosis." Jackson comments, "A vast gap is opened up between knowledge (as scientific investigation and rational inquiry) and gnosis (a knowledge of ultimate truths, a kind of spiritual wisdom)." In the end, Victor's and the monster's split is not resolved "but is re-located in a final darkness." In this way, says Jackson, "*Frankenstein* marks the establishment of a tradition of disenchanted, secular fantasies, becoming increasingly grotesque and horrific" (*Fantasy* 101).

At this point, we might reasonably ask what the alternative to this situation would be. What might Victor have done that would have averted the tragedy, that might even have led to his (and therefore the monster's) spiritual fulfillment? Oddly, the answer may be found in a figure of speech that he himself utters. At the point in his narrative where he describes how Elizabeth fell into a black despair after the deaths of William and Justine, Victor comments, "The first of those sorrows which are sent to wean us from the earth, had visited her, and its dimming influence quenched her dearest smiles" (84–85). It is the greatest of the book's many ironies that Victor cannot recognize in his own words the path that he could have taken to find healing and fulfillment. One of the oldest spiritual themes in the world, perhaps *the* oldest, is the necessity of suffering for salvation. In Christianity this is seen in the crucifixion of Christ, the mystical idea of the "dark night of the soul," and the doctrine of the *felix culpa,* the "happy fall" (from paradise) that sets in motion the plan of humanity's redemption through Christ. In Buddhism it is seen in the first of the Buddha's Four Noble Truths, which is simply that "all life is suffering (or impermanence)." Buddhists of all stripes agree that this suffering is necessary and good, for without it none of us would ever feel the need to transcend our unenlightened state.

The contemporary spiritual teacher and writer Eckhart Tolle states the matter as follows, in terms of the suffering that arises from striving for some worldly goal in the future (which for our purpose we might conceive as Victor's quest to conquer death):

> Ultimately, suffering arises from not finding. And that is the beginning of an awakening—when the realization dawns that "Perhaps this is not the way. Perhaps I will never get to where I am striving to reach; perhaps it's not in the future at all." After having been lost in the world, suddenly, through all the pressure of suffering, the realization comes that the answers may not be found out there in worldly attainment and in the future. That's an important point for many people to reach. That sense of deep crisis—where the world as they have known it and the sense of self that they have known that is identified with the world, become meaningless. . . . The purpose of the world is for you to be lost in it, ultimately. The purpose of the world is for you to suffer, to create the suffering that seems to be what is needed for the awakening to happen. And then once the awakening happens, with it comes the realization that the suffering is unnecessary now. You have reached the end of suffering because you have transcended the world. It is a place free of suffering. (Cohen)

I do not need to quote names and page numbers to point out that a multitude of critics have recognized that one of the functions of the monster as Victor's double is to take away all that Victor loves. The monster himself explicitly states this as his mission when Victor refuses to create a mate for him. Above, I quoted Shattuck as saying that Victor's ruin can in no way be construed as a fortunate fall. While I agree with him, it is at least possible to see, in light of Tolle's words, how it *could* have been a fortunate fall if Victor had decided to let the sorrows wean him from the earth and show him the way to transcendence and spiritual fulfillment. He might have decided to endure the sufferings as his dark night of the soul, and on the other side he would have found that he had become whole again. Small has recognized this possibility, too, and I shall give him the final word on the matter, which he frames in terms of the Christian idea of forgiveness: "In the last situation, when metaphor vanishes, it is not possible to reject [the monster], for he is no longer separate, he is quite simply ourselves. When by his agency, which is ours, we are bereft of everything, we will forgive him for being us as he will forgive us for trying to deny it; by which, merged with each other, we may ask to be forgiven" (331).

VII. Conclusion: The Presence or Absence of Hope

Not all readers agree that the conclusion of *Frankenstein* is steeped in utter despair. Kawin, for instance, sees in Walton the symbol of the integration that eludes Frankenstein and his monster: "One could add up Frankenstein and the Monster and have something resembling an integrated person: a figure who would in fact resemble Walton, who is an overreacher with both scientific and poetic interests." Although "this synthesis would add to the figure of Walton . . . the element of tragic experience" (194–195), it would also seem to hint that the novel contains at least a trace of the satisfaction that I am claiming it denies the reader. We might note, though, that Steven Glickman, Kawin's student at the University of Colorado, writes that while Kawin's idea seems plausible, the novel leaves the reader to "do the math" for him or herself (127–28). And of course there is no guarantee that everyone will see this or agree with it. On a more insidious note, Glickman considers the triple-framing device of *Frankenstein's* narrative structure (something about which I have said nothing in this paper so far), and says that "multiple framing suggest [*sic*] to me an outward trajectory, a movement from within the Chinese-box structure out beyond the text to its reader" (123). He quotes Peter Brooks as saying that the text of the novel "contaminates us with a residue of meaning that cannot be explained or rationalized, but is passed on as affect, as taint" (124).[4] In light of what I have proposed in this paper, the "affective taint" that *Frankenstein* may pass on to its reader will have a powerful effect indeed, since it will be confirming to the modern reader, living perhaps in the midst of the spiritually alienated West, that the situation is beyond repair.

From a scientific standpoint as well as a literary one, there are those who do not think the situation is as hopeless as Mary Shelley has made it out to be. Chet Raymo, a physicist, astronomer, and popular writer about scientific matters for laypeople, has written about the scientific objectivity that Roszak so deplores, and has said that he sees nothing inherently wrong with it. He points out that many modern scientists were influenced by the positivist philosophers of the nineteenth and early twentieth century. Recalling Bacon's disdain for alchemy, he writes, "We were weary of the seemingly endless squabbles of metaphysicians and dreamed of objectivity, even if it meant focusing our attention on the small part of human experience that is amenable to logical analysis. We sought clarity at the cost of completeness" (170). He

---

4. The quotation is from Peter Brooks, "Godlike Science/Unhallowed Arts," in George Levine and U. C. Knoepflmacher, ed. *The Endurance of* Frankenstein: *Essays on Mary Shelley's Novel* (Berkeley: University of California Press, 1979), 220.

acknowledges that scientific objectivity involves an incomplete view of the human self, and he justifies this by explaining that science "is willing to temporarily suppress part of what it means to be human in order to gather to itself more reliable knowledge of the nonhuman world" (54). In words that are strikingly reminiscent of Roszak's, and which recall at once both the position Roszak advances and the one he critiques, Raymo writes:

> Scientific literature emphasizes the part of our experience that is common to anyone who makes the observations in the same way. The quantitative prose of science is a way of separating the world "out there" from the world "in here." Ordinary language is laden with cultural and personal baggage. It transfers too much of ourselves onto the thing that is described. The struggle for objectivity is what makes science a source of reliable knowledge. (230)

But he also readily acknowledges that "a diet of purely objective knowledge is oppressive" (230). He sees art and science as complementary, not competing (perhaps in the way that I have portrayed Victor and the monster as complementary halves of a single self), writing that "art and science are each sublime activities of the human mind. We are less than human without either. . . . The scientist who does not allow herself to be spiritually empowered by art is the poorer for it. And the artist who dismisses science has closed himself off from half of the human adventure" (54, 55).

I have devoted so much space to quoting Raymo simply to reinforce that from the scientific quarter itself, there are voices that would call Roszak's, Smith's, and Mary Shelley's positions absurd. Raymo himself appears to be a man possessed of a deep spiritual consciousness, as witnessed by the book of his from which I am quoting. It is a book in which he indeed manages to make the connection named in the title (between science and religion) seem exhilarating, and it is an eloquent testimony of one scientist's desire to honor both sides of his nature. It is not my place to agree or disagree with him, although I might point out that Roszak would find much to argue with in his statements, especially in the idea that science provides "more reliable knowledge of the nonhuman world." As we have seen, Roszak would deny the desirability of viewing things in terms of a "nonhuman world" at all. Instead, he would argue that a harmonious relationship between scientific knowledge, conceived explicitly in terms of the "In Here/Out There" dichotomy, and the visionary side of human nature, is infinitely more difficult to achieve than Raymo has made it appear, if indeed it is achievable at all.

Ultimately, my point is that this issue is central to the relationship Western culture has had with itself for the past two centuries, and that we can find in *Frankenstein* a parable about what it means to commit ourselves to the quest for power over nature through scientific objectivity. One does not have to agree with Mary Shelley's dire prognosis any more than one has to agree with Roszak, Raymo, or anybody of the other people I have quoted. But I do think we cannot afford to ignore "the first great myth of the industrial age," "the central myth of Western culture." And I suspect that in the future, as we in the West continue our journey through the dark night of psychic alienation in the urban-industrial technological landscape that we have created, we may find ourselves turning more and more to *Frankenstein* as a subject for entertainment, reflection, and even guidance. I am inclined to think that this is as it should be, for as MacAndrew has said, "Gothic fiction symbolizes the unresolvable, shifting, but perpetual paradox of human nature. Until the human condition changes, we will find such fantasies to embody the dilemma of our existence, to face us with it, so that we, too, may face the dark" (250).

2001

Works Cited

Aldiss, Brian W. *Billion Year Spree: The True History of Science Fiction.* Garden City, NY: Doubleday, 1973.

Clemens, Valdine. *The Return of the Repressed: Gothic Horror from* The Castle of Otranto *to* Alien. Albany: State University of New York Press, 1999.

Cohen, Andrew. "Ripples on the Surface of Being: An Interview with Eckhart Tolle." *What Is Enlightenment?* Accessed 24 July 2001. www.wie.org/ j18/tolle.asp. vortex144.wordpress.com/2013/09/15/ripples-on-the-surface-of-being-an-interview-with-eckhart-tolle-by-andrew-cohen/

Crook, Nora. "Mary Shelley, Author of *Frankenstein.*" In David Punter, ed. *A Companion to the Gothic.* Malden, MA: Blackwell, 2000. 58–69.

Glickman, Steven R. "Forbidden Knowledge: The Ambivalence of Knowledge and Writing in Horror Fiction from Mary Shelley to Stephen King." Ph.D. diss.: University of Colorado, 1997.

Jackson, Rosemary. *Fantasy: The Literature of Subversion.* New York: Methuen, 1981.

———. "Narcissism and Beyond: A Psychoanalytic Reading of Frankenstein and Fantasies of the Double." In William Coyle, ed. *Aspects of Fantasy: Selected Essays from the Second International Conference on the Fantastic in Literature and Film.* Westport, CT: Greenwood Press, 1986. 43–53.

Jung, Carl F. *Man and His Symbols*. New York: Dell, 1964.

Kawin, Bruce. *The Mind of the Novel: Reflexive Fiction and the Ineffable*. Princeton: Princeton University Press, 1982.

Ketterer, David. *Frankenstein's Creation*. Victoria, BC: University of Victoria, 1979.

Kilgour, Maggie. *The Rise of the Gothic Novel*. London: Routledge, 1995.

MacAndrew, Elizabeth. *The Gothic Tradition in Fiction*. New York: Columbia University Press, 1979.

Monleon, José. *1848: The Assault on Reason* (extract). In Ken Gelder, ed., *The Horror Reader*. London: Routledge, 2000. 20–28.

Oates, Joyce Carol. "Frankenstein's Fallen Angel." *Critical Inquiry* 10 (March 1984): 543–54.

Paul, Terri Goldberg. "Blasted Hopes: A Thematic Survey of Nineteenth-Century British Science Fiction." Ph.D. diss.: Ohio State University, 1979.

"Puritanical Physics: Theodore Roszak Attacks Sexual Stereotypes Dominating Today's Scientific Community" (interview). *Grace Online: Life from a Spiritual Perspective*. 5 April 2000. www.gracecathedral.org/enrichment /interviews.int_20000405.shtml

Raymo, Chet. *Skeptics and True Believers: The Exhilarating Connection between Science and Religion*. New York: Walker & Co., 1998.

Roszak, Theodore. *Where the Wasteland Ends: Politics and Transcendence in Postindustrial Society*. 1972. Berkeley, CA: Celestial Arts, 1989.

Shattuck, Roger. *Forbidden Knowledge: From Prometheus to Pornography*. New York: St. Martin's Press, 1996.

Shelley, Mary. *Frankenstein*. Ed. Johanna M. Smith. Boston: Bedford Books, 1992.

Small, Christopher. *Mary Shelley's Frankenstein: Tracing the Myth*. Pittsburgh: University of Pittsburgh Press, 1973.

Smith, Huston. *Beyond the Post-Modern Mind*. New York: Crossroad, 1982.

Tropp, Martin. *Mary Shelley's Monster: The Story of Frankenstein*. Boston: Houghton Mifflin, 1976.

Wexelblatt, Robert. "The Ambivalence of Frankenstein." *Arizona Quarterly* 36 (1980): 101–17.

Gods and Monsters, Worms and Fire: A Horrific Reading of Isaiah

I. Introduction: Troubling Questions and Taxonomic Schemes

Most educated people are familiar with the common moral and aesthetic problems that confront modern readers of certain Old Testament texts. *The NIV Study Bible,* a modern English translation with accompanying study notes that is widely used among contemporary evangelicals, devotes space in its introduction to the Book of Joshua to point out one of these common problems: "Many readers of Joshua (and other OT books) are deeply troubled by the role that warfare plays in this account of God's dealings with his people." The introduction goes on to justify the pervasive practice of war and conquest by God's people in the Book of Joshua (and, by implication, in the rest of the Old Testament) by framing it as "the story of how God, to whom the whole world belongs, at one stage in the history of redemption reconquered a portion of the earth from the powers of this world that had claimed it for themselves, defending their claims by force of arms and reliance on their false gods" (Barker 290).

That the editors of such a prominent, mainstream publication should feel it necessary to devote space to justifying the morality of the Old Testament is witness to the fact that much of what appears in this ancient library of texts seems bizarre and brutal to a host of modern readers. I, for one, feel that Joshua is hardly the only Old Testament book that warrants such a walking-on-eggshells approach. Many other books call for equal treatment, and not only because they, like Joshua, feature scenes of slaughter and cruelty performed at the behest, and sometimes directly by the hand, of the biblical God, but also because of the outright horror, in a cosmic supernatural sense, that they generate.

Isaiah ranks among those other books that the authors and editors of *The NIV Study Bible* would have done well to approach with care. As a reader with

251

a particular personal interest in matters of both religion and supernatural horror, I am fascinated by the fact that much of what appears in Isaiah might have been lifted right out of a horror story. Layered in with the familiar passages about the suffering servant and the comfort that Yahweh offers his people are disturbing scenes of bloodshed and mayhem, and even wholesale cosmic destruction, that clash violently with this softer stuff. Add to these the fact that the book's closing verse—chapter 66, verse 24—rounds things out on an explicit note of graphic horror, and you have a situation in which an all-out horrific reading seems warranted.

In order to present such a reading, I will make use of a taxonomic tool formulated by Roger C. Schlobin and presented in his paper "Prototypic Horror: The Genre of the Book of Job." Schlobin offers a three-part scheme for judging whether or not a given text should be understood as a horror story, and he applies this scheme to the Book of Job in an effort to answer the longstanding question of the book's proper genre. In what follows, I demonstrate that when the same scheme is applied to Isaiah, the book easily meets every one of Schlobin's stated requirements. My evidence, in addition to 66:24, will include passages from chapters 24 and 34, in which Yahweh reduces the created world to a state of primeval chaos, and from chapter 40, which describes Yahweh's absolute aloofness and transcendence in forceful detail. I will argue that 66:24, coming as it does on the heels of these other passages, cements the validity of reading Isaiah as a horror story. Or rather, I will argue that it cements the *possibility* of such a reading (a distinction that I will return to in my concluding thoughts).

On a methodological note, I should pause here to specify that my approach in this essay is explicitly reader-oriented. I make unabashed leaps of the imagination, all founded on the personal base of knowledge and set of interests that define me as a culturally and historically situated reader. Of course, such leaps may seem unwarranted to more traditionally minded readers who adhere to the historical-critical or social-scientific schools of thought. My entire essay, I suspect, may seem to such readers like nothing more (and, I hope, nothing less) than a flight of fancy. In my defense, I will say only that I identify mightily with the words of Edgar W. Conrad, which I feel comfortable in appropriating as my own:

> My reading, like every reading of every text, will produce meaning only because of my active participation in creating meaning in the reading process. Every reading is of necessity a reading *into,* or eisegesis. Indeed, the worst kind of eisegesis may be readings in which interpreters remain unaware of their involvement because they think they are reading meaning *out of* the text. (29; Conrad's emphases)

In what follows I will be concerned, like Conrad, "with the text's aesthetic momentum, not its historical development" (29). And like Kathryn Darr, but in contrast to Conrad's self-described mingling of objective methods with reader-oriented methods, I will take the further step of "remember[ing] that readers are required to actualize that potential aesthetic momentum" (20). This means that I will largely pass over the question of authorial intent, for I will be relying on the fact that, as stated by Darr, "because readers themselves play a role in actualizing texts . . . we must leave open the possibility that they discern relationships between texts not, consciously or unconsciously, in the redactors' thoughts" (22).

To begin with, let us turn to Schlobin's identification of the "three, critical elements of horror": "(1) its distortion of cosmology . . . (2) its dark inversion of signs, symbols, processes, and expectations that cause this aberrant world; and (3) its monster-victim relationship with its archetypal devastation of individual will" (24). Since Schlobin gives no instruction that these criteria must be considered in this specific order, I will rearrange them to suit my purpose, considering the third element second and the second one last. That said, it is to the first of these elements—the distortion of cosmology—that I now turn.

II. Distorted Cosmology in Isaiah: The Return to Chaos

"In all of horror's refractions," Schlobin writes, "the aberrant world or distorted cosmology is one of its required characteristics." The world of a horror sotry "must initially begin as a normal one" but then "crumble to chaos," even as it holds out "the futile hopes of success, triumph, and/or escape" (24). The Book of Job conforms to this criterion, Schlobin says, through its presentation of Job's initial state of prosperity and divine favor, followed by his period of great suffering during which he cries for justice, concluded by the revelation to him of Yahweh's transcendent unknowability.

This same element of distorted cosmology is present in Isaiah in the passages describing Yahweh's wrathful reduction of the world to a state of primordial chaos. Although a few other passages scattered throughout the book also make use of this motif, the bulk of them are concentrated in chapters 24 and 34, which, as we do well to note, occupy places of considerable significance in the text. Chapter 24 is the first chapter of what has often been termed the "Isaiah Apocalypse," consisting of chapters 24–27. In the words of Brevard Childs, "Few sections within the book of Isaiah have called forth such a wide measure of scholarly disagreement on their analysis and interpretation as have these four chapters" (171). Childs calls attention to the importance of this section for the book as a whole when he asserts that it portrays "God's final purpose . . . by means of a reuse of the entire corpus of Isaianic material" (174). Jensen asserts a similar point when he writes that the section "gives a unified conception of how God's work in history will finally reach its term" and maintains that "its position after the collection of oracles against the nations (chaps. 13–23) is neither haphazard nor purposeless," since "it provides a framework within which to understand those other oracles" (192).

Chapter 34, for its part, when taken in tandem with its companion chapter 35, has been called the "Little Apocalypse." According to Childs, this chapter supports a "holistic reading [of the book] by setting up a resonance with major themes taken from both before and after these chapters." It "function[s] redactionally as a diptych to form an editorial bridge combining the first part of Isaiah with the second" (200, 253). With greater brevity, Peter D. Miscall says chapters 34 and 35 "stand in the physical center of the book and can perhaps tell us something about the whole book" (18). For my own purpose here, the point of noting all this is simply to highlight the fact that these two sections of Isaiah occupy positions of major importance in Isaiah's overall scheme, and thus the implications for the rest of the book will be profound if these particular parts can be read horrifically.

Beginning with chapter 24, we see that the first verse states, "Now the LORD is about to lay waste the earth and make it desolate, and he will twist its surface and scatter its inhabitants." Commenting on this, John H. Hayes and Stuart A. Irvine observe that "Isaiah's proclamation that Yahweh is now moving to refashion and reorder the world opens with what appears as almost a thesis sentence" (300). And what a terrifying thesis sentence it is! The chapter that follows goes on to speak of the earth being "utterly laid waste and utterly despoiled" (v. 3). Early on the text makes reference to "the city of chaos" being "broken down, every house is shut up so that no one can enter" (v. 10). "City of chaos," as Hayes and Irvine point out, refers to the Assyrian citadel (the Assyrians being the primary human/earthly threat to Israel throughout the Book of Isaiah) and may be literally rendered as "*tohu*-town." The "name fits the imagery being employed by Isaiah . . . recalling as it does the imagery reflected in Genesis 1:2, in which the earth is *tohu* [formless, chaotic] before God's creation. The destruction of the citadel is thus viewed by Isaiah as part of the reversion to disorder and chaos out of which new order can arise" (301).

Other images of primordial chaos are found in v. 18, which describes "the windows of heaven" being opened and "the foundations of the earth" trembling. Hayes and Irvine note that through the use of these images, Isaiah demonstrates "the universality of Yahweh's actions. . . . As at the time of the flood, the earth is undergoing radical change" (304). Nor is the imagery itself the whole of the matter, for as Joseph Jensen incisively points out, the image of the "windows of heaven" carries with it an entire worldview:

> The opening of the windows of heaven alludes not only to P's account of the great flood (see Gen 7:11; 8:2) but also to the cosmology behind it. In Gen 1:6–7 God separated the waters above from the waters below, thus marking off from the primal chaos what he was going to organize into earth and sea and sky; to allow the waters above to pour in again is a way of returning all to the original chaos. The author [of Isaiah] is invoking images to convey something of the cosmic nature of the calamity; so also the earthquake imagery which follows [in vv. 18c–20] points to something beyond a merely natural disaster. (196)[1]

Such a sweeping, cosmic interpretation seems quite appropriate for the content of the first chapter of the "Isaiah Apocalypse." John B. Geyer, paraphrasing a point made by R. Murray in *The Cosmic Covenant*, emphasizes that although the imagery of Isaiah 24 may seem, on one level, to refer to the destruction of the land by enemy forces of a decidedly human, non-supernatural nature, they actually depict "the undoing of nature and its order" (49). And, as Harry Bultema points out in his commentary on this chapter, for the human inhabitants of the earth who experience these things, "the horror will be unspeakably great" (236).

Moving ahead ten chapters, we see that once again Isaiah chooses to focus loving attention upon horrific depictions of Yahweh's wrath. Chapter 34 depicts Yahweh as "enraged against all the nations, and furious against all their hoards; he has doomed them, has given them over for slaughter" (v. 2). Images of staggering violence populate the chapter, as in, for example, verse 3: "The slain shall be cast out, and the stench of their corpses shall rise; the mountains shall flow with their blood." Yahweh's sword is said to have "drunk its fill in the heavens," and "will descend upon Edom, upon the people I have doomed to judgment. . . . For the LORD has a great sacrifice in Bozrah, a great slaughter in the land of Edom" (vv. 5, 6c). A. S. Herbert describes the language of the chapter as "violent and terrifying" and says that as with chapter 24, the destruction being depicted has universal connotations:

> The specific mention of Edom (verse 6) must be understood in relation to the cruel advantage taken by the Edomites of the Babylonian invasion of Judah in 598–587 B.C., referred to in Lam. 4:21–2 ; Ps.137:7. But in this chapter Edom has become a symbolic name for all the enemies of the peo-

---

1. "P's account" refers to the so-called "documentary hypothesis," which holds that the Pentateuch was assembled from the work of at least four different sources, conventionally known as the Yahwist (or J), Elohist (E), Deuteronomist (D), and Priestly (P) documents.

ple of God, as it does in Obadiah. The prophet sees the whole universe as involved in the divine judgment; it is a return to primeval chaos. (193)

Philip D. Stern agrees. "[I]n Isaiah 34, a breakdown of order and the reestablishment of primordial-type chaos are being described" (389). In fact, according to Stern, "Images of chaos appear in this chapter far more than anywhere else in the Bible" (387). He appears especially impressed with the description in verses 11–15 of the land being given over to wild animals, "goat-demons," and the demoness Lilith, calling the passage "an ingenious evocation of chaos-imageries" (399).[2] The import of all these chaos images is reinforced, he says, by the fact that the opening verse of the chapter, "an appeal to all the earth and its fullness to give heed, makes the point that the message to follow is one of cosmic dimensions" (388).

Having established that chapters 24 and 34 do indeed portray scenes of cosmic destruction and the reduction of the created order to primordial chaos, let us pause here to recall that our purpose is to establish that the chapters fulfill Schlobin's requirement that a horror story must display evidence of a distorted cosmology. In elaborating the meaning of this requirement, Schlobin quotes from H. P. Lovecraft's seminal essay "Supernatural Horror in Literature," and since Lovecraft's words sharpen my argument considerably by narrowing the type of horror we are seeking to establish, I shall quote them in full (in contrast to Schlobin's fragmentary presentation of them). According to Lovecraft, for a story to be classified as a true tale of supernatural horror,

> a certain atmosphere of breathless and unexplainable dread of outer, unknown forces must be present; and there must be a hint, expressed with a

---

2. The same, or a similar, motif appears in the Song of the Vineyard in 5:5–6, where the prophet speaks of punishing the unruly vineyard by "remov[ing] its hedge, and it shall be devoured; I will break down its wall, and it shall be trampled down. I will make it a waste; it shall not be pruned or hoed, and it shall be overgrown with briers and thorns; I will also command the clouds that they rain no rain upon it." Commenting on this passage, Victor Matthews writes that the "only solution" to the problem of the wicked vine that produces the wrong sort of grapes "is the complete destruction of the vine and a return to the 'chaos' that existed prior to the establishment of the vineyard (compare the flood epic of Genesis 6–9)." In an observation that recalls the overrunning of the land by wild animals mentioned in chapter 34, Matthews says of the vineyard, "With the terraces destroyed, the soil will erode away and what remains will only nurture thorns and weeds. Wild animals will prowl through this once civilized place and the withholding of the rains is the final insult that can be applied to an unclean place. It spells disaster for all" (28).

seriousness and portentousness becoming its subject, of that most terrible conception of the human brain—a malign and particular suspension or defeat of those fixed laws of Nature which are our only safeguard against the assaults of chaos and the daemons of unplumbed space. (368)

A glimpse into an internal debate among horror theorists may help to clarify still further the type of horror in question. Certain genre scholars have maintained that Lovecraft's description of the necessary atmosphere of supernatural horror applies not to the genre as a whole but more specifically to the subgenre of "cosmic fear," a.k.a. "the weird tale." Noël Carroll, for example, argues in *The Philosophy of Horror* that cosmic fear

> may be relevant to explaining why some works of horror attract their audiences (though, I suspect, not as many works as Lovecraft has in mind); but it is not fundamental enough to explain the attractiveness of horror across the board. This point may be obscured while reading Lovecraft since, given his putative classificatory scheme of things, the genre is identified in terms of cosmic fear; but once we see that Lovecraft's classificatory scheme really represents a covert preference for one sort of (possibly) especially commendatory, horrific effect, we note that cosmic fear is a special source of interest, occurring only in some works of horror, and that it is not pervasive enough to account for generic fascination with the genre. (165)

Regardless of whether Lovecraft or his critics are correct in this matter, the very point of disagreement brings out more clearly the type of horror referenced by the term "distorted cosmology." What we are looking for in Isaiah is a situation in which the cosmos is assaulted from without by an unknown and unknowable force. The horror of cosmological distortion is the horror of knowing that the laws of nature are subject to violation, that creation might one day split open like an eggshell and reveal those "daemons of unplumbed space"—that is, the monsters of chaos. This is the horror of cosmic fear, of realizing that the limited human view of the cosmos is hopelessly myopic, because there are forces out there that may well break through into our cozy world and destroy us, or at the very least shatter our sense of metaphysical security. Schlobin does not specify the way in which this threat must present itself. In the Book of Job, Yahweh threatens Job's comfortable cosmology by overturning Job's cherished belief in a cosmic moral order in which righteousness will always be rewarded.[3] In Isaiah, Yahweh literally undoes the cre-

---

3. See, for example, Job's lament in Job 21, where he expresses horror at the inverted morality that he sees at work in the world: "When I think of it I am dismayed, and shuddering seizes my flesh. Why do the wicked live on, reach old age, and grow mighty in power? Their children are established in their presence, and their off-

ated world in an orgy of bloody violence. In both instances, he functions as exactly the type of threat Lovecraft describes.

But this means that in Isaiah, Yahweh plays the part of Lovecraft's "daemons of unplumbed space." In other words, Yahweh, in a very important way, functions as a chaos monster. And this leads us to our next point.

III. Yahweh, King of the Monsters

According to Schlobin, a second crucial factor in any horror story is

> its monster-victim relationship with its archetypal devastation of individual will. . . . In general, horror's creatures are blatantly oblivious to any human sense of order, ethics, or morality. They are so evil that good is either unknown to them or has no impact on them. . . . Their natures are incomprehensible to the epistemologies of their victims . . . and monsters are completely capable of disintegrating their victims' bodies and souls. (24, 30)

In the story of Job, as read by Schlobin, Yahweh is revealed as precisely this sort of monster by his incomprehensible maltreatment of the eponymous sufferer: "Job is helpless before the irrational forces and punishments forced upon him. Yahweh is a divine solipsist who has no expectation of losing the wager or suffering any consequences" (31).

Yahweh's monstrous role in Isaiah is seen, as stated above, in the fact of his assuming the role of a chaos monster. The idea of chaos monsters that threaten the created order is of course an old one. Mircea Eliade is only the most famous among many scholars who have written of the motif's prevalence among, and meaning for, virtually all traditionally religious societies. "Since 'our world' is a cosmos," Eliade wrote,

> any attack from without threatens to turn it into chaos. . . . [T]he enemies who attack it are assimilated to the enemies of the gods, the demons, and especially the archdemon, the primordial dragon conquered by the gods at the beginning of time. An attack on "our world" is equivalent to an act of revenge by the mythical dragon, who rebels against the work of the gods, the cosmos, and struggles to annihilate it. (47–48)

The Old Testament is rife with instances of this motif in action. From the veiled references to the Babylonian chaos dragon Tiamat in the Hebrew cognate *tehom*, "the deep," found in Genesis 1:2 and elsewhere (such as Isaiah 24:10, already noted), to such direct references as—significantly—Isaiah's

---

spring before their eyes. Their houses are safe from fear, and no rod of God is upon them" (vv. 6–9).

mention of Yahweh's victorious encounters with the chaos dragons Leviathan (27:1) and Rahab (51:9), Old Testament theology displays abundant evidence of being rooted in chaos mythology. "In the Hebrew Bible," writes David Penchansky, "great sea creatures and land giants lay waiting in the chaos just outside the imposed order of God's creation." But, as Penchansky also notes, "sometimes . . . the divine figure itself functions as a monster" (43).

Timothy Beal has written at length about this duality in the Hebrew conception of the deity. Beal points out that while in some cases, as with the above-named battles between Yahweh and Leviathan and Rahab, the biblical God's relationship with primordial chaos monsters is adversarial and results in battles whose ultimate purpose is cosmogonic, at other times God actually allies himself with the chaos monsters or even becomes one himself. An example is found in Isaiah 8, where

> Assyria is imagined as God's monstrous means of pronouncing judgment on Judah. . . . Here the king of Assyria . . . is personified as the flood waters of the great river Euphrates, which is associated with primordial chaos waters. Isaiah's audacious and horrifying claim is that God is raising up these mighty and massive flood waters against Judah. God is taking sides with the monstrous enemy against Judah. (32)

While Beal's recognition that God in this passage has allied himself with the forces of chaos against Judah is indeed full of import, I cannot help but feel that Beal missed an opportunity when he failed to acknowledge that in chapters 24 and 34 of this same book Yahweh takes an even more direct role as an agent of chaos, in that he accomplishes what he has prevented the classical chaos dragons themselves from doing: he destroys the creation from top to bottom, making it all like the "city of chaos" described in 24:10. And he can do this precisely because of his absolute and ultimate authority and control over the created order. Douglas A. Knight has pointed out that "the Hebrew myths dealing with the birth of the cosmos envision no struggle between the creator and any other beings or substances." Even though, as noted above, the ancient Babylonian chaos dragon Tiamat appears in veiled form in the Old Testament, and even though Leviathan and others are mentioned in various places, these "mythic figures offer no resistance whatsoever to YHWH, not even as a narrative foil" (142).

In the reading of Isaiah that I am proposing, Yahweh, without any force to oppose him, becomes the very type of chaos monster that he has defeated. He slew Rahab and cut her into pieces, presumably as part of his original cosmogonic act. He is prophesied to kill Leviathan, "the fleeing serpent . . . the twisting serpent . . . the dragon that is in the sea," on "that day," i.e., the Day of Yahweh, the Day of Divine Judgment, when he will punish all evildoers and bring about the consummation of the creation (27:1). But it appears that the whole meaning of these acts has been merely to clear the way for

Yahweh to bring about an even worse cosmic destruction than what these sinister serpents could have accomplished. Yahweh has saved the world from the archetypal chaos monsters only to *become* a chaos monster who, in his unopposed power, outdoes the others at their own horrific game.

Obviously, I am, as promised in my introduction, engaging in a deliberately creative reading at this point. I am picking certain signals, certain indicators in the text, and running with them. But aside from my own half-playful (and half-serious) desire to see how much horror I can wring from Isaiah, there is also the manifest fact that the biblical God is often portrayed as a source of horror as much as he is a source of comfort and blessing. One interesting speculation about this demonic or horrific aspect of the deity focuses on the fact that in a monotheistic worldview, all aspects of divinity must necessarily be channeled into a single entity. "Since the divine sphere is held to be the cause of all that is inexplicable in the human sphere," writes Knight, inexplicable things therefore

> go to the account of the gods. In polytheistic religions demons or malicious gods are typically held responsible for things that seem bizarre and are otherwise unable to be accounted for within a given cosmology. Yahwism, however, could not tolerate any divine or semi-divine rivals to God. . . . Presumably the demonic element became "absorbed" into the developing conception of YHWH, associated with his numinous character, and identified frequently with his theophanic appearances, not the least in the image of the divine warrior. (146)

Such an understanding goes a long way toward explaining the world's terror at God's self-manifestation as described in Isaiah and elsewhere. For instance, in Isaiah 2:10 the reader is warned to "enter into the rock, and hide in the dust, from the terror of the LORD, and from the glory of his majesty." Jensen points out that "the primary source of the terror" is in fact "the glory of his majesty" itself (62). One is reminded of Rudolf Otto's famous thesis about the origin of religious awe in "daemonic dread." Otto claimed that the first stirrings of mature religious awe were presaged in "the feeling of 'something uncanny', 'eerie', or 'weird'" (14). Although he believed this level of religious apprehension was crude and rightly superseded by "higher" forms as human religious traditions developed, he maintained that

> even when the worship of "daemons" has long since reached the higher level of worship of "gods," these gods still retain as *numina* something of the "ghost" in the impress they make on the feelings of the worshipper, viz. the peculiar quality of the "uncanny" and "awful," which survives with the quality of exaltedness and sublimity or is symbolized by means of it. And this element, softened though it is, does not disappear even on the highest level of all, where the worship of God is at its purest. (17)

In light of these thoughts, it is hardly inconsequential that Otto, in talking of the biblical God specifically, wrote,

> Specially noticeable is the ʾ*ēmāh* of Yahweh ("fear of God"), which Yahweh can pour forth, dispatching almost like a daemon, and which seizes upon a man with paralyzing effect. . . . Here we have a terror fraught with an inward shuddering such as not even the most menacing and overpowering created thing can instil. It has something spectral about it. (13–14)

This persistence of the original element of creeping dread in the more exalted forms of religious awe—including the theology of ancient Israel—leaves us in a position where we have only a short imaginative leap to make from the theologically orthodox position, which maintains that Yahweh appears as a horror only because his absolute holiness reveals the nature of a sinful world to itself, to the burgeoning suspicion that Yahweh, in his very nature, may be horrific, may in fact be a monster.

This leads us to the final issue to be considered in this regard, an issue that Schlobin hits upon when he claims that in horror stories, the monsters' "natures are incomprehensible to the epistemologies of their victims." Isaiah chapter 40—the first chapter of Second Isaiah, the beginning of what *The NIV Study Bible* calls (with unintentional irony, in my view) "The Book of Comfort"—speaks famously of Yahweh's absolute transcendence and incomprehensibility. In words that echo Yahweh's divine self-concealment at the end of Job,[4] verses 12–14 ask rhetorically,

> Who has measured the waters in the hollow of his hand, and marked off the heavens with a span, enclosed the dust of the earth in a measure, and weighted the mountains in scales and the hills in a balance? Who has directed the spirit of the LORD, or as his counselor has instructed him? Whom did he consult in his enlightenment, and who taught him the path of justice?

The answer to all these questions is, of course, *nobody*. Nobody helped Yahweh create the universe. Nobody can know as much of creation's mysteries as he does. Yahweh transcends everything that we puny mortals can possibly understand or accomplish. He alone is supreme in power and knowledge

Verses 15–24 present a creedal statement that emphasizes Yahweh's supreme superiority and authority over all the earth's rulers and inhabitants: the

---

4. See, for example, Job 38:4–7: "Where were you when I laid the foundation of the earth? Tell me, if you have understanding. Who determined its measurements— surely you know! Or who stretched the line upon it? On what were its bases sunk, or who laid its cornerstone when the morning stars sang together and all the heavenly beings shouted for joy?"

nations are nothing before him (vv. 15–17); nothing is comparable to him (18–20); he "sits above the circle of the earth, and its inhabitants are like grasshoppers," and he can do whatever he wants with earthly rulers (21–24). He is absolute, unapproachable, unknowable, unsearchable, supreme.

This leads inevitably to a rather cold conclusion about Yahweh's character as portrayed in Isaiah. First notice that the book focuses intensely on the issue of Yahweh's *holiness*. "Yahweh's holiness," writes Jensen, "is the quality that comes most to the fore in Isaiah's teaching" (33). John N. Oswalt concurs when he points out that "Isaiah's favorite appellation for God is 'the Holy One of Israel'" (33). But as Jensen notes, "God's holiness . . . implies power even more than it implies moral goodness" (21). Herbert elaborates: "The word 'holy' is primarily not an ethical term, but one indicating the otherness, the incalculable power, of God, his inaccessibility. He is 'the great stranger in the human world'. . . . *Holy* expressed the mysterious, incalculable, unapproachable quality of the divine in contrast to the human" (15, 59). Oswalt points out that this aspect of Yahweh's nature is the one most emphasized in Isaiah's famous call narrative: "Above everything else the realization which struck the prophet in his call experience (ch. 6) was the realization of the terrifying 'otherness' of god. He was not merely superhuman, as were the pagan gods, nor was he a great 'grandfather in the sky.' He was of a completely different order from his creatures" (33).[5] This again calls to mind the words of Otto, who described the holy or numinous in terms of its awe-fullness, its overpoweringness, and of the sense one derives from it of being "a creature, submerged and overwhelmed by its own nothingness in contrast to that which is supreme above all creatures" (10).

The upshot for my argument is this: that if the above descriptions correctly express the way Yahweh is portrayed in Isaiah, and if Otto's words are an accurate description of the way humans are meant to feel and react toward Yahweh—and a rereading of chapter 40 indicates to me that the answer is affirmative on both counts—then the Book of Isaiah most certainly meets Schlobin's requirement that the monsters in horror stories must be incomprehensible to their victims.[6]

---

5. I should point out that Oswalt, who is a conservative evangelical scholar, disagrees with the point I am making here about Yahweh's holiness in Isaiah meaning primarily ontological separation and power. "It was not merely God's ontological otherness which captured Isaiah's thinking," Oswalt writes. "In fact, the primary characteristic that set this God apart from humanity, made him holy, was his moral and ethical perfection."

6. For intertextual support for the idea of Yahweh's incomprehensibility, we might look to the opening chapters of Ezekiel, which constitute the prophet's call narrative, and which famously describe a theophanic vision of Yahweh and his attendants that inspires equal measures of stunned awe and giddy terror. See, for example,

This issue of incomprehensibility also factors into the final criterion of Schlobin's scheme that I will apply to Isaiah. Schlobin said that in the world of horror, signs, symbols, processes, and expectations will be inverted. Because of this, the monster's victims will not be able to understand the meaning of what has happened to them. This describes all too well the state of those people whom Yahweh chooses to destroy in the Book of Isaiah.

IV. Cosmic Inversion and Closure in Corpses

Horror, says Schlobin, "generally . . . substitute[s] new meanings for signs. Rather than stripping significance from signs, horror fills them with inverted and deadly meanings, repugnant to the victims and attractive to the monsters (or to those who relish horror's punishment of its victims)" (27). In the Book of Job, this can be seen in the inefficacy of Job's righteousness in protecting him from divine punishment.[7] "The most obvious" inversion, Schlobin says, "is the inversion of Job's relationship with Yahweh, which changes from covenant to betrayal" (28–29). Job's very righteousness, and also the presence and words of his well-intentioned friends, then go from being sources of meaning and comfort to reminders of the horrific distortion that has been revealed to him at the heart of things.

In Isaiah, this horrific inversion of signs can be clearly seen, first, in the way chapters 24 and 34 frame their depictions of cosmic destruction in positive terms. The reader will surely be aware that, as mentioned several para-

---

the four-faced, four-winged creatures described in Ezekiel 1:5–14, and the four wheels within wheels, rimmed with eyes, in vv. 15–21, and then in vv. 26–28 the awesome vision of "the likeness of the glory of the LORD": "There was something like a throne, in appearance like sapphire; and seated above the likeness of a throne was something that seemed like a human form. Upward from what appeared like the loins I saw something like gleaming amber, something that looked like fire enclosed all around; and downward from what looked like the loins I saw something that looked like fire, and there was a splendor all around. Like the bow in a cloud on a rainy day, such was the appearance of the splendor all around. This was the appearance of the likeness of the glory of the LORD."

7. See, for example, Job 16:16–17: "My face is red with weeping, and deep darkness is on my eyelids, though there is no violence in my hands, and my prayer is pure." To the possible observation/criticism that Job is technically not a victim of divine punishment, but simply of Yahweh's permissiveness in allowing Satan to attack Job, I would point out that Satan was merely fulfilling the task Yahweh had ordained for him, which was to test the mettle of creation, and that this makes Yahweh all the more monstrous in the story. For a detailed investigation of Yahweh's status as a monster in the Book of Job, I refer the reader, of course, to Schlobin's article.

graphs ago, in the overall scheme of the text these catastrophes are meant to be seen in a positive light. As Hayes and Irvine noted, cosmic destruction in Isaiah is a "reversion to disorder and chaos *out of which new order can arise*" (301; emphasis added). Yahweh undertakes these acts as part of his plan to sweep the evil out of the world and create a new world, "new heavens and a new earth," in which "the former things shall not be remembered or come to mind" (65:17). There will be no more suffering or weeping, everyone will live to a ripe old age (as in the pre-flood era), and there will be such a total absence of strife and contention that "the wolf and the lamb shall feed together, the lion shall eat straw like the ox" (65:25)—imagery that recalls the conditions that existed in Eden. These are the intended theological complements of the scenes of bloody cosmic destruction to which I have given such lengthy attention. There can be no doubt that, in light of this glorious outcome, the reader is being encouraged to view the withering of the earth, "terror, and the pit, and the snare" (24:17), stinking corpses and mountains stained with blood, wild animals and demons, and all the rest of the shocking and violent images of chapters 24 and 34, in an ultimately positive light. After all, these are the necessary precursors to the beautiful new creation! Such a reframing of what would intuitively seem to be horrific imagery into categories of desirability constitutes a radical inversion of the normal meanings attached to such signs, and thus shows that Isaiah, in this respect, meets Schlobin's criterion.

But I am getting ahead of myself. For of course the reader is meant to be *horrified* by chapters 24 and 34. The reader is meant to view these things as horrific examples of what will happen to people who are not found righteous by the Holy One of Israel. This means that for my interpretation of the text to be justified, there has to be some other element in Isaiah, an element that we haven't examined yet, for thus far nothing that I have pointed out has indicated that Isaiah *ought* to be read in a horrific light. I have merely managed to prove that it *can* be read this way.

This final element is found in book's final verse, chapter 66, verse 24, which rounds off Isaiah on a note of horror that resounds all the way back to the first chapter. The final verse comes at the tail end of a long description of the new heavens and new earth, and of the requirements of worship in the new order of things. Of these requirements, the final one is this: "And they shall go out and look at the dead bodies of the people who have rebelled against me [Yahweh]; for their worm shall not die, their fire shall not be quenched, and they shall be an abhorrence to all flesh" (66:24). In other words, the ultimate act of worship in the new creation will be to gaze upon the corpses of Yahweh's slain enemies (who, according to verse 16, will be numerous). "Concluding the magisterial Book of Isaiah," writes P. D. Hanson, "with its celebration of the Holy God whose infinite love reaches out for lost mortals is a verse that holds up as an eternal memorial the worm-invested, smoldering bodies of those who have rebelled against their creator" (quoted in Miscall 126n11).

The interpretative problems posed by such a concluding verse are obvious. Miscall points out that "most commentators are troubled by the harshness of the judgments expressed in vv. 15–17 and 24 and by the sharp contrast with the positive tones of the other verses" (126). Conrad describes the verse as "jolting" and says that "as a contemporary reader, I do not know what to do with this verse. I want to delete it as well as others of its kind" (162).

This reaction is not confined to contemporary readers alone; as Hanson observes, "Modern readers are not the first to flinch at the sight." Ancient readers recognized the problem, too. In fact, they found it so troubling that they tried to get around it by disobeying the text as it came to them: "According to the Masoretic notation," Hanson says, "verse 24 is to be repeated by the repetition of verse 23 in the synagogue" (quoted in Miscall 126n11). Childs says critical scholars "are virtually unanimous that v. 24 is a later and unfortunate addition, which is then described as an apocalyptic portrayal of Gehenna." He says the ancient injunction to repeat verse 23 was motivated by the desire "to end the book on a note of promise" (542). But as Miscall points out, the problem may not be so easily solved, and in fact might be compounded by this proposed solution, since "repeating v. 23 . . . can have the effect of emphasizing v. 24 by framing it in a chiastic structure" (126n11).

What all this discomfort amounts to is the recognition that we *want* Isaiah to end on a note of promise. Given the exalted message the book as a unified entity tries to put forth, we want it to end with more of those comforting words about the joy and happiness and utter absence of suffering in the new creation. We do not want to be reminded of Yahweh's wrath, which seems— let us admit it—disturbingly capricious. The picture of those eternally abused corpses in 66:24 bears much of the flavor of what Otto referred to when he said Yahweh's wrath often seems to have "no concern whatever with moral qualities. There is something very baffling in the way in which is 'is kindled' and manifested. It is, as has been well said, 'like a hidden force of nature', like stored-up electricity, discharging itself upon anyone who comes too near. It is 'incalculable' and 'arbitrary'" (18).

Perhaps not tangentially, we might note that if by chance the reader is wondering at this point in my argument what has become of the theology of the covenant—the theology that holds that Yahweh pours out his wrath not arbitrarily, but in response to human evils and in accord with principles that he has laid down clearly in advance—it merely takes a slight shift in perspective to recognize that the covenant itself is arbitrary. Yahweh is under no obligation to conform to human standards of morality and justice, and as we saw in the preceding section, we may not be able to look to his self-nature as a guarantor of his justice and lovingkindness. Indeed, the famous imagery of the potter and the clay, in which Yahweh is compared to a potter who can do whatever he wants with his "clay" (that is, humans)—not excluding turning them against himself through no fault of their own, and thus making them subject to his punishment—may be best known to many Christian readers from its presentation in Paul's letter to the Romans (cf. Romans 9:14–21), but it actually has its origin in Isaiah, where it appears not once but twice.[8] Paul's commentary on the matter, wherein he attempts to mount a smooth dismissal of the subject, is most instructive, and it reminds us yet again of Job, and of Schlobin's contention that Job suffers under the nightmarish torments of a monstrous God: "You will say to me then, 'Why then does he still find fault? For who can resist his will?'" But who indeed are you, a human being, to argue with God?" (Romans 9:19–20a).

To return to our main subject: Schlobin said tales of horror strip from signs their accustomed meanings and substitute new and "deadly" meanings that are repugnant to the victims but attractive to the monsters. In the final verse of Isaiah, we see this principle at work in the form of human corpses being gnawed by worms and scorched by flames, and being presented to those who view them, and to the reader, as things attractive and desirable. It is a holy duty to watch these corpses being desecrated, no matter how repugnant the thought, let alone the sight.

We should note that the idea of exposing enemy corpses hardly begins with Isaiah 66:24. The practice was well established in the ancient Middle East, where remaining unburied after death "was the worst that could befall someone. . . . Exposing the corpse represented a final humiliation and a desecration, for most ancient peoples believed that proper, timely burial affected the quality of the afterlife" (Walton et al. 373). The final verse of Isaiah thus employs a known motif in its depiction of the fate of Yahweh's enemies. But the motif may have been especially detestable to the Israelites, who took the necessity and propriety of corpse burial so seriously that their "law required even the body of an impaled criminal to be removed and buried at sunset rather than left to be devoured by birds and other animals" (Walton et al. 373).[9]

---

8. See Isaiah 29:16 and 45:9.

9. For instances of this motif being used in the Hebrew scriptures other than Isaiah, see, for example, 1 Samuel 31:8–13, in which the Philistines behead Saul's corpse and hang it on a wall, only to have it stolen by the inhabitants of Jabesh-gilead, who burn it and bury the bones. See also 2 Samuel 21:4–14, in which David halts a

Furthermore—and here we hit upon the heart of the horror contained in Isaiah's final verse—the depiction of the peculiar state of the desecrated corpses in the new creation makes for a particularly potent inversion of signs, for one can see within the nature of the corpses' punishment a previously unsuspected aspect of Yahweh's hidden nature. The two punishments specific to the corpses in 66:24 are worms and fire. The worms we may take as a standard symbol of putrefaction, and also, perhaps, as an invocation of the "wormlike" connotations of the ancient chaos serpents; Yahweh has given the corpses over to a figurative eternal assault by the likes of Leviathan.

But what of the fire? What is its function? Where does it come from? Why does it continue to scorch eternally?

The Hebrew word for "fire" in this verse is *'esh*. While the same word is used to refer simply to normal, physical fire, it is also used throughout the Old Testament to refer to the supernatural fire accompanying a theophany, and also, figuratively, to God's anger. The fire that burns the corpses of Yahweh's slain enemies in the final verse of Isaiah is the same fire that is explicitly identified with Yahweh himself in Deuteronomy 4:24, which says, "For the LORD your God is a devouring fire." It is what the Israelites saw when Moses spent forty days and nights with Yahweh on Mount Sinai, and "the appearance of the LORD was like a devouring fire on the top of the mountain" (Exodus 24:17). It is the fire Yahweh rained down on Sodom and Gomorrah (Genesis 19:24). It is the fire the Israelites associated with Yahweh after they received the Ten Commandments and said, "For this great fire will consume us; if we hear the voice of the LORD our God any longer, we shall die. For who is there of all flesh that has heard the voice of the living God speaking out of fire, as we have, and has remained alive?" (Deuteronomy 5:25–26).

It is also the fire that appears in one of the Bible's most famous theophanies: "Then the angel of the LORD appeared to [Moses] in a flame of fire out of a bush; he looked, and the bush was blazing, yet it was not consumed" (Exodus 3:2). When we consider this in light of the other instances of *'esh*

---

three-year famine by handing over seven of Saul's descendants to the Gibeonites, whom Saul had nearly wiped out. The Gibeonites impale these seven men "before the Lord" and leave their bodies exposed. Rizpah, the mother of two of them, protects the bodies from being defiled by birds and wild animals "until rain [falls] on them from the heavens" (i.e., until the drought, the cause of the famine, breaks). David hears of it and brings Saul and Jonathan's bones back from the people of Jabeth-gilead to be properly buried in the rightful tomb. He also gathers up the remains of the seven who had been impaled. "After that, God heeded the supplications for the land" (v. 14).

mentioned above, and when we consider also the parallel between the bush that burns but is not consumed, and the corpses in the new creation whose "fire shall not be quenched," the answer to the riddle of the fire starts to become clear: The corpses in Isaiah 66:24 have become theophanies on the order of the burning bush in Exodus. Like the bush, they burn without being consumed, and the fire, *'esh*, that burns them, *is the essence or manifestation of Yahweh himself*. If we may be permitted to take a final leap of the imagination, the entire Book of Isaiah has been a "setup" that Yahweh has employed to get us to the point where we can see him exercising his true purpose: he has redeemed a select group of people from out of the mass of doomed humanity, for the ultimate purpose of forcing them to witness his awful flaming essence eternally scorching and corrupting the corpses of those who opposed him. His motives, as we have seen, are inscrutable, and his power, inescapable. Thus, the best indication we have of his true nature and intentions comes from what we see him actually do. And what we see is appalling at every level. "Isaiah's whole vision," writes Miscall, "ends with a scene of perdition: undying worms, perpetual fire and finally 'a horror for all flesh'" (136).

The conclusion is clear: there is no escape. Yahweh is a chaos monster, a demon from beyond space, and the Book of Isaiah is the story of this monster breaking into the ordered world of life and light for the purpose of staging a show full of suffering and sickening violence, all for his own unfathomable reasons.

V. Concluding Thoughts on Closure, Anticlosure, and Cognitive Dissonance

I said above that the note of horror at the end of Isaiah "resounds all the way back to the first chapter." This is the case not only because of the intensity of the verse's imagery and message, nor is it only because several elements found in chapter 66, including the fire in the final verse, are also found in chapter 1, which has long been recognized as a kind of "table of contents" that must have been added in one of the final redactions of the book.[10] A large measure of 66:24's power arises from the simple fact that it comes at the end. We have already seen that readers both ancient and modern have struggled with this ostensibly odd placement of such a difficult verse. Now the time has come to consider this matter more closely.

---

10. See 1:31: "The strong shall become like tinder, and their work like a spark; they and their work shall burn together, with no one to quench them."

What galls those who try to find a way to assimilate 66:24 into their interpretative grids is the inescapable working of the literary element known as *closure*. Closure, according to Holman and Harmon's *A Handbook to Literature*, is "the principle that structured things do not just stop, they come to an end with a sense of conclusion, completeness, wholeness, integrity, finality, and termination" (91). Terry Heller, a literary theorist and student of the horror genre, says closure is "one of the features of a literary work that makes it seem whole. . . . At some point at or shortly after the end of the text, we expect to see all the prominent features of the work forming a harmony that can recede in memory as we turn to other objects in the world." In essence, says Heller, the achievement of closure gives a literary work a sense of being "rounded off," of having reached a conclusion that emerges organically from what has led up to it.

The question before us is: does the final verse of Isaiah achieve closure? Does it sum up everything that has come before it and provide us with a stopping point that seems organically related to what led up to it? Although, as noted, the verse refers to an image that first appears at the end of the first chapter, its obvious shock value and the trouble it has caused readers down through the centuries would seem to indicate that it does not, in fact, achieve closure in the traditional sense. It is too radically removed from the tenor of some of the other things in the book—the more comforting and uplifting things—for it to achieve closure as Heller has described it. Ronald E. Clements has even written an entire article based on this very recognition, titled "Isaiah: A Book without an Ending?" According to Clements, "When we read [66:24], we are not at all surprised that neither ancient readers nor modern scholars have been happy to regard this brief verse as the appropriate closure to the book. It is not at all typical of its overall message" (109). Clements says closure is a "significant feature of a narrative ending. . . . Certainly it is this that we should look for in a collection of prophecies in which a 'final' prophecy, even if it does not actually occur at the end of a book, indicates a sense of fulfillment and completion" (114–15). He identifies the true—by which he means the thematically appropriate—close of the book as coming at the end of chapter 60, or possibly 61 or 62 (109).

So the Isaian text in its received form definitely does not achieve closure in the traditional narrative or literary sense. But according to Holman and Harmon and Clements, it *should* achieve some sort of closure, since it is definitely a structured work and thus calls for "a sense of fulfillment and completion." Clements uses this as an excuse to find closure elsewhere and to characterize the text in its received form as literarily defective. But in contrast to this strategy, I want to dwell upon the text as it stands and to ask a new, slightly modified question: what exactly is the lasting, lingering effect of Isaiah's closing verse as has come down to us? With 66:24 screaming at us to be understood in some fashion, what is the subjective impact or meaning—or as

Darr would call it, the "synchronic impact"—of closing the book on such a note of horror?

Again, Heller—drawing heavily on the seminal work of philosopher Tzvetan Todorov in *The Fantastic: A Structural Approach to Literary Genre*—comes to our aid by offering the following thoughts on *anti*closure, which he sees as characterizing a particular type of terror tale, the "terror fantasy":

> Like all literary texts, a terror fantasy invites the reader to use the signals of the text to construct an implied reader and to establish thereby an aesthetic relation to the text. Unlike most literary works, a terror fantasy offers at least two simultaneously valid but opposed readings, each of which illuminates the strengths of the other and betrays its own weaknesses. This splitting of the role of implied reader precludes the ending of that role. As a result, the terror fantasy produces anticlosure; it pointedly refuses to end.
>
> Anticlosure is not merely a failure to resolve thematic complications, nor is it a thematic assertion of the openness of reality. It is not at all like the story with its last page removed nor the "slice of life" in which it is presumed that life goes on after the arbitrary ending of the history. Anticlosure results from a tale's turning back on itself to form a closed loop. It is not the text that fails to end, but the reading, the activity of concretizing the work. This activity cannot stop because each of its possible resting places is disturbed by the presence of another.
>
> In these tales, then, the role of implied reader becomes a snare. And the trap by itself produces anxiety.

I have quoted Heller at such length regarding anticlosure because his words are so pertinent to my own personal situation as a reader of Isaiah (and of many other biblical texts). Heller says anticlosure occurs when a text holds out two equally valid but opposed readings that mutually illuminate each other. Readers find themselves torn between these readings, unable to settle on either one, and ultimately this unresolved tension keeps readers in a state of permanent terror and prevents them from ever reaching a satisfactory state of mind regarding the work. I have experienced this repeatedly over time with virtually every biblical text that I have read. Isaiah is only one of the most pointed, owing to its overt intimations of horror.

Perhaps it is inappropriate to end an academic exploration like this one on a pointedly personal note, but since everything I have said in this paper stems from my personal motivations in tackling such a subject, I will go ahead and take the risk. For many years now, I have been torn between reading biblical texts in a conventionally pious way and an imaginatively horrific way.[11] The intimations of a darker interpretation lurking beneath the more common one(s) have come to me almost involuntarily as I have studied the Bible in increasing depth over time and seen the various ways in which darkness might enter through the cracks, as it were, and pervade everything with an underlying mood of shadow. The reading of Isaiah that I have been pursuing here is only one example of this type of thinking—and, I fear, not an entirely successful one. To prove my point, I have had to focus at length upon isolated sections of the text while ignoring others altogether. I have indeed demonstrated that Isaiah meets Schlobin's three requirements for a horror story, but had I chosen other passages, I would have found my horrific interpretation challenged at many steps.

But then again, and hopefully not in marked conflict with my self-avowed reader-oriented approach, I do believe many of the elements of horror that I have noted in Isaiah are there for the reading, and are not merely the result of willful eisegesis. The fact that readers have struggled for centuries to figure out how to handle 66:24 is sufficient evidence to assure me that I am not stranded alone on an island of imaginative thinking.

This dithering back and forth is, I believe, evidence that Isaiah indeed presents us with an instance of anticlosure as described by Heller. The questions posed by my horrific reading and the recognition of its largely arbitrary nature are insoluble. Should Yahweh be viewed as a majestic, holy, compassionate God—or as a secret trickster, a chaos monster in disguise, who engineers everything in order to arrive at the point where he can enjoy the horrified gaze of his chosen ones as they watch him commit an eternal, meaningless act of vindictiveness? Should the cosmic destructions of chapters 24 and 34 be viewed as the just rewards of a world that has rejected the transcendent source of goodness and light, or should they be viewed as assaults by a monstrous alien force that in its very nature rightly induces not love and reverence, but horror? The more I consider these issues, the more I find that I am unable to decide which is the more purely imaginative—which is to say, *fictional*—interpretation, and thus I find I am stuck in a state of anticlosure that will not let me rest. Appropriately enough, this effect of my reading harks back to my explicitly subjective methodological approach, since, as Edgar V. McKnight has pointed out, "reader-oriented theories not only emphasize the reader's role in the process of achieving meaning but also see the result of reading in terms of an effect upon the reader" (203).

It is perhaps tangential but not totally insignificant that Lovecraft, whose quotation from "Supernatural Horror in Literature" helped to define the spe-

---

11. Another obvious possibility—the noncommittal scholarly approach, based simply on secular interest—is not an option for me, since I am not able (or willing) to pay attention to a text at all unless it engages my emotions, interests, and energies on a deeply personal level.

cific type of horror we were seeking in Isaiah, harbored a similar disparity in his own temperament. We have already seen that he deemed the breaking or suspension of natural laws to be the "most terrible conception of the human brain." But in another context, when discussing his motivations and methods as an author of horror fiction, he wrote something of an entirely different tenor:

> I choose weird stories because they suit my inclination best—one of my strongest and most persistent wishes being to achieve, momentarily, the illusion of some strange suspension or violation of the galling limitations of time, space, and natural law which forever imprison us and frustrate our curiosity about the infinite cosmic spaces beyond the radius of our sight and analysis. ("Notes" 113)

Here and elsewhere, Lovecraft was a bundle of contradictions, and we may view it as appropriate that the man whose words about those "daemons from unplumbed space" have guided us on a large part of our journey through Isaiah could not even agree with himself, as we cannot agree with ourselves, on the question of whether the assaults of those extracosmic demons on the brittle shell of the created universe—assaults that are as existentially real as anything we encounter in empirical reality—should be received joyously, as opportunities for ultimate liberation, or with abject horror, as confirmations of our most awful metaphysical and ontological fears.

1998

Works Cited

Barker, Kenneth, general ed. *The NIV Study Bible.* Grand Rapids, MI: Zondervan, 1985.

Beal, Timothy. *Religion and Its Monsters.* New York: Routledge, 2002.

Bultema, Harry. *Commentary on Isaiah.* Grand Rapids, MI: Kregel Publications, 1981.

Carroll, Noël. *The Philosophy of Horror.* New York: Routledge, 1990.

Childs, Brevard S. *Isaiah.* Louisville, KY: Westminster John Knox Press, 2001.

Clements, Ronald E. "Isaiah: A Book without an Ending?" *Journal for the Study of the Old Testament* 97 (2002): 109–26.

Conrad, Edgar W. *Reading Isaiah.* Minneapolis, MN: Fortress Press, 1991.

Darr, Katheryn Pfisterer. *Isaiah's Vision and the Family of God.* Louisville, KY: Westminster John Knox Press, 1994.

Eliade, Mircea. *The Sacred and the Profane: The Nature of Religion.* Tr. Willard R. Trask. 1957. San Diego: Harcourt, 1987.

Geyer, John B. "Desolation and Cosmos." *Vetus Testamentum* 49, No. 1 (1999): 49–64.

Hayes, John H., and Stuart A. Irvine. *Isaiah, the Eighth-century Prophet: His Times and Preaching.* Nashville, TN: Abingdon, 1987.

Heller, Terry. *The Delights of Terror: An Aesthetics of the Tale of Terror.* Urbana: University of Illinois Press, 1987. Internet edition published 2002. www.public.coe.edu/~theller/essays/delights/dt1.html. Site accessed 25 February 2003.

Herbert, A. S. *Isaiah 1–39.* Cambridge: Cambridge University Press, 1973.

Holman, C. Hugh, and William Harmon. *A Handbook to Literature.* 6th ed. New York: Macmillan, 1992.

Jensen, Joseph, O.S.B. *Isaiah 1–39.* Wilmington, DE: Michael Glazier, 1984.

Knight, Douglas A. "Cosmogony and Order in the Hebrew Tradition." In Robin W. Lovin and Frank E. Reynolds, ed. *Cosmogony and Ethical Order: New Studies in Comparative Ethics.* Chicago: University of Chicago Press, 1985. 133–57.

Lovecraft, H. P. "Notes on the Writing of Weird Fiction." In Lovecraft's *Miscellaneous Writings.* Ed. S. T. Joshi. Sauk City, WI: Arkham House, 1995. 113–16.

———. "Supernatural Horror in Literature." 1927. In Lovecraft's *Dagon and Other Macabre Tales.* Ed. August Derleth; texts ed. S. T. Joshi. Sauk City, WI: Arkham House, 1987. 365–436.

Matthews, Victor. "Treading the Winepress: Actual and Metaphorical Viticulture in the Ancient Near East." *Semeia* 86 (1999): 19–32.

McKnight, Edgar V. "Reader-Response Criticism." In Steven L. McKenzie and Stephen R. Haynes, ed. *To Each Its Own Meaning: An Introduction to Biblical Criticisms and Their Application.* Louisville, KY: Westminster/John Knox Press, 1993. 197–219.

Miscall, Peter D. *Isaiah 34–35: A Nightmare/A Dream.* Sheffield, UK: Sheffield Academic Press, 1999.

Oswalt, John N. *The Book of Isaiah: Chapters 1–39.* Grand Rapids, MI: William B. Eerdmans, 1986.

Otto, Rudolf. *The Idea of the Holy.* Tr. John W. Harvey. New York: Oxford University Press, 1958.

Penchansky, David. "God the Monster: Fantasy in the Garden of Eden." In George Aichele & Tina Pippin, ed. *The Monstrous and the Unspeakable: The Bible as Fantastic Literature*. Sheffield, UK: Sheffield Academic Press, 1997. 40–58.

Schlobin, Roger C. "Protoypic Horror: The Genre of the Book of Job." *Semeia* 60 (1992): 23–38.

Stern, Philip D. "Isaiah 34, Chaos, and the Ban." In Robert Chazan, William W. Hallo, and Lawrence H. Schiffman, ed. *Ki Baruch Hu: Ancient Near Eastern, Biblical, and Judaic Studies in Honor of Baruch A. Levine*. Winona Lake, IN: Eisenbrauns, 1999. 387–400.

Walton, John H.; Matthews, Victor H.; and Chavalas, Mark W. *The IVP Bible Background Commentary: Old Testament*. Downers Grove, IL: InterVarsity Press, 2000.

The Spaces Between

Fantasy, Horror, and Infinite Longing

It's currently October, the spiritual heart of autumn, season of darkening skies and shivering shadows, when death and life, fantasy and reality, night and day, bleed briefly into each other to generate a sense of infinite vistas lying just beyond our ability to grasp. Or at least that's how it unfolds in the Missouri Ozarks, my lifelong home until a couple of years ago. In 2008 my family and I relocated to Central Texas, and down here in my new native country, daytime temperatures are still climbing into the 80s. There's nary a red or golden leaf in sight. The forecast for Halloween itself, the spiritual focal point of the whole month, calls for sunny skies and a high of 85. I don't often quote Charles Schulz, but since it was he who conceived the figure of the Great Pumpkin, it seems appropriate under current circumstances: Rats.

Still, none of this means the season is failing to inspire its archetypal mood, a pungent emotional coloration composed of equal parts wistful longing, melancholic brooding, and shadowy fascination. And this has got me to reflecting seriously on the significance of this mood for the religion-spirituality-speculative fiction crossover arena that has long been my special interest. To cut to the chase: the archetypal mood that I and millions of other people have come to associate with autumn in general and October in particular touches on a peculiar emotional/spiritual upwelling that is central to the concerns of fantasy and horror, and that I first began to experience consciously as an early adolescent.

It makes itself known as a peculiar longing of an especially poignant and piercing sort. It comes over a person without warning, manifesting itself as a kind of heightened emotional intensity that feels like wonder, excitement, and nostalgia all mixed up together and mingled with the sense of some imminent revelation and/or the resurfacing of a tantalizing lost memory whose content is vague, but whose import seems vast. For me personally, as indicated above, this feeling is often tangled up with the kaleidoscopic impressions accompanying the advent of autumn. Sometimes it happens in conjunction with certain scents, or with the soft feeling of the air on my skin on certain delicate days, or in conjunction with spontaneous memories of the past. But more often it is triggered by visual images: sunsets and sunrises, cloudscapes, scenic vistas both pastoral and urban. Music can trigger it, too. So can certain books and movies.

Oddly, one of the surest triggers for me is the sight of huge metal electrical poles draped with cables and marching away toward the distant horizon. For some reason the sight of those latticed structures and clustered lines framed against the landscape and sky, and converging toward the vanishing point, makes me almost sick with yearning. Something about the perspective of it all, which calls out and underscores the eternal complementarity between my single-pointed, finite perspective and the never-seen possibilities that lie on the far side of the horizon, generates a palpable sense of delicious revelation and fulfillment lying barely, and perpetually, beyond my grasp.

I knew this experience for years, and vaguely knew that it was connected to my love for fantasy, horror, and some science fiction, before I finally found a name for it in the writings of C. S. Lewis. I was in my twenties when I discovered that Lewis, some of whose Narnia books I had read as a child, had in fact spent his adult life writing about precisely this experience of infinite longing. He borrowed the German word *Sehnsucht* to refer to it, and described it *in The Pilgrim's Regress* as an "intense longing" for "that unnamable something, desire for which pierces us like a rapier at the smell of a bonfire, the sound of wild ducks flying overhead, the title of *The Well at the World's End,* the opening lines of *Kubla Khan,* the morning cobwebs in late summer, or the noise of falling waves. . . . [T]he mere wanting is found somehow to be a delight" (234, 237, 234). In what I soon came to recognize as a common development, I found that reading Lewis's description of the whole thing actually served to evoke the longing itself.

Importantly, Lewis emphasized "the peculiar mystery about the *object* of this Desire," which always remains beyond our ability to clearly conceive or articulate. He wrote,

> [I]f it comes to a child while he is looking at a far off hillside he at once thinks "if only I were there"; if it comes when he is remembering some event in the past, he thinks "if only I could go back to those days." If it comes (a little later) while he is reading a "romantic" tale or poem of "perilous seas and faerie lands forlorn," he thinks he is wishing that such places really existed and that he could reach them. (210; Lewis's emphasis)

None of these things, Lewis points out, will actually satisfy the desire even if they are attained, which leads to the strange and tantalizing realization that it is as if the desire somehow comes *through* the objects that arouse it instead of being embodied *in* them.

When I first read Lewis's exposition of these things and realized that he was describing what I myself had experienced but been unable to explain, I immediately understood, for the first time, the clear link between this phenomenon and some of my favorite fantasy-horror writers. Lovecraft, for example, wrote repeatedly in his letters of finding himself overcome by aesthetic rapture and a sense of longing and "adventurous expectancy" at the sight of sunsets, cloudscapes, winding streets, rooftops angled in certain suggestive arrangements, and so on. As a fiction writer, he threaded this emotional current through nearly all his stories, alternately balancing himself on one side or the other of the divide between the transcendent rapture and cosmic horror that were, in his personal experience, equally embedded in this infinite yearning.

This comes through intensely in, for instance, his "Dreamland" stories, such as the epic, unpolished, astounding short novel of ethereal fantasy and cosmic horror *The Dream-Quest of Unknown Kadath,* where the narrative opens with Lovecraft's fictional alter ego, Randolph Carter, gazing downward in a dream upon a mystical golden city:

> [A]s Carter stood breathless and expectant on that balustraded parapet there swept up to him the poignancy and suspense of almost-vanished memory, the pain of lost things and the maddening need to place again what once had had an awesome and momentous place. . . . [He was] sick with longing for those glittering sunset streets and cryptical hill lanes among ancient tiled roofs. (*Dream Cycle* 106, 107)

There is no mistaking that kind of language. It fairly glitters with *Sehnsucht.* Lovecraft even went so far as to assert that this heightened emotional responsiveness to a scene of beauty that seems to hint at a transcendent world of absolute aesthetic fulfillment is the very warrant for literature itself:

> [This is] the impulse which justifies authorship. . . . The time to begin writing is when the events of the world seem to suggest things larger than the world—strangenesses and patterns and rhythms and uniquities of combination which no one ever saw or heard before, but which are so vast and marvellous and beautiful that they absolutely demand proclamation with a fanfare of silver trumpets. Space and time become vitalised with literary significance when they begin to make us subtly homesick for something 'out of space, out of time'. . . . *To find those other lives, other worlds, and other dreamlands, is the true author's task.* That is what literature is; and if any piece of writing is motivated by anything apart from this mystic and never-finished

quest, it is base and unjustified imitation. (*Selected Letters* 3.97; Lovecraft's emphasis)

Over time, my ongoing reading about these matters turned up other seminal authors talking about the same thing. These included, naturally, the nineteenth-century Romantics, among whom this longing was well known. But what struck me as much as anything was its prevalence among writers who were oriented toward fantasy and horror—genres that, yes, were inheritors of Romanticism's well-established Gothic-fantastic strain.

In his monolithic *The Occult*, for example, Colin Wilson described an experience that had struck him in childhood, and that seemed to him pregnant with profound meaning. He wrote of it in words that echo Lewis's description of the irreducible elusiveness of the object of *Sehnsucht:*

> Who has not experienced this strange frustration that comes in moments of pleasure and fulfilment? As a child, I had this feeling about water. If my parents took me on a bus excursion, I used to crane out of the window every time we went over a bridge; something about large sheets of water excited a painful desire that I found incomprehensible. For if I actually approached the water, what could I *do* to satisfy this feeling? Drink it? Swim in it? (126; Wilson's emphasis)

Wilson viewed this experience as the effect of a latent human sense, specifically, "man's evolutionary appetite, the drive to make contact with reality" (126). He dubbed it Faculty X and, like Lewis and Lovecraft, regarded it as pointing toward the infinite, the absolute, Reality with a capital "R." Each of these writers took this same experience as the emotional and philosophical foundation upon which to erect his life's work, although Lovecraft differed from the other two with his view that the object of the longing is an illusion. This was in line with his overall view of reality, which he regarded as the blind, meaningless, and ultimately unfathomable fluctuations of a purely material cosmos. Lewis and Wilson, by contrast, viewed *Sehnsucht* or Faculty X as really having an object, a possible eventual fulfillment in an experience of transcendent union between the knower and the known, in which the ontological primacy of mind over matter would be realized and revealed.

You don't have to take sides in this issue to feel its resonance with what Stephen King so evocatively identified as the role of fantasy and horror writers in the penultimate "Last Waltz" section of his *Danse Macabre:* "The job of the fantasy writer, or the horror writer, is to bust the walls of [adult] tunnel vision wide for a little while; to provide a single powerful spectacle for that third eye. The job of the fantasy-horror writer is to make you, for a little while, a child again" (378).

Speculative fiction expands the human perspective by transforming literal, factual reality into imaginary reality. Not imaginary as in unreal, but imaginary as in remade by the human mind and spirit into something more, something visionary and spiritually magnetic. You don't have to be religious, you don't even have to consider yourself "spiritual"—but you don't have to be irreligious or anti-spiritual, either—to recognize the valid use of these words as indicators of a real impact that speculative fiction really does have on the human spirit, or call it mind or psyche or whatever you prefer: the knowing self, you-as-conscious-subject.

Still further: if Lewis and Wilson are right (contra Lovecraft)—and many years of experiential and intellectual engagement in philosophical, religious, and spiritual explorations have left me, at least, with no doubt that they are—then this effect isn't just a private emotional experience that has no meaning beyond the feeling of it, but a genuine window on a wider reality than the one most of customarily recognize in our workaday mode. It literally expands our personal horizon. In other words, and in short, it is possible to argue without hyperbole or silliness that the greatest works of fantasy, horror, and science fiction serve as religious or spiritual texts—not only, not even primarily, in terms of their specific content, but in terms of the potent effect they have on our outlook (and inlook), simply because they're aimed at inflaming Faculty X and expanding the domain of our imaginings.

2010

Works Cited

King, Stephen. *Danse Macabre*. New York: Everest House, 1978.

Lewis, C. S. *The Pilgrim's Regress: An Allegorical Apology for Christianity, Reason, and Romanticism*. 1933. Grand Rapids, MI: William B. Eerdmans, 2014.

Lovecraft, H. P. *The Dream Cycle of H. P. Lovecraft: Dreams of Terror and Death*. New York: Ballantine, 1995.

———. *Selected Letters*. Ed. August Derleth, Donald Wandrei, and James Turner. Sauk City, WI: Arkham House, 1964–76. 5 vols.

Wilson, Colin. *The Essential Colin Wilson*. London: Harrap, 1985.

In Search of Higher Intelligence: The Daemonic Muse(s) of Aleister Crowley, Timothy Leary, and Robert Anton Wilson

I. Introduction: The Riddle of Inspiration

The question of inspired creativity's ultimate source—I mean creativity as the human act of birthing new ideas and works of art—is an old and fascinating one. Historically, attempts to answer it have led, almost without exception, into the realms of the spiritual, the esoteric, and the occult, where muses and daimons and daemons and genii hover all around us in imaginal hyperspace, whispering into the ears of poets, artists, historians, philosophers, and madmen. More recently, in the past couple of centuries, creativity has become a popular topic in the realms of psychology and neurology, where the id, the collective unconscious, the right cerebral hemisphere, the temporal lobe, the cerebellum, and various other psychological and neurobiological structures and interrelationships have been named and championed as the real "muse." The shift has been away from belief in an objectively real spiritual source to the belief that inspiration is a purely subjective experience with biological and psychological causes. Which direction a given person tends—toward a forthrightly spiritual(ish) or a reductive materialist/scientific interpretation—depends on his or her philosophical sensibility and cast of mind. Some intrepid souls with fertile imaginations and the gift or curse of divergent thinking have embraced both.

Of all the myriad strands in the lively cultural conversation on this issue, it would be hard to identify a more colorful and fascinating one than the line of influence that extends from the infamous occultist Aleister Crowley to psychedelic guru Timothy Leary to counterculture novelist-psychologist-philosopher and "guerrilla ontologist" Robert Anton Wilson. The lives of these three men, both individually and collectively, illustrate some of the most far-out reaches of the daemonic muse question, including, especially, the dividing line between objective and subjective interpretations of it. Notably, this is highlighted not only in their individual biographies but in the plotline that interconnects their collective lives and thought.

In what follows, I delve into Crowley's, Leary's, and Wilson's respective experiences of receiving communication from a seemingly autonomous spiritual, psychic, or even extraterrestrial intelligence. I consider each man's interpretative stance toward such experiences, and I detail the line of succession, as it were, that links them all together. I conclude by ruminating briefly on the implications of this story for our understanding of the daemonic muse experience itself, with particular attention given to Wilson, whose attitude of absolute agnosticism, combined with his posture of deep openness to experiences of seeming engagement with a transcendental intelligence, provides a model for vibrant creative living and working.

II. The Great Beast and His Holy Guardian Angel

Aleister Crowley (1875–1947) was arguably the most influential occultist of the twentieth century. His relevance to the muse-based or daemon-based approach to writing and creativity is found in his lifelong engagement with the idea of the Holy Guardian Angel, which stands as a specific iteration of the fundamental concept of the muse, daemon, or genius. By the time Crowley came along, the concept of the Holy Guardian Angel as a person's presiding spiritual guide, helper, and exemplar, the accessing of which was the chief goal of magical or esoteric work, had already been around for several centuries in Western occult and mystical circles, or even longer if you factor in its long prehistory in Neoplatonism and various sister schools of philosophical mysticism. Crowley himself borrowed the term from an English translation of a medieval occult text. So there was nothing particularly original in his use of it, or even in his fundamental philosophical framing of it. But he was the one who made it central and definitive for subsequent generations when he founded the new religion of Thelema and devoted the remainder of his life to explicating and promoting its principles.

The founding event itself, which Thelemites still celebrate every year on the spring equinox as the Feast of the Equinox of the Gods, was the writing of *Liber AL vel Legis* or *The Book of the Law*. As the story goes, in April 1904, while Crowley was on honeymoon in Cairo with his new wife, Rose, *Liber AL* was dictated to him over a span of three days by a voice that identified itself as Aiwass or Aiwaz, messenger of the Egyptian god Horus. The book became Thelema's central scripture, and Crowley identified Aiwass as his own Holy Guardian Angel. He also identified the event as a dividing point in history that signaled the end of the former "Aeon of Osiris," a period characterized by belief in patriarchal monotheism and all that goes with it, and the new "Aeon of Horus," whose guiding ethos would be individual liberty and the discovery of each person's "True Will" in communion with his or her own Holy Guardian Angel.

Interestingly and importantly, Crowley's championing of Thelema and *Liber AL* did not happen right away in the immediate wake of his Cairo experience. In fact, he was initially not all that enamored of the book, and he spoke more than once of the way its ideas were distasteful and contrary to his own thoughts. Robert Anton Wilson and his co-author Miriam Joe Hill elaborate on this briefly in their encyclopedia *Everything Is under Control: Conspiracies, Cults, and Cover-ups,* and their comments again underscore the question of what Crowley's experience with Aiwass "really was":

> At first, Crowley did not like the experience or the book, and managed to largely ignore them for ten years. After 1914, however, he felt increasingly under their spell, and eventually he devoted the rest of his life to the "mission" the book imposed on him. After 1919, he spoke of the Cairo experience as an encounter with a superhuman intelligence; one of his disciples, Kenneth Grant, has claimed the communicating entity emanated from the system of the double star, Sirius, while another student, Israel Regardie, prefers to say Crowley reached the depths of the human evolutionary unconscious unknown to either Freud or Jung. (134)

Thelema is erected entirely upon and around the idea of the Holy Guardian Angel. Its central organizing concept is the necessity for each adherent to achieve the "knowledge and conversation" of his or her own Angel, and thereby to discover the aforementioned True Will, a term that is basically coeval with the idea of a life mission or divine purpose. The most famous statement from *Liber AL*—the oft-quoted "Do what thou wilt shall be the whole of the law"—was borrowed and modified from Rabelais, but in Thelema it assumes the radically specific and transformative meaning of *discovering one's guiding daimon and thereby accessing, activating, and actualizing one's cosmic/divine destiny.* The classical daimon/daemon or genius encapsulated the idea of an invisible spirit that accompanies a person through life and exerts a kind of existential gravity or magnetism that evokes experiences in accordance with the divinely ordained life plan. When Crowley spoke and wrote about the Holy Guardian Angel, and also, significantly, when similar-minded people and organizations in his time did the same—as with the influential Hermetic Order of the Golden Dawn, whose founder was in fact the translator of the book that provided Crowley with the term "Holy Guardian Angel"—he was pursuing the same thing from a different angle.

Crowley's experience is also relevant because his interpretation of it, which continued to evolve throughout his lifetime, underscored the tension or confusion between objective and subjective views. Until the end of his life, he kept issuing what seemed to be contradictory statements about the matter. Sometimes he even planted them side-by-side in the same writing, as in *The Equinox of the Gods* (1936), the book where he told the story of how *The Book of the Law* came to be written. At one point he described the Holy Guardian Angel as "our Secret Self—our Subconscious Ego," clearly favoring an interpretation of the Angel as a layer or presence within the psyche. But in the same chapter he said that even though the words of *The Book of the Law* were physically written by him as "ink on paper, in the material sense," still they

> are not My words, unless Aiwaz be taken to be no more than my subconscious self, or some part of it: in that case, my conscious self being ignorant of the Truth in the Book and hostile to most of the ethics and philosophy of the Book, Aiwaz is a severely suppressed part of me. Such a theory would further imply that I am, unknown to myself, possessed of all sorts of praeternatural knowledge and power. (Maroney 168–69)

In other words, Crowley says here that the simplest and therefore best explanation is to consider the Holy Guardian Angel an independent intelligence, since the subconscious explanation strains credulity even more.

Four decades after Crowley wrote these words, in June 1973, Robert Anton Wilson took "a programmed trip on something an underground Alchemist told [me] was LSD," where part of the "program" involved listening to a taped reading of Crowley's Invocation of the Holy Guardian Angel. As Wilson recounted in *Cosmic Trigger: The Final Secret of the Illuminati*, he achieved, among other experiences, "a rush of Jungian archetypes, strongly influenced by the imagery of Crowley's Invocation, but nonetheless having that peculiar quality of external reality and *alien intelligence* emphasized by Jung in his discussion of the archetypes" (83; Wilson's emphasis). He also "laughed merrily at Crowley's joking seriousness in telling one disciple, Frank Bennett, that the Holy Guardian Angel invoked in this ritual is merely 'our own unconsciousness' and meanwhile telling another disciple, Jane Wolf, that the Holy Guardian Angel is 'a separate being of superhuman intelligence'" (84). Again, the paradox or contradiction is deliberate and central.

The reference to Frank Bennett, not incidentally, comes from a conversation that Bennett and Crowley both recorded separately, Crowley in his autobiography and Bennett in his diary of the time he spent with Crowley in 1921. Bennett was a British-born Australian who became one of Crowley's chief disciples, and Crowley wrote in his *Confessions* that he once revealed something to Bennett that shocked him into an initiatory experience of his Holy Guardian Angel. Editors John Symonds and Kenneth Grant fill in the other half of this story in a footnote to their edition of the book: "We know from Frank Bennett's diary what Crowley said to him on this occasion. . . . Crowley told him that it was all a matter of getting the subconscious mind to work; and when this subconscious mind was allowed full sway, without interference from the conscious mind, then illumination could be said to have begun; for the subconscious mind was our Holy Guardian Angel" (Crowley 936n4).

For our present purposes, perhaps the most helpful expression of this interpretative tension comes from Israel Regardie, who served as Crowley's personal secretary from 1928 to 1932 and went on to become one of the most influential figures in modern Western occultism. In his introduction to *The Law Is for All*, a collection of Crowley's commentary on *The Book of the Law*, Regardie wrote, "It really makes little difference in the long run whether *The Book of the Law* was dictated to him by a preterhuman intelligence named Aiwass or whether it stemmed from the creative deeps of Aleister Crowley. The book was written. And he became the mouthpiece for the Zeitgeist, accurately expressing the intrinsic nature of our time as no one else has done to date" (quoted in Sutin 133). One is free to disagree with Regardie regarding Crowley's prophetic value and insight, but his basic point—that it doesn't matter whether one opts for the supernatural or psychological explanation, because the end result is the same—is worth pondering at length and in depth by those who seek to navigate a relationship with their own deep creative selves.

III. The Strange Case of Timothy Leary

The leap from Crowley to Leary is, culturally speaking, a drastic one. It is a leap from Edwardian and post-Edwardian England to the America of Woodstock and rock and roll; from World Wars I and II to the Vietnam era; from black-and-white movies and the age of radio to the shimmering visual-electronic culture of McLuhan's global village. But even so, the basic theme of perceived guidance and communication from an invisible, alien presence remains constant. Moreover, the fact that the early twenty-first century saw a resurgence of interest in Leary's life and legacy, and also in the general history of the psychedelic movement and the possible therapeutic and spiritual uses of psychedelic drugs, only reinforces the pertinence of attempting to understand the nature of this internal guidance and its emergence as an alien-seeming force—something that is characteristic of many psychedelic experiences.

More than just well known, the basic outline of Timothy Leary's life is legendary. His "first career," as it were, was as a mainstream psychologist and professor. In the 1950s he taught psychology at Berkeley and performed research for the Kaiser Family Foundation, after which, most famously, he taught at Harvard from 1959 to 1963. Some of this early work has had a lasting influence; while serving as head of psychological research for the Kaiser Family Foundation, Leary came up with a system of analyzing human personality along two axes, love-hate and dominance-submission, that produced eight possible personality types, each with two subdivisions. It was a brilliant idea (with roots in the work of earlier psychologists) that ended up expressed in a diagram that has come to be known as the "interpersonal circle" or the "Leary circumplex." Leary's insights helped to lay the foundation for what would become the standard personality tests that are still in use today, such as the Myers-Briggs Type Indicator, which is mostly extrapolated from Jung—who had deeply influenced Leary.

Leary's fall (or ascent, depending on your perspective) from formal respectability was initiated in 1960 when, encouraged by the cultural tenor of the time and the specific incitements of friends and colleagues from both academia and the emerging counterculture, he traveled to Mexico and ingested psilocybin mushrooms. Some years later he said, "I learned more about my brain and its possibilities, and I learned more about psychology, in the five hours after taking these mushrooms than I had in the preceding 15 years of studying, human research and psychology" (cited in *Ram Dass*). When he returned to Harvard, he enlisted the aid of his colleague Richard Alpert, who would later achieve fame as writer and spiritual teacher Ram Dass, to launch a formal study of the psychological effects and possible therapeutic uses of psychedelic drugs.

The story of how the whole thing spun out of control is long and fascinating, but the short version is that after achieving some interesting and promising initial results—such as an indication that the integration of psychedelics into the counseling programs offered to criminal offenders might drastically reduce recidivism rates—Leary, who was naturally anti-authoritarian and free-wheeling, grew fed up with the constraints of conventional research, reputation, and respectability, and in 1963 ended up getting fired from Harvard along with Alpert. The university shut the research program down, and within a few years the U.S. government had banned the use of all psychedelic drugs for any purposes, scientific or otherwise.

The provocation for the government ban was traceable at least partly to Leary himself, who upon his departure from Harvard rapidly transformed himself into the colorful prophet of psychedelic liberation that he is best remembered as today. Naturally, this incurred the wrath of civil authority, and so began a trend that was eventually epitomized by Richard Nixon's televised proclamation circa 1970 that Leary was "the most dangerous man in America."

Irrepressible to the core, Leary refused to back down, and his life path rapidly mutated into something like a thriller novel with a plot involving imprisonment, escape, flight from the U.S., entanglement with prominent antigovernment groups (including the Black Panthers and the Weather Underground), kidnapping, flight from country to country, and eventual return to the U.S. in 1973, at which point he was thrown back in prison, first at Folsom and then at the California Medical Facility at Vacaville. At Folsom he was kept in solitary confinement and also, for a time, in a cell next to Charles Manson.

It was in those prisons that his story dovetailed with our overarching theme of guidance by the muse/daimon/genius, for it was there that he began to experiment consciously with opening himself to thoughts and ideas that, as it seemed, "wanted" to be expressed through him—in other words, with channeling. Viewing the operation as a form of telepathy, and setting as his goal the contacting of "Higher Intelligence" (his specific term) of an expressly extraterrestrial sort, he recruited his wife, Joanna, a fellow prisoner named Wayne Benner, and Benner's girlfriend, a journalist, to participate. The resulting writings—*Starseed* (1973), *Neurologic* (1973), and *Terra II: A Way Out* (1974)—introduced his famous eight-circuit model of consciousness and advanced the idea that life originally came to earth from outer space, and that humanity is destined by DNA coding and evolutionary impulse to colonize space and return to the stars for transcendence and fulfillment via reunion with the galactic source of our being, which is none other than the Higher Intelligence that Leary and his team were in contact with.

To back up a bit and draw a crucial connection, by this point in his life Leary had come to see himself as deeply connected to Aleister Crowley. He had long felt an interest in Crowley's life and ideas, but by the time he arrived at Vacaville in 1974 this had advanced to a point where he viewed his own life as a "continuation" of Crowley and his work (as distinct from a reincarnation, since his and Crowley's lifespans overlapped). In the words of John Higgs, author of *I Have America Surrounded: The Life of Timothy Leary*, in the early 1970s Leary came to believe "that his role in life was to continue Crowley's 'Great Work,' that of bringing about a fundamental shift in human consciousness" (15). This was the result of several mind-blowing events that seemed to Leary to indicate a profound connection to Crowley. Most dramatically, in 1971 Leary and the English beatnik artist and writer Brian Barritt tripped together on LSD in the Sahara desert at Bou Saada, "City of Happiness," reputedly a site of magical influence. It was the night of Easter Saturday and Sunday, and Leary and Barrett witnessed massive celestial imagery and visionary symbolism. A year later they discovered that some of the things they had seen and experienced paralleled with uncanny precision a series of visions that Crowley had reported in his *Confessions*. Unknown to them at the time of their Sahara experience, Crowley had engaged in a weeks-long magical ritual in 1909 with the poet Victor Neuberg on the very same site in the very same riverbed at Bou Saada. Barritt later wrote that he and Leary were "pretty freaked out" when they discovered this, and he speculated about a "mysterious force" in the form of an "unconscious directive" that had dictated in parallel fashion the motivations and even the life events and circumstances of Crowley-Neuberg and Leary-Barritt across a span of decades (Barritt 155, 152).

The Crowleyan vibe was further augmented in 1972 when Leary asked a deck of Crowley-designed tarot cards, "Who am I and what is my destiny?" and then randomly cut the deck to the Ace of Discs—the very card that Crowley had identified as his own representation. In his autobiography, *Confessions of a Hope Fiend*—a title that he chose by deliberately blending Crowley's *Confessions* with another of his books, *Diary of a Dope Fiend*—Leary wrote, "The eerie synchronicities between our lives [i.e., his and Barritt's] and that of Crowley, which were later to preoccupy us, were still unfolding with such precision as to make us wonder if one can escape the programmed imprinting with which we are born" (Barritt 153).

It was in the wake of all these Crowleyan synchronicities that the incarcerated Leary began his channeling experiments. He approached them in the full sway of his sense of carrying on Crowley's planetary consciousness-altering mission, and in full awareness of the fact that Crowley had attempted similar contact with a higher intelligence. And although Leary made no mention of the Holy Guardian Angel, his emerging extraterrestrial hypothesis corresponded to the views of a subset of Thelemites who thought contact with one's Holy Guardian Angel was actually a form of contact with a literal extraterrestrial intelligence. (Others, by contrast, vehemently insisted and still insist today that such a view is false, ridiculous, and detrimental to the cause.)

Wilson began exchanging letters with Leary a few month after the commencement of Leary's telepathic "transmissions" and later offered a succinct description of the concrete nature of the experiments: "The Starseed Transmissions—'hallucinations' or whatever—were received in 19 bursts, seldom in recognizable English sentences, requiring considerable meditation and discussion between the four Receivers before they could be summarized" (*Cosmic Trigger* 105). What is of prime interest to us here is that even though the resulting writings clearly advanced and proceeded from the extraterrestrial view of higher intelligence rather than the unconscious or daemonic muse-based one such—in *Terra II*, for example, Leary asserts that humanity's age-old belief in higher intelligences (as in religious beliefs) is accurate, but he modifies it in a science fictional direction: "The goal of the evolutionary process is to produce nervous systems capable of communicating with the galactic network. Contacting the Higher Intelligence" ("Starseed" 15)—other things said by other people about the Learyan view of communicating with perceived higher or external intelligences, and even things said by Leary himself, clearly link his experiences to a more traditionally muse-like view.

For instance, in a bit of archival footage featured in the "Summer of Love" episode of PBS's *American Experience* series, Leary describes the LSD experience by saying, "It is a sense of being in communion with powers greater than yourself, and intelligence which far outstrips the human mind, and energies which are very ancient." There is no indication of the context or time period in which he said this, but it resonates interestingly with something he told Wilson when the latter came to visit him at the Vacaville prison:

> [Leary said] Interstellar ESP may have been going on for all our history . . . but we just haven't understood. Our nervous systems have translated their messages in terms we *could* understand. The "angels" who spoke to Dr. Dee, the Elizabethan scientist-magician [who had figured in both Crowley-Neuberg's and Leary-Barritt's visionary experiences in the Sahara], were extraterrestrials, but Dee couldn't comprehend them in those terms and considered them "messengers from God." The same is true of many other shamans and mystics. (*Cosmic Trigger* 118; Wilson's emphasis)

Note that despite the outrageous-sounding nature of such speculations to the modern secular-materialist ear, Leary was not insane. Or at least that was the medical-psychological opinion of the mental health professionals who evaluated him, according to Wilson:

> It should be remembered, in evaluating the Starseed signals, that, a few months before this experiment, three government psychiatrists testified (at the escape trial) that Dr. Leary was perfectly sane and possessed of a high I.Q. Since so many extremists of Left and Right have impugned Leary's sanity, it should also be entered in the record that Dr. Wesley Hiler, a staff psychologist at Vacaville who spoke to Dr. Leary every day (often to ask Tim's advice), emphatically agrees with that verdict. "Timothy Leary is totally, radiantly sane," he told me in a 1973 interview. (*Cosmic Trigger* 104–5)

Nor did Hiler make this judgment in ignorance of the telepathy/channeling experiments that Leary was engaged in. In fact, Wilson says Hiler regarded Leary's project as existing within the long historical and psychological record of humanity's experiments and experiences with such things. Hiler's actual words resonate wonderfully with the vibe of ontological uncertainty that we are exploring here:

> I asked Hiler what he *really* thought of Dr. Leary's extraterrestrial contacts. Specifically, since he didn't regard Leary as crazy or hallucinating, what was

happening when Leary thought he was receiving extraterrestrial communications? "Every man and woman who reaches the higher levels of spiritual
and intellectual development," Dr. Hiler said calmly, "feels the presence of
a Higher Intelligence. Our theories are all unproven. Socrates called it his
daemon. Others call it gods or angels. Leary calls it extraterrestrial. Maybe it's
just another part of our brain, a part we usually don't use. Who knows?"
(*Cosmic Trigger* 163; Wilson's emphasis)

IV. Bob Wilson's Excellent Adventure

As already indicated by the above discussions, Wilson's thought resonated
deeply with the ideas of both Leary and Crowley, and he was in direct contact
with the former during the Starseed period. He even helped Leary crystallize
and promulgate his eight-circuit model of consciousness; although Leary first
laid out the model in *Neurologic* (1973) and *Exo-Psychology* (1977), Wilson gave
it an energetic and entertaining publicity boost, and also provided a work of
genuine substance in its own right, in his 1983 book *Prometheus Rising*, which
featured an introduction by former Crowley secretary Israel Regardie. So it is
unsurprising that in addition to being aware of and interested in Crowley's
and Leary's experiences of communicating with angels and aliens, Wilson had
his own encounters with "higher intelligence."

The primary account of it is found in his *Cosmic Trigger* (1977; later retitled *Cosmic Trigger I* when Wilson wrote two sequels). Richard Metzger zeroes
in on the emotional heart of the matter when he writes that even though
many people had delighted in the trippy and subversive delights of Wilson's
famous *Illuminatus!* trilogy (co-written with Robert Shea and published in
1975), "*Cosmic Trigger* was different. This time the mask came off. In this
book, Wilson came clean, in the most intellectually honest way that anyone
ever has, on the subject of 'What happens when you start fooling around with
occult things? What happens when you do psychedelic drugs and try to contact higher dimensional entities through ritual magick?'" (14).

Wilson, who had a Ph.D. in psychology, contextualized the book's content
in a valuable introduction that he wrote for a new edition published in 1986.
"*Cosmic Trigger*," he explained, "deals with a process of *deliberately induced brain
change* through which I put myself in the years 1962–76. This process is called
'initiation' or 'vision quest' in many traditional societies and can loosely be considered some dangerous variety of self-psychotherapy in modern terminology"
(ii; Wilson's emphasis). In the course of this "initiation," he came into perceived
contact with a number of external-seeming intelligences and was thrust into the
same surreal world that Leary and Crowley had likewise explored.

The high point came after he commenced a new "course of neuropsy-chological experiments" in 1971 in response to the impression that he had deciphered a hidden message in Crowley's *The Book of Lies*. "The outstanding result," he wrote, "was that I entered a belief system, from 1973 until around October 1974, in which I was receiving telepathic messages from entities residing on a planet of the double star Sirius" (8). Although Wilson never describes anything like the experience of supernatural dictation that resulted in Crowley's *The Book of the Law,* or like Leary's experience of extraterrestrial telepathy that resulted in the Starseed books, the question of his supposed Sirius contact, and of the general idea of psychic contact with alien-seeming forces or entities, dominates the bulk of *Cosmic Trigger* and forms the guiding thread of Wilson's journey through "Chapel Perilous," his term, borrowed from Arthurian legend, for the frightening and transformative state of psychological uncertainty in which the walls of a person's belief system have been breached by the intrusion of events that seem equally amenable to paranormal/supernatural and naturalistic, non-supernatural explanations.

In describing the various synchronicities and paranormal events that began to unfold in his life, Wilson forcefully foregrounds the questions of ontology and epistemology—of what's really real and how or whether we're even capable of making that determination—and he describes various reversals and mutations in his own viewpoint. For example, he explains that it was a meeting in October 1974 with Dr. Jacques Vallée, the internationally renowned astronomer and ufologist, that led him away from the belief that he (Wilson) was literally receiving telepathic transmissions from Sirius. Wilson says Vallée told him this type of otherworldly communication is a centuries-old phenomenon "and will probably not turn out to be extraterrestrial," since the extraterrestrial slant can be chalked up to the influence of modern cultural beliefs. In former eras, Vallée said, "The phenomenon took other and spookier forms" (*Cosmic Trigger* 9).[1]

Wilson says Vallée's viewpoint

> made perfect sense to me, since I had originally gotten in touch with "the entity" by means of Crowleyan occultism. The extraterrestrial explanation was not the *real* explanation, as I had thought; it was just the latest model for the Experience, as angels had been a model for it in the Middle Ages, or dead relatives speaking through mediums had been a model in the nineteenth century. (*Cosmic Trigger* 9; Wilson's emphasis)

---

1. The veracity of Wilson's recollection here is supported by the fact that Vallée himself said largely the same things in his 2010 book *Wonders in the Sky: Unexplained Aerial Objects from Antiquity to Modern Times.*

This framing of all belief systems in relativistic and provisional terms—an attitude that, as we might do well to notice, is implicit in the very concept of a "belief system" itself, since to recognize belief systems as such automatically subverts the unreflective and wholesale adoption of any of them—became for Wilson the touchstone of his whole outlook. He began that new preface to *Cosmic Trigger*, written ten years after the book's first publication, by proclaiming in all capital letters, "I DO NOT BELIEVE ANYTHING" (i). In explaining this position over several pages, he quoted approvingly Alan Watts's characterization of the universe as "a giant Rorshach [*sic*] ink-blot" and described his own position as "neurological model agnosticism—the application of the Copenhagen Interpretation beyond physics to consciousness itself" (iv).

Most significant for the question of the daemonic muse and its ontological status are Wilson's specific thoughts about the status of all invisible entities/intelligences that are encountered in psychic space:

> Personally, I also suspect, or guess, or intuit, that the more unconventional of my models here—the ones involving Higher Intelligence, such as the Cabalistic Holy Guardian Angel or the extraterrestrial from Sirius—are *necessary* working tools at certain stages in the metaprogramming process [i.e., the process of accessing and altering one's fundamental psychological imprints].
>
> That is, whether such entities exist anywhere outside our own imaginations, some areas of brain functioning cannot be accessed without using these "keys" to open the locks. I do not insist on this; it is just my own opinion. (v; Wilson's emphasis)

With this, we are back once again to Crowley and his continual dance on the edge of mutually exclusive interpretations. "I don't believe anything," Wilson insisted, and so did Crowley and Leary, at least in spirit. The question at hand is: can we learn anything from this?

V. Conclusion: Angels, Daemons, and Haunted Artists

For our specific purpose here, what is valuable in the stories of Crowley, Leary, and Wilson is the vivid picture they show us of people struggling to interpret and live with forces in the psyche that really do present themselves as independent of the ego and possessed of their own intelligence and will. As already mentioned, the Holy Guardian Angel and its supernatural and extraterrestrial kin are explicitly connected in historical-cultural-conceptual-psychological terms to the ancient muse, daimon, and genius, and a Wilsonian attitude of thoroughgoing "neurological model agnosticism" toward them simply removes categorical interpretations of what is happening in the perceived experience of inner communication, not—*not*—the fact of the experience itself. Regardless of what we think or how we feel about it, this experience of being in perceived contact with a "higher intelligence" really did happen to these three men. It really has happened to people throughout history. And it really can happen to you and me. It doesn't necessarily mean audible voices and telepathic transmissions, but it does mean a sense of something impinging on or communicating with our conscious self "from the outside," or perhaps from the deep *inside,* which experientially amounts to the same thing. The really electrifying jolt comes when we realize, as our three present case subjects all did, that such impinging and communicating are *always* happening, regardless of whether or not we are consciously aware of it, as a constant psychic undercurrent. If we are skilled and sensitive enough to tune in and hear it, the rewards in terms of creative vibrancy can be exquisite.

Entirely aside from all the far-out details of his (possibly) paranormal experiences, at least twice in his life Wilson directly equated the autonomous-feeling force in the psyche that drives artistic creativity with the ontologically indeterminate Higher Intelligence that seemingly communicated with him, Leary, and Crowley. One of these instances came in an essay he wrote about the life and work of Raymond Chandler, under the pseudonym of one of his (Wilson's) own fictional creations, book critic Epicene Wildeblood. In describing the fifteen-year hiatus from fiction-writing that Chandler once experienced, Wilson said, "Chandler spent 15 years, the prime years of a man's life, in the oil-executive game before *the Daemon or Holy Guardian Angel that haunts artists got its teeth into him again*" (*Illuminati Papers* 127 [emphasis added]).

The other instance is found in a 1981 interview Wilson gave to the late great genre magazine *Starship: The Magazine about Science Fiction.* The interviewer asked him, "Is a book fully organized in your mind before you start writing or does it take shape as it unfolds?" Wilson responded:

> Sometimes I have a clearer idea of where I'm going than other times, but it always surprises me. In the course of writing, I'm always drawing on my unconscious creativity, and I find things creeping into my writing that I wasn't aware of at the time. That's part of the pleasure of writing. After you've written something, you say to yourself, "Where in the hell did that come from?" Faulkner called it the "demon" that directs the writer. The Kabalists call it the "holy guardian angel." Every writer experiences this sensation. Robert E. Howard said he felt there was somebody dictating the Conan stories to him. There's some deep level of the unconscious that knows a lot more than the conscious mind of the writer knows. (Elliot)

The unconscious mind? The daemon? The Holy Guardian Angel? All and none of the above? For purposes of accessing and aligning with the experience of creative inspiration, *does it really matter?*

2011–2012

Works Cited

Barritt, Brian. *The Road of Excess: A Psychedelic Autobiography* (excerpt). In Richard Metzger, ed. *Book of Lies: The Disinformation Guide to Magick and the Occult.* New York: The Disinformation Co., 2003. 149–55.

Crowley, Aleister. *The Confessions of Aleister Crowley: An Autohagiography.* 1929. New York: Penguin Arkana, 1989.

Elliot, Jeffrey. "Robert Anton Wilson: Searching for Cosmic Intelligence." *Robert Anton Wilson Fans.* Accessed 3 October 2012, from www.rawilsonfans. com/articles/Starship.htm. Reprinted from *Starship: The Magazine about Science Fiction* 19, No. 1 (Spring 1981).

Higgs, John. "The High Priest and the Great Beast." *Sub Rosa* 4 (March 2006): 15–22.

Leary, Timothy. "Starseed: A Way Out." In Brad Steiger and John White, ed. *Other Worlds, Other Universes.* Pomeroy, WA: Health Research Books, 1986. 15–27. Excerpted and reprinted from Timothy Leary, *Terra II: A Way Out.* San Francisco: Starseed, 1974.

Maroney, Tim. "Six Voices on Crowley." In Richard Metzger, ed. *Book of Lies: The Disinformation Guide to Magick and the Occult.* New York: The Disinformation Co., 2003. 164–83.

Metzger, Richard. *Disinformation: The Interviews.* New York: The Disinformation Co., 2002.

Ram Dass: Fierce Grace. Lemle, Mickey, prod. and dir. 2001; New York: Zeitgeist Video, 2003. DVD.

"Summer of Love" (television transcript). Gail Dolgin and Vicente Franco, writers and directors. *American Experience,* season 19, episode 12, 2007. Accessed 3 October 2012, from www.pbs.org/wgbh/americanexperience/films/summer-of-love/.

Sutin, Lawrence. *Do What Thou Wilt: A Life of Aleister Crowley.* New York: St. Martin's Press, 2000.

Wilson, Robert Anton. *Cosmic Trigger: The Final Secret of the Illuminati.* 1977. Tempe, AZ: New Falcon Publications, 1991.

———. *The Illuminati Papers.* Berkeley: Ronin Publishing, 1980.

Wilson, Robert Anton, and Miriam Joe Hill. *Everything Is under Control: Conspiracies, Cults, and Cover-ups.* New York: HarperCollins, 1998.

Scratches on the Universe's Utmost Rim

In the first chapter/lecture in *Psychology and Religion*, titled "The Autonomy of the Unconscious Mind," Carl Jung wrote:

> It is an almost ridiculous prejudice to assume that existence can only be physical. As a matter of fact the only form of existence we know of immediately is psychic. We might well say, on the contrary, that physical existence is merely an inference, since we know of matter only in so far as we perceive psychic images transmitted by the senses. We are surely making a great mistake when we forget this simple yet fundamental truth. . . . Imaginations do exist and they may be just as real and just as obnoxious or dangerous as physical conditions. (11)

Elsewhere, expanding on the same point, he wrote:

> [W]e shall do well to admit there is justification for the old view of the soul as an objective reality—as something independent, and therefore capricious and dangerous. The further assumption that this being, so mysterious and terrifying, is at the same time the source of life, is also understandable in the light of psychology. (*Modern Man* 183)

The great secret of life, which, in order to be grasped as more than a mere philosophical abstraction, requires not just intellectual understanding but a true awakening along the lines of the 180-degree perspective reversal produced by Douglas Harding's headlessness experiments, is simply this: contrary to popular, ingrained, pre-programmed, deep-rooted assumptions, subjectivity is not an abstraction or reduction from objectivity. Rather, objectivity is a reduction from subjectivity. We think of ourselves as private little islands of mind living in a big open space called the Real World (meaning the objective, disenchanted, de-souled universe of materiality and physicality) and jostling frequently up against a human society of similarly isolated little minds. We think that we ourselves are encompassed and contained by "The World."

But in point of phenomenological fact, the opposite is true. The World exists and subsists within us.

Again, this is no idle philosophical speculation. Philip K. Dick once defined reality as that which continues to exist when you have stopped believing in it (261). The reality of this inversion of our customary view of the relative relationship between subject and object, ourselves and our world, qualifies as precisely that.

*   *   *

A seminal moment in the formation of Jung's concept of *synchronicity* came as he was treating a highly educated woman who, by his description, was locked in a rigid Cartesian rationalism that hindered her therapy. The basis of all depth psychotherapy is the airing of unconscious psychic content and the integrating of this with the conscious sense of self, but this woman was centered in a view of reality that denied the existence or significance of such things and kept her wholly imprisoned in her rational ego.

One day as they sat together in Jung's office, the woman told him of a dream from the previous night in which she was given a golden scarab beetle. An iconic symbol of death and transformation in ancient Egypt, the scarab is a figure resonant with psychological meanings, as Jung was well aware. But the situation quickly transcended the realm of purely abstract symbolism when Jung heard a gentle, insistent tapping on the window behind him. As he later recounted,

> I turned round and saw a fairly large flying insect that was knocking against the window-pane from outside in the obvious attempt to get into the dark room. That seemed to me very strange. I opened the window immediately and caught the insect in the air as it flew in. It was a scarabaeid beetle, or common rose-chafer (*Cetonia aurata*), whose gold-green colour most nearly resembles that of a golden scarab. I handed the beetle to my patient with the words, "Here is your scarab." The experience punctured the desired hole in her rationalism and broke the ice of her intellectual resistance. The treatment could now be continued with satisfactory results. (*Portable Jung* 512)

This event went on to become the chief instance that Jung regularly referred to as an illustration of synchronicity in action.

*   *   *

The term "liminality" comes from early twentieth-century anthropology. It was first developed by the French ethnologist and folklorist Arnold van Gennep and then taken up famously by British cultural anthropologist Victor

Turner. Both used it to describe the status of people undergoing cultural initiations and rites of passage into adulthood, during which, according to the rules and beliefs of a given society, such people have left childhood behind but not yet achieved full adult status. During this interim such people are, in van Gennep's and Turner's terms, "liminal beings," meaning they stand not inside the culturally established categories of identity but *between,* in a position of interstitial suspension.

The word "liminal" itself comes from the Latin *limen,* or threshold, as in the threshold of a doorway. It refers metaphorically to an interstice, a halfway position, a zone of betweenness, a location or position or status that "falls between the cracks."

It is instructive to draw a connection between this and sociologist Peter Berger's idea, laid out in his classic book *The Sacred Canopy: Elements of Sociological Theory of Religion,* of the "nomos," the socioculturally constructed universe of shared beliefs and meanings that represents the boundaries of what a given people recognize—and are able to accept—as "reality." To be separated from the nomizing influence of society, says Berger, is to be in danger of experiencing a sense of meaninglessness, which in his view is

> the nightmare *par excellence,* in which the individual is submerged in a world of disorder, senselessness and madness. Reality and identity are malignantly transformed into meaningless figures of horror. To be in society is to be "sane" precisely in the sense of being shielded from the ultimate "insanity" of such anomic terror. (22)

And for a still further dose of eldritch resonance, we can recall Lovecraft's famous statement of monstrous liminality and teratological interstitiality in the famous passage from his "The Dunwich Horror," presented as a fictional excerpt from the Necronomicon, asserting that "The Old Ones were, the Old Ones are, and the Old Ones shall be. Not in the spaces we know, but *between* them, they walk Serene and Primal, undimensioned and to us unseen" (*Thing on the Doorstep* 219; Lovecraft's emphasis).

Would it represent an unwarranted stretching of the point if we noted that, from the perspective of a Lovecraftian-Bergerian hybrid philosophy of outsideness and in-betweenness, read in terms of van Gennep's and Turner's anthropological observations and theories, we ourselves become proximally equivalent to the Old Ones when we step through the cracks of psyche and society to inhabit the spaces between? Or if we observed that Turner's and van Gennep's "liminal beings" are in fact separated for a time from the nomizing influence of society? And that, therefore, people undergoing true initiatory experiences are themselves "malignantly transformed" for the duration of the experience into "meaningless figures of horror" who embody, in their very (non)persons, the ultimate insanity of anomic terror?

*   *   *

The implications of these things for life-as-lived, and for our understandings of art, self, society, and reality, are darkly profound and profoundly dark.

As Jung defined it, synchronicity is an "acausal connecting principle" that manifests itself in the form of "spontaneous, meaningful coincidences of so high a degree of improbability as to appear flatly unbelievable" (*Portable Jung* 510). That potent little word "meaningful" is the key: a synchronicity is the convergence of two or more events in a mesh of meaningfulness, so that instead of one of them *causing* the other—a relationship that is the basis of physics, and also of material science in general—they mutually *illuminate* and *say something* about each other. It thus bridges the gap between the subjective world of the psyche and the objective world of (seemingly) external phenomena. Something happens, a particular concentration of objective events presents itself, that harmonizes uncannily with a person's psychic state and effectively serves as an *expression* of this state by "the world" at large. Jung wrote, "Take for instance my case of the scarab: at the moment my patient was telling me her dream a real 'scarab' tried to get into the room as if it had understood that it must play a mythological role as a symbol of rebirth" (*Jung on Synchronicity* 105).

In his essay "A Way of Writing," the late poet William Stafford spoke of the "strange bonus" that sometimes happened to him when he pursued the act of writing in a deliberate attitude of ignorance. Instead of planning and thinking ahead of time, he said he made a discipline of setting aside time each morning for writing, and then he spent that time noting down whatever came to him. "At times," he said,

> without my insisting on it, my writings become coherent; the successive elements that occur to me are clearly related. They lead by themselves to new connections. Sometimes the language, even the syllables that happen along, may start a trend. Sometimes the materials alert me to something waiting in my mind, ready for sustained attention. At such times, I allow myself to be eloquent, or intentional, or for great swoops (Treacherous! Not to be trusted!) reasonable. But I do not insist on any of that; for I know that back of my activity there will be the coherence of my self, and that indulgence of my impulses will bring recurrent patterns and meanings again. (18–19)

In *On Not Being Able to Paint*, the classic Freudian study of artistic creativity first published in 1950, British author and psychotherapist Marion Milner, writing under the pseudonym Joanna Field, recounted and reflected on her experience of learning to produce meaningful drawings and paintings by surrendering to the subjective pressures within her psyche. She described how she deliberately worked for a while in accordance with the idea, gleaned from a book she had read, that in learning to paint one should start simply by trying to discover what one's eye seems to "like." Following this advice, over a span of weeks she produced a series of drawings that she collectively titled "Earth." Only afterward did she realize that the figures she had drawn—an approaching storm over a dark sea where a mythic snake and a New Mexican Indian drum rose from the waves; a dove hovering over water; messy, chaotic scribbles; a tree; a sea wall—were united by the theme of chaos encroaching on order, as in the biblical story of Noah and the great deluge with its waters of primal uncreation that wiped out the world, after which a dove brought back evidence of solidity's reappearance from beneath the deep.

This was all in harmony with an unsettling recognition about the nature of perception and subjective identity that had been subtly emerging out of certain experiments that Milner had lately been making in perceiving the world's visual appearance nakedly and truly, without preconception. At the time she made the "Earth" series, she had been noticing for a time that "the effort needed in order to see the edges of objects as they really look stirred a dim fear, a fear of what might happen if one let go one's mental hold on the outline which kept everything separate and in its place" (18). This was in turn a facet of the wider realization that had begun to grip her as she saw that "original work in painting, if it was ever to get beyond the stage of happy flukes, would demand facing certain facts about oneself as a separate being, facts that could often perhaps be successfully by-passed in ordinary living" (14).

And suddenly we are back to Berger with his concept of the "sacred canopy," that is, the matrix of cultural meanings that gives order and coherence to the chaos of raw experience. As with all articulations of an inside, the concept of the sacred canopy necessarily entails a profane *outside,* and Berger rivetingly describes the way this outer darkness forms an all-enveloping and all-menacing anti-cosmos whose very outsideness automatically renders it nameless and horrifying to those on the inside. He also identifies its appallingly intimate point of access, which is none other than our own deepest psychic interiority:

> It would be erroneous to think of these situations [in which the reality of everyday life is put into question] as being rare. On the contrary, every individual passes through such a situation every twenty hours or so—in the experience of sleep and, very importantly, in the transition stages between

sleep and wakefulness. In the world of dreams the reality of everyday life is definitely left behind. In the transition stages of falling asleep and waking up again the contours of everyday reality are, at the least, less firm than in the state of fully awake consciousness. The reality of everyday life, therefore, is continuously surrounded by a penumbra of vastly different realities. These, to be sure, are segregated in consciousness as having a special cognitive status (in the consciousness of modern man, a lesser one) and thus generally prevented from massively threatening the primary reality of fully awake existence. Even then, however, the "dikes" of everyday reality are not always impermeable to the invasion of those other realities that insinuate themselves into consciousness during sleep. There are always the "nightmares" that continue to haunt in the daytime—specifically, with the "nightmarish" thought that daytime reality may not be what it purports to be, that behind it lurks a totally different reality that may have as much validity, that indeed world and self may ultimately be something quite different from what they are defined to be by the society in which one lives one's daytime existence. (42)

* * *

For many readers—perhaps for you—the concept of synchronicity sounds pointedly absurd. Coincidences, we are wont to say, even the most highly improbable ones, are simply random events with no intrinsic meaning. Any meaning they seem to possess is simply our own projection. Subjective and objective reality represent discrete categories. To muddle them is to engage in "magical thinking" of a grossly primitive, naïve, and, when it comes right down to it, foolish and destructive sort.

And as for the in-between spaces of liminality, well, to state it bluntly, who really cares? Liminality is fine as a sociological theory or whatever, but it doesn't have anything to do with the real, workaday world of everyday life.

This line of thinking, however plausible and reasonable it may sound to some ears, is the expression of a cultural bias, and specifically, a worldview based on reductionism and materialism. Its claims are really begged questions, but because we inhabitants of modern-day, post-industrial, corporate-consumer technocracies live, move, and have our being within its all-encompassing philosophical and ideological fog, we generally fail to see this.

Sometimes, however, we find that events line up as if in direct challenge to that dogmatic slumber. Someone hands us our golden scarab, flown fresh on glistening wings from the dark mind of our dreams into the clear light of day, and the seams of our world split open all around us, and suddenly we're floating and stumbling through a real-life Twilight Zone. As Lovecraft evocatively wrote:

> Children will always be afraid of the dark, and men with minds sensitive to hereditary impulse will always tremble at the thought of the hidden and

fathomless worlds of strange life which may pulsate in the gulfs beyond the stars, or press hideously upon our own globe in unholy dimensions which only the dead and the moonstruck can glimpse. . . . The one test of the really weird is simply this—whether or not there be excited in the reader a profound sense of dread, and of contact with unknown spheres and powers; a subtle attitude of awed listening, as if for the beating of black wings or the scratching of outside shapes and entities on the known universe's utmost rim. (*H. P. Lovecraft: The Fiction* 1043–44)

Some of us are constitutionally prevented from regarding these words as merely fictional, poetic, or symbolic.

*   *   *

In my horror novelette "Teeth," there is a scene where the narrator reads a private notebook filled with ruminations on the convergence of philosophy and religion with cosmic horror in the context of quantum physics. He is a graduate student in philosophy, and the reading of these things initiates a transformative change in his psyche that gives him a different sort of philosophical education than the one he had previously pursued.

When I first wrote that story in the mid-1990s, I was enwrapped in a pattern of inner and outer events and circumstances—personal, professional, psychological, spiritual—that seemed either starkly meaningless or evilly intended, and I was utterly unable to decide which possibility, a meaningless cosmos or a malevolent one, seemed more likely. Amid the indecision, regardless of the causes, I was suffering.

Lovecraft's celebrated opening paragraph to "The Call of Cthulhu," which I quoted in that story, wasn't just something that I found interesting for intellectual or literary reasons. It struck right to my core and articulated my lurking fear that life, the universe, and everything in general might well turn out to be not meaningless at all, that it might flow from and be invested with a very definite and pervasive overall meaning—and that this meaning might well turn out to be unbearably awful.

Here is how Lovecraft put it:

> The most merciful thing in the world, I think, is the inability of the human mind to correlate all its contents. We live on a placid island of ignorance in the midst of black seas of infinity, and it was not meant that we should voyage far. The sciences, each straining in its own direction, have hitherto harmed us little. But some day the piecing together of dissociated knowledge will open up such terrifying vistas of reality, and of our frightful position therein, that we shall either go mad from the revelation or flee from the deadly light into the peace and safety of a new dark age. (*Dunwich Horror* 125)

Recall William Stafford's words: "At times, without my insisting on it, my writings become coherent. . . . *I know that back of my activity there will be the coherence of my self.*"

Is it possible that a horrific meaning inhering in the cosmos at large could also inhere in the self? If it really is possible through the practice of writing or some other art to hit upon and uncover "the coherence of my self" as seen in "recurrent patterns and meanings" that emerge from "the indulgence of my impulses," might I perhaps find that this isn't all I had hoped it would be? Might I find that self-actualization isn't automatically joyful and fulfilling? Might I find that the coherence within my self—or *beneath* or *behind* my self—turns out to correspond to Lovecraft's nightmare of deadly meaning in the universe as a whole, and to the ravenous cosmic outsideness pressing inward on the seams of Berger's sacred canopy? If so, how might the accessing and actualizing of this self transform the very world, this particular cosmic *nomos,* in unforeseen and unnatural ways?

"As above, so below" says the ancient Hermetic maxim. In esoteric spiritual terms, this is understood as referring to the identity between the deep reality of the individual soul and the transcendent reality of absolute deity that encompasses and lies beyond the rim of the cosmos. In the words of religion scholar Huston Smith,

> Envisioned externally, as residing outside of man and apart from him, the Good dons metaphors of height: "I shall lift up mine eyes unto the hills . . ."; "in the year that King Uzziah died, I saw the Lord, high and lifted up." When man reverses his gaze and looks inward, his value-imagery likewise transposes; it turns over. Within man, the best lies deepest; it is basic, fundamental, the ground of his being. All the levels of reality are within man, for microcosm mirrors macrocosm; man mirrors the Infinite. But mirrors invert; hence symbolism's "law of inverse analogy." That which man seeks externally in the highest heavens he seeks internally in the depths of his soul. Spiritual space, like physical, is curved. We journey far to reach our origin. (20–21)

But what if the reality "above," the one we "seek externally in the highest heavens," were to be something like what Lovecraft described in "Supernatural Horror in Literature" as the extra-cosmic nightmare whose evocation constitutes the essence of weird supernatural horror? Yes, what *then?* What if those "hidden and fathomless worlds of strange life" may pulsate not only "in the gulfs beyond the stars" but in the depths of our own souls? What if those dark entities and outside shapes with their claws and black wings may scratch not just on the *outer* rim of the known universe but the inner rim of our unknown depths? Behind the brain, beneath the breath, below the deepest layers of the personal unconscious with its skeleton closet of rapacious Freudian id-ness, in the place where we reach Jung's and Hillman's archetypes, and then be-yond even that, delving into the daimonic substratum of the Self which is the primal residing place of angels, aliens, shadow people, and discarnates—in that deepest, darkest depth of personal selfhood, might we find the very essence of the monstrous, a slumbering cosmic Leviathan? Might we be confronted by the crimson glowing eyes and tentacular visage of something beyond endur-ance, but also beyond escaping, because it is in fact the Zen master's whale upon which we stand while fishing heedlessly for minnows?

*   *   *

To some people, this kind of speculation sounds ridiculous and pointless. It seems a patent waste of time, words, and imaginative energy. To others, espe-cially those who enjoy cosmic horror stories, it is very interesting indeed, even if it sounds purely fanciful. Both responses miss the mark. Both miss the na-ked experience of turning the eyes upward and gazing at the diseased yellow moon to which the words are but a dark Taoist gesture. When the reality in question arises to grip you from within, it is neither interesting nor fanciful. Nor is it ridiculous or pointless. Rather, it is awful—and also aweful—in the most pointed, particular, and agonizing sense of that word. Furthermore, it is undeniable, inexorable, and inescapable.

In his essay "The Consolations of Horror," Thomas Ligotti argues that artistic horror offers only a single valid consolation: "simply that someone shares some of your own feelings and has made of these a work of art which you have the insight, sensitivity, and—like it or not—peculiar set of experi-ences to appreciate" (xxi). In achieving the unenviable status of an initiate in-to the "peculiar set of experiences" that will lead a person to appreciate—truly, deeply, existentially—the works of a Ligotti or Lovecraft, or to sense in every statement of religious, mystical, and non-dual truth the implied threat of some living nightmare that is poised to erupt through the veneer of mun-dane surface realities—in achieving this particular state of mind and soul, a person may find that all the synchronicities that typically attend a real en-gagement with matters mythic, daimonic, and esoteric begin to appear like the workings of some vast conspiracy whose masterminds are always multiple steps ahead, always planning a million moves in advance, always hiding just around the next dark corner and beyond the next fold in the twilight landscape, always playing a game whose rules, strategies, and fundamental purpose remain obscure. You never asked to play this game. You don't even know its name or nature. But now you realize that you are, and always have been, a pawn.

Patrick Harpur observes in *Daimonic Reality* that a personal awakening to the liminal zone of daimonic entities and realities is often accompanied by the heightened sense of a network of meaningful interconnections. Synchronicities begin to abound. Harpur also notes that, for some people, this can all become deranged into a genuine case of paranoid schizophrenia based on the sense of some grand, overarching cosmic conspiracy (91–96). In *The Secret Life of Puppets*, Victoria Nelson draws an extended comparison between the psyches and writings of Lovecraft and the celebrated schizophrenic Daniel Paul Schreber, whose pathology fascinated Freud, and who believed, among many other things, that mysterious "rays" were penetrating, deforming, and controlling his mind and body. Schreber believed he was under the domination of alien intelligences. "The inner worlds of Lovecraft and Schreber," writes Nelson, "are full of fear and suffering, painful metamorphoses, debasement: transformation minus transfiguration" (130). She also argues from various angles and with various evocative means of support that schizophrenics are "failed mystics" and that supernatural horror fiction serves the equivalent of a religious function.

Near the end of "Teeth," the narrator intuits a possible escape from his metaphysical-ontological trap:

> Over the years I have become an assiduous student of Lovecraft, not just his stories but his essays and letters. And I have marveled at the man's uncanny ability to see so deeply into the truth and yet remain so composed and kindhearted. Perhaps this gentle New Englander knew something that I do not, something he tried to convey when he wrote of the "vast conceit of those who babble of the *malignant* Ancient Ones." Perhaps the horror exists only in me, not in reality itself. . . . After all, It knows only Itself, and maybe I will not perceive It as horrific after I die. Perhaps I will be so thoroughly consumed by and identified with it that "I" will not even exist at all, and my sense of horror will prove to be as fleeting and finite as the self that sensed it. (119)

Does he actually mean what he is saying? Does he actually understand it? For that matter, do I? For there's the rub: here, in one of the darkest corridors of Chapel Perilous, you can never be sure. Of anything. At all.

You can only know for certain that you don't want anybody to turn on the lights, because after a while you come to realize the darkness is as much a comfort as a threat. When the monster lies in shadows—its native domain— at least you don't have to look at it, lock eyes with it, and recognize its gaze as the depth of your own.

2012

Works Cited

Berger, Peter. *The Sacred Canopy: Notes toward a Sociological Theory of Religion.* Garden City, NY: Doubleday, 1967.

Cardin, Matt. *To Rouse Leviathan.* New York: Hippocampus Press, 2019.

Dick, Philip K. *The Shifting Realities of Philip K. Dick: Selected Literary and Philosophical Writings.* Ed. Lawrence Sutin. New York: Vintage Books, 1995.

Harding, Douglas. *On Having No Head: Zen and the Rediscovery of the Obvious.* Rev. ed. New York: Penguin Arkana, 1988.

Harpur, Patrick. *Daimonic Reality: A Field Guide to the Otherworld.* Enumclaw, WA: Pine Winds Press, 1994.

Jung, C. G. *Jung on Synchronicity and the Paranormal.* Ed. Roderick Main. London: Routledge, 1997.

———. *Modern Man in Search of a Soul.* Tr. W. S. Dell and Cary F. Baynes. San Diego: Harcourt, 1955.

———. *The Portable Jung.* Ed. Joseph Campbell. New York: Penguin Books, 1976.

———. *Psychology and Religion.* New Haven: Yale University Press, 1938.

Ligotti, Thomas. *The Nightmare Factory.* New York: Carroll & Graf, 1996.

Lovecraft, H. P. *The Dunwich Horror and Others.* Ed. August Derleth; texts ed. S. T. Joshi. Sauk City, WI: Arkham House, 1984.

———. *H.P. Lovecraft: The Fiction.* Ed. S. T. Joshi New York: Barnes & Noble, 2008.

———. *The Thing on the Doorstep and Other Weird Stories.* Ed. S. T. Joshi. New York: Penguin Classics, 2002.

Milner, Marion. *On Not Being Able to Paint.* New York: Routledge, 2010.

Nelson, Victoria. *The Secret Life of Puppets.* Cambridge, MA: Harvard University Press, 2001.

Smith, Huston. *Forgotten Truth: The Common Vision of the World's Religions.* San Francisco: HarperSanFrancisco, 1992.

Stafford, William. "A Way of Writing." In *Writing the Australian Crawl.* Ann Arbor: University of Michigan Press, 1978. 17–20.

Initiation by Nightmare:
Cosmic Horror and Chapel Perilous

When the first of many sleep paralysis attacks happened to me in the early 1990s, I had no idea that it was the onset of a period that I would later come to regard as a spontaneous shamanic-type initiation via nightmare. I didn't know it would shatter the psychological, spiritual, ontological, metaphysical, and interpersonal assumptions that had undergirded my worldview and daily experience for so long that I had forgotten they were assumptions instead of givens. Terence McKenna, among others, has argued that, in accordance with the same principle that keeps a fish oblivious to the existence of water, the perturbation of consciousness is necessary for us even to become aware of the reality of consciousness as such. For me this was confirmed with lasting impact by the experience of waking up from a profoundly deep sleep to encounter a darkly luminous, vaguely man-shaped outline of a being that stood over me at the foot of the bed, and that shone with sizzling rays of shadow, and that represented a thunderous and *sui generis*—intended solely for me—black hole of a negative singularity, a presence whose entire reason for being was to draw me in and annihilate me. In the manner of dreams and daemons, the experience was as much cognitive and emotional as it was perceptual. There was no separation between these usually discrete categories. Nor was there a separation between the categories of self and other, between "me" and the assaulting presence. Horror was literally all there was, all that existed, all that was real— not as a reaction to the experience but as an organic and inevitable symmetry of being. I was not horrified. The experience was purely and simply horror.

When this proved to be not an isolated episode but an ongoing crisis spanning a period of months and years, and when the psychic effects began to leak into the daylight world and contaminate my daily life with a distinct and inescapable background static of creeping nightmarishness, I knew something dire had happened. I had crossed some sort of threshold, and the most likely vocabulary for thinking and talking about it was the vocabulary of cosmic horror, which I had learned from years of obsessively reading Lovecraft, Lovecraft criticism, and a whole host of associated authors.

There was, however, another vocabulary that I could have used, and it would have complemented the cosmic horrific one in mutually illuminating fashion. It was the vocabulary of consciousness change and high paranormal weirdness encoded in the idea of Chapel Perilous as explicated by Robert Anton Wilson. But this did not occur to me until much later.

* * *

Wikipedia has a brief article on Chapel Perilous that defines the term in its psychological use as "an occult term referring to a psychological state in which an individual cannot be certain if they have been aided or hindered by some force outside the realm of the natural world, or if what appeared to be supernatural interference was a product of their own imagination." I can't think of a better succinct summary. But it only "works," it only carries the appropriate vibe of electrifying significance, if you are aware of the details that lie behind it, including its origin story.

At the time when my crisis unfolded, I had already been enraptured for years by Wilson's books, vibe, and guerrilla ontological charm. *Illuminatus!*, the *Schrödinger's Cat* trilogy, *The Illuminati Papers*, the Historical Illuminatus Chronicles, *Prometheus Rising*, *The New Inquisition*, *Quantum Psychology*, *Cosmic Trigger*, and several of his other books were canonical texts for me. So I was very well acquainted with his concept of Chapel Perilous, which was a central theme, perhaps *the* central theme, not just in his writing but in his life. And yet somehow I did not draw the obvious connection between this concept and my spiraling spiritual-existential crisis.

When *Cosmic Trigger* was published in 1977, Wilson was already associated with the idea of global occult conspiracies due to his co-authorship of the *Illuminatus!* trilogy, which he and Robert Shea wrote with epic satirical intent. In *Cosmic Trigger*'s introduction, titled "Thinking about the Unthinkable," he announced, "I no longer disbelieve in the Illuminati, but I don't believe in them yet either." He then explained what he meant by this weird statement, and in doing so he described a particular state of mind and soul that permanently established the term Chapel Perilous as a core entry in the lexicon of spiritual edge-realm explorers:

> In researching occult conspiracies, one eventually faces a crossroad of mythic proportions (called Chapel Perilous in the trade). You come out the other side either stone paranoid or an agnostic; there is no third way. I came out agnostic.

Chapel Perilous, like the mysterious entity called "I," cannot be located in the space-time continuum; it is weightless, odorless, tasteless and undetectable by ordinary instruments. Indeed, like the Ego, it is even possible to deny that it is there. And yet, even more like the Ego, once you are inside it, there doesn't seem to be any way to ever get out again, until you suddenly discover that it has been brought into existence by thought and does not exist outside thought. Everything you fear is waiting with slavering jaws in Chapel Perilous, but if you are armed with the wand of intuition, the cup of sympathy, the sword of reason, and the pentacle of valor, you will find there (the legends say) the Medicine of Metals, the Elixir of Life, the Philosopher's Stone, True Wisdom and Perfect Happiness.

That's what the legends always say, and the language of myth is poetically precise. For instance, if you go into that realm without the sword of reason, you will lose your mind, but at the same time, if you take only the sword of reason without the cup of sympathy, you will lose your heart. Even more remarkably, if you approach without the wand of intuition, you can stand at the door for decades never realizing you have arrived. You might think you are just waiting for a bus, or wandering from room to room looking for your cigarettes, watching a TV show, or reading a cryptic and ambiguous book. Chapel Perilous is tricky that way. (6–7)

Additional valuable explanation came two decades later in *Maybe Logic,* the 2003 documentary about Wilson's life and thought, wherein Wilson explained that

Chapel Perilous is a stage in the magickal quest in which your maps turn out to be totally inadequate for the territory, and you're completely lost. And at that point you get an ally who helps you find your way back to something you can understand. And then after that for the rest of your life you've got this question: Was that ally a supernatural helper, or was it just part of my own mind trying to save me from going totally bonkers with this stuff? And the people I know who've had that kind of experience, very few of them have come to an absolutely certain conclusion about that.

He also shared some of the personal background that lay behind his discovery of the ontologically and epistemologically indeterminate nature of encounters with what seem like supernatural and/or paranormal intelligences and entities:

Around 1973 I became convinced for a while that I was receiving messages from outer space. But then a psychic reader told me I was actually channeling an ancient Chinese philosopher, and another psychic reader told me I was channeling a medieval Irish bard. And at that time I started reading neurology, and I decided it was just my right brain talking to my left brain. And then I went to Ireland and found out it was actually a six-foot-tall white rabbit. They call it the Pooka, and the Irish know all about it. (*Maybe Logic*)

To reiterate, in *Cosmic Trigger* Wilson wrote that when you enter this state—when you cross the threshold into Chapel Perilous and find that although all kinds of bizarre and seemingly impossible things are undeniably happening, you are completely unable to decide whether they are objectively real or purely imaginary—"you come out the other side either stone paranoid or an agnostic; there is no third way." In a sense, though, nobody ever really leaves Chapel Perilous. The memory of it becomes a living and present part of your everyday experience. When Wilson says he came out as an agnostic, he means he emerged with a permanently altered understanding and sense of things. For many people who casually call themselves agnostic in everyday life, what they really mean is that they're too lazy or shallow to think deeply about things. Unlike, say, a T. H. Huxley or a Bertrand Russell, who energetically considered the implications of a deep and clear agnosticism, the lazy agnostic poseur lacks the energy, will, and/or intellect to engage in a focused and meaningful interrogation of epistemological foundations. Dismissing ultimate questions with a metaphorical (or perhaps literal) wave of the hand, such a person says, "Ah, we can't even know the answers, so what does it even matter?" By contrast, the type of agnosticism that is truly vital is the one that realizes ultimate questions a) really do matter and b) are revealed as insoluble mysteries, vast blanknesses, the deeper we dig. Wilson's agnosticism was of the latter variety. It was existential.

I didn't realize it at the time, but in the early 1990s my seeming experiences of supernatural/demonic assault represented a kind of epistemological shakedown that was calibrated to result in exactly this same realization of ontological, metaphysical, and cosmological indeterminacy. And it wasn't until I started to realize and own this fact some years later, thanks to a wide-focus course of reading and study combined with various online and in-person conversations and interactions, that I discovered there was an existing spiritual and philosophical counterculture—much of it directly associated with the newly minted neo-shamanism movement, as vibrating in deep concord with the reborn psychedelic movement—whose members already knew all about this type of thing. I just happened to be the last one to know.

*   *   *

The term "Chapel Perilous" comes from Sir Thomas Malory's *Le Morte d'Arthur*, which contains an episode in which Sir Lancelot visits said chapel and successfully resists the seduction attempts of a sorceress named Hellawes. Although Malory's story is apparently the first time that Chapel Perilous, or the Perilous Chapel, is explicitly so named, this type of setting—a mysterious chapel where a hero undergoes a trial or temptation while on a sacred quest—was already a staple of the Grail legends by the time Malory wrote and compiled his now-classic collection of Arthurian romance tales in the late fifteenth century.

In 1922, T. S. Eliot incorporated Chapel Perilous into the apocalyptic-cosmic doomscape of *The Waste Land.* In the poem's accompanying notes, he explicitly referred the reader to another book for explanation and commentary on his central use of the grail motif, stating that "not only the title but the plan and a good deal of the incidental symbolism of the poem were suggested by Miss Jessie L. Weston's book on the Grail legend: *From Ritual to Romance*" (51).

Published in 1920, *From Ritual to Romance* is a landmark work of anthropological and mythological scholarship in which Weston, an independent scholar and folklorist specializing in medieval Arthurian texts, uncovers ostensible links between the various components of the grail legends and the myths, beliefs, and rituals of Europe's ancient, pre-Christian mystery cults. She focuses especially on the tale of the Fisher King, which in its primal/archetypal form involves a king whose kingdom becomes desolate when he himself falls gravely ill or becomes impotent, and he therefore sends out a brave knight—Perceval in some versions, Gawain in others, or sometimes somebody else—to find the Holy Grail, which will restore himself and his kingdom to health. At the far end of the quest, the knight stumbles into the nightmarish Chapel Perilous (which, as noted above, is not always named such, and occasionally is not a chapel at all but a Perilous Cemetery), where he undergoes a severe trial and eventually emerges to bring home the grail.

Weston's commentaries and analyses to accompany her summaries of such matters are darkly evocative. She devotes her energies to developing the idea that the ancient roots of the grail legend in general and the Chapel Perilous experience in particular reside in older stories of a dreadful initiation involving a plunge into the otherworld, with possibly dire consequences extending into the physical realm:

> *[T]his is the story of an initiation* (or perhaps it would be more correct to say the test of fitness for an initiation) *carried out on the astral plane, and reacting with fatal results upon the physical.* . . . [T]he Mystery ritual comprised a double initiation, the Lower, into the mysteries of generation, i.e., of physical Life; the higher, into the Spiritual Divine Life, where man is made one with God.
>
> [I suggest] that the test for the primary initiation, that into the sources of physical life, would probably consist in a contact with the horrors of

> physical death, and that the tradition of the Perilous Chapel, which survives in the Grail romances in confused and contaminated form, was a reminiscence of the test for this lower initiation. (Weston's emphasis)

At one point she chides some of her fellow scholars for focusing exclusively on the supposed Celtic roots of the tradition in question. Weston argues that this tradition has a far deeper and wider pedigree, both historically and spiritually, than many were accustomed to imagining:

> Visits to the Otherworld are not always derivations from Celtic Fairy-lore. Unless I am mistaken the root of this theme is far more deeply imbedded than in the shifting sands of Folk and Fairy tale. I believe it to be essentially a Mystery tradition; the Otherworld is not a myth, but a reality, and in all ages there have been souls who have been willing to brave the great adventure, and to risk all for the chance of bringing back with them some assurance of the future life. Naturally these ventures passed into tradition with the men who risked them. The early races of men became semi-mythic, their beliefs, their experiences, receded into a land of mist, where their figures assumed fantastic outlines, and the record of their deeds departed more and more widely from historic accuracy.
>
> The poets and dreamers wove their magic webs, and a world apart from the world of actual experience came to life. But it was not all myth, nor all fantasy; there was a basis of truth and reality at the foundation of the mystic growth, and a true criticism will not rest content with wandering in these enchanted lands, and holding all it meets with for the outcome of human imagination. ... The Grail romances repose eventually, not upon a poet's imagination, but upon the ruins of an august and ancient ritual, a ritual which once claimed to be the accredited guardian of the deepest secrets of Life. Driven from its high estate by the relentless force of religious evolution—for after all Adonis, Attis, and their congeners, were but the "half-gods" who must needs yield place when "the Gods" themselves arrive—it yet lingered on; openly, in Folk practice, in Fast and Feast, whereby the well-being of the land might be assured; secretly, in cave or mountain-fastness, or island isolation, where those who craved for a more sensible (not necessarily sensuous) contact with the unseen Spiritual forces of Life than the orthodox development of Christianity afforded, might, and did, find satisfaction.

The entire grail legend, then, at least according to this analysis, can be read as an encoded story about a sometimes dreadful initiation into otherworldly realities with implications extending into the physical world. Chapel Perilous is the primary symbolic site of this defining trial and transition.

But—and this is crucial—is Chapel Perilous necessarily *somewhere that you go*, even in a symbolic, metaphorical, and/or psychological sense? Or can it perhaps be *something that comes to you?* In *Daimonic Reality,* Harpur writes provocatively about various types of initiation into daimonic/liminal/otherworldly things, including not just the customary (but shattering) visionary death-and-rebirth experiences of shamans but the spontaneous initiatory power of *dreaming* that is open to everyone. Then he suddenly moves on to consider a separate type of initiation, one that is qualitatively different from the rest:

> I am led to consider another form of initiation. It is difficult to describe—indeed it may not be appropriate to call it initiation at all since it does not apparently involve the death and rebirth experience of the shaman's subterranean and celestial journeys. But it does involve a change, sometimes dramatic, in the recipient, usually in the form of an expanded awareness of the Otherworld and a greater degree of wisdom in encountering it.
>
> Unlike the Shaman's experience of the Otherworld as a daimonic realm entered during altered states of consciousness, this different kind of initiation happens the other way around: the Otherworld enters this world. Our everyday reality becomes heightened, full of extraordinary synchronicities, significances, and paranormal events. People who investigate the daimonic are particularly prone to these—although they can happen to anyone who is engaged on a search for some sort of knowledge or truth (every scholar, for instance, knows how the very book he requires can fall off a library shelf at his feet!). (242–43)

He finishes with a capstone statement that resounds and resonates all the way back to the Grail legends with their dreadful daimonic initiatory setting of Chapel Perilous: "In other words, it is a goal-oriented kind of initiation and, as such, might be called a *quest*" (243; Harpur's emphasis).

This is riveting. This is revolutionary. However, based on my own experience, and also that of a handful of friends and acquaintances, as well as the testimony of cosmic horror fiction with its vibrant and venerable trope of unexpected and unpleasant liftings and rendings of reality's veil (as in, for example, Blackwood's "The Willows" and "The Wendigo," Lovecraft's "The Call of Cthulhu" and "The Music of Erich Zann," Ligotti's "The Sect of the Idiot" and "Nethescurial," Klein's "The Events at Poroth Farm" and "Black Man with a Horn")—based on all this, I have to wonder whether the kind of initiation Harpur describes, in which the Otherworld breaks through into this one, might happen *not because someone has sought it out, but simply because it wants to happen.* Spontaneously. Unexpectedly. Inevitably. Unavoidably.

Put differently, I have to wonder whether this initiation might sometimes take place not as the result of a quest, not because you have been pursuing it, but as the result of what we might call a "reversed" or "inverted" quest, because *it* has been pursuing *you.*

*   *   *

Terence McKenna, in talking about the psychedelic undermining and transmutation of a person's experience of reality (as was his lifelong wont and mission), once gave a really able exposition of Chapel Perilous:

> Robert Anton Wilson ... coined the term Chapel Perilous. This is when
> something happens in your life and it all begins to fit together and make
> sense, too much sense. Because it's coming from the exterior and it seems
> to either mean that you're losing your mind or you are somehow the central
> focus of a universal conspiracy that is leading you toward some unimagina-
> ble breakthrough. Along the way to the mystery lie the realms of loving eve-
> rybody, moving fields of geometric color, past lives, you name it. But these
> are just milestones on the way. When you finally get to "the thing," the way
> you will know that you've arrived is that you will be struck dumb with won-
> der. That you will say, "My God, this is impossible. This is inherently im-
> possible. This is what impossible was invented to talk about. This cannot
> be!" Then we're in the ballpark. Then we're in the presence of the true *coin-
> cidentia oppositorum.* (thelakeysisters)

In July 2012 it was revealed, via a public reading of a portion of Dennis
McKenna's forthcoming memoir *The Brotherhood of the Screaming Abyss: My Life
with Terence McKenna,* that his brother Terence suffered a horrific experience
during a psychedelic mushroom trip in 1988 or 1989 that proved so traumat-
ic, it put him off taking psychedelics, except for tiny doses on infrequent oc-
casions, for the rest of his life. This came as a bombshell in the sizable
community that pays attention to such things, since Terence was known for
advocating "heroic" doses of psychedelics for many years after that in his
books and talks, and since Dennis claimed in the book excerpt that many of
the things Terence continued to espouse in his later years, including most of
his wilder speculations about 2012, Timewave Zero, the alien intelligences of
the psychedelic hyperrealm, and the future spontaneous organization of organic intelligence through the global Internet—in other words, the things for
which he was most popular—were just show business, just philosophical performance art that paid the bills. The excerpt was read aloud by Bruce Damer
to an audience at the Esalen Institute, at an event organized by Damer and
Lorenzo Hagerty (host and creator of the Psychedelic Salon podcast) under
the title "A Deep Dive into the Mind of Terence McKenna." It also went out
as a Psychedelic Salon episode. But then, rather shockingly, it was pulled, and
Hagerty put up a note at the podcast's website explaining that this had been
done at the request of Dennis McKenna and the McKenna family, and that
the excerpts in question were from a portion of an early draft of the memoir

that would not appear in the final book.

What Dennis revealed in that now-lost portion of his memoir was Terence's horrific mushroom experience. The details were hazy, said Dennis, but apparently the episode involved Terence being introduced to the formerly wise and benevolent mushroom spirit, which he had related to for years as a nurturing teacher, in a nightmarish new guise as it "turned on him" and precipitated a kind of negative enlightenment. He saw the cosmos or multiverse in the stark, horrifying light of "a lack of all meaning"—a phrase he kept repeating over and over. According to Dennis, among the most deeply and transformatively disturbing aspects of the experience was its utter unexpectedness. It caught Terence, a seasoned psychedelic traveler, completely off-guard.

I find this to be extraordinarily fascinating, not just because it offers a revelatory look at a previously unknown side of Terence McKenna, whose life and wisdom have become important to me in recent years, but because it dovetails with a kind of galling perfection with what I described in my horror story "Teeth" as the all-encompassing psychological/spiritual effect on the narrator when he is forcibly initiated into an experience of cosmic supernatural horror. Several days after this inciting event, which occurs when the narrator looks at a mandala and sees it open onto a hellish abyss of devouring teeth, he becomes aware of a catastrophic change in his psyche that involves a vision of his future as "nothing but an endless black tunnel lined with painful and meaningless experiences. . . . Was my life, was existence itself, truly what I now perceived it to be: nothing more than a short interlude in an otherwise unbroken continuum of horror, a sometimes distracting but ultimately vain dream that was destined to end with a terrible awakening to the abiding reality of chaos, of madness, of nightmare?" (Cardin 108–9).

That this essentially describes my own real-world internal state when I wrote the words—a state that had evolved inexorably out of those soul-draining nocturnal, supernatural(-seeming) assaults—and that today, some seventeen years after writing that story, it is now known that Terence McKenna, figurehead of the newly mature and hopeful psychedelic renaissance, and an increasingly important figure in my own intellectual pantheon, may have had a life-changing encounter with just such a soul-sucking vacuum of total, horrific meaninglessness while communing with his beloved plant teacher—that this could happen not only startles me but reinforces a suspicion that has grown on me over time, even as I have lived my way out of that mental-emotional-philosophical hellhole.

We are all playing with fire, those of us who actively perturb consciousness, and also those of us who have such perturbations forced upon us by powers outside our ken or control. In the words of the weekly closing narration from a classic horror television series that I enjoyed in my youth, "The dark side is always there, waiting for us to enter, waiting to enter us." What I didn't understand as an adolescent was that this is not mere poetic speech, nor is it mere aesthetic or intellectual entertainment for those drawn to the dark side of fiction, film, philosophy, and spirituality. This is deadly truth.

Wilson spoke of Chapel Perilous in terms of the perceived arrival of a spiritual ally that helps one through a crisis. But there is another corridor of the chapel where the ally's aspect is decidedly darker, and it is damned difficult to see him, her, or it as an ally at all. The fact that the classic ally in the Western esoteric and occult traditions is one's daemon, one's genius, one's Holy Guardian Angel, makes this darker aspect of the experience all the more disturbing. For what does it mean when your own "higher self," the daemon or daimon who, according to the ancient Western understanding, represents the divine template and design for your life—and which in a modern-day context we can metaphorize as the "unconscious mind," especially in a Jungian sense—what does it mean when *this*, the most intimate and personal-to-you of all possible psychological/spiritual realities, appears in the form of a demonic, assaulting presence?

2012

Works Cited

Cardin, Matt. *To Rouse Leviathan*. New York: Hippocampus Press, 2019.

"Chapel Perilous." *Wikipedia*. Modified 24 September 2012, en.wikipedia. org/wiki/Chapel_perilous.

Eliot, T. S. *The Waste Land and Other Writings*. New York: Modern Library, 2002.

Harpur, Patrick. *Daimonic Reality: A Field Guide to the Otherworld*. Enumclaw, WA: Pine Winds Press, 1994.

thelakeysisters. "Chapel Perilous—Along the Way to the Mystery." YouTube Video, 3:04. 26 November 2010. www.youtube.com/watch?v=vZeomwPriDQ.

Maybe Logic: The Lives and Ideas of Robert Anton Wilson. Lance Bauscher, dir. 2003. Santa Cruz, CA: Deepleaf Productions, 2003. DVD.

Weston, Jessie L. *From Ritual to Romance*. 1920. Accessed 24 September 2012. www.fullbooks.com/From-Ritual-to-Romance1.html

Wilson, Robert Anton. *Cosmic Trigger: The Final Secret of the Illuminati*. 1977. Tempe, AZ: New Falcon Publications, 1991.

Interviews

Interview with Matt Cardin

Interview by Stuart Young

SY: Many of your stories revolve around matters of spiritual horror. Indeed, your short fiction collection *Divinations of the Deep* dealt exclusively with this theme. What exactly are your own spiritual beliefs?

MC: Not to sound contentious, but I'd rather not espouse a belief in anything, since to *believe* implies that one doesn't *know*. I'd rather be like Jiddu Krishnamurti and claim up front that I have no beliefs whatsoever.

At present my spiritual life and practice, such as they are, consist primarily of remaining mindful of the present moment and focusing upon my immediate experience of first personhood. This is very much in line with the idea or realization of headlessness as taught by your fellow Englishman, the philosopher Douglas Harding. Beyond that, I hold all beliefs, doctrines, dogmas, and so on at arm's length, as objects of interest and occasional study—sometimes very intense personal interest and study, but distanced nonetheless. I was raised an evangelical Christian and have remained formally involved in and affiliated with various Protestant churches throughout my adulthood, so it's probably no surprise that I'm still overcome now and then by lingering inner tendencies toward Protestant theological orthodoxy. I've pretty much learned to follow Emerson's advice by simply yielding to those devout motions of the soul whenever they occur. But this predisposition for experiencing wholesale inner revolutions made for a very stormy ride a few years back, especially during the early and mid-1990s when I had just graduated from college and gotten married. I could tell you a long, detailed story about the near philosophical and psychological meltdown that I experienced during those years when I was overcome by a kind of philosophical schizophrenia. I could go on and on about the literally hundreds of authors and books that both contributed to this problem and helped me through it. But I suspect this account would be of interest only to me, and to tell the truth, I'm tired of rehashing it (as I've done many times before in my private journals). Suffice it to say that the point where I now find myself in my religious, spiritual, and philosophical understanding of things is to a considerable extent the result or outgrowth of everything I experienced, read, reflected upon, and struggled with during that time. What it has really amounted to is learning to wake up to the reality of my immediate experience, stop abstracting away into various invented dream worlds that lead to nowhere but more suffering, and embrace the fact that truth, meaning the fundamental nature of things, can't be encompassed intellectually or stated propositionally.

SY: You studied Okinawan Goju-ryu karate for several years. Was that due to your interest in Zen or was it just in preparation for dealing with anyone who gave your stories bad reviews?

MC: Actually, I studied Japanese Goju, not Okinawan. A man named Gogen Yamaguchi studied under Chojun Miyagi, the founder of Okinawan Goju, and then took it to mainland Japan where he formed the Japanese version.

The main reason I got into karate at all, at age twelve, was that I had seen it performed in movies and on television and had come to believe that it was absolutely the coolest thing in the world. My chief interest in Zen came afterward, after I had stopped my formal martial arts practice. I practiced for a total of six years and earned the rank of Shodan (first degree black belt). Now I feel like something of a bum for allowing this part of me to lie dormant for so many years, especially since I was fortunate enough to fall by complete accident into a very impressive teaching lineage. My first teacher was Jeff Speakman. I studied under him for almost two years before he left for California to study Kenpo under Ed Parker. He then went on to star in *The Perfect Weapon* and a few other martial arts movies. When he departed for the West Coast, I moved up to study under his teacher, a man named Lou Angel, who is today a living legend. He in turn had studied under both Peter Urban, who brought Goju to America in the 1950s, and then Gogen Yamaguchi himself, under whom Mr. Urban had studied. What with all this impressiveness in the background of the senseis under whom I studied, I feel a little sheepish that the only thing I did with my training after quitting it at the age of seventeen was to play a ninja warrior in a satirical fantasy movie that my roommates and I made in college.

SY: Do you go out of your way to research esoteric topics for your stories or do you just kind of stumble across them?

MC: The esoteric topics that find their ways into my stories do so naturally, simply because they're the things that fascinate me. My story "Teeth," for example, which appeared in the Del Rey anthology *The Children of Cthulhu,* contains a slew of philosophical quotations and dark metaphysical speculations because I had been obsessing over such things for quite some time when I wrote it. I actually wrote the first version of that one back in 1995, when I was in the thick of my personal philosophical problems. All the stories I've written since then have similarly been literary outpourings based on various issues that have preoccupied me for extended periods, and these have invariably revolved around sundry dark spiritual things.

SY: Given the way that the general public tends to view horror as the tackiest of all genres, it might seem strange to them that you deal with spiritual matters in horror stories. Do you ever feel that perhaps the concerns you wish to address would be better served by being examined in the context of another, more respected, genre?

MC: I don't think about genre at all when I go to write a story. I mean, I do consider myself a horror fan, and I know that the stories I have written are properly classified as horror. But all this means is that I'm deeply, personally drawn to things that just happen to fall under the horror category label. I'm independently interested in both religion and spirituality on the one hand and horror as an emotion, experience, and aesthetic mode on the other. This means I am extremely exhilarated by stories, films, philosophical and spiritual ideas, poems, and so on that display a distinct interface between these two realms. I really couldn't care less whether anybody views this connection as unfortunate or demeaning to either subject.

And anyway, the deep connection between spirituality and art horror is well established. To a large extent, the whole subgenre of the weird tale, which has been my personal favorite area of endeavor as both a reader and a writer, revolves around this very connection. I mean, look into the tales of Machen, Blackwood, Hodgson, Lovecraft, Aickman, Ligotti, and many more, and you immediately see dark spiritual themes interacting with classic horror themes all over the place. In a more general sense, supernaturalism is one of the major classic themes of horror as a literary mode, and supernaturalism is closely bound up with religion and spirituality. So I think it's perfectly legitimate from a historical and aesthetic viewpoint to explore spiritual matters in the context of horror fiction.

From the other end of things, I also think it's completely appropriate and legitimate to explore horror in the context of religion and spirituality. Within the Christian tradition and the Judeo-Christian scriptures alone, you can see horror breaking out all over the place and playing a central role. What in the world is up with that awful darkness and dread that come over Abram in Genesis when he's visited by Yahweh and informed of the future enslavement of his people in Egypt? Why does the New Testament author of Hebrews assert that "it is a dreadful thing to fall into the hands of the living God"? Why does Yahweh sometimes come across in the Book of Isaiah as a chaos monster who is even more terrible in his character, intentions, and ultimate nature than the primeval chaos dragons Leviathan and Rahab, against whom he is supposedly working to save the cosmos? Why does the original ending of the Gospel of Mark—not the longer ending, which appears in many New Testament translations, and which is now known to have been tacked on at a later date, but the original ending, which comes several verses before that—why does this original ending show the two Marys and Salome discovering Jesus' tomb standing empty after the resurrection, tell of their encounter with the angel inside, and then conclude the account simply by saying that they ran away from the tomb in extreme fear, for trembling and astonishment had come upon them—*and that's it?* Why are people seized with fear and awe in the New Testament whenever Jesus calms a storm or performs an exorcism or raises a person from the dead? Why is the Book of Revelation full of intense horrific imagery? In short, why does it so often happen, and not only with Judaism and Christianity, but in many other religious traditions as well— think, for example, of Arjuna's horror when Krishna reveals his true appearance in the Bhagavad Gita—that the unveiling of God, Ultimate Reality, the Ground of Being, whatever, is portrayed as an occasion for intense horror?

This is something that fascinates me. Certainly, there are orthodox theological answers to all these questions, answers that manage to keep the traditional, reassuring view of things intact. But I find that I'm drawn to subversive speculations that tend to invert traditional notions of the character of divinity and deep reality. Rudolf Otto, the great German scholar of religions, claimed in his seminal book *The Idea of the Holy* that the earliest stirring of religious or spiritual emotion in the human race wasn't a sense of comfort, peace, or divine joy, but was instead an intense emotion of daemonic dread. He goes on to state that this primal emotion was elaborated into all the higher religions and still maintains a place of great importance within them today. Whether or not one thinks it's reasonable to agree with Otto about this, the idea itself is so potent that it's positively stunning, and it has had quite a long, varied, and fruitful life in the field of religious studies.

So the point I'm making here, and at such length that I fear my answer would make even Colin Wilson blush, is that whether we consider the matter from the viewpoint of horror and its internal integrity as a genre or mode, or from the viewpoint of religion/spirituality with its own internal integrity, the crossover between the two fields is longstanding, permanent, well-established, fascinating, potent, and extremely profitable for further investigation.

SY: Your horror fiction is very bleak, particularly as it's not just gross-out physical horror. Often during the course of one of your stories, it seems that you take your protagonist and then actually crush their soul. But religion, generally speaking, is quite optimistic. How do you reconcile these two very different outlooks?

MC: In general terms, I reconcile them by making reference to all the stuff I just talked about. I tend to think of modern industrial civilization as being characterized by its spiritual desolation, and I speculate that one obvious and effective way for people to experience an actual opening-up to the forgotten spiritual side of life is to seek out and undergo the sort of dark initiation into transcendence that one finds in the reading of horror fiction. But this is a somewhat trite answer, no matter how attractive is sometimes seems to me.

As far as my own work as a writer goes, I've sometimes said the outlook I put forth in my stories is rather like the dark underbelly of my actual spiritual attitude. But in reality the relationship between the two is a little more complicated than that. I seem to exist in a perpetual state of suspension between believing the worst and believing the best about life, the universe, and everything. By "worst" I mean the kind of twisted metaphysic I build up as the spiritual foundation of my stories, where individual conscious existence is framed as a nightmare, and where the reality to which one awakens through spiritual illumination is even worse. By "best" I mean a world in which ultimate reality turns out to be what all the great mystics and gurus have pointed toward: the experience of ecstasy in divine union, the sat-chit-ananda or being-consciousness-bliss of Vedantic Hinduism. I lead my life as a consumer of ideas according to what moves and excites me, and for some reason I find that both of these scenarios excite my imagination equally at different times. I find that I'm forced to put on a kind of fiction-maker's attitude in order to maintain the dark view, whereas when I'm truly mindful and aware, the fears that accompany the dark view seem somewhat silly and impossible. So in essence, I hold to the darker view with a quasi-fictional attitude and the lighter view with a greater sense of its existential validity. Why they should both happen to engage my intellect and emotions with such intensity is anyone's guess. I've never been able to figure it out myself.

SY: You teach English at a high school. Do you ever slip any horror fiction into the syllabus in an attempt to corrupt America's youth? Or do you leave that to MTV?

MC: All I've done in this direction is to incorporate *Frankenstein* into the sophomore English class that I teach. I make it something of a multimedia event by supplementing the novel with information about the Frankenstein myth's long and varied history in show business. I screen extended clips from James Whale's *Frankenstein* and *Bride of Frankenstein,* as well as from *Young Frankenstein.* I show the full-length Branagh-directed film adaptation, which, despite its many failings, still has much to recommend it. I also fill in a little bit on the history of the various nineteenth-century stage adaptations, such as *Presumption, or the Fate of Frankenstein,* which provided more of the basis for the 1931 Whale-directed version than did the novel itself. And of course this is all subordinate to the goal of having my students read the novel and get a handle on the various philosophical, scientific, and literary allusions that pepper it. For the past two years I've had us all read the whole thing together out loud, since, as I discovered during my first year of teaching the book, Ms. Shelley's imposing vocabulary and complex early nineteenth-century English prose style can be quite baffling to contemporary American sixteen-year-olds.

Besides that, I did include a passage from Tim Lebbon's *The Nature of Balance* in a final exam I wrote a couple of years ago. But I think that's as far as I'll go with the idea of bringing horror into my teaching job. I've thought several times about bringing Lovecraft and Ligotti into the classroom in minimal form, but I know I'll never do it, because it would undoubtedly be a disaster in terms of student comprehension and interest, and I can't stand the thought of encountering all the bewilderment and distaste that many (although certainly not all) of my students would exhibit toward two of my most cherished authors. Besides, I think the best introduction to HPL and Ligotti is to discover them by accident, on your own, and to gain the impression that you have uncovered a magnificent secret.

SY: Okay, I'm just going to throw some names at you. These are various people who I know have influenced your writing and/or your philosophy. If you could just give me a quick summary of how and why each person has influenced you. First off, Thomas Ligotti.

MC: I "read around" Thomas Ligotti for a few years before I actually set out to read his work. By this I mean I saw his name cropping up in various places, heard him compared to Lovecraft, and even thumbed through his collection *Grimscribe* on a Walmart bookrack. (Today, in retrospect, the thought of encountering his work in a Walmart blows my mind.) And from what I saw, I knew this was somebody whose work I would eventually have to read. Two things finally clinched it. First, I browsed through editor John Pelan's first *Darkside* anthology (this time standing in a supermarket) and read the final lines of Tom's story "The Nightmare Network," which describe a camera view that zooms out to encompass the entire universe. The story ends by saying, "Long shot of the universe. There is no one behind the camera." That dovetailed so perfectly with certain things I had been thinking and feeling for a very long time that it set off a kind of alchemical explosion in my brain.

The other deciding factor was my bumping into, and then becoming fast friends with, a man named Jonathan Padgett in the alt.horror.cthulhu newsgroup in late 1997 or early 1998. Jonathan was a longtime Ligotti fanatic, and he had been nursing a plan to create a Ligotti website for several years. Our mutual enthusiasm, mine that of a newbie and his that of a veteran, influenced us both. He created first a Ligotti newsgroup and then the Thomas Ligotti Online Website, while I set about reading Tom's books, starting with *Grimscribe*.

I don't want to make too much of this, but it really did feel as if I had been waiting my whole life to read something like what I encountered in *Grimscribe*. The overpowering emotional and intellectual impact of reading the first few stories was literally life-changing. Here was an author who was saying things, and even using various specific expressions, figures of speech, and symbols, that I had been brooding over for a very long time in the privacy of my own thoughts. I had already written "Teeth" at that point, and I saw in Tom's "The Last Feast of Harlequin," "The Spectacles in the Drawer," "Flowers of the Abyss," and "Nethescurial" a kind of confirmation, fulfillment, and awesome extension of everything that had driven me to want to write a horror story in the first place.

Now, these several years later, I have read Tom's entire body of work. I have written extensively about his stories both singularly and collectively. I have been fortunate enough to strike up a friendship with him via email correspondence. And perhaps not surprisingly, I seem to have linked my name and reputation inextricably to his (at least among the tiny handful of people who have read my work). I've seen myself described online as someone who tirelessly promotes Tom's work. I've been told to my face by a well-known figure in the fantasy/horror field that I'm simply trying to ride Tom's coattails to success. I've seen someone comment that my *Divinations of the Deep* collection, while enjoyable, is a little too Ligottian. The irony here is that I've never imitated him or anybody else. I've written solely from the depths of my personal passion. Any influence that Tom has exercised over me has simply been in the form of inspiring me *to* write, not in determining *what* or *how* I write. He and I just happen to share a remarkably close kinship of vision and disposition when it comes to certain things. I've had this impression confirmed from his end by things he has said to me in private about both my stories and my essays about his work.

Please excuse the unsolicited mini-rant. I just thought I'd set the record straight. And of course I have nobody to blame but myself if indeed I seem to have been laboring willfully in Tom's shadow.

SY: H. P. Lovecraft.

MC: Lovecraft was my arch-passion before I encountered Ligotti. He will always remain one of my literary lights. I devoured his complete works in high school and college, as well as a mountain of secondary information in the form of biographies, critical studies, appreciations, and so on. His cosmic nihilism played an enormous part in undergirding my emotional and philosophical outlook during those turbulent years of my philosophical disease. I would give anything to have been able to meet the man or correspond with him.

SY: Stephen King.

MC: The first book I read by King was *Pet Sematary*. The most recent was *Dreamcatcher*. I've only read a comparative handful of his novels (compared to how many he's written, that is), and among those, *It* is far and away my favorite. I've not really turned out to be much of a novel reader, although back in high school I was a fan of epic fantasy and read lots of thick paperback fantasy novels. My later predilection for shorter works has kept me from making King a staple of my literary diet. In my various academic writings about horror, I have referred several times to his *Danse Macabre*, which I consider to be a really wonderful resource, as well as a thoroughly enjoyable read. From what I hear, his *Dark Tower* mythos is fairly grandiose and interesting, but there's no way that I'm ever going to make time to read all those gargantuan novels in which he lays it out. Many years ago I read *The Gunslinger*. Today I can hardly remember a thing about it, other than the mescaline scene. *Dreamcatcher* was diverting but disappointing. I'm more inclined to admire King from afar for who he is and what he's done—because writing such an enormous amount of popular fiction, much of it displaying real literary merit, is no mean feat—than to count myself an active fan and actually keep up with his work.

SY: T.E.D. Klein.

MC: I read *The Ceremonies* and then *Dark Gods* back in the early and mid-1990s. Both of them enthralled me with their dark cosmic visions of horror, and I sensed the intelligence and literary skill of a magnificently talented author behind them. I certainly wish the man would write more, although if he's anything like me, he's not really in control of his output. I'll remain happy to wait for whatever projects satisfy him when they reach their organic completion. Interestingly, Gene O'Neill, who is friends with Klein, has told me that Klein and I would probably have a lot to talk about, since we share many interests in common and also share, according to Gene, a kind of common outlook or mindset.

SY: Robert Anton Wilson.

MC: Wilson blew open a lot of mental doors for me and gave me a delicious feeling that I was absorbing all kinds of subversive, secret knowledge. I've speculated in the past that a certain amount of my philosophical schizophrenia may have been due to Wilson's influence. When I was in the middle of that painful period, I thought back several times to Wilson's and his co-author Robert Shea's claim in the appendices to *Illuminatus!* that they had covertly programmed the reader in all sorts of strange ways through various hidden things coded into the book, and that many of the results of this programming might not become apparent until years afterward. All things considered, I think I've been influenced more by the inspiration and excitement that I derived from reading Wilson's books than from any actual content or methods that I gleaned from them, although God knows I did absorb a huge amount of formerly unknown information. When I was an undergraduate, I wrote him a very fanboyish letter that I can only hope he never received.

SY: Ken Wilber.

MC: I get a real charge out of seeing Wilber's native brilliance on display in his various writings. The first thing I ever read by him was an article titled "A Spirituality That Transforms," wherein he delineates two distinct functions of religion, which he terms "translation" and "transformation." The first, he says, refers to the role of religion in helping to create meaning for the separate self by giving it moral rules, formulating interpretative myths for it, providing rituals for it to perform and participate in, and so on. The second function, transformation, cuts directly across this first function and is intended not to fortify, bolster, or console the separate self, but rather to shatter or explode it in the service of allowing the individual to recognize higher and wider levels of being. Both functions, he says, are vitally important, for without translation we could never stabilize and learn to live authentically at the level where we presently find ourselves, while without transformation there would be no possibility of a real liberation or awakening to higher levels of being.

It's that kind of clarity that endears him to me. I didn't start reading his work until fairly late in my spiritual education, so he hasn't impacted me as much as some of the people I encountered earlier, such as Alan Watts and Huston Smith. But I still really enjoy what he does, and I feel I've derived real benefit from it. He lays things out so very lucidly—such as his contention that the mystical or non-dual vision is something that simply requires cultivation to achieve, just as you have to train yourself in science or literary criticism if you want to understand the subjects they deal with—that I think it's difficult not to be charmed by him. In particular, his identification of the pre/trans fallacy has been of real personal value to me. That's the mistake, common among Romantics, of equating pre-rational thinking, which is actually *ir*rational, with the higher level of *trans*-rational thinking.

SY: Is there anyone else you'd like to mention that hasn't been covered so far?

MC: Interesting that you would ask. Some months ago I found myself stranded in the midst of an extremely boring group training session at my school. The subject was brain-based learning, which is only the latest in a seemingly endless string of fads to march through the world of education theory. Since I know that by the time anybody actually learns what the new theoretical model is trying to teach, the next theory in line will already have taken its place, I didn't feel any obligation to listen to the presentation. And I found myself idly making a list of the authors who have meant the most to me throughout my life. I ended up with a list of nearly 120 names. Then I went back through and tried to identify the ones who have *really* meant the most, my personal pantheon of literary gods.

Thanks to your asking this question, I now possess a justification for having ignored the training session and made my list. By the way, I generally skip such lists of favorite authors when I find other people reciting them in interviews, because I find them boring. So I'll fully understand if nobody gives a damn about the names that follow. But anyway, in addition to Ligotti, Lovecraft, and Robert Anton Wilson, about whom you've already asked me, my list of finalists includes, in no particular order, Homer, Douglas Harding, E. F. Schumacher, Eckhart Tolle, Alan Watts, Thaddeus Golas, Richard Bach, Oswald Chambers, the Bible, Jan van de Wetering, Allan Bloom, the *Tao Te Ching*, Shunryu Suzuki, Scott Morrison, Ray Bradbury, Carl Jung, Nietzsche, Kierkegaard, William Barrett (the philosopher and existentialist writer), Huston Smith, Joseph Campbell, Ayn Rand, C. S. Lewis, J. R. R. Tolkien, Lloyd Alexander, Hugh Prather, Walker Percy, Richard Tarnas, Theodore Roszak, and Robert Pirsig.

2004

Interview with Matt Cardin: Dark Awakenings and Cosmic Horror

Interview by Lovecraft News Network

LNN: Your new collection, *Dark Awakenings,* raises the following questions: "What if the spiritual awakening coveted by so many religious seekers is in fact the ultimate doom? What if the object of religious longing might prove to be the very heart of horror? Could salvation, liberation, enlightenment then be achieved only by identifying with that apotheosis of metaphysical loathing?"

Disregarding the knee-jerk emotional reactions these questions might elicit from those whose concept of cosmology is based on bumper stickers and slogans, is it really that farfetched? The god of the Old Testament, for example, is unquestionably more malevolent than the apathetic entities of Lovecraft. You discussed this a bit in your interview with Stuart Young in *Terror Tales* when you asked, "Why does the New Testament author of Hebrews assert, 'It is a dreadful thing to fall into the hands of the living God?'" I mean, is not conventional Christian teleology dolefully misanthropic by definition? Is Pat Robertson and his worldview not proof enough that your premise is beyond the realm of speculation? I suppose what I am really getting at is this: since cosmic horror does seem so readily apparent, why is it not more openly acknowledged by more people? Of course this sort of thinking is unpleasant, but pollution, climate change, and child slavery are also unpleasant, and we still talk about these things at least somewhat openly in society. Whence the difference?

MC: Of course you're correct that the dark and horrific side of Christian theology and teleology, and also, I think, of world religion in general, is central to the whole thing. But as you also point out, it's not openly acknowledged by a lot of people. How come? I think it has something to do with the softening and sanitizing of the human race that has occurred during the past few centuries. The post-Enlightenment attitude and worldview based on universal rights and dignity and so on represents a brand-new meme in human history. By the antiseptic standards of our current Western and Westernized nations, every civilization in history has been inconceivably violent, not just in act but in attitude, and this includes their religious conceptions. Today we denizens of Western consumer society have largely cut ourselves off from such things, although the worldwide resurgence of fundamentalism, and also the increasingly bloody and trippy nature of our mass entertainments, shows the same impulses reentering through the back door. As you point out, you can watch Robertson on *The 700 Club* or listen to any number of old-style fundamentalist Protestant preachers to get some of this classic vibe of divine terribleness.

But the cosmic horror I'm getting at in *Dark Awakenings* is something besides that. I'm interested in the idea of a cosmic horror that's absolute, that nobody could find comfort in or fit into a remotely palatable theological framework. The traditional bloody Judeo-Christian cosmology and anthropology have rested on the idea that somehow things are being "set right" on the planet and in the universe through all of this horror. Even the terror of the deity, which is so expertly evoked in a lot of biblical apocalypticism, is supposed to apply only, ultimately, to those who oppose him. The "winners," Yahweh's chosen ones, get to enjoy his everlasting beneficence in the end. That's where the whole idea of the *felix culpa*, the "happy fall" from divine grace, comes in. The bloody drama of human history is justified by the fact that it's somehow necessary to achieve God's blissfully perfect result. In contrast to this, what has long interested me is the speculation that maybe there's something fundamentally horrific about God or the Ground of Being from the human perspective—in other words, that cosmic horror is final and absolute, not provisional. Just this morning I finished reading John Keel's *The Mothman Prophecies*, which Keel concludes with a quote (incorrectly attributed to Charles Fort; it was actually penned by Damon Knight in his Fort bio) that gets at a major aspect of this idea with marvelous clarity: "If there is a universal mind, must it be sane?" I would add: or good or wholesome or reassuring? Could ultimate reality in its essence be something noxious, toxic, nightmarish? Not even Pat Robertson wants to go there.

LNN: What does this (cosmic horror) mean for us as a species from a biological/Darwinian perspective?

MC: I suppose it could mean we're the unluckiest beings on the planet, since our particular set of biological adaptations has resulted in the development of a nervous system capable of self-aware thought, which is now able to recognize with full, stark, staring horror the awfulness of our situation, cosmically and ontologically speaking. "Consciousness is a disease" and all that.

Note that whenever I talk about these things, I do so hypothetically, in a kind of philosophical hyperspace. I'm not saying I actually believe in this type of cosmic-horrific situation. But I'm not saying I don't, either. Just two days ago my nine-year-old niece asked me if I believe in ghosts. I tried to turn the question back at her, but she really wanted to hear my answer. If it's possible for a person to hem and haw in deeply philosophical language while trying to talk in terms that a nine-year-old can understand, then that's what I did. Do I believe in ghosts? How the hell do you even answer such a question when "I," "believe in," and "ghosts" are all terms that beg a thousand questions? The same knee-jerk tendency to poke through spiritual claims in search of the assumptions behind them keeps my thoughts about cosmic horror floating in a safely hypothetical space. That said, the very idea of this kind of horror still feels connected to me in a deeply personal and existential fashion.

LNN: How do you feel about the transition of Lovecraft and his work from obscurity to a more mainstream, or at least more populous, status? And what does this say about contemporary culture?

MC: I'm still really pleased about Lovecraft's canonization. I have that dumb thing in me that feels disappointed whenever some obscure love of mine becomes widely popular, but Lovecraft's rising reputation hasn't managed to trip that alarm yet, since I still find that in my daily life nobody has heard of him. This is true even at the community college where I teach. Ask any ten faculty members in the English department about Lovecraft, and you might get one or two hits, if that. The rest are blank stares. Tom Ligotti is fond of saying, "There is no obscurity like minor renown." Lovecraft enjoyed this kind of renown for decades as a cult author. I've got to wonder how long it's going to take for him to break out of it, if indeed he ever will. I do think his movement into widespread mainstream consciousness may simply happen as a result of generational passings, since a lot of young fantasy and horror fans are hearing more about him all the time.

As for what the rising awareness of him says about contemporary culture, I think it just underscores the increasing tendency of marginal obsessions to go mainstream in our brave new world of 24/7 digital connectedness. I never thought the doomer meme—peak oil, apocalyptic climate change, total economic collapse, and so on—would move to the mainstream as it has, but now you can look anywhere and find Joe Sixpack, John Lawyer, and half a dozen network talking heads going on about it. Just in the past week I've been astonished to read about the inroads being made into popular mainstream awareness by the general idea of a 9/11 conspiracy. It's enough to make a person wonder just what's going to be left in the way of pleasantly private obsessions that aren't defiled by the light of mass popular attention.

LNN: Depending on how pretentious we want to be, we could make the claim that life in a (post-)postmodern world allows for one to embrace both cosmic horror and humanism simultaneously. This is something that I believe is not discussed often enough when it comes to Lovecraft. I think our recent articles at Lovecraft News Network on Cthulhu Cakes and Plush Cthulhu are great examples. Beyond the simple pleasures of irony and the moral paradox of these items, could these not also be signifiers of an ability to produce a gleeful acceptance of one's lugubrious plight in a terrifying universe?

MC: Oh, certainly. But we could also argue that the act of portraying the high priest of the Old Ones in such cutesy-kitschy form represents an attempt to tame, defang, and neuter the shrieking horror of our plight instead of gleefully accepting it.

I'm personally fascinated by the whole idea of "quaffing the brew of nothingness," as somebody, I forget who, once said, and finding it invigorating instead of devastating, or maybe invigorating *because* devastating. Maybe in the current context that should be amended to read "quaffing the brew of horror." It would be great if glee, or at least equanimity, could coexist and maybe even be symbiotic with cosmic nightmarishness. But in my own experience, which has included recurrent bouts of real psychological and existential horror, such a position isn't actually achievable. The horror really is insupportable and absolutely corrosive. It eats right through all attempts to box it up into any sort of category that would make it manageable.

LNN: Robert Bloch thought that Lovecraft wrote about supernatural horror as a means to an end. He said,

> Consider the phenomenon of exorcism, this time from the view-point of the artist rather than the audience. Most writers who chose to work within the horror genre do so to exorcise their own fears by exposing and expressing them to an audience. . . . Drawing upon a common heritage of myth, legend, and fairy tales, they employ a technique of conveying their visions in terms of convincing reality. . . . Lovecraft intended to present an explana-

tion of why horror fiction appealed to certain types of readers. And in so doing he unconsciously revealed his own reasons for writing—as attempts to come to grips with a lifelong fear of the unknown.

Without worrying too much about the fallacy of authorial intent, do you agree with this, and would it be a stretch to say that you, too, are involved in a similar sort of process as you write?

MC: I think Bloch nailed Lovecraft, and I think you've nailed me. Bloch's idea of authorial self-exorcism seems well conceived. It's also splendidly absorbing. But in my own case it's not so much fear of the unknown that drives me as it is a sense of numinous uncanniness, verging into Rudolf Otto's "daemonic dread," at the very fact of existence itself—which, crucially, includes not just the disenchanted world of physical nature that's visible to empirical science but the world of immediate, first-person experience with all its daimonic psychological oddities.

A procedural note about Bloch's diagnosis of Lovecraft: it wasn't just fear of the unknown that drove Lovecraft's authorial attempts. As Lovecraft made starkly and resonantly clear in his personal correspondence, and also in his "Notes on Writing Weird Fiction," he wrote horror fiction as a means of capturing and crystallizing his lifelong impressions of an infinite, transcendent reality that seemed to peer through the cracks of the world. These cracks, for him, included skyscapes and vistas of architectural beauty. And his response to these transcendent intimations was deliciously paradoxical. He was both enchanted and terrified by them. He passionately longed for an experience of boundlessness, of freedom from the restraints of physical reality, which he of course knew all too well, both materially, due to his increasing monetary poverty over time, and intellectually, with his vast knowledge of natural science as underwritten by a nineteenth-century mechanistic-materialistic viewpoint. He said over and over that his most powerful emotional experiences were eruptions of infinite longing whenever he observed sunsets or contemplated scenic New England streets and buildings. But as everybody knows, he also experienced those same perceived gaps and that same perceived reality as horrifying, something he probably said most directly and powerfully in the introduction to "Supernatural Horror in Literature." So his career as a horror writer wasn't motivated just by fear of the unknown but by a two-sided emotional coin that was fear on one side and exhilarated longing on the other.

And again, I find myself in kinship with him, because in my focus on religious, philosophical, and spiritual horror, I'm walking an analogous line between the paradisiacal potentials of these things and the nightmarish ones.

LNN: Along these lines, the French Lovecraft scholar Maurice Lévy echoed this sentiment when he wrote,

> Lovecraft was, as we have seen, a man without hope. Unstable, sick, unhappy, obstinately rejecting what he considered the delusions of faith, fed on nihilistic philosophies, he had frequently thought of suicide. Only his dreams—his correspondence testifies to it—permitted him to overcome each crisis and to try once again to live. Did he not in dream find, in the blackest moments, the unexpected help of secret and vitalizing forces? We are then tempted to regard the Cthulhu Mythos, whose elaboration was slow, progressive, and continuous, as the adequate receptacle for the author's anguish, where, in the waters of dream, it could "precipitate," form deposits in precise, horrible, monstrous shapes at the bottom of a structure ready to receive them and give them meaning. Driven by myth ... horror can only be expressed by and in sacrilege: the impious cults, hideous ceremonies, blasphemous rites elsewhere mentioned, which tell a reverse history of salvation. It is at this deep level that the cure operates: because the sick man recognizes these images of horror as his own, he is in a position to assume them fully and thereby overcome them. To give a material representation to anguish is in itself to be freed from it. ... For we can never totally invent our monsters; they express our inner selves too much for that.

This quote reminds me of one of my favorite moments in your short story "Teeth" in which the protagonist starts to re-evaluate the world after his own encounter with cosmic horror: "The once-familiar moon was now the dead, decaying fetal carcass of some unimaginably monstrous creature, and as I looked on I saw it beginning to mutate into something more monstrous still." Might Lévy and Bloch then be an answer to the question you once posed to Stuart Young: "Why [horror] should happen to engage my intellect and emotions with such intensity is anyone's guess. I've never been able to figure it out myself."

MC: Indeed, I think whenever one experiences this kind of electric-magnetic attraction to any subject matter in the way that you and I—not to mention Lovecraft, Bloch, and Lévy—are attracted to horror, there's a deep psychological reason, and it has to do with the drive built into every organism to achieve comfort and equilibrium. As I mentioned above, with our exquisitely developed hyper-self-awareness—not just vegetable or animal consciousness but the added faculty of self-consciousness—we're constantly engaged in an astoundingly complex act of inner housekeeping, usually on a preconscious or unconscious level, and this surely relates to why Lovecraft wrote what he did, and why I write what I do, and why every other author and artist feels magically and helplessly bound to a specific subject or theme. Victoria Nelson argued in *The Secret Life of Puppets* that genre stories stoke or play on a type of compulsion neurosis among readers who don't want to confront a psychological reality directly but instead want to flirt with it again and again in formulaic stories that always bring them right up the point of confrontation and then shy away. She identified Lovecraft's work as being a fairly archetypal example. She also engaged in some subtle psychological analysis of the old gent. She may well be right.

On the other hand, in the past few years I've also grown increasingly attached to the daimonic theory of consciousness, which invokes in quasi-metaphorical fashion the ancient idea of the daimon or personal genius, the accompanying spirit that houses a person's deep character, life, pattern, and destiny. I'm inclined to refer to it in explanation of the overtly mythic cast which Lévy attributes—correctly, I think—to Lovecraft's and everybody else's deep psychic life, and also to our tendency to circle back to the same themes over and over.

LNN: The scholar and linguist Bradley Will claimed Lovecraft's depictions of cosmic horror could be called a "semiotic crisis." Denying his characters an adequate system of signification suggests something "so far beyond the edges of our language, so far removed from our frame of reference, that it defeats the system. . . . Its only designation can be its lack of designation. It is, if you will, a blank spot. This 'blank spot'—a signified with no signifier or a signifier with no signified—is a failure of the system of language."

From the perspective of an author, how does this notion of the "semiotic crisis" fit into the writing process as you perceive and practice it?

MC: No amount of authorial work, no experience of blissful creative flow, and no inherent quality of intellectual or artistic genius will ever allow an author to really, truly capture the essence of the inspiration that drove him or her to write something. Language is necessarily a reduction. I forget which modern poet said that "the poem is always perfect in the mind," but he was speaking truth. The very fact that actually committing words to paper will inevitably result in some quality of diminishment in the idea itself is probably what led Cioran to say, I think it was in *The Trouble with Being Born,* that as he grew older it became progressively more difficult for him to summon the motivation to blacken a page.

But fantasy fiction, and especially horror fiction, stands in an interesting relationship to this point, since fantasy and horror often deal in their actual subject matter with the idea of inexpressible truth. This makes horror fiction a choice literary vehicle for exploring the concept itself. Although all authorship is ultimately failure, as judged by its inability to express the pure essence of an inspiration or idea, writing can sidestep and even subvert, after a fashion, this inbuilt inability by deliberately generating a sense that the words are reductions of awesome truths that loom behind them. Blackwood's success in achieving this feat in "The Willows" is legendary, and it's what led Lovecraft to praise that story so highly. Lovecraft's success in achieving this in "The Call of Cthulhu," "The Music of Erich Zann," and several others is equally legendary, and largely accounts for his enduring audience. Ditto for the successes of—to name two more authors in my personal pantheon—Ted Klein and Tom Ligotti. Tom's direct dealing with this whole idea in, for instance, "Nethescurial" and "Vastarien" is maybe the quintessential example. The inherent artistic-ontological limitations of language and art can become a positive strength when they're incorporated into works that directly reference the inherent artistic-ontological limitations of language and art.

As for my own work, I've abandoned far more stories than I've completed, often because of what we're talking about. William Stafford said in "A Way of Writing" that one of the tricks he employed to keep himself productive was to deliberately lower his standards during composition, to the point where he could consider himself successful if he simply got something, anything, written down on paper. I'm still learning the wisdom of that. When actually sitting down to write, forget all about the inherent semiotic crisis. Just cough up whatever wants to lodge on the page or screen.

2010

Matt Cardin Unleashes His Teeming Brain

Interview by T. E. Grau

TEG: Thank you, Matt, for sitting down with me across this table varnished in the smooth ethery veneer of time and space and mysterious electrical connectivity. To start out, I'll ignore everything I've learned from Charlie Rose and go the lazy route by asking you to give us a bit of your background as a writer. What compelled you to start writing fiction? And what steered this endeavor toward the darker stuff?

MC: Remember the movie *Broadcast News*? It starts by showing a few scenes of the main characters as children. Each kid displays a distinct set of personality traits and predispositions, and each scene concludes by announcing, with a freeze frame and a superimposed title card, which career the kid grew up to pursue as an adult. As I recall, the point was that people's later lives really do "foreshadow certain ends," as Dickens's Scrooge would say.

I bring this up because it's a shorthand way of answering your question about why I started writing fiction. One of my earliest expressed desires of the "what I want to be when I grow up" variety was "I want to be a writer," and I had the innate set of childhood tendencies—I was verbally intelligent, a voracious reader, "gifted" (whatever that means), creatively agitated—to make good on that desire.

As for why I *ultimately* started writing fiction, and why it has always been of the dark variety, I think interrogating the question itself shows that it is, at bottom, unanswerable. In fact, interrogating the question opens up a vast, murky, electrifying, terrifying realm of unknown and unknowable realities that hold us all perpetually in their grip. This is along the lines of the thought experiment that Robert Anton Wilson recommends in, I think, *Prometheus Rising*, or maybe it's in *Quantum Psychology*—and anyway, he borrowed it from Aleister Crowley, who said he got it from somebody else—where you stop, as in really and truly, for a long pause, and you engage in a deep questioning of the reasons for why you're right there, in that location and circumstance, at that precise moment, doing what you're doing and thinking what you're thinking and feeling what you're feeling. Keep pressing the question "Why, why, why?" to each and every answer that presents itself, and if you really dig down and follow this backward trail of causation and justification, eventually you'll find, not just as an intellectual matter but as a startling existential realization, that *you have absolutely no idea*. You don't know, ultimately, why you're right there, right then, doing that. In a sense, everything about your life is just arbitrary, just happening by itself, and any story you tell yourself to explain *why* stands as more of a rationalization than an explanation.

What's more, those unknowable reasons—which also, pointedly, include the reasons for *why you are who you are*—shade directly into the unknowable reasons behind everything else. The impenetrable mystery that lies behind the entire universe, and that makes it be what it is and do what it does, is not something you can write off as abstract and distant and unimportant for daily life, because it happens to be the mystery of your very own being.

I think the fact that I'm the type of person who instantly and helplessly goes for the über-philosophical end of things even when nobody's asking for it—as in, you know, the way I'm going on and on right now in answer to your reasonable and straightforward question—is linked to why I write, and to why my writing always inhabits dark territory. I could have just mentioned *Broadcast News* when it came to mind and then said a few things about my childhood tendencies and the way they foreshadowed my authorial leanings. But that kind of answer always strikes me as a begged question. I mean, okay, so you were a certain type of kid with certain interests and traits and talents. But *why were you like that? Where do innate qualities ultimately come from?* Instantly, the mystery of human personhood is all up in our face, and for me this leads to inevitable ruminations about the metaphysical and ontological origins of individual selfhood and consciousness, and the ancient idea of the genius daemon that makes each person's life and self be what it is, and the Zen koan where the master orders the student, "Show me your original face, the one you had before your parents were born."

I could also mention the fact that I entered a very dark place late in college and an even darker one in the years following it, a development abetted by a kind of spontaneous initiatory experience into certain nightmarish things by the onset of sleep paralysis attacks that were accompanied by visionary/imaginary assaults by a demonic-seeming entity. This permanently and profoundly altered me and set the tone and direction for what I now write. Or maybe it just realized, as in made real, what was always wanting to be written through me anyway.

TEG: If you feel comfortable, please elaborate a bit on this "demonic-seeming entity." Do you believe it to be something real and, indeed, supernatural? Or a creation of lucid dreaming or some other between-consciousness state? I ask because belief in the reality of this entity would definitely alter one's writing, making the term "horror FICTION" a bit of a misnomer.

MC: The problem with trying to give any kind of reasonable or accurate answer here is that the question of "real" or "unreal" is embedded in a fog of assumptions that don't necessarily apply to whatever "real reality" may be involved in the experiences I'm talking about. For the past couple of centuries, ever since the massive revolution in consciousness that was the Western Enlightenment, to ask if something is real has meant to ask if it's real according to the standards of empirical measurement and evidence. In other words, it's to ask it in terms of material science. This is the nature of the rhetorical-philosophical playing field these days, and it's really deep-set, really dug in as a universal cultural and psychological orientation, to the point where even people who may consciously grasp the point when somebody explains it as I'm doing right now can remain unaware of just how deep its unconscious roots extend into their fundamental way of thinking about everything. In other words, for a lot of people, and for what's come to stand as the mainstream view of reality, regardless of whether you classify yourself as a "skeptic" or a "believer," the rules and boundaries of any conversation about the supernatural or paranormal, and therefore the basic direction the conversation will automatically take, are all set in psychic stone before you've even spoken a word or exchanged an idea.

But—and here's the thing—what's encountered in sleep paralysis or any other spiritual experience categorically eludes this whole philosophical gameboard. Or at least it calls it into question and underscores its limited and arbitrary boundaries. This is because entity encounters and many other paranormal, parapsychological, and supernatural experiences are bound up with the very subjectivity of the person who considers the question of their reality. Is it possible to set up cameras and instruments and conclude that a ghost did not actually appear in a supposedly haunted room, or that no demon-like entity approached me during the night? In point of fact, the answer is no. You can prove that nothing measurable, recordable, or empirically-materially provable showed up in a given room at a given time, but you can never prove that a person, or a dozen or a hundred people, did not in fact see or experience something that possessed some sort of reality whose nature just happens to transcend the physical entirely and exist on a level that's not verifiable by any instrumental means. In other words, there may be things that objectively exist *within subjectivity itself,* and their reality may be just as existentially significant and pressing for us, and maybe even more so, than things "out there" that can be encountered and measured and proved or disproved in materiality.

When it comes right down to it, our modern categories of "real" and "unreal," and also the subdivision of the unreal into "imaginary" and "hallucinated," are essentially linguistic and conceptual political plays. They're ways of policing consciousness by giving people ways to pigeonhole their experiences in prefabricated ontological slots. And, to grossly misquote Shakespeare, reality itself flows right through and past those slots, because there are more things in heaven and earth than are dreamt of in our current flatland versions of philosophy and psychology. Fortunately, recent developments like the resurgence of psychedelic research and thought, the birth of the "paranthropology" movement as exemplified by Jack Hunter's excellent journal of that title, and the serious philosophical attention being given to shamanism are all addressing the imperialism and shortcomings of the modern Western mindset.

So, was my demonic-seeming entity real? I have to answer that it was as real as I am, as real as the consciousness from which I'm giving you this semblance of an answer.

TEG: Give me a few writers/artist/philosophers and seminal works of fiction that may have inspired or affected your work.

MC: I think my answer at the moment may go in directions it wouldn't normally go, because during the past several weeks, for reasons I can't figure out, I've found myself thinking about some of my favorite childhood authors. As I suspect was also the case for you, and as is probably the case for nearly everybody who reads our blog, I was entranced with books when I was young. I mean, I still am today, but the magnetic-hypnotic pull of books that voracious readers feel especially in their youth was definitely there for me from as far back as I can remember, and it shaped my inner world at a crucial age.

I devoured books by Ray Bradbury, Madeleine L'Engle, Lloyd Alexander, C. S. Lewis, Susan Cooper, and J. R. R. Tolkien all through school. Lots of science fiction and fantasy. I also read some of Lewis's nonfiction work about Christianity and religion, and was very moved by it. As an adult I reread book four of Lloyd Alexander's Chronicles of Prydain, titled *Taran Wanderer,* and discovered depths in it that I hadn't been able to appreciate before. The same thing happened with Ms. L'Engle's *A Wrinkle in Time* and *A Wind in the Door,* two books that I credit with programming me at a young age to appreciate and resonate with stories that combine cosmic terror, horror, wonder, and awe, along with a taste for dystopian storytelling (think Camazotz, the dark planet in *A Wrinkle in Time*) and a fascination with the use of fantasy, science fiction, and horror for philosophical and spiritual exploration. They also gave me a taste for the positive deliciousness of scientific ideas as they relate to questions of cosmic reality and its human meanings.

Anne Rice knocked me for a serious loop when I was sixteen and seventeen; the emotional, philosophical, historical, and stylistic depth and darkness and lushness of *Interview with the Vampire* and, especially, *The Vampire Lestat* marked me permanently, but I found with surprise that I just couldn't read her later work, which struck me as irredeemably shitty.

I went nuts over Jack London in junior high and read *White Fang* and *The Call of the Wild* multiple times. Oddly, I remember reading an old novelization of the original *King Kong* movie over and over at around the same time. In my seventh grade English class, I wrote a short story sequel to *The Call of the Wild* that impressed the teacher so much, she submitted it to *Stone Soup,* the long-running literary magazine of stories by kids aged eight to thirteen. (It was rejected.)

Throughout childhood, and actually into adulthood, I read any and all books about horror and science fiction movies that I could get my hands on. The same was true for books about the supernatural and paranormal, as in the many young adult books on those subjects by Daniel Cohen. I'm partly defined by the early memories of those books with their glorious pictures, mostly in black and white, of Count Orlok, Kong, Dr. Caligari, Cesar, Karloff's Frankenstein, Karloff's mummy, Lugosi's Dracula, Christopher Lee's Dracula, the Gill-Man, Godzilla, Klaatu, ghosts, Nessie, UFOs, and more. A lot of that was in pre–home video days, and cable television didn't come to my neighborhood until I was in seventh grade, so for years I only knew all those movies through the books with their loads of pictures and their sometimes inaccurate plot summaries. This generated a truly mythic sense of them that I wouldn't exchange for the world. I remember Tom Ligotti once saying that he, too, first came to know *The Cabinet of Dr. Caligari* by reading about it, and even though he didn't like the film when he finally saw it, he has always lived with a kind of mythic-perfect version of it existing in his head thanks to those gorgeous movie stills. That's exactly what I'm talking about (although I like the actual *Caligari* film better than Tom does).

As for what has influenced me in a more adult vein, people who read my work, both fiction and nonfiction, are aware of the deep mark that Lovecraft and Ligotti have made on me, along with a roster of additional masters of weird fiction: Klein, Poe, and so on. My authorial sensibility is also shaped by, and is in fact inseparable from, my lifelong deep reading of the Bible, Christian theology, Gnosticism, Zen Buddhism, Vedanta, world religions, and a host of philosophers and spiritual thinkers and teachers: Alan Watts, Eckhart Tolle, Douglas Harding, Robert Anton Wilson, Jung, Nietzsche, Kierkegaard, William James, and others. A more recent addition to the pantheon is Patrick Harpur, author of *Daimonic Reality* and several other books that I will inevitably end up reading.

TEG: The movies of the mind are often better than those on the screen . . . Getting more specific, I read your short story "Teeth" a few years back and became an ardent fan. Due to the thematic elements in the piece—and not that this classifies or pigeonholes all your work—but do you consider yourself a "Lovecraftian"? If so, what does being identified as such mean to you? If not, why not?

MC: I'm a Lovecraftian by temperament but not by conscious intent. I'm no more or less a Lovecraftian writer than I am a Ligottian writer, a Jungian writer, or an apocalyptic-esoteric-occult-paranormal-Zen-Christian-agnostic writer. "Teeth" was my first published work, both electronically and in print. It appeared first at Thomas Ligotti Online and then in Del Rey's *The Children of Cthulhu*, and it quotes the first paragraph of "The Call of Cthulhu" in full, and mentions Lovecraft directly, and explicitly invokes his master themes of cosmic horror and cosmic monstrousness as illustrations or explanations of the narrator's personal spiritual-philosophical destruction. So that established a Lovecraftian pedigree for it and for me right from the start of my publishing career. But I'm not at all interested in trying to write deliberately in a Lovecraftian vein, and especially not—Cthulhu save us—in a *mythos* vein. The Lovecraftian resonances in some of my stories are simply spontaneous reflections of the fact that Lovecraft, in his person and philosophy and writings—including his essays and letters as much as his stories—has become a part of my universe. I wanted to read him before I had ever heard of him, and when we finally met, it was like finding a lost part of myself. The same thing has happened with Ligotti and many of the other writers I was just talking about.

Steve Rasnic Tem said something in his contributor's bio for *The Children of Cthulhu* that has always struck me as a neat explanation of what I'm getting at: "I'm not particularly interested in playing in other writers' universes, but I am interested in what happens when my own particular obsessions encounter those of another writer." Or actually, even that description goes too far for me. It's not exactly that I'm interested in exploring how my particular obsessions interface with those of Lovecraft or any other writer, but simply that the organic expression of my own sensibility always turns out to involve a constellation of other writers, and also filmmakers and composers and musicians, whose ideas and emotions have become part of me. I read a cool recent interview with Woody Allen where the interviewer brought up one of Allen's favorite novels and asked him, "How did it influence you?" And Allen just said, "It's not that it influenced me; it resonated with me, in the same way as when I see movies by Ingmar Bergman. They mean something to me because of his preoccupations and his view of life. It rang a bell in me." That's what I'm talking about.

Or even shorter: In my 2006 Ligotti interview, when I asked Tom to talk about *The Conspiracy against the Human Race,* he described the book as "a synthesis of ideas I've formed over my life and of other people's ideas that rhyme with mine." I find that beautiful and insightful, and am happy to steal it as a description of almost everything I've written.

TEG: "Resonance" instead of "influence." I think that describes what many writers feel when they come across another writer whose work jibes with what they personally do. It doesn't necessarily alter the course of one's fiction, but a previously unknown harmony is discovered, that could add more confidence and surety to a writer's path, as they know they're not working alone in the dark.

MC: And I think that's one of the most valuable things that can happen to a writer, or to any person, really. It's one of those deep mysteries of human life that our own most personal and fate-filled paths are often activated for us, or at least they're called out and made more conscious for us, when we come into contact with other people and are "influenced" by them. I'd also like to point out that this often works just as well when the reaction isn't one of sympathetic resonance but of deep rejection. Your own path can be revealed and clarified quite well by coming up against that which you are most pointedly *not.*

TEG: I know a little about your background and the religious underpinnings of your upbringing. But I'll ask anyway, as it seems to mirror some of my childhood experiences: What is it about a devout/strict Christian childhood that leads one to develop a fascination with cosmic horror, or dark things in general?

MC: In a way this brings me back to my questioning of the question, because I think people, including me, are not just products of their environment but bearers of an inbuilt disposition from birth. Environment and upbringing shape this disposition, but they don't create it. So my fascination with cosmic horror and dark things in general was, I think, part of the seed self, the "psychic acorn" James Hillman talked about, that was born with me.

But as for how a devout Christian upbringing like mine affected all that, I can say that it certainly provided a rich trove of apocalyptic theological ideas. I grew up in a church that hovered somewhere between conservative evangelical and fundamentalist, but its basic moral and social environment fit hand-in-glove with the culture of the Missouri Ozarks at the time, so for most of my youth I was kind of like the fish that couldn't become aware of the water around it. I didn't know that my church was part of a very specific denominational movement within Protestant evangelicalism called the Independent Christian Church, which was and is one of those conservative restoration movements that view themselves as reviving primitive Christianity the way it was practiced in New Testament times. I didn't know its theology and politics and social attitudes and puritanical morality fell mostly on the conservative, uptight, reactionary end of the spectrum. I didn't even really understand that there *was* a spectrum. My religious environment, which was pretty much inseparable from my cultural and family environment, formed a totally enveloping backdrop to my view of the world for a huge portion of my youth.

So all that, along with the fact that some of the preaching and teaching and general social culture was caught up in the 1970s version of today's Left Behind-type apocalypticism—I'm talking about, you know, the Hal Lindsey school of "end times" thought—made for a heady mythological-mental environment. And I was innately fascinated with it all, and inclined to take it all very seriously. Along with the fantasy and horror reading, I studied my Bible and went to church every Sunday, and to church camp every summer, and to youth group meetings every week. For a while I thought I wanted to be a preacher.

So when I started to get disillusioned with a lot of that during my teens, the snapback was pretty severe. I didn't realize until then—and it was a realization that kept growing for many years—that the same set of passions and inclinations that led me to take my religion so personally and seriously also accounted for my inbuilt fascination with supernatural horror. That's why, when I dove into the serious reading and study of Lovecraft, I was completely bowled over by the spiritual, psychological, and metaphysical aspects of his thought world. In addition to his stories, I read his "Supernatural Horror in Literature" and found him saying that weird fiction involves "a psychological pattern or tradition as real and as deeply grounded in mental experience as any other pattern or tradition of mankind; coeval with the religious feeling and closely related to many aspects of it." Much later, in grad school, I read Rudolf Otto's *The Idea of the Holy* and found Otto linking the prehistoric origin of the human religious capacity and sensibility to a fear-response of "daemonic dread" and awed trembling before a great and fascinating cosmic mystery, and I saw him saying that this primal aspect of human psychology was culturally elaborated not only into religions but into the ancient tradition of stories about ghosts and other supernatural horrors. And all this was like reading a deep analysis of my own inner world, written decades before I was even born.

TEG: You possess a master's in religion. This has already been touched upon above, but which came first, the M.A. or the horror writing? Meaning, did pursuing terrifying things lead you to explore the deeper mysteries of varied religions, or the other way around?

MC: I wrote the first version of "Teeth" circa 1995. I started pursuing my master's degree in religious studies in 1996. So the timing was right in line with that whole life entanglement between loving fantasy and horror fiction and being devoutly religious. The grad school career and the horror writing took off almost simultaneously. They both augmented each other, too, because I wrote the stories that ended up in *Divinations of the Deep* while I was immersing myself in my grad studies, and lots of the ideas and emotions that went into them were caused by or involved with the stuff I was studying. As I already said, I was introduced to Otto in grad school, and that was a flat-out game-changer. So was the time I spent studying Gnosticism under Dr. Charles Hedrick, one of the world's leading scholars of the subject. Anybody who reads "An Abhorrence to All Flesh," "Notes of a Mad Copyist," or "Judas of the Infinite" in *Divinations* will instantly be able to spot my incorporation and reprocessing of lots of Gnostic themes in a supernatural horrific context—something that was helped along by the fact that if you study the second-century Gnostics, and also the older and wider tradition they're a part of, you discover that some of them believed they were living in a supernaturally horrific cosmos already.

TEG: What do you see as the connective tissue between horror, religion, consciousness, spirituality, creativity, and enlightenment? Yes, I'm making you work for this answer.

MC: Work, you say? Doesn't everybody like to talk about these things?

I hope this makes sense: To be conscious, and especially to be *self-aware* in the singular way that appears to be exclusively or predominantly human, is to be, in principle, capable of horror. Horror is built into human consciousness. This is because we're all ensconced or trapped—depending on how you spin it—in our subjective points of view. To say it another way, we *are subjectivity*. And this means there's a kind of horizon to our experience, and beyond that there's an outside reality that confronts us with the so-called "mystery of the other." Each of us is confronted by, and situated at the subjective center of, the "outer world." Both the structure of our consciousness and the cues from our cultures tell us what's "natural," how things are "supposed to be," what the world and universe "really are." And our sense of normalcy and cosmic security comes to rest on this. In other words, this really amounts to a personal "cosmos" for each individual, an ordering of experience and perceived reality with its own definite structure and boundaries.

But sometimes, something rips through what sociologist Peter Berger called the "sacred canopy" of our established understanding of the universe, and the result is pure horror. Not necessarily *terror*, which is something different, but *horror*, defined as a combination of fear and revulsion. Being physically assaulted, or having someone close to you die (even if peacefully, but especially if horribly), or having your entire sensibility overwhelmed like what happened on 9/11 or like what happens in the middle of a war, or being hideously injured and seeing your own innards, or having your deeply held moral view of things violated by things that "should not be"—these cause horror because they punch through that subjective-objective divide and threaten to assault us in our core. Whatever lies "outside" is potentially, and inherently, horrifying, which is why the Lovecraftian trope of cosmic outsideness represents a kind of apotheosis of horror as such.

But the thing is, religion and spirituality are likewise concerned with what lies outside or beyond the cosmic horizon. Their point is to reconnect with and, depending on your tradition, to *identify with* and/or *be transformed by* the reality beyond the veil: God, Buddha nature, Brahman, spirit, whatever. The same "place" where cosmic horror is "located" is the place where the object of religious and spiritual longing resides. And maybe, just maybe, both realities are really the same. From the human point of view, we can't actually know. But we can suspect, and sometimes we can fall into heaven or hell realms of experience that seem to confirm one way or the other.

As for how this all relates to creativity, the creative process involves the unconscious mind, and when we talk about that we open a whole new can of horror, because when you really come to understand what the term "unconscious mind" means, you see that they refer to an interior counterpart or analog to cosmic outsideness. In our ego selves we're confronted from both in front and behind, above and below, by an ungovernable and dangerous realm of otherness. The unconscious mind is the source of dreaming, visions, creative inspiration, and all those innate passions and predispositions I was talking about a minute ago. And they're beyond our conscious control. They're part of us, but we experience them as autonomous and often dangerous and disturbing, as in complexes and schizophrenia and nightmares and—to mention something I've personally grappled with—experiences of hypnagogia during sleep paralysis where demonic-seeming stuff erupts into conscious experience. The recognition of all this is what led to my fascination with the ancient symbolic figures of the genius, the daemon, and the muse, because these refer to spiritual or psychic entities or intelligences that speak as independent beings from inside the psyche itself. And the potential for horror is therefore massive, although it's balanced by an equal potential for enlightenment, awakening, and spiritual communion of the blissful sort.

Spirituality, religion, creativity, enlightenment—these all open us up to what presents itself as something outside, something that exists beyond the horizon of our personal consciousness but is still somehow entangled with our identities, and this opens up the possibility of a truly uncanny experience of life that makes it the existential equivalent of living in a weird supernatural horror story.

TEG: Among your many impressive accomplishments, one that ranks up there is actually more based on what you currently aren't doing than what you are, which is your bold move to unplug from Facebook and other mainstream bastions of social media. Or at least you were unplugged until recently, and you took five whole months off in 2011 as well. This shouldn't be such a big deal, but based on the current climate of overall communication (both cyber and fleshy), and the means of marketing one's work, it truly is, at least to me. What prompted this move? How has it affected your writing, your daily routine, and your overall endeavors?

MC: I've gone through several cycles of energy, attitude, creativity, and overall outlook during my life online, which started in 1996. I'm convinced that the Internet has the potential for truly dystopian destruction on both a personal and a collective, societal level. I'm talking about authentic cultural collapse and a new dark age along the lines of *Fahrenheit 451* and *Brave New World*. At the same time, its valid uses and benefits are also clear. I really respect the opinions of Daniel Pinchbeck, and a couple of years ago in an opinion piece for Alternet he called the Internet "ground zero in the global consciousness revolution," since it decentralizes the former hegemonic power of governments and corporations, and enables grassroots communicating, organizing, learning, and intellectual enlightenment in an unprecedented way. But he also pointed out that Facebook, for instance, has as many inherent problems as benefits. The Catch-22 is that Facebook and its ilk are somewhat inescapable if you want to reach anybody these days, because that's where all the people are. I resonate with this, as I do with the recent media pieces about Facebook's fifty-first employee, Katherine Losse, who quit the company over dire concerns about what social media are doing to human relationships and societies, and moved to the remote town of Marfa, Texas, to write a book on the subject. After a while, she found that she just couldn't keep her Facebook account turned off if she wanted to be viable in the current writing and publishing environment, so she re-approached it with a new wariness and determination to ride the Facebook railroad instead of letting it ride her.

In my own life, my publishing career and personal relationships have been enhanced by my online activities—my publishing career, in fact, grew directly out of my involvement in Usenet in the 1990s—but they've also been hindered by it, such as when I find that the cyberworld has become a psychic vampire that drains my time and creative energy, leaving me anhedonic, or when I find that the endless parade of information and distractions, some of which are pure trash but some of which take the form of validly worthwhile articles and films and so on, distracts me from the real world of family, friends, and coworkers. Neil Postman and Marshall McLuhan both talked about how technologies aren't neutral, contrary to most people's unreflective opinions. All technologies come with inbuilt "programs" for social change, such as the automobile, which ended up creating cities that are designed for cars instead of people. Communication technologies are the most insidious and profoundly impactful because they directly affect how we even think and talk about their effects.

So that's all a long-winded way of saying that I've unplugged for a couple of extended periods in order to regroup and recover my attention, energy, and soul. Last year's extended Internet sabbatical resulted in a significant upsurge in motivation and inspiration to write. I found that I was thinking more clearly and feeling more calm and centered. In fact, my overall sense of calm and peace was positively blissful. I did an extra lot of meditation and mental/spiritual centering—something I've done off and on since my late teens—and reached some deeper levels than I'd ever encountered. That bled out into my personal daily interactions, too. There's a passage in a book by Oliver Sacks where he talks about a kind of spiritual epiphany that he experienced while recovering from a leg injury. What he describes is what I experienced for several months last year:

> After breakfast I wandered out—it was a particularly glorious September morning—and settled myself on a stone seat with a large view in all directions, and filled and lit my pipe. This was a new, or at least an almost-forgotten, experience. *I had never had the leisure to light a pipe before,* or not, it seemed to me, for fourteen years at least. Now, suddenly, I had an immense sense of leisure, an unhurriedness, a freedom I had almost forgotten—but which, now it had returned, seemed the most precious thing in life. There was an intense sense of stillness, peacefulness, joy, a pure delight in the "now," freed from drive or desire. I was intensely conscious of each leaf, autumn-tinted, on the ground; intensely conscious of the Eden around me. The world was motionless, frozen—everything concentrated in an intensity of sheer being. . . . Now, on this morning, as though on the first morning of Creation, I felt like Adam beholding a new world with wonder. I had not known, or had forgotten, that there could be such beauty, such completeness, in every moment. I had no sense at all of moments, of the serial, only of the perfection and beauty of the timeless now.[1]

When I first encountered that passage several years ago, I was already very familiar with the literature of awakening—I had read obsessively about Zen and such for many years—so Sacks's words were just a particularly engaging and lovely description of things that I had read about many times before. But during last year's Internet sabbatical, I actually fell into a state exactly like what he describes. That was a new experience, and it lasted several months. I figured my horror writing days were done. At one point I said as much at my Teeming Brain blog. Then some kind of inner motion kicked back in, and, well, here I am.

I find the whole "unplugging" movement that's now taking root to be fascinating. Currently Paul Miller, a tech writer for *The Verge,* is spending a year offline. Less than a week ago at the time I'm talking with you now, *The Verge* checked in with him, and he told them that the first two weeks were a Zen-like paradise of blissful peace and focus. And even now that the newness

---

1. Oliver Sacks, *A Leg to Stand On* (New York: Touchstone, 1998), 143–44; Sacks's emphasis.

has worn off, he told them, "I have zero regrets about leaving the internet. I'm only three months in, and I can honestly say that this is turning into the best year of my life." From my own experience, I can tell you that he's not just blowing smoke.

TEG: Tell me a bit about your music. How does it fit into your life, and your creative pursuits?

MC: In the past few years, playing the piano has become more and more central to my enjoyment of everyday life. On most evenings I spend at least a little time playing a few of Bach's two-part inventions, a little Beethoven, maybe some modern piano pieces along the lines of the Windham Hill albums, and maybe noodling around with improvisational stuff. I'm struck with a sense of time's numinosity when I reflect on the fact that I've been playing piano and keyboards for over thirty years now. It's just an integral part of living for me, and it has become a kind of discipline, or maybe a pressing need, or actually both, that helps to get me in the right inner state for writing, the state where I can actually hear and feel the promptings of my daemon muse and successfully wrangle them into some tangible form. And of course the music itself has been the location of my creativity in the past, as when I spent three or four years obsessively creating an album of electronic music. That whole project just flooded out of me, from the same inner place where my short fiction arises, the place that's the source of both my horror writing and my religious and spiritual turning. It's all connected at the root.

TEG: Eight years elapsed between your *Divinations of the Deep* (one of the best titles I've encountered, for my money) and *Dark Awakenings*. Why the relatively long span between books? If I'm prying too much about your creative process, tell me to sod off.

MC: I'll answer by talking about other people. Victoria Nelson is the author of two of my favorite books. One is *On Writer's Block: A New Approach to Creativity*, which entrances me with its blazingly lucid and lovely exposition of creativity as a relationship with the "other" of the unconscious mind. Her entire thesis is that deep creativity involves getting into rhythm and relationship with this other self and letting its innate needs and movements shape the work. At one point she talks about the case of Joseph Joubert, the eighteenth- and nineteenth-century writer who produced brilliant aphorisms and journal entries but froze whenever he tried to write longer works or organize his thoughts into a book. His friends constantly encouraged him to apply himself to the creation of something that would last. But, says Nelson, in the end he realized that the aphorism was the direction his native talent wanted to go. It was what he was meant to write. He published nothing in his lifetime, but his works were organized and published after his death.

Ms. Nelson also looks at examples like that of Philip Larkin, who told the *Paris Review* that he only produced on average three poems a year. Nelson mentions many such instances, and she encourages slow writers to honor their native creative pace and refuse to punish themselves and their unconscious partner for not being what they are neither able nor intended to be.

Ms. Nelson herself bears witness to this wisdom. Her other book that has been so significant to me, *The Secret Life of Puppets*, is a brilliant, deep, complex examination of the way the irreducible Platonic/mystical impulse in the human psyche, which is repressed and expelled by the dominant scientific materialist cast of contemporary Western culture, has managed to creep back into our lives through the back door of popular culture, especially in the realms of science fiction, fantasy, and horror. She says wonderfully insightful things about Lovecraft, Bruno Schulz, Philip K. Dick, Freud, Jung, *The Matrix*, religion, psychology, occultism, esotericism, and more. And the book itself took her, basically, forever to write. In her acknowledgments at the end of it, she notes that it was seeded over the course of many separate essays, and she thanks her editor at Harvard University Press for her "long-term enthusiasm." She also refers at one point to "the Lovecraftian entity this book became"—something evocatively appropriate in relation to cyclopean cycles of time.

Just a few months ago, ten years after *The Secret Life of Puppets* appeared, her new book finally came out: *Gothicka: Vampire Heroes, Human Gods, and the New Supernatural.*

To draw the point, I'll simply say that I think my own creative cycle and my own unconscious partner, which I relate to as a genius daemon, operate on roughly the same schedule as Ms. Nelson's.

TEG: Where do you see your place in the horror/speculative fiction scene, and where do you see yourself in ten years? How about thirty?

MC: I really don't expect my work to reach more than a few people in my lifetime, and I don't know if it will be remembered when I'm gone. Something about the way I relate to life and people in my authorial capacity seems destined to make my work appeal to a very small crowd. I also identify deeply and completely with Lovecraft's sense of repugnance, horror, and paralysis at the very thought of doing what's necessary to market oneself in a money-based culture. I don't know why exactly this is the case, since I don't share his faux aristocratic pose, although I do have very strong philosophical thoughts and feelings about the ugliness of money and its inbuilt program—like those embedded in technologies—to vampirize real value from art, goods, services, relationships, and life at large. Money isn't something I've ever been able to attract in more than lower-middle to middle-middle class amounts, so I certainly won't be remembered as a rich author, nor, I think, as a famous one.

Ten years from now? Maybe I'll be publishing my next book and still speaking to that microscopic sliver of readers who know of and appreciate my work. Thirty years from now? Pretty much the same, although I feel no more confident of my projections about such a thing than I do of the government's projections about the fate of Social Security or anything else three decades down the road. We all stand now at a technological, ecological, and civilizational inflection point, and things thirty years down the road will likely look even more dramatically different—perhaps unrecognizably so—than today's world looks compared to 1982.

So hey, maybe that's what I'll spend the next thirty years writing about.

TEG: Any parting words from one of the most Teemingest Brains working all non-Euclidean angles of not just horror/speculative fiction, but total consciousness and philosophy today?

MC: Apropos to what I said earlier about life online and offline, I'm thinking of adopting a new motto, which might make for a good bumper sticker: "Explore disconnection." This has resonances beyond the issue of digitally interconnected existence, too. In our rage to be social and connected, disconnection becomes a romantic alternative. We're all like Cypher in *The Matrix,* pining to be plugged into unreality because we think it's better than the real world. Or maybe we can actually transform the virtual into the real instead of the opposite happening, an idea that was just about the only worthwhile thing to come out of the lamentable last film in the Matrix trilogy, which should never have gone past part one. Whatever the case, I shall now retreat into the sanctity (but not solitude, since there's somebody in here with me) of my private thoughts, and I encourage anybody reading this to consider doing the same, as often as possible, exploring nominal disconnection and finding that it's actually a more deep and intimate type of connection than what can be found through any computer network.

2012

Matt Cardin: Life and Mind of a Teeming Brain

Interview by Rafael Tages

RT: For all who don't know you yet, tell us all a little bit about yourself.

MC: I'm always a bit stymied by this type of request. Maybe it's just that I don't know what to lead with, or how to frame the boundaries of the question. A little bit about myself? How about just the basic demographic facts, to begin with. I'm American, white, forty-three years old, middle class, married. By cultural upbringing I'm an evangelical Protestant. By spiritual and philosophical predilection I'm a kind of Zen Christian agnostic/skeptic with occult and esoteric leanings. I'm a native of the Missouri Ozarks but now I live in Central Texas. I teach college English. I formerly taught high school, sold Yamaha pianos and digital keyboards, worked as a communications specialist and loan originator for a mortgage company, produced video courses for a state university, and did live video production work for Glen Campbell, the Mandrells, Eddie Rabbitt, the Oak Ridge Boys, Kenny Rogers, and a bunch of other country and pop music stars in Branson, Missouri. My general lifestyle on an average daily basis is intensely mundane.

RT: What do you think helped you to become a writer?

MC: I have a deeply depressive personality that I mostly show only in my writing. This has been crucial. So has the fact that my psyche kind of came apart when I was in my twenties due to some pretty grim and frightful experiences with sleep paralysis and accompanying paranormal assault–type episodes. I wrote more frequently and obsessively during that period than at any other time in my life. It lasted from about 1992 to 2000, during my first few years after college, and most of what I wrote went into private journals and was driven by a real, piercing, and pretty much unendurable sense of despair. But the basic desire to write goes back farther than that. I can't really say why I wanted to "be a writer"—something I started saying when I was very young—but the type of writer that I would turn out to be was virtually written in the stars, or at least it feels that way.

RT: What is your writing process? Do you follow any rules or rituals when you are planning to write?

MC: It seems to happen differently each time, when it happens at all. I've written stories, papers, and essays that started with notes I made from ideas bubbling up from my unconscious, and I've also started "cold" by just diving in without any plan and seeing what comes up. I've started writing when I felt inspired and driven by an idea that excited me, and I've started writing mechanically, just for the sheer purpose of getting something down on paper, or on a computer screen.

This has all been part of a long process of experimentation to find out what works best for me. I'm very self-conscious, in fact probably too much so, about the creative act itself. In recent years it has turned out that the best thing is for me to wait until I'm actually moved by some mesmerizing idea that makes me want to commit it to written words so that I can uncover what it's really about. This approach runs directly counter to a great deal of advice about writing that I've dearly loved, and that I've gained from the likes of Ray Bradbury, Natalie Goldberg, Dorothea Brande, Julia Cameron, and others, who all stressed the importance of writing regularly and freely to establish a constant outpouring of words. Bradbury was fond of emphasizing the importance of sheer quantity, which he said would inevitably, spontaneously, at some point, result in quality. I love that idea in theory, and the occasional disciplined practice of it has jump-started a few valuable creative projects for me. But in the long run, for the most part, it just doesn't work for me. I dry up and start to hate writing when I make myself do it all the time. So this means I'm a writer who goes for very long periods without writing anything at all. I frequently begin to think or fear that I may never write again.

RT: What are your main influences for writing in the horror genre?

MC: My major horror influences include Lovecraft, Ligotti, Klein, and a host of other writers in the weird fiction tradition and the wider tradition of supernatural horror in general. When I was young I read a lot of Poe's and Bradbury's horror stories, and this proved significant. So did a horror record that a friend played for me at his house one late summer afternoon. It featured some spooky sound effects plus a few readings of classic horror stories, including a deliriously unhinged performance of Poe's "The Telltale Heart." I can still hear the narrator's voice as he goes for broke in an over-the-top reading of the final line: "Here! Here! It is the beating of his hideous heart!" That flat-out marked me.

Although I don't usually name him in this regard, I suppose I ought to mention Stephen King, since I imbibed a large number of his books in my youth, along with the movies adapted from them, and this was influential. My parents didn't let me watch scary stuff when I was young, so when the movie versions of *Carrie* and *The Shining* and the television miniseries of *'Salem's Lot* came out in the 1970s, I saw the ads but didn't get to see the movies themselves, and my mind generated all kinds of vague expectations of the colossally frightening things that must be in them. The same thing happened with non–Stephen King movies, too, including *Hell Night*, *Silent Scream*, and several more. Whenever I accidentally caught the television ads, I was so frightened that I couldn't stop seeing them in my mind's eye for hours afterward. Quite seriously, these commercials filled me with a sense of terror and dread. But at the same time, I found them hypnotically fascinating.

I've realized in recent years that my parents did me a wonderful creative favor by forbidding me to watch such things, because this, working in tandem with a native bent in my personality, inculcated a deep and tantalizing sense of some elusive horror that's loose in the world and that can never really be seen or known directly, but that would absolutely fry you if you saw it face to face.

My horror writing is also influenced by a number of nonfiction writers whose works have been deeply important to me, including Rudolf Otto, Theodore Roszak, Alan Watts, Huston Smith, Richard Tarnas, and about a dozen others who have written in the areas of theology, spirituality, philosophy, science, scientism, and wide-scope criticism of modern/postmodern industrial technocratic civilization. My attraction to supernatural horror is bound up with all these ideas. And I've noticed that I'm not alone in this; I was pretty excited when I first read Ted Klein's "Children of the Kingdom" and saw that he began it with a quote from Huston Smith (who was quoting Rebecca West) that had likewise lodged in my own consciousness. It said the prevailing mood of the late twentieth century was "a desperate search for a pattern."

RT: Do you align yourself with any other kind of genre in fiction?

MC: Although all the fiction that I've written is horror, with much of it falling in the specific subgenre of weird horror, I'm also influenced by fantasy and science fiction, and elements of these have found their way into my work, too. I'm especially wrapped up in dystopian fiction, with Ray Bradbury's *Fahrenheit 451* standing at the top of the heap.

RT: Which other kinds of media do you find amusing? Do you follow any series or shows?

MC: I'm kind of surprised to report that the only television shows I've been following with any dedication for the past few years have been distinctly realistic instead of speculative. I binge-watched all the *Friday Night Lights* television series a couple of years ago with my wife and absolutely loved it. I'm currently watching *Person of Interest*, which has gone full-on dystopian sci-fi in the past season, much to my increased enjoyment. My favorite show right now is *The Good Wife*, which is as rich, complex, entertaining, and engrossing as any great film or novel has ever been. I don't know exactly why this shift toward realism has happened, since for most of my life I got very deeply into fantasy, SF, and horror TV shows like *The X-Files*, *The Twilight Zone*, *Star Trek: TOS*, *Tales from the Darkside*, *The Outer Limits*, *Night Gallery*, and such. On a practical level, part of the change is due to the fact that I always watch television with my wife now, and she's totally uninterested in the speculative genres, so I've accidentally discovered a new taste for realism that was apparently just waiting to come out.

RT: What about some nonfiction and your philosophic worldview? Tell us a little bit of your whole take on things, philosophically speaking. We see that you mix your fiction with your essays in some ways that are very interesting, like in your *Dark Awakenings* collection. Your research on the origins of angels and demons is particularly intriguing. How does it all connect, in your view?

MC: It occurs to me that something approaching an answer to this question is scattered throughout my previous answers like pieces of a jumbled-up puzzle. Remember what I said about that sense of a presence that's always lurking behind everything, and that is somehow related to the ultimately fearsome whatever-it-is that I imagined into all of those horror movies I wasn't allowed to watch as a kid? Philosophically speaking, my whole life as a horror writer, and also as someone with a real spiritual outlook and set of practices, and as someone who has found it bizarre and often difficult to be a human being among and around other human beings, and who has been alternately depressed and elated in a kind of undiagnosed life of bipolarity—philosophically speaking, all this has been about the attempt to figure out, or at least come to terms with, that hidden presence.

Writing about the origins of angels and demons is just more of the same, because angels and demons, especially when we trace them to their roots in Western occult and esoteric philosophy and ancient Greco-Roman and Middle Eastern religious and philosophical concepts, are names and symbols for forces or presences or powers that we can never definitely pigeonhole as being either purely subjective/psychological or purely objective in nature. The ancient view is that each person's highest/deepest/truest self is a daimon or daemon, what some members of the Western gnostic, esoteric, and occult subcultures call the Holy Guardian Angel and regard as something that may not really be an aspect of one's self at all but a truly independent entity. This can all sound abstract, but it goes right back to the most immediately and inescapably real experience for each of us, which is that our perception of an objective world around us is mirrored from "behind" or "within" by the complementary perception of a presence that stands behind or prior to our very act of looking and seeing and knowing. Basically, there's someone or something "in here" with us. A long time ago I began to realize that this is mirrored for me on the external level by all the various symbols for the ultimate mystery of God, including the monstrous symbols for this that appear in various supernatural horror stories, especially in the area of weird fiction. When Lovecraft invokes the idea of unspeakable horrors and sanity-blasting cosmic gods and monsters, and when he says the fundamental supernatural horrific response is basically coeval with the ancient category of consciousness that we call "religious experience," I hear him developing an eccentric version of negative/apophatic theology and helping to clarify the very thing that drives me personally.

I hope at least gestured toward answering your question.

RT: In one of your stories, a very interesting one, you praised coffee a lot. Do you drink a lot of coffee?

MC: I have no idea why coffee ended up featuring so highly in that story, which is titled "The Devil and One Lump." That just sort of happened on its own, aside from any intention I brought to the writing. But I do drink coffee myself, although only in the morning, and then only a couple of cups. If I drink more than that, or drink it at any other time of day, much digestive distress and crippling hypoglycemia ensues. I'm definitely no Balzac, although I've always been fascinated by the stories of the obsessive coffee drinking that fueled his writing and killed him early.

RT: In your writings, both fiction and essays, you always talk about academia. What do you think of modern academia these days, both in the U.S and outside? Do you stand by the side of modern academia or do you think it can change its ways to accommodate other types and modes of thinking? I mean, these days academia seems to be rather strict and hierarchical. Student theses are long and boring because they are required to make extensive use of quotations and pre-approved material. Other than that, scholarships and grants and so on serve to narrow a lot of what students may want to delve into in their papers. Do you agree with all this, or not? What's your take?

MC: Your characterization of the situation as strict and hierarchical, with an overabundance of red tape and a capitulation of much scholarship to monetary concerns, sounds accurate enough to me. That said, I'm mainly familiar with just the American situation. I only have a glancing acquaintance with the situation elsewhere, although I am in contact with a global network of scholars at various universities. Personally, I think the attempt in America—which has been almost entirely successful over the past thirty years, mind you—to remake and transform universities into institutions that operate according to corporate business principles has been an unmitigated disaster, and I think this is the real story, as in the foundational explanatory narrative ("a desperate search for a pattern"), of what has transpired in American higher education during the past several decades. Well, that, plus the advent of postmodernism and the various schools of "criticism" that arose from the 1960s through the 1990s. We're all still living in the fallout from that. Oh, and there's the stranglehold of scientism and skepticism on the intellectual outlook and cultural tone of the universities. And the rise of Internet-based classes, including the shining example the MOOC (Massively Open Online Class), which exemplifies how easily anything, including a college education, can be turned into a digital parody of itself when it's reconceived to serve the ideology of the Internet. I find much to criticize about the system both institutionally and intellectually.

There are also very smart and wise and honorably intentioned people working within this system. I know many of them myself, some of them in person and more of them through email and other correspondence. I like to think that people like Jeffrey Kripal, for example, may represent a sea change or turning point in what counts as acceptable intellectual and scholarly discourse within the academic community. Jeff is doing mainstream work as a religion scholar while writing and saying things about religion, spirituality, science, and the paranormal that clash directly and dramatically with the reigning orthodoxy of scientific materialism. And there are many others who think like him throughout the U.S., and also in Canada and Europe and elsewhere. It's an interesting time to be involved in academia, what with all the current tumult. Systemically speaking, I'm inclined to see much more that's negative than positive. But who knows, the negatives may well drive, and may well currently be driving, some or all of us toward some positive change. My expectation, for what it's worth, is to see things become positively dystopian before they get any better. But then, that's an outlook that has come to apply to most things for me, and I've become more and more hesitant over time to ascribe any real objective validity to it.

2014

Shadows in the Corner of His Transcendental Eye: A Conversation with Matt Cardin

Interview by Jon Padgett

JP: Can you describe the dark night of the soul you experienced as a young man? How did this lead to an interest in horror fiction writing, and how has it informed your development as an artist and a thinker since that time?

MC: An easy way to answer this—easy for me, anyway, and therefore a copout—would be to direct people to the several things I've written about the matter at *The Teeming Brain,* probably most pointedly in two posts/essays titled "Initiation by Nightmare: Cosmic Horror and Chapel Perilous" and "Shadow Visitors: Sleep Paralysis and Discarnate 'Dark Ones.'" But to answer your question here at the moment, shortly after graduating from college in the early 1990s and instantly becoming a husband, father, and breadwinner, I began to experience sleep paralysis attacks that included dramatic visionary assaults by a demon-type entity. These episodes were truly, totally, and terribly shattering.

But to back up: Before that I had been intensely and equally interested in both religion and horror fiction and film for many years, and since earliest childhood I had led a pretty profligate emotional life full of too-intense highs and lows, although I wasn't aware that such a thing was anything besides normal. I was raised an evangelical Protestant—a religious life that I took with the utmost seriousness—and then I spent a good portion of my college years neglecting my formally assigned studies in favor of educating myself in weird supernatural horror fiction, especially the works of Lovecraft plus the associated criticism by the likes of Mosig, Joshi, Burleson, Schweitzer, and so on. So my mental-emotional cast and basic sensibility were already thoroughly suited to being impacted with dreadful force by those supernatural or supernatural-seeming assaults when they hit me out of nowhere. Rather swiftly, it all got bound up with what basically amounted to an early mid-life crisis in which I fell into total, and I mean total, anguish and despair as all the sense of meaning, except for icy depression and horror, drained out of my inner life. This was not a good state for a young husband, father, and twenty-something professional (specifically, a videographer) to be in. But there you have it.

Oh, and I forgot to mention that I was also reading insatiably and encyclopedically about all the above-named subjects and many related ones. I was also journaling with something like fanatical devotion. Sometimes I even did these things while in the very act of directing the video part of the show at Glen Campbell's theater in Branson, Missouri. My guys on the camera crew were astounded and amused. Anyway, eventually it all resulted in my writing a decent horror story that I titled "Teeth"—with which you are of course familiar, since you provided some valuable editorial input on it when I met you a few years later, and you published it at the then brand new *Thomas Ligotti Online*, making it my first published work. I think "Teeth" and my novella *The God of Foulness*, and maybe the ending of my story "Desert Places," do the best job of communicating to the reader an accurate sense of how I was experiencing the world and my own self at that time.

As for my development as an artist and thinker since then, the horror has now faded, and a deeper layer below it, one that's characterized by a profound sense of inner peace, has come to reign inside me instead. This is tied to much ongoing study and active spiritual practice. But I'm still interested, although sometimes only theoretically, in all the same things that came before. Authorially, my fiction writer's muse appears to have deserted me and moved on to inspire someone else. Either that or she has fallen into a deep, deep sleep.

JP: We've talked in the past at some length about the "profound inner peace" you've discovered within yourself. Would you expound on the development of your spiritual practice and perhaps discuss how it has changed your perceptions and influenced the way you think about the literature you're drawn towards both as a writer and a reader?

MC: In late high school and throughout college, I largely rejected my evangelical upbringing in favor of reading about Zen, Taoism, Vedanta, magickal theory and praxis, Western esotericism, Christian mysticism, general Western philosophy, and more. Favorite writers and writings included Alan Watts, Robert Anton Wilson, Theodore Roszak, Nietzsche, *Reality Hackers* magazine (later retitled *Mondo 2000*), Jan van de Wetering's books about being a Westerner studying Zen in a Japanese monastery, and many, many more. I also dabbled in various meditation practices and spiritual exercises, a trend that was abetted by the cultural diversity at the University of Missouri—a far cry from my mono-tone small Ozarks hometown—where I met real Buddhists and Hindus and more, and where one of my professors who became a kind of personal mentor was a Tibetan Buddhist. This was all contemporaneous with my hardcore self-education in weird fiction. Then after college my family situation reintroduced me into the evangelical and fundamentalist Protestant world, and pretty soon I was a church pianist—something I had previously done during my teen years in my home church—as well as a deacon and Sunday School teacher, even as I was still pursuing all those other things in private and adding a bunch of new writers, writings, and ideas to the mix: Ken Wilber, Huston Smith, Pema Cho-dron, plus Scott Morrison and many other representatives of the neo-Advaita non-dual crowd who were so prominent and popular in the 1990s. Discovering Eckhart Tolle and his The *Power of Now* in, I think, 2000 probably climaxed that whole wing of things. I also first read Kierkegaard and some other major phi-losophers, including Schopenhauer and Bertrand Russell, during that same '90s period. And I read a lot of ancient Greek literature in translation. Homer, Aeschylus, Sophocles, Euripides, Aristophanes, Plato, Aristotle.

Basically, I was catching up on a bunch of things that I had only been able to focus on very briefly and superficially while minoring in philosophy and taking lots of humanities classes at Mizzou. It was really an obsessive and frantically driven thing, all that reading and meditating and praying and jour-naling. The whole roiling mass of it made for a very weird, and weirdly rich, mishmash of spiritual self-perception, especially as I was going through all those nightmarish disruptions at the same time.

That became a long-term trend, my being simultaneously involved in formal institutional Protestant settings on the one hand and a private life made up of all that other stuff on the other hand, even as I was still dosing heavily on Lovecraft—his stories, poems, letters, essays, and the increasing slew of critical writings about him—while adding lots of Blackwood, Machen, Klein, and, beginning circa 1997, Ligotti to the mix.

So, after all that, in answer to your actual question, beginning in the early 2000s and increasing over time, the crisis phase somehow flamed out, and that sense of peace started to make itself known. I don't do all the obsessive reading anymore, although I do still read what I suppose is a titanic amount of material of all sorts, including nominally spiritual, religious, and philosophical texts. What has become really central is a consistent prayer and meditation practice. I do half an hour of dedicated daily sitting in the early mornings, and when I use the word "prayer," I mean actual formal Christian prayer that mingles men-tal/verbal aspects with a silent, contemplative, Zen-like component. Focused awareness on the inner or subtle body is also important. And I make a point of practicing mindfulness or presence as consistently as possible throughout the day, although nowadays it almost sounds distastefully trendy to say this in light of how the very idea of mindfulness has become significantly corrupted in America through its association with the spiritual pretensions of Silicon Valley.

As for how this fits or interacts with my longtime involvement in supernatural horror fiction as a writer, editor, and scholar, I suppose this is similar to the question, which I have been asked a few times, of why my main focus has always been on the intersection of horror with religion and religious experience. For me they're fused at a very deep level. Religion and spirituality are genetically inseparable from everything that goes into the supernatural horror response. They're not just related or mingled, they share much of the exact same psychological, cultural, literary, artistic, and spiritual DNA. In a way I think supernatural horror and religion/spirituality are like those optical illusion pictures that are used as psychological perception tests, like the one where you can see either two human profiles or a vase, or the one where you can see either a young woman or an old woman. The exact same pictures can be perceived in two distinctly and dramatically different ways. It's an inner shift from one perceptual interpretation to another that makes one image or the other visible. The difference is truly in the eye—and the psyche—of the beholder.

The same holds true for those "magic eye" computer-generated pictures that were so popular in the 1990s, where you stare for a while at what looks like a generic textural pattern and then have your mind blown when suddenly it morphs into something else and you see a three-dimensional picture that was formerly invisible to you. For me, religious experience and supernatural horror are like that. They're the same thing, perceived differently. I do think it's possible for a person to cultivate and maximize an experience of one aspect or the other with some deliberateness. But it's also possible for one or the other experience to force itself upon a person for reasons that are ultimately obscure. I had a negative version of it, the horrific experience of it, forced on me existentially for a number of years. I've come to view this in terms of a spontaneous initiatory experience of the type that Patrick Harpur describes in *Daimonic Reality*. It was my doorway to Chapel Perilous.

The peaceful obverse or complement that more defines my experience now is certainly a nice change, especially when things go down like this year, when my dad and one of my closest uncles died after losing battles with brutally swift-moving cancers. 2015 has been surreal, like a sustained time warp or underwater sleepwalk. Oddly, the deep peace has not only maintained itself but intensified, and I'm glad for this and am doing everything I can to honor, appreciate, and reinforce it. However, for me this state is always going to exist in permanent communion with an awareness of the present reality, however obscured or dormant, of its less pleasant flipside.

Not coincidentally, whenever I seek out art, literature, or film, I'm generally looking for something that displays a familiarity, whether fleeting or central, superficial or profound, with this very understanding and experience of things.

JP: As you know, I've also been personally, positively affected by the work of Eckhart Tolle (at your suggestion!)—specifically his repeated call to presence and continuous, internal watchfulness/awareness. And lately I've been musing about the role of compulsive thinking in horror (both real world and literary) and its flip side. As I've been writing and revising my own horror stories recently, I've been keeping this Kafka quote in mind: "You do not need to leave your house. Stay at your table and listen. Do not even listen, simply wait. Don't even wait, be quiet, still and solitary. And the world will offer itself to you to be unmasked, it can't do otherwise, in a trance it will writhe before you." I'm wondering if this instruction from the late master speaks as deeply to you as it does to me.

MC: Short answer: yes, it speaks to me. Very deeply. Piercingly deeply.

Longer answer, consisting of a list of things this calls to mind:

The great Indian sage Shankara stated at the end of his life that one of his only regrets was that he had traveled so much in search of a guru, because this was a distraction from the fact that reality itself, Brahman, is always present right here.

Lao Tzu in chapter 47 of the *Tao Te Ching* said (in Stephen Mitchell's wonderful translation), "Without opening your door, you can open your heart to the world. Without looking out your window, you can see the essence of the Tao. The more you know, the less you understand. The Master arrives without leaving, sees the light without looking, achieves without doing a thing."

I think of Wallace Shawn and Andre Gregory talking together at the table in that French restaurant in *My Dinner with Andre*. And Wally, fresh from being dazzled and disturbed by Andre's ongoing revelation of many fantastic and dramatic life experiences in locales around the globe that have led him to points of view of a decidedly offbeat nature, asserts with some passion and heat that he thinks there's just as much reality to be found in the cigar store next door to the restaurant as there is at, say, Mount Everest, and that the problem is that none of us can usually *see* it. And here I offer a close paraphrase of Wally's point: "But I think if you could really see the full reality that's there in the cigar store, it would just blow your brains out!" His point being that you don't have to go to Everest. And Andre counters that although Wally's general point may be true, we're all so deeply asleep these days that in order for somebody to wake up like that, it's *absolutely necessary* for them to be taken to Everest in one way or another, whether literally or metaphorically. And Wally is basically discomfited by this response.

And then of course along with all this, there's the weird/cosmic horrific vibe that one can catch quite easily from those quoted Kafka words. If, that is, your're is a person whose ear is inclined that way, as mine definitely is, and as I know yours is, too, Jon. The world will unmask itself and "writhe before you" if you sit quietly and alone? Hell, then keep moving and keep people around you. Keep the damned world shut up and fully masked, especially if you're someone who has read and truly understood the most famous opening lines to some of HPL's stories: "The most merciful thing in the world is the inability of the mind to correlate all its contents." "Life is a hideous thing, and from the background behind what we know of it peer daemoniacal hints of truth which make it sometimes a thousandfold more hideous." Same thing if you've read any of Ligotti's stories with their inevitable revelations that what lies behind the surface veil is really, really unpleasant. Or if you've read, and not just read but been marked by, Nietzsche's insight in *The Birth of Tragedy* to the effect that the only way anybody can keep on acting, moving, and living in the usual sense is by being buried in illusion, because a glimpse of the real truth is paralyzing. "In the consciousness of once having glimpsed the truth," says old Friedrich, "the man now sees everywhere only the horror or absurdity of being."

Yes, I'm rambling. But that line from Kafka really strikes a nerve with me, especially since all this stuff I'm spouting is also accompanied, for me, by the typical warm glow that I get every time I hear anybody say something wonderful in that vein—the vein of wisdom about writing, creativity, inspiration, and artistic insight, I mean—because it hits right in the middle of my longtime personal fascination with the idea and experience of inspired creativity, the daimon, the muse, and all that. I guess I'm seeing a paradox here, because although I think Kafka is in large measure correct, I also think he's playing with fire. It's possible for the unmasking of reality to paralyze, for reality to reveal itself as a Medusa at heart, and for this to kill or at least constrict the spirit, including the creative will to produce some bit of writing, art, music, whatever. I know whereof I speak. On a more practical note, I don't think what he describes will work for absolutely everybody. I don't think the opening of a deep or transcendent power of surplus vision that I take him to be referring to will automatically happen for just any person. I think it only works for those who are somehow prepared for it to happen, whether through deliberate training, natural endowment such as the incontestable genius of Kafka himself, or, in some cases, a purely accidental and unsuspected propensity that may prove to be disastrous.

JP: Speaking of the Medusa and the flipside of Kafka's quote, Tom Ligotti and I were having an email conversation last spring about his masterful story, "The Bungalow House." In my message, I observed that his tale never struck me as explicitly belonging to either the psychological horror or supernatural horror subgenres. Ligotti responded, in part, as follows: "I think what you say about 'The Bungalow House' applies to all good horror stories. If the theme is ambitious enough and intensely felt by the writer, then a good story emerges that's beyond labels. Still, I said myself [in *The Conspiracy against the Human Race*] that 'the supernatural may be regarded as the metaphysical counterpart of insanity'—the best possible vehicle for conveying the uncanny. And the uncanny is to me the defining trait of this strange and terrible world and our strange and terrible minds. In my stories, the psychological and the supernatural do tend to bleed into each other. And everything is madness." This impromptu Ligotti quote has haunted and fascinated me for months, and I would love to hear your response to his words on the supernatural as "the best possible vehicle for conveying the uncanny" in light of your previous observations regarding the stories you have written and the way you see the world. I assume you agree with at least part of what Ligotti was expressing.

MC: Yeah, I truly do agree with it. Tom's line about the supernatural being validly regarded as the metaphysical counterpart of insanity entered my bloodstream when I first read it in, as I recall, one of those early, dramatically different versions of *Conspiracy* that he distributed to some of us. It struck me as expressing a quintessential insight that acts like a skeleton key to understanding, well, a whole hell of a lot about both the dark side of "real world" religious and supernatural matters and the entirety of supernatural horror fiction and its fundamental effect and *raison d'être*.

As for the supernatural being "the best possible vehicle for conveying the uncanny," I think that's borne out in both personal and collective human experience. Although a number of important literary scholars—I'm thinking for example of Joshi and, especially, Peter Penzoldt in his seminal 1952 study *The Supernatural in Fiction*—have insightfully observed that the rise of horror fiction as its own separate genre necessarily coincided with the rise of modern science, since the supernatural horrific emotional effect that lies at the heart of this genre could only fully emerge in contrast to the age of science and its cultural milieu of secular disenchantment, you don't have to look very far to see that manifestations of what's clearly framed as the supernatural, and therefore an already existing idea about what constitutes the proper and wholesome boundaries of the natural, are very, very old in art and literature. Some of my favorite examples of this—and I've mentioned this in interviews before—come in the New Testament, where most of the miracles performed by Jesus and the apostles are greeted not with joy but with expressions of absolute terror and dread by the crowds. And do you remember that wonderful passage in Machen's prologue to "The White People"? Cotgrave asks Ambrose, "What is sin?" And Ambrose replies, "What would your feelings be, seriously, if your cat or your dog began to talk to you, and to dispute with you in human accents? You would be overwhelmed with horror. I am sure of it. And if the roses in your garden sang a weird song, you would go mad. And suppose the stones in the road began to swell and grow before your eyes, and if the pebble that you noticed at night had shot out stony blossoms in the morning?" I first read that passage when Ted Klein quoted it in *The Ceremonies*, and it has stayed close to me ever since. Sin isn't an act of moral evil as customarily conceived. It's a blasphemous violation of the natural order. And it's utterly horrifying, no matter how mundane in ostensible scope.

Those are the kind of things that I think of, and agree with, and resonate with, when I hear people say things like what Tom said. Well, those and also, of course, Rudolf Otto's characterization of religion in *The Idea of the Holy* as being all about fear and trembling before the *mysterium tremendum et fascinans* that is the Godhead, and about religion's primal basis in a primary experience of "daemonic dread" that is apparently hardwired into human consciousness. Our self-conscious human existence truly is uncanny right down to the root. Often we're successful at blocking this out for a time. Expressions of the supernatural, including those in horror fiction and religion, have the power to shock us out of that defensive trance and therefore into a more direct confrontation with and experience of the reality of our situation.

JP: Speaking of expressions of the supernatural, what are your thoughts about Penguin Classics reprinting Ligotti's *Songs of a Dead Dreamer* and *Grimscribe*? He'll be one of ten living authors published by them, which just blows my mind. I can't help but think about the fact that Lovecraft himself was published by PC just six years before the Library of America reprinted Tom. Do you think that Ligotti's work is approaching inclusion within the Western Canon?

MC: I'm truly thrilled over the Penguin Classics deal. I don't know what went on behind the scenes, but I think credit for this development has to go at least in part to Tom's burst of mainstream prominence in 2014 via the *True Detective* connection. I like to think it may also be evidence that his work is experiencing a genuine, organic elevation in general literary status due to its intrinsic excellence. Whatever the case, I consider the whole thing to be wonderful, and I'm looking forward to adding the book to my Ligotti collection. I also find it fascinating to witness how the Epic Rise of Ligotti is currently feeding on itself and becoming something of a self-perpetuating phenomenon. The major case in point as I type these words is the piece about Tom and the Penguin Classics book in the *Wall Street Journal* by Michael Calia, which was published recently along with an accompanying interview.

As for Tom's status relative to the Western Canon, the Penguin Classics edition is a strong move in the direction of his being included, and of course any future Library of America edition would all but clinch it. That said, I view the question of canon as relating more to issues of broad awareness and acceptance across multiple cultural strata than to any specific indicators like these. People who have never read a word of Emily Dickinson or F. Scott Fitzgerald or Jack Kerouac still know their names and some of their most famous works, although now that I've said that my spirit sinks as I think of the scores of my students for whom this has been resoundingly untrue. My personal view, which grips me at a gut level, is that an author hasn't achieved canonical status, at least in the sense that I want that word to carry, unless and until an awareness of his or her work has become a necessary component of general cultural literacy. On that count, Tom has a long way to go, and it'll be a long time before it happens, if it ever does. I hasten to add that I don't think this is necessarily unfortunate. Some authors are built for cult status. Witness the case of Lovecraft, who currently straddles mainstream and cult status in the weirdest of ways, and whose work is a major driver of collective cultural life in many parts of the world, even for the multitudes of people who would draw a blank on his name. I suspect Tom's legacy may end up inhabiting similar territory, only on a more rarefied and sophisticated level.

JP: What do you think most Ligotti readers would be surprised to learn about him?

MC: Some years ago I probably would have pointed to his strong sense of humor. But that might have been just a lingering prejudice from my own blind spot during the first few years when I read him. Back then I was so transfixed by his mystical nihilism and the way it resonated all the way to my core, and I took it so very seriously, that I was pretty much oblivious to the darkly and distinctly funny aspects of some of his stories. But that facet of his personality is more prominent now, and not just to me, since Tom has displayed his caustic wit in many of his interviews, including the recent WSJ one, where he's in prime form. Or then again, maybe my original answer to your question might still hold, because maybe most Ligotti readers would be surprised to learn that he can be just as funny, if not funnier, in his private correspondence.

JP: As a reader and writer of weird fiction, what do you most value in a story?

MC: What I value most are stories that move me deeply on multiple levels: intellectually, emotionally, spiritually, even physically. As many sensitive readers are well aware, the literary *frisson* isn't just a fancy word that's kicked around by overwrought littérateurs. It's a real thing, a real response. What I crave when it comes to weird fiction is a story that provides a genuine philosophical-spiritual *frisson*, a response that's a fusion of the psychological and physiological. I look for stories that do for me what David Hartwell describes in the introduction to his *Dark Descent* anthology when he describes horror stories of the fantastic: they generate the sense that I'm gaining a wider or deeper vision of a dark and fantastic reality that always trembles on the edge of perception, intuition, and effability, like a transcendental field of peripheral vision. It sounds coldly clinical to describe it this way, but the reality of the thing is electrical and warm, or sometimes icy, and in any case it's deeply affecting. I guess at bottom I value stories that speak to a pointedly shadowy type of *Sehnsucht*. If a given story both ignites and briefly fulfills that deep, tantalizing longing, and if it leaves me kind of suspended between wonder and horror, then it's a winner.

The specific stories that I'm liable to name in this connection are probably pretty standard, and they represent just one segment of the wider field of weird fiction that Ann and Jeff VanderMeer have so ably surveyed in their mega-anthology *The Weird*. Lovecraft "does it" for me with "The Call of Cthulhu," "The Music of Erich Zann," "Nyarlathotep," "The Silver Key," and a few others. Blackwood does it for me with "The Willows" and especially "The Wendigo," which has practically come to haunt me. Machen does it with "The Great God Pan" and "The White People." Klein does it with *Dark Gods* and "The Events at Poroth Farm" and *The Ceremonies*. Stephen King does it in very long-form fashion with *It*. Ligotti does it with nearly everything he writes, although in his case my response is augmented or accompanied by something else, a kind of dreadful pleasure and strange solace in the appalling, consuming nihilism of it all. High on the list here are "Nethescurial," "The Shadow at the Bottom of the World," "The Last Feast of Harlequin," "The Bungalow House," "I Have a Special Plan for This World" (the poem cycle), "Dr. Locrian's Asylum," "The Frolic," "Notes on the Writing of Horror," "The Tsalal," "The Sect of the Idiot," "The Red Tower," and others I could name. I could also go on naming additional authors and stories both old and new, but you get the idea.

JP: What element is most often missing in weird fiction? Or, as an author, what is the most difficult to capture?

MC: When an author, including me, blows it in this area, what's usually missing is the inspiration, the electricity, the real first-person experience of the wonder, terror, horror, longing, unease, surreality, and sometimes despair that ought to invest a story like this. I've read far too many stories that obviously—too obviously—strain and strive to be weird fiction, but that end up being nothing more than empty exercises in atmosphere. And I've found that these failed stories are more unreadable to me than any other type of fiction. Their sheer deadness galls me to the point where I literally experience a cognitive block. I can't keep plowing through the prose. It starts to lose all sense. I reread a few sentences or paragraphs multiple times in search of that dark current, and it feels as if some force is actively attacking my ability to focus and make sense of the words. Eventually I just give up. I have no idea how to quantify or objectively analyze what has gone wrong in these cases. I like to think it's ultimately due to an element that is categorically unquantifiable.

The other main thing that can go wrong is simply a deficient prose style that destroys the atmosphere. Weird fiction requires a more skilled and delicate creation of atmosphere than maybe any other kind. This is intrinsic to its fundamental purpose and effect. So on the technical end of things, this is its Achilles' heel. I don't think the strength of an author's vision and the level of his or her skill and sophistication on the craft end of things can be separated when it comes to weird fiction. Both are crucial. I think quite a few people who find themselves moved by weird fiction and feel the desire to write some of it themselves simply aren't up to the task, whether because they lack the innate inner equipment or because they haven't put in the necessary work to refine their capacity for expression.

JP: You've mentioned the absence (or quiescence) of your writer's muse. What's next for Matt Cardin?

MC: Fiction-wise, ideas for stories do in fact continue to suggest themselves on a pretty regular basis. Some are interesting enough to keep me brooding on them for a time. But none of them has to be written. None of them presses on me with such force that I'm positively driven to write it, as happened with the stories in *Divinations of the Deep* and *Dark Awakenings*. And quite honestly, I'm not at all inclined to make the serious investment of time, effort, and self that goes into writing something, especially a fictional story, unless it flat-out demands that I do so. Fiction asks more of me than other types of writing. For a story to emerge in any kind of condition besides stillborn, I have to let it become a veritable obsession for whatever length of time it requires. So in a way I'm relieved that there's an ongoing hiatus.

In the past my inner life has suffered due to longterm fictional fixations. More importantly, so has my family life. I was a starkly lousy husband in the early years, for various reasons. Some of the psychic stuff that made me that way reawakens whenever I try to focus on writing fiction. You know that story about Rilke's refusal to attend his daughter's wedding because he was in a creatively inspired state and wouldn't agree to withdraw an ounce of his attention from that? Some consider this a remarkable story of wholehearted dedication to one's creative calling. Others find it appalling.

Well over a decade ago, I read Richard Bausch's "Letter to a Young Writer" and saw him saying the following among his Ten Commandments for writers of fiction, or of anything else: "Remember that it is an absurdity to put writing before the life you have to lead. I'm not talking about leisure. I'm talking about the responsibility you have to the people you love and who love you back. No arduousness in the craft or arts should ever occupy one second of the time you're supposed to be spending that way. It has never been a question of the one or the other and writers who say it is are lying to themselves or providing an excuse for bad behavior." At the time I thought instantly of Rilke and felt more inclined to side with him. These many years later, my allegiance has shifted, and Bausch may as well be speaking for me. The life I have with my family is central, followed closely by relationships with friends, coworkers, and so on. The justice I do or fail to do on this front is largely determined by the tenor of my inner state, and for me, for the time being, despite Bausch's claim that writing and life aren't mutually exclusive, I really can't have both.

Beyond that, there's the additional fact that I have a pretty poor attitude toward the value of writing in general these days. I'm increasingly gripped by the sense that most of what I would write if I put forth the effort would be useless. I mean, really, what's the point? What would it ultimately mean or accomplish? The world is littered with too many books as it is. This same sense also infects my regard for most of what's being published by everybody else these days. I still enjoy visiting bookstores, but sometimes the pleasure feels distinctly vestigial.

JP: Thanks so much for this fascinating conversation, Matt. It's always such a pleasure.

MC: Likewise, Jon. To end on a note that may be cryptic to everybody but you and me: I am becalmed in virtue.

2015

Publication History

"A Brief History of the Angel and the Demon." First published in shorter form as "The Angel and the Demon" in *Icons of Horror and the Supernatural: An Encyclopedia of Our Worst Nightmares*, edited by S. T. Joshi (Greenwood Press, 2006). Also in *Dark Awakenings* by Matt Cardin (Mythos Books, 2010), where it appeared in significantly revised and expanded form. The version appearing in the present volume has been expanded still further with previously unpublished material.

"Fantasy, Horror, and Infinite Longing." First published at *SF Signal*, 28 October 2010.

Foreword to *Beneath the Surface* by Simon Strantzas (revised and expanded electronic edition, Dark Regions Press, 2015).

"A Formless Shade of Divinity: Chasing Down the Demiurge in Thomas Ligotti's 'The Red Tower,' *I Have a Special Plan for This World*, and *This Degenerate Little Down*." First published as a booklet accompanying a vinyl audio recording of *The Red Tower* (Cadabra Records, 2020).

"Gods and Monsters, Worms and Fire: A Horrific Reading of Isaiah." First published in *Dark Awakenings* by Matt Cardin (Mythos Books, 2010) (written in 1998).

"Icy Bleakness and Killing Sadness: The Desolating Impact of Thomas Ligotti's 'The Bungalow House.'" First published as a booklet accompanying a vinyl audio recording of Ligotti's "The Bungalow House" (Cadabra Records, 2018). Also in *Penumbra* No. 1 (2020).

"In Search of Higher Intelligence: The Daemonic Muse(s) of Aleister Crowley, Timothy Leary, and Robert Anton Wilson." First published at *Demon Muse*, 2 June 2011. Also in *Paranthropology: Anthropological Approaches to the Paranormal* 3, No. 4 (October 2012) Also in *Daimonic Imagination: Uncanny Intelligence*, edited by Angela Voss and William Rowlandson (Cambridge Scholars Publishing, 2013).

"Initiation by Nightmare: Cosmic Horror and Chapel Perilous." First published at *The Teeming Brain,* 13 August 2012.

"Interview with Matt Cardin." Interview by Stuart Young. First published in *Terror Tales* (March 2004).

"Interview with Matt Cardin: Dark Awakenings and Cosmic Horror." First published at *Lovecraft News Network,* 3 March 2010.

Introduction to *Portraits of Ruin* by Joseph S. Pulver, Sr. (Hippocampus Press, 2012).

Introduction to *The Secret of Ventriloquism* by Jon Padgett (Dunhams Manor Press, 2016).

"Liminal Terror and Collective Identity in Thomas Ligotti's 'The Shadow at the Bottom of the World.'" First published at *The Art of Grimscribe,* 2002. Also in *The Thomas Ligotti Reader,* edited by Darrell Schweitzer (Wildside Press, 2003).

"Loathsome Objects: George Romero's Living Dead Films as Contemplative Tools." First published in *Dark Awakenings* by Matt Cardin (Mythos Books, 2010) (written in 1999).

"The Master's Eyes, Shining with Secrets: H. P. Lovecraft and His Influence on Thomas Ligotti." First published at *Thomas Ligotti Online,* 2005. Also in *Lovecraft Annual* No. 1 (2007).

"Matt Cardin: Life and Mind of a Teeming Brain." Interview by Rafael Tages. First published at *Cloudy Sky,* 28 May 2014.

"Matt Cardin Unleashes His Teeming Brain." Interview by T. E. Grau. First published at *The Cosmicomicon,* 20 September 2012.

"Of Masks and Mystagogues." Introduction to *Born to Fear: Interviews with Thomas Ligotti,* edited by Matt Cardin (Subterranean Press, 2014).

"Religion and Vampires." First published in *Encyclopedia of the Vampire: The Living Dead in Myth, Legend, and Popular Culture,* edited by S. T. Joshi (Greenwood Press, 2010).

"Scratches on the Universe's Utmost Rim." First published at *The Teeming Brain* in two parts, as "Liminality, Synchronicity, and the Walls of Everyday Reality" (23 July 2012) and "Horror, Meaning, and Madness: Dangers of Lifting the Cosmic Veil" (6 August 2012).

"Shadows in the Corner of His Transcendental Eye: A Conversation with Matt Cardin." Interview by Jon Padgett. First published in *Xnoybis: A Journal of Weird Fiction* No. 2 (Fall 2015).

"Spookhouses, Catharsis, and Dark Consolations." Introduction to *Horror Literature through History*, edited by Matt Cardin (Greenwood Press, 2017).

"Thomas Ligotti's Career of Nightmares." First published in *Terror Tales* (April 2000). Also at *The Art of Grimscribe*, 2002. Also in *The Thomas Ligotti Reader*, edited by Darrell Schweitzer (Wildside Press, 2003).

"Those Sorrows Which Are Sent to Wean Us from the Earth: The Failed Quest for Enlightenment in Mary Shelley's *Frankenstein*." First published in *Penny Dreadful* No. 14 (December 2001).

"The Transition from Literary Horror to Existential Nightmare in Thomas Ligotti's 'Nethescurial.'" First published at *Thomas Ligotti Online*, April 2000. Also in *The Thomas Ligotti Reader*, edited by Darrell Schweitzer (Wildside Press, 2003).

Acknowledgments

A book like this, bringing together material written over a span of many years, involves relationships with an unusually extended group of people. Some of these take place only through an author-reader interaction. The multitude of references to and citations of various books and authors in these pages effectively serves as my expression of gratitude to those people. Other relationships are more direct and personal. Over the years, many individuals have helped to shape my ideas and outlook and elicit my creative impulses in a variety of ways both direct and indirect, through friendship, conversation, collaboration, and project invitations. I especially want to thank the following: Tom Ligotti, Jon Padgett, S. T. Joshi, Simon Strantzas, Joe Pulver (RIP), Richard Gavin, Mark Samuels, Stu Young, Ted Grau, Monika Angerhuber, Michael Cisco, John Langan, Terry Wright (RIP), Kim Paffenroth, Stephen Jones, Nick Mamatas, Quentin S. Crisp, Jason Van Hollander, Ryan Hurd, David Metcalfe, Jack Hunter, Erik Davis, Jim Fadiman, J. F. Martel, John DeNardo, Derrick Hussey, Jonathan Dennison, Victor Matthews, Martha Finch, Darrell Schweitzer, Rafael Tages, John Morehead, and George Butler.

Index

CPSIA information can be obtained
at www.ICGtesting.com
Printed in the USA
BVHW050744240223
659125BV00006B/85